THE BOOK OF SECRETS

I DEDICATE THIS BOOK TO MY ENTIRE FAMILY.
—M. T.

Text copyright © 2020 by Mat Tonti
Illustrations copyright © 2020 by Mat Tonti
Color work by Dan Silber

KAR-BEN PUBLISHING®
An imprint of Lerner Publishing Group, Inc.
241 First Avenue North
Minneapolis, MN 55401 USA
Website address: www.karben.com

Main body text set in CCComicrazy.
Typeface provided by Comicraft.

Library of Congress Cataloging-in-Publication Data

Names: Tonti, Mat, author, illustrator.
Title: The book of secrets / Mat Tonti.
Description: Minneapolis : Kar-Ben Publishing, [2020] | Audience: Ages
    8–11. |
    Audience: Grades 4–6. | Summary: Rose and Ben receive a
    mysterious package from their Bubbe containing Jewish stories about
    outwitting fate through action and personal agency, and soon are on
    the run from a sorceress seeking the book.
Identifiers: LCCN 2019041618 (print) | LCCN 2019041619 (ebook) |
    ISBN 9781541578258 (library binding) | ISBN 9781541578265
    (paperback) | ISBN 9781541599574 (ebook)
Subjects: LCSH: Graphic novels. | CYAC: Graphic novels. | Books
    and reading—Fiction. | Fate and fatalism—Fiction. | Adventure and
    adventurers—Fiction. | Jews—Fiction. | Storytelling—Fiction.
Classification: LCC PZ7.7.T64 Boo 2020 (print) | LCC PZ7.7.T64
    (ebook) | DDC 741.5/973—dc23

LC record available at https://lccn.loc.gov/2019041618
LC ebook record available at https://lccn.loc.gov/2019041619

Manufactured in the United States of America
1-46932-47810-11/18/2019

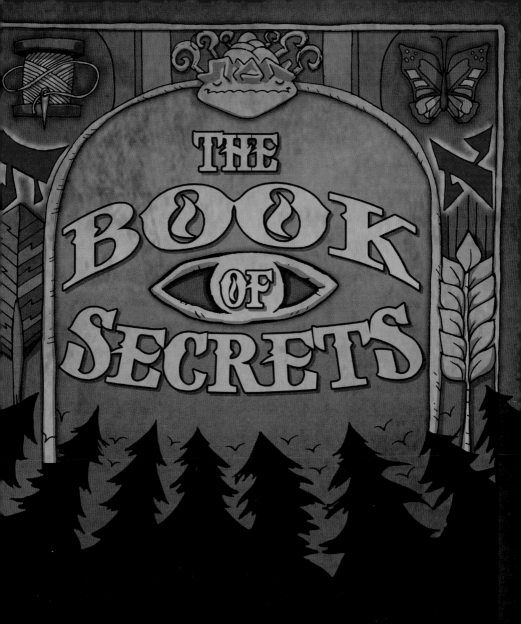

THE BOOK OF SECRETS

Mat Tonti

Color work by Dan Silber

KAR-BEN
PUBLISHING

MOST PEOPLE TELL YOU STORIES TO PUT YOU TO SLEEP,
I TELL YOU STORIES TO WAKE YOU UP.

—REBBE NACHMAN

Table of Contents

INTRODUCTION 6

THE BUTTERFLY IN THE HAND 22

THE SCRIBE AND THE PRINCESS . . . 32

THE TAINTED GRAIN 46

OG AND THE TAILOR 68

UNDER THE BRIDGE 86

BEFORE THE GATE 118

AND THE STORY WAS ENOUGH . . . 136

THE BOOK OF SECRETS 150

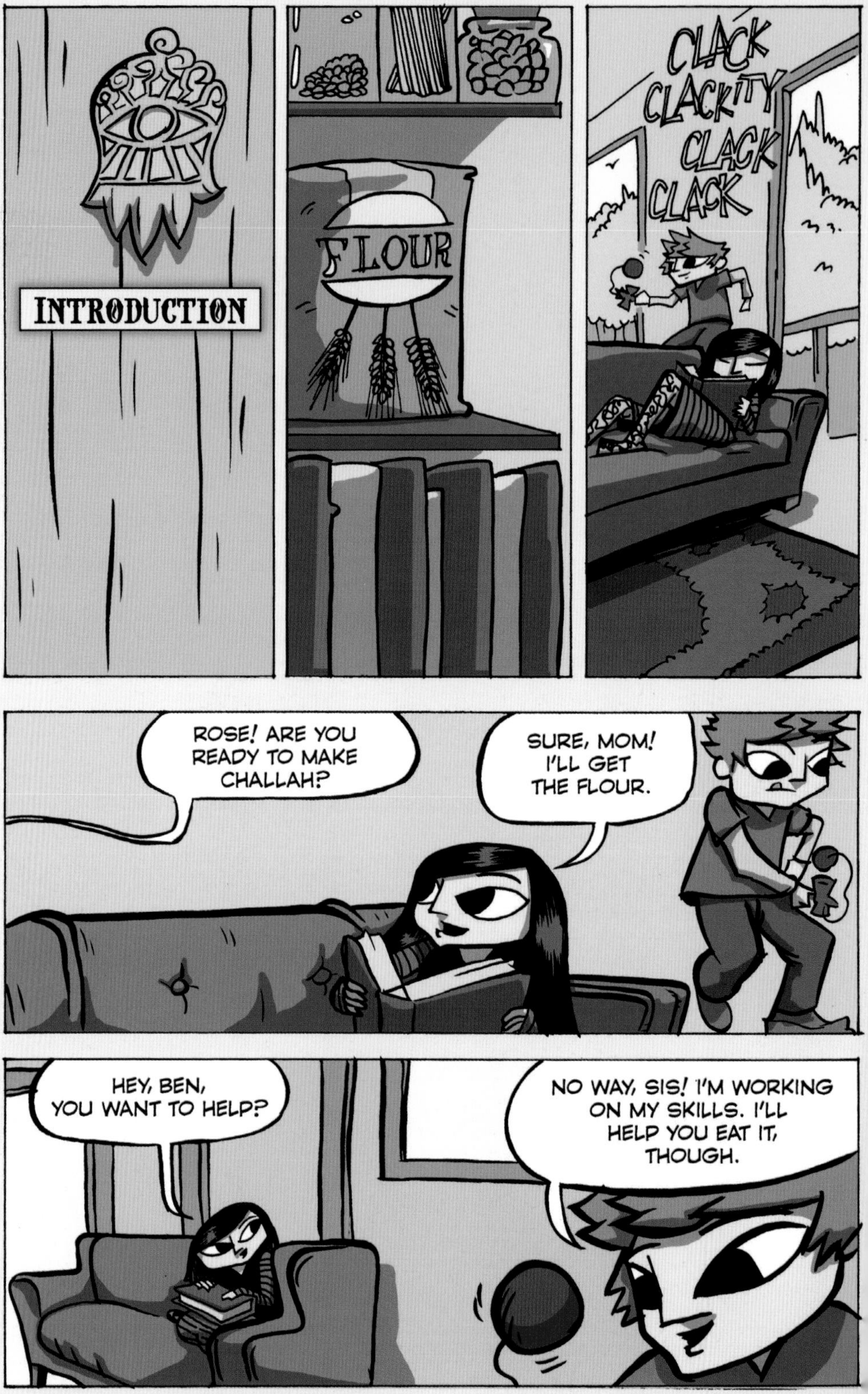
INTRODUCTION
FLOUR
CLACK
CLACKITY
CLACK
CLACK
ROSE! ARE YOU READY TO MAKE CHALLAH?
SURE, MOM! I'LL GET THE FLOUR.
HEY, BEN, YOU WANT TO HELP?
NO WAY, SIS! I'M WORKING ON MY SKILLS. I'LL HELP YOU EAT IT, THOUGH.

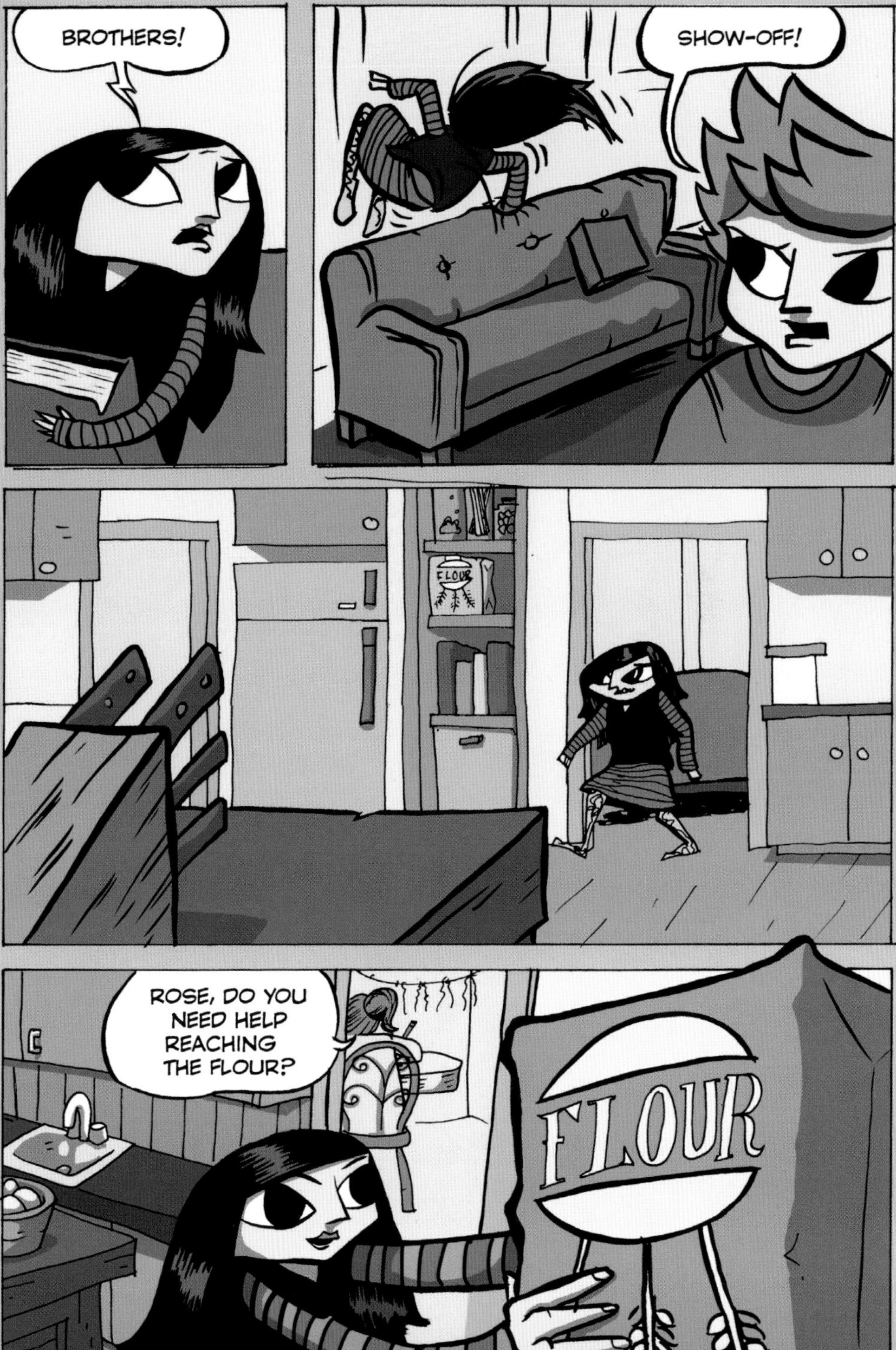
BROTHERS!
SHOW-OFF!
FLOUR
ROSE, DO YOU NEED HELP REACHING THE FLOUR?
FLOUR

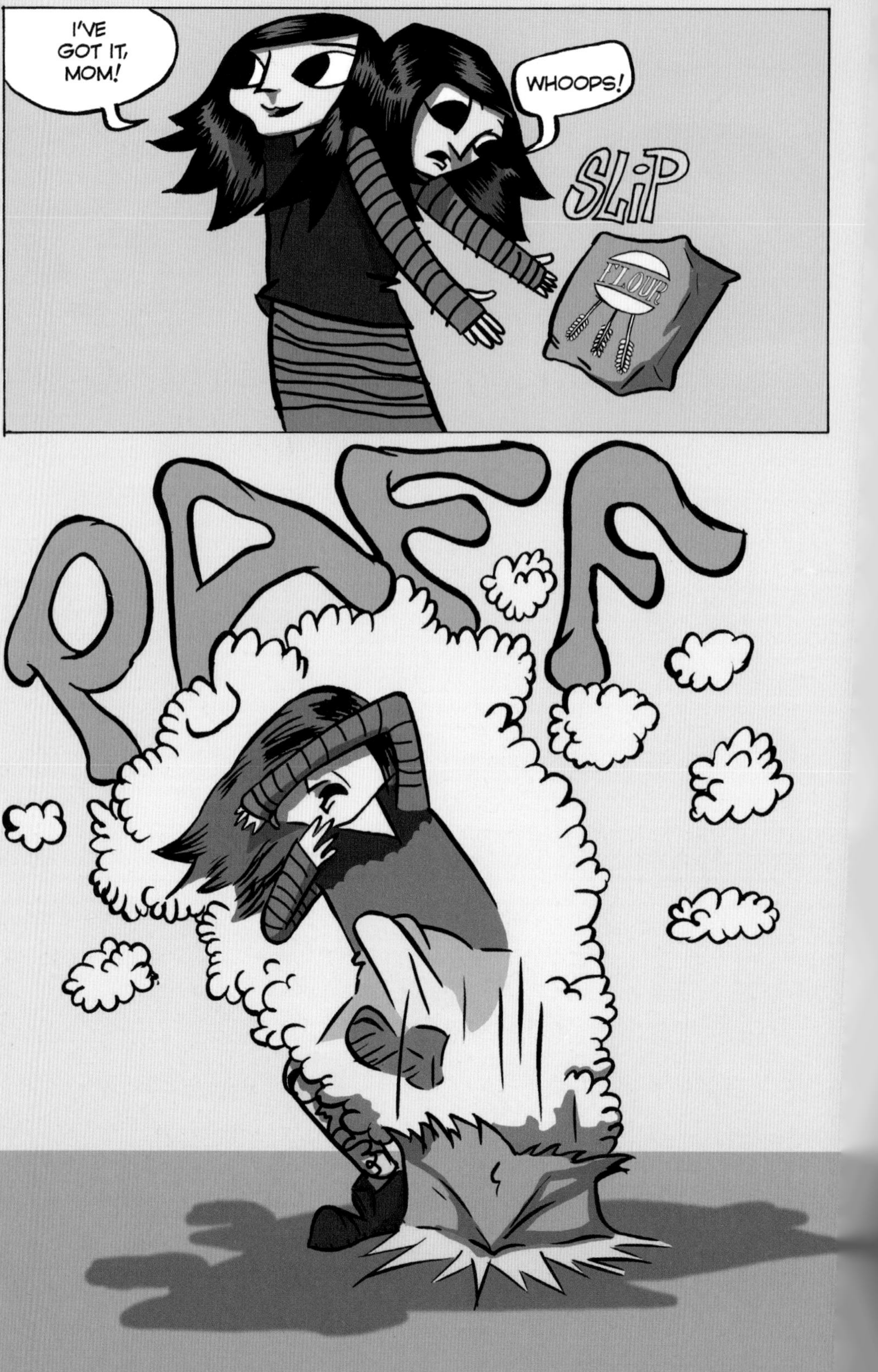
I'VE GOT IT, MOM!
WHOOPS!
SLIP
FLOUR
PAFF

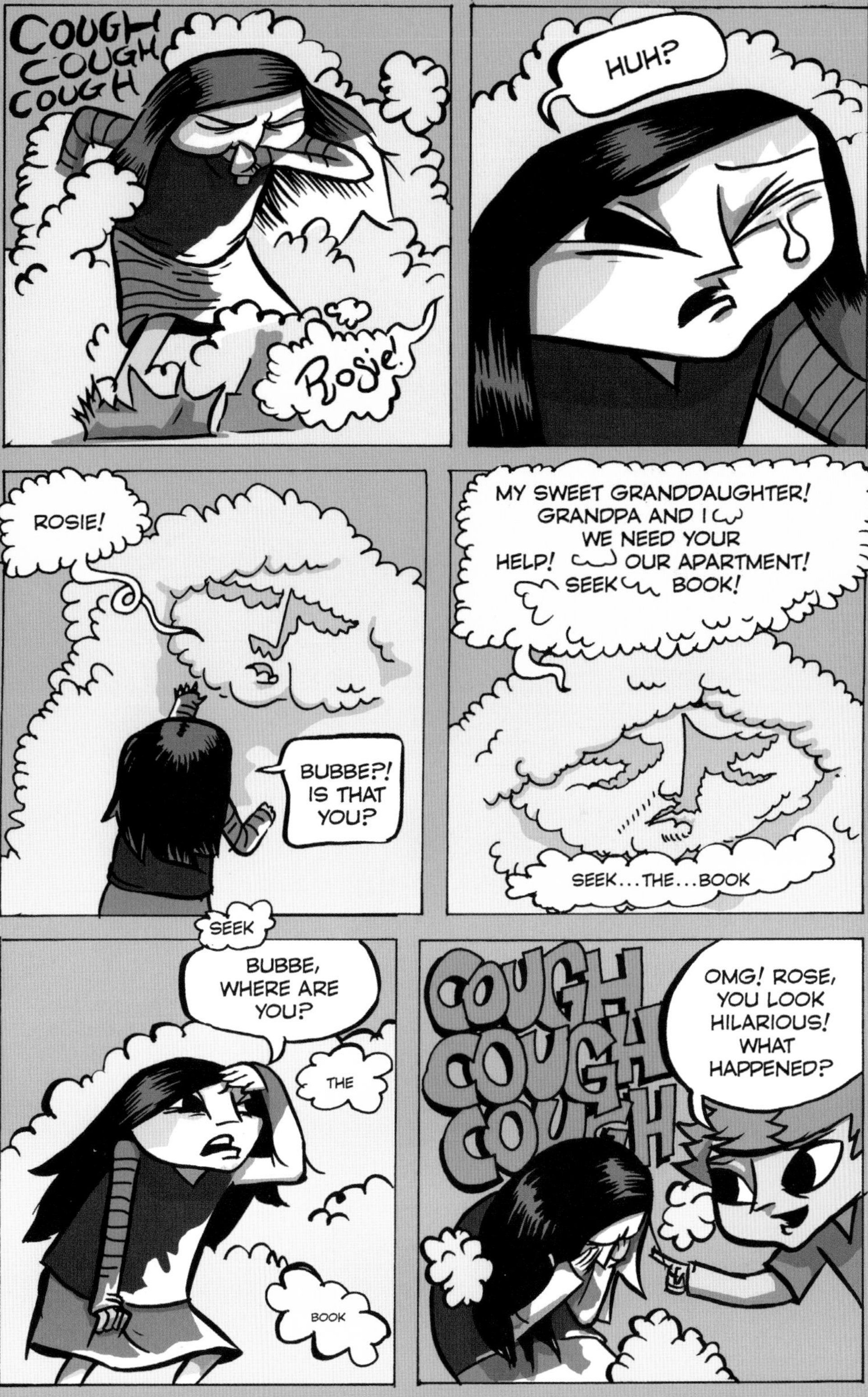
COUGH COUGH COUGH
Rosie!
HUH?
ROSIE!
BUBBE?! IS THAT YOU?
MY SWEET GRANDDAUGHTER! GRANDPA AND I
WE NEED YOUR HELP!
OUR APARTMENT!
SEEK
BOOK!
SEEK...THE...BOOK
SEEK
BUBBE, WHERE ARE YOU?
THE
BOOK
COUGH COUGH COUGH
OMG! ROSE, YOU LOOK HILARIOUS! WHAT HAPPENED?

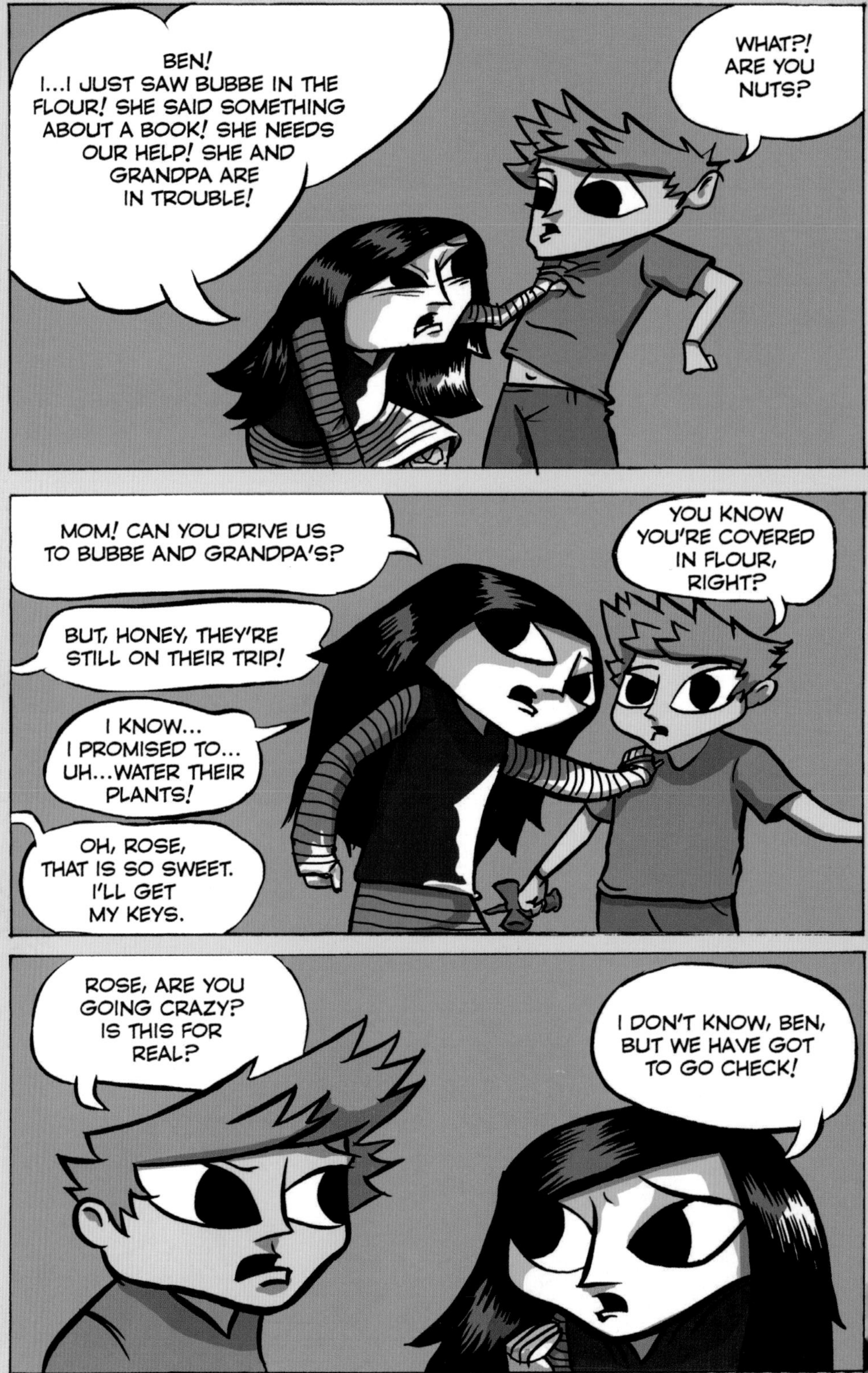
BEN! I...I JUST SAW BUBBE IN THE FLOUR! SHE SAID SOMETHING ABOUT A BOOK! SHE NEEDS OUR HELP! SHE AND GRANDPA ARE IN TROUBLE!
WHAT?! ARE YOU NUTS?
MOM! CAN YOU DRIVE US TO BUBBE AND GRANDPA'S?
BUT, HONEY, THEY'RE STILL ON THEIR TRIP!
YOU KNOW YOU'RE COVERED IN FLOUR, RIGHT?
I KNOW... I PROMISED TO... UH...WATER THEIR PLANTS!
OH, ROSE, THAT IS SO SWEET. I'LL GET MY KEYS.
ROSE, ARE YOU GOING CRAZY? IS THIS FOR REAL?
I DON'T KNOW, BEN, BUT WE HAVE GOT TO GO CHECK!

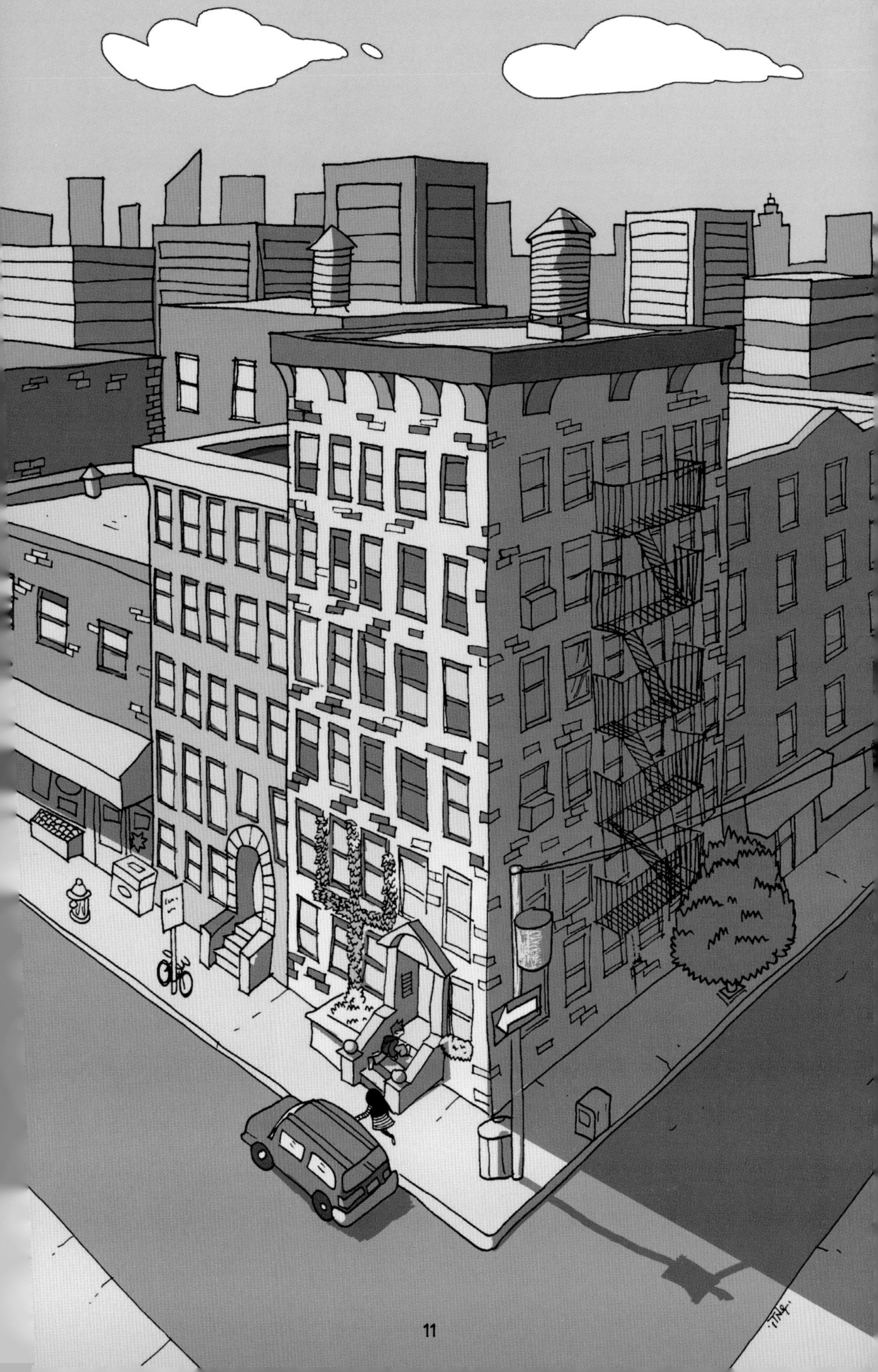

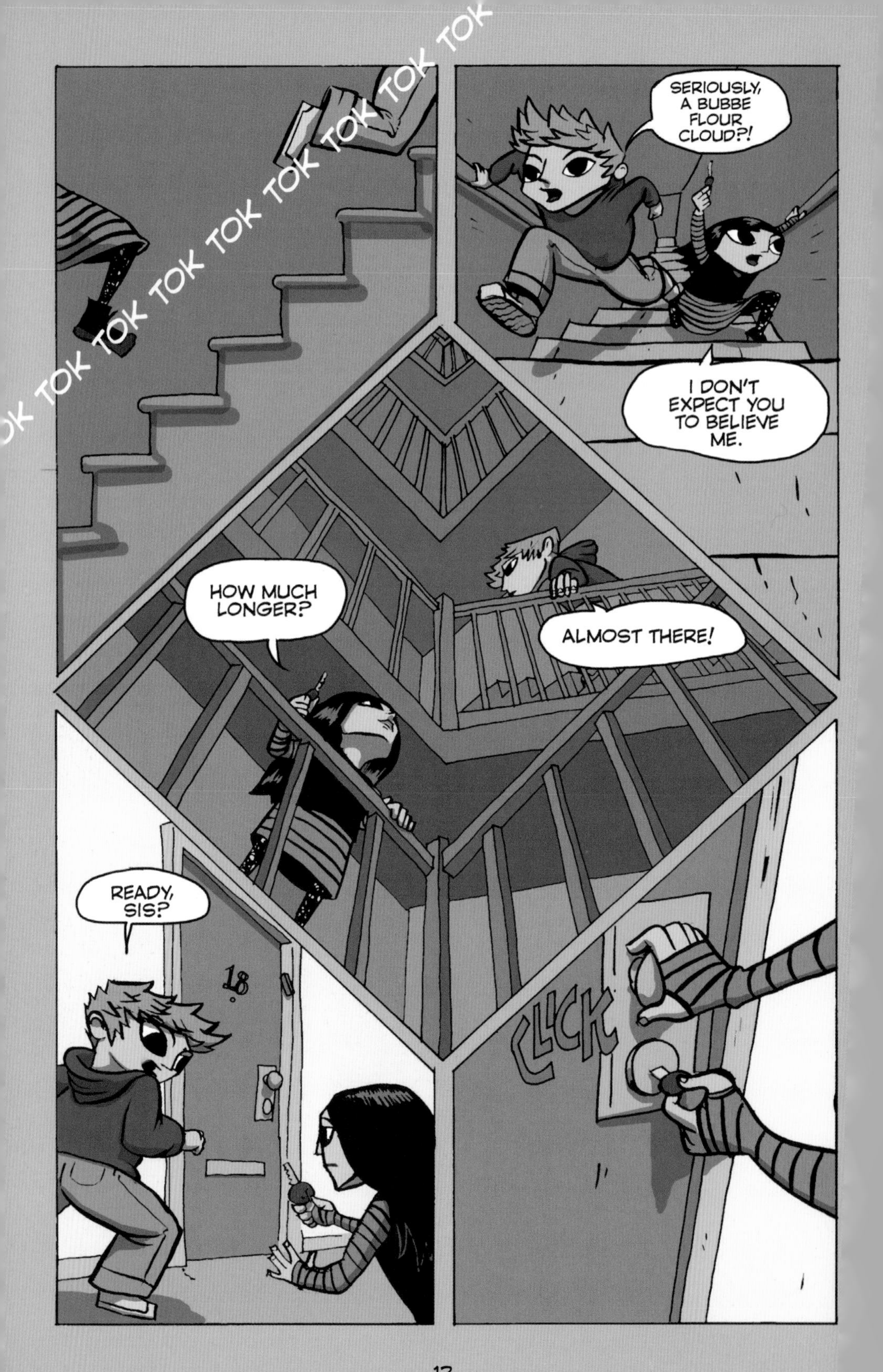
TOK TOK TOK TOK TOK TOK TOK TOK
SERIOUSLY, A BUBBE FLOUR CLOUD?!
I DON'T EXPECT YOU TO BELIEVE ME.
HOW MUCH LONGER?
ALMOST THERE!
READY, SIS?
18
CLICK

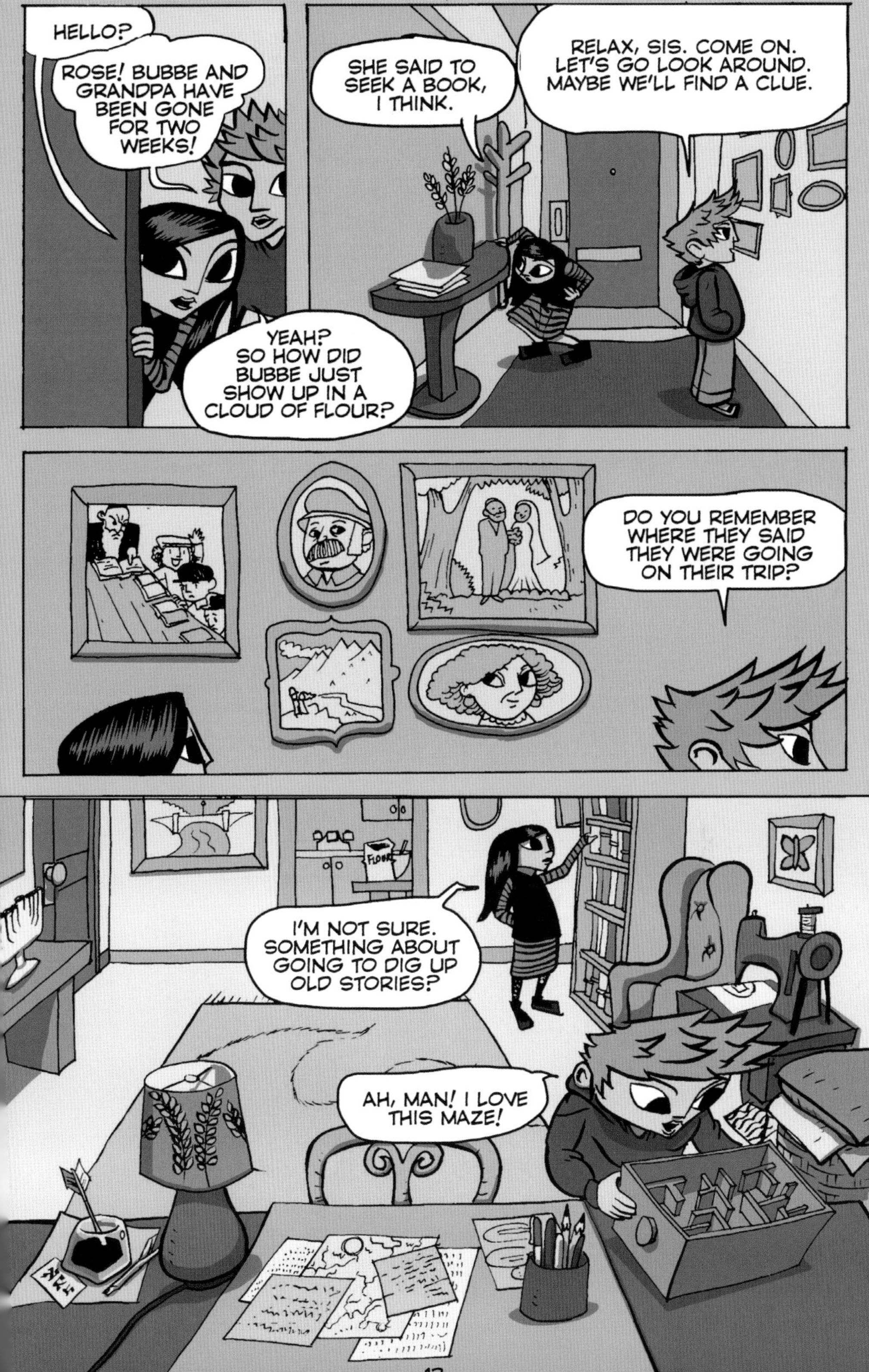
HELLO?
ROSE! BUBBE AND GRANDPA HAVE BEEN GONE FOR TWO WEEKS!
YEAH? SO HOW DID BUBBE JUST SHOW UP IN A CLOUD OF FLOUR?
SHE SAID TO SEEK A BOOK, I THINK.
RELAX, SIS. COME ON. LET'S GO LOOK AROUND. MAYBE WE'LL FIND A CLUE.
DO YOU REMEMBER WHERE THEY SAID THEY WERE GOING ON THEIR TRIP?
I'M NOT SURE. SOMETHING ABOUT GOING TO DIG UP OLD STORIES?
FLOUR
AH, MAN! I LOVE THIS MAZE!

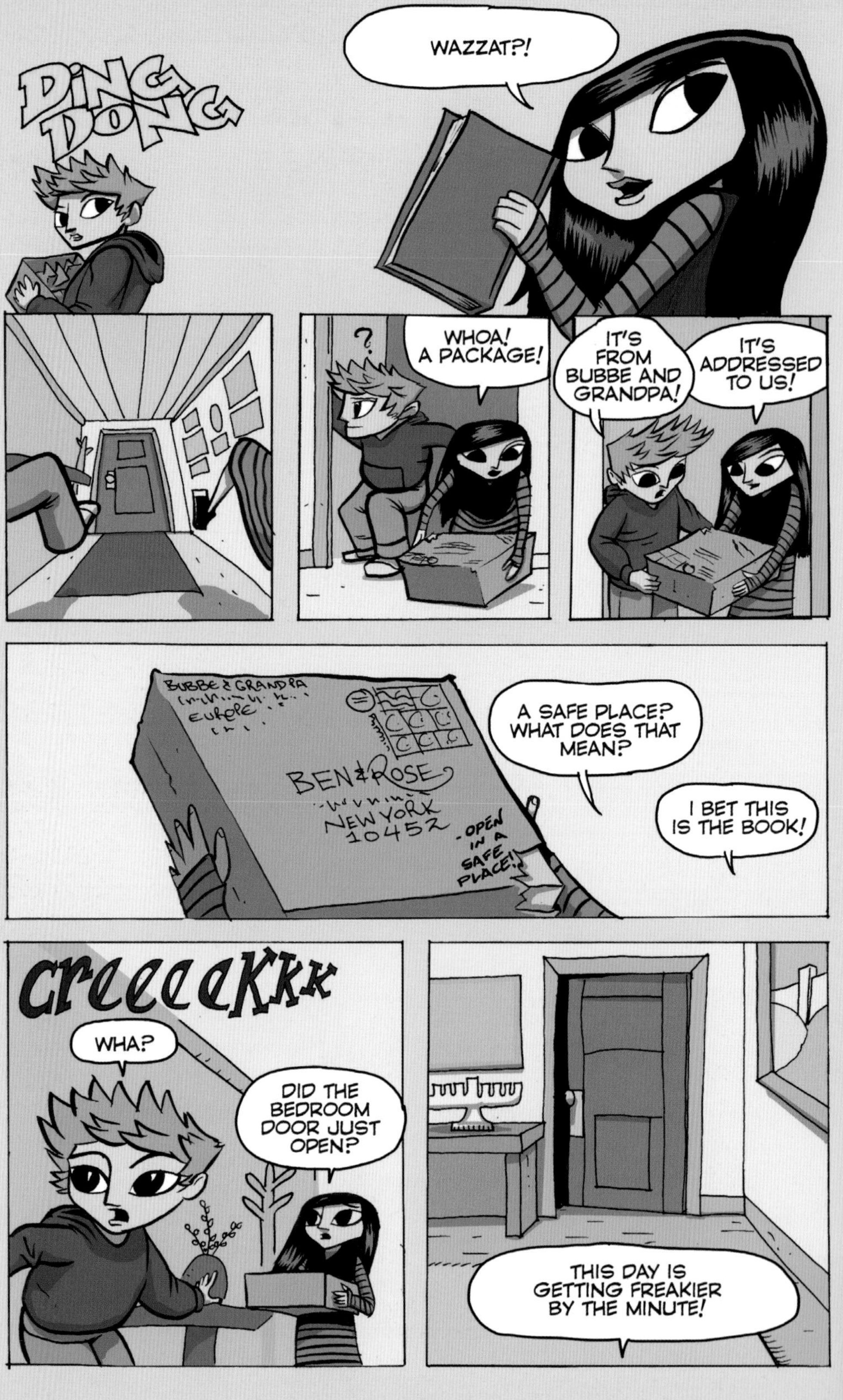
DING DONG
WAZZAT?!
WHOA! A PACKAGE!
IT'S FROM BUBBE AND GRANDPA!
IT'S ADDRESSED TO US!
BUBBE & GRANDPA
EUROPE
BEN & ROSE
NEW YORK 10452
OPEN IN A SAFE PLACE!
A SAFE PLACE? WHAT DOES THAT MEAN?
I BET THIS IS THE BOOK!
CREEEEKKK
WHA?
DID THE BEDROOM DOOR JUST OPEN?
THIS DAY IS GETTING FREAKIER BY THE MINUTE!

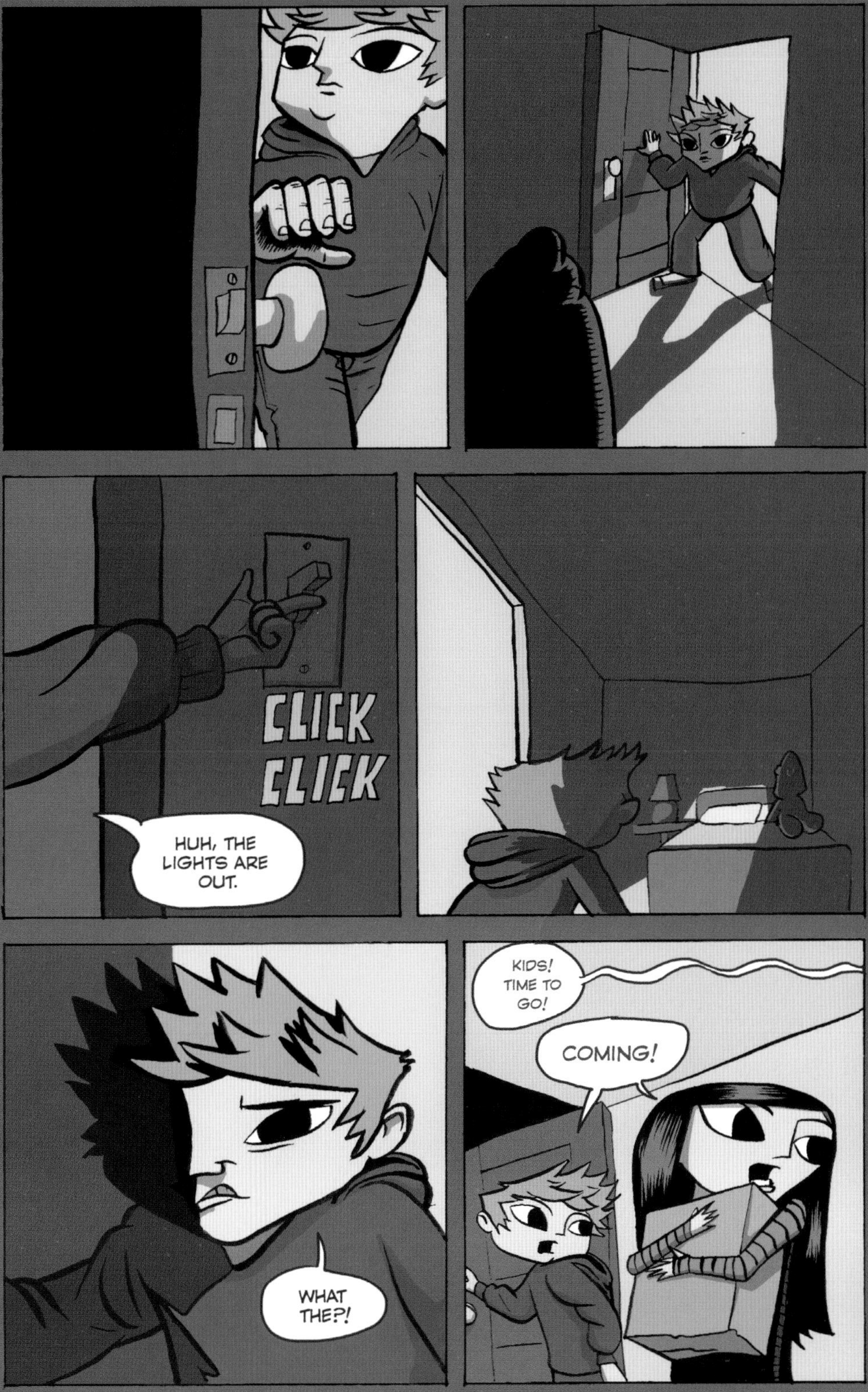
CLICK
CLICK
HUH, THE LIGHTS ARE OUT.
WHAT THE?!
KIDS! TIME TO GO!
COMING!

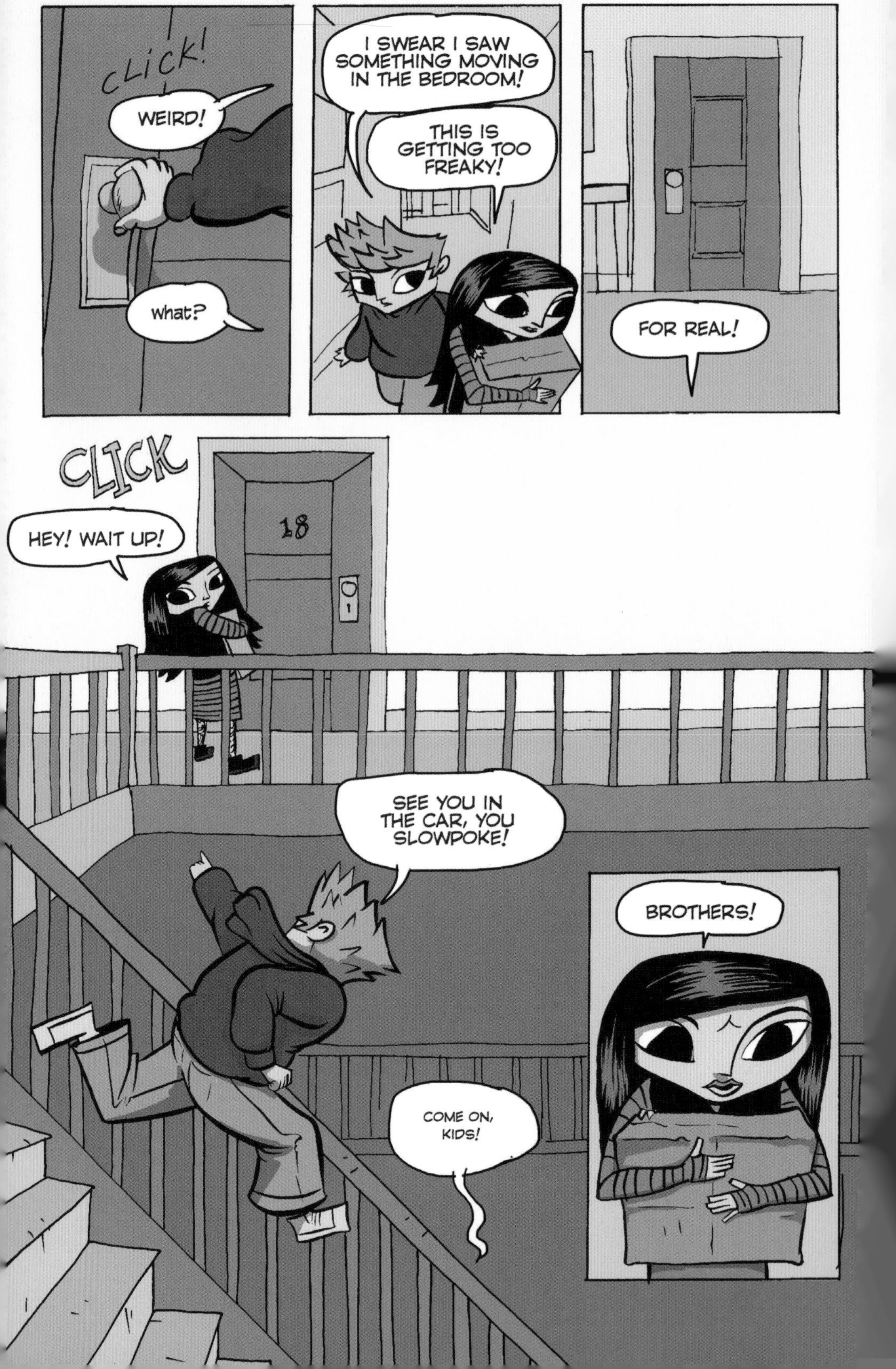
CLICK!
WEIRD!
what?
I SWEAR I SAW SOMETHING MOVING IN THE BEDROOM!
THIS IS GETTING TOO FREAKY!
FOR REAL!
CLICK
HEY! WAIT UP!
18
SEE YOU IN THE CAR, YOU SLOWPOKE!
BROTHERS!
COME ON, KIDS!

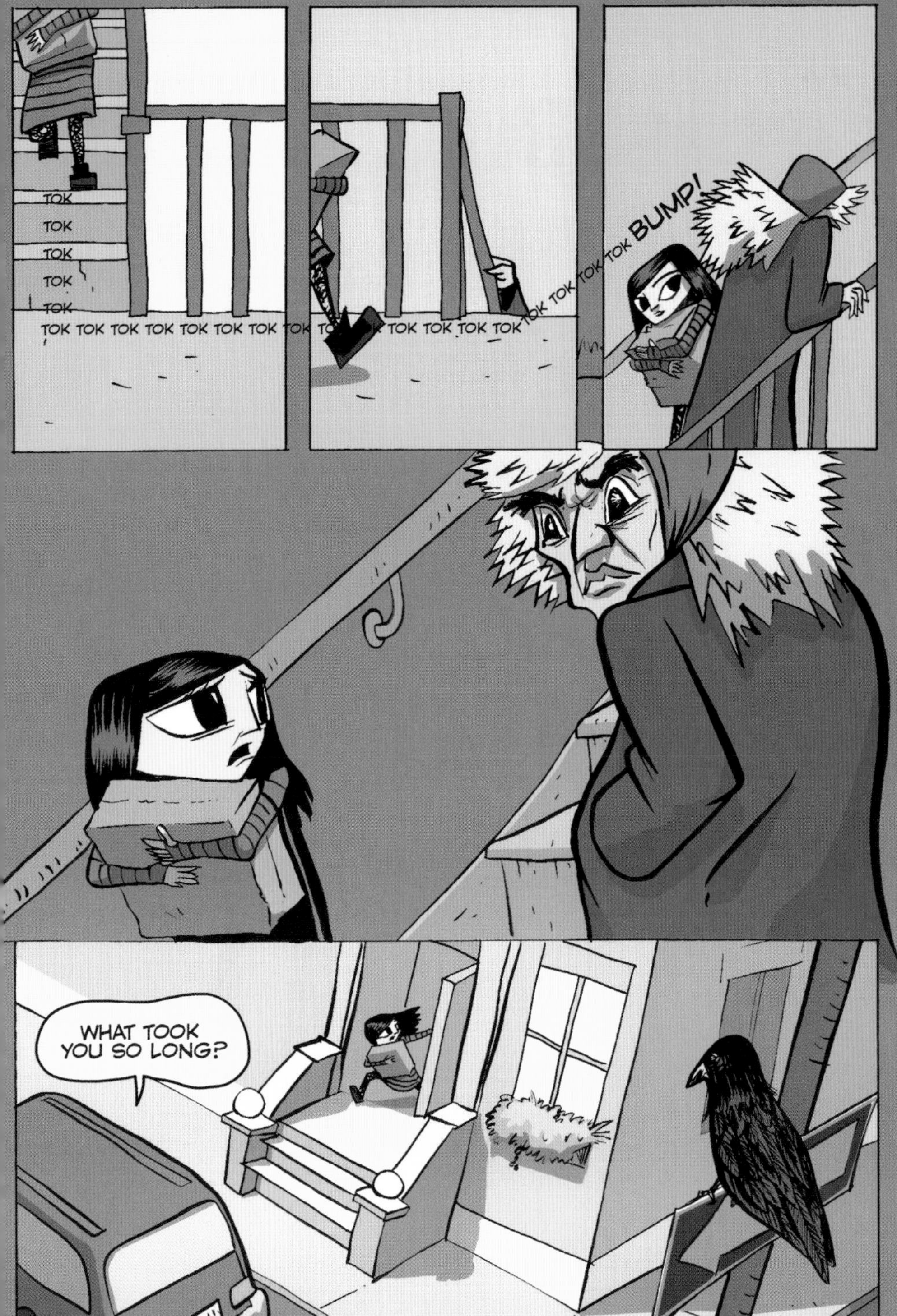
TOK
TOK
TOK
TOK
TOK
TOK TOK TOK TOK TOK TOK TOK
TOK TOK TOK TOK
TOK TOK TOK TOK BUMP!
WHAT TOOK YOU SO LONG?

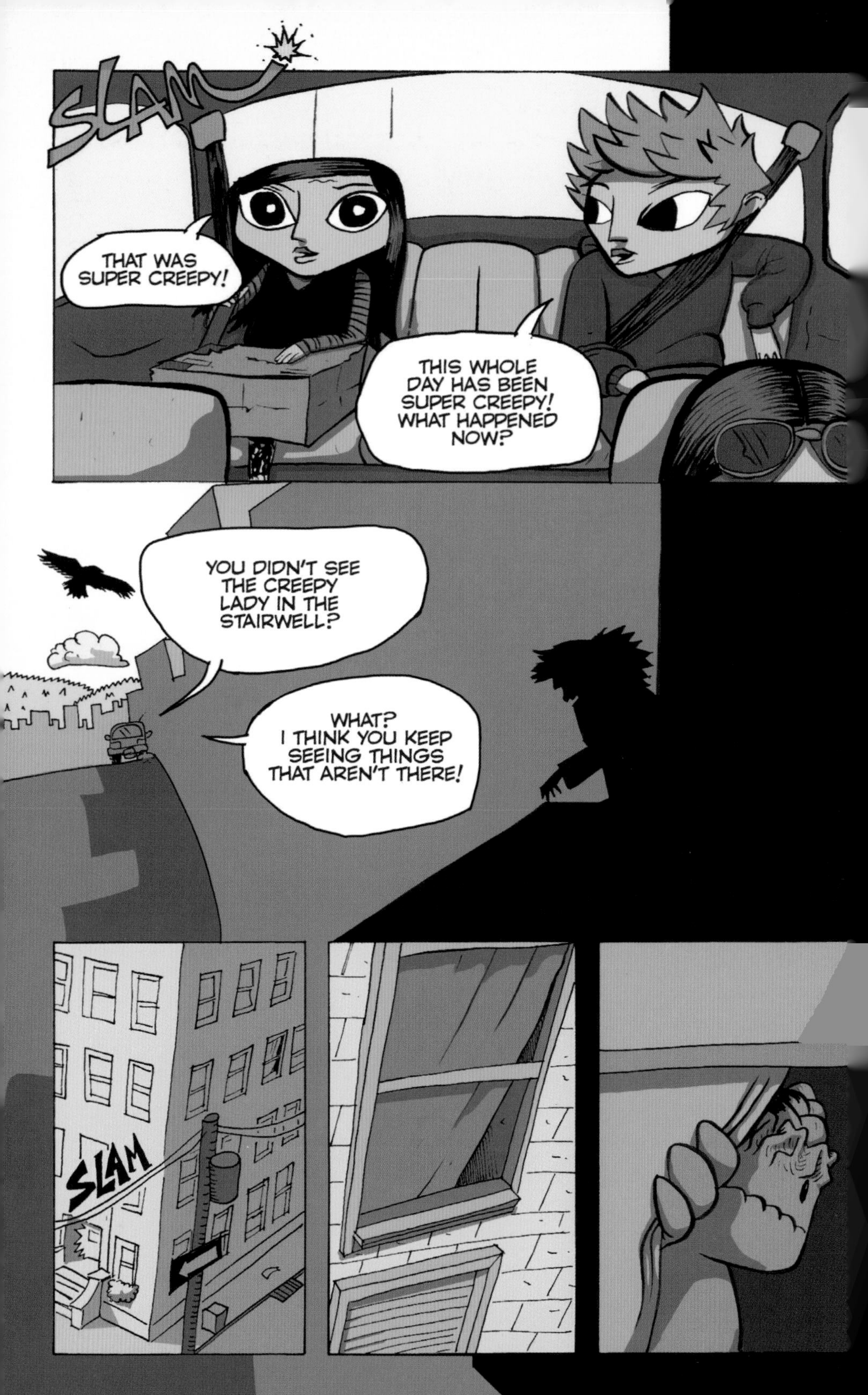
SLAM
THAT WAS SUPER CREEPY!
THIS WHOLE DAY HAS BEEN SUPER CREEPY! WHAT HAPPENED NOW?
YOU DIDN'T SEE THE CREEPY LADY IN THE STAIRWELL?
WHAT? I THINK YOU KEEP SEEING THINGS THAT AREN'T THERE!
SLAM

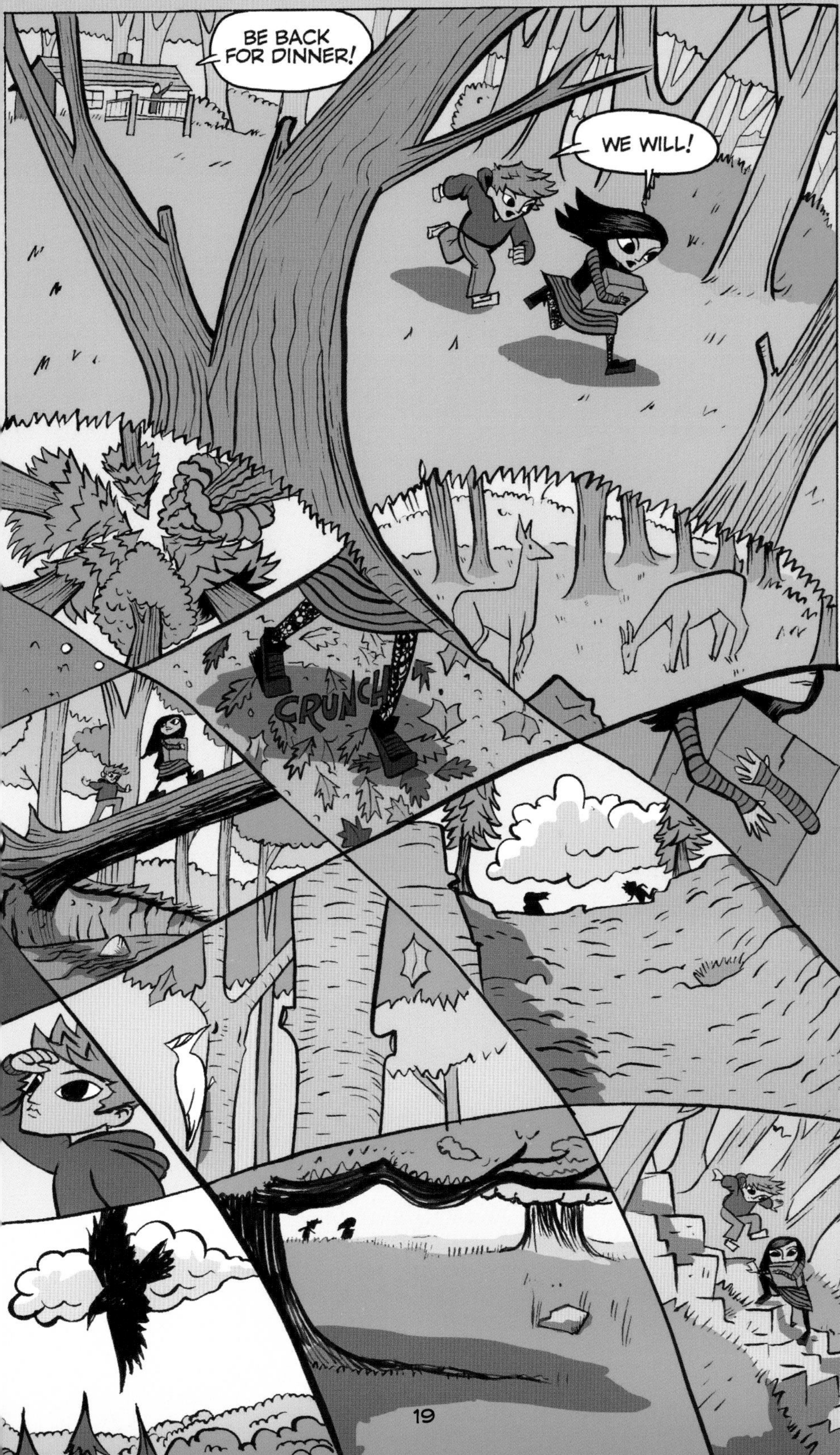
BE BACK FOR DINNER!
WE WILL!
CRUNCH

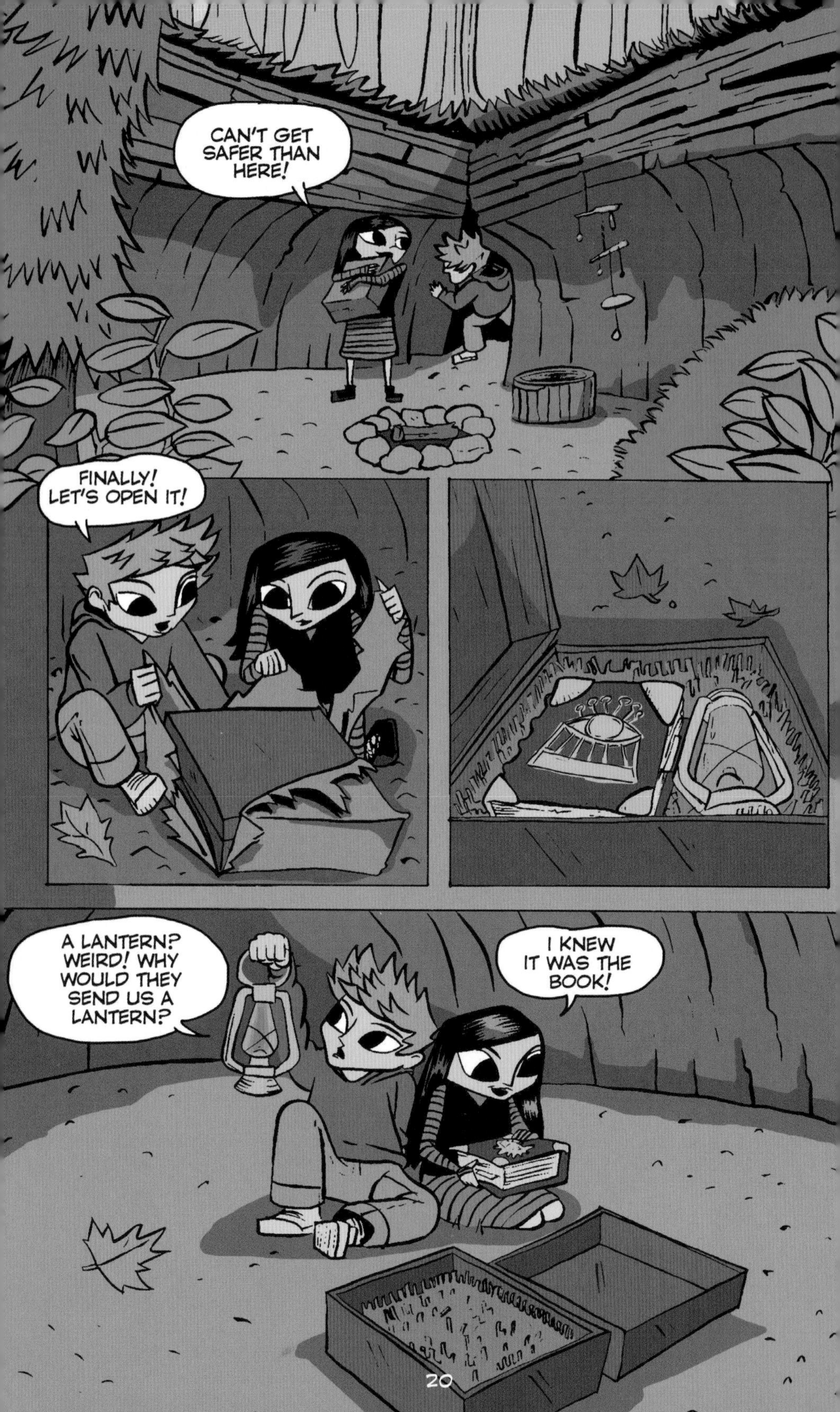
CAN'T GET SAFER THAN HERE!
FINALLY! LET'S OPEN IT!
A LANTERN? WEIRD! WHY WOULD THEY SEND US A LANTERN?
I KNEW IT WAS THE BOOK!

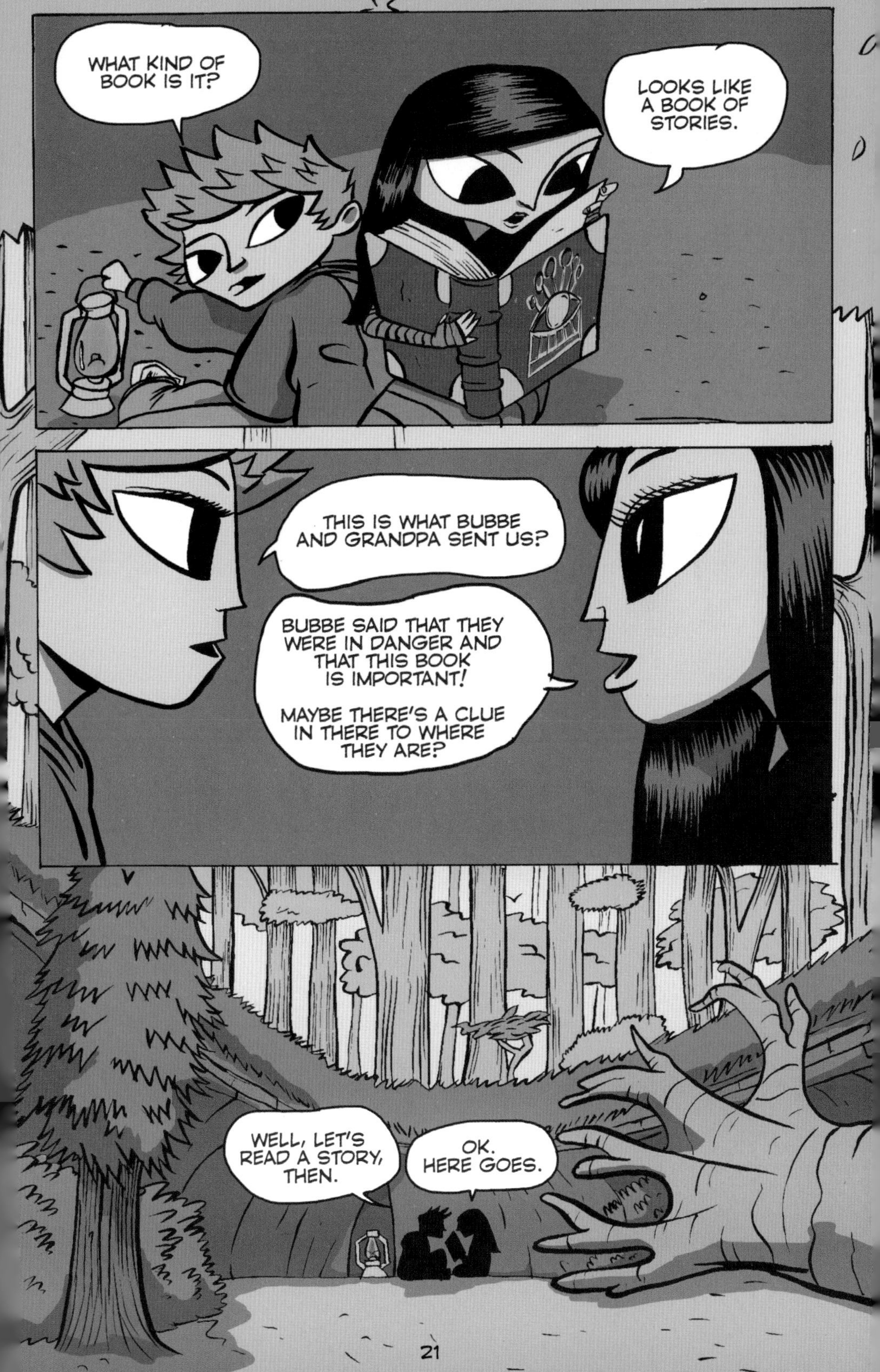
WHAT KIND OF BOOK IS IT?
LOOKS LIKE A BOOK OF STORIES.
THIS IS WHAT BUBBE AND GRANDPA SENT US?
BUBBE SAID THAT THEY WERE IN DANGER AND THAT THIS BOOK IS IMPORTANT!
MAYBE THERE'S A CLUE IN THERE TO WHERE THEY ARE?
WELL, LET'S READ A STORY, THEN.
OK. HERE GOES.

THE BUTTERFLY IN THE HAND

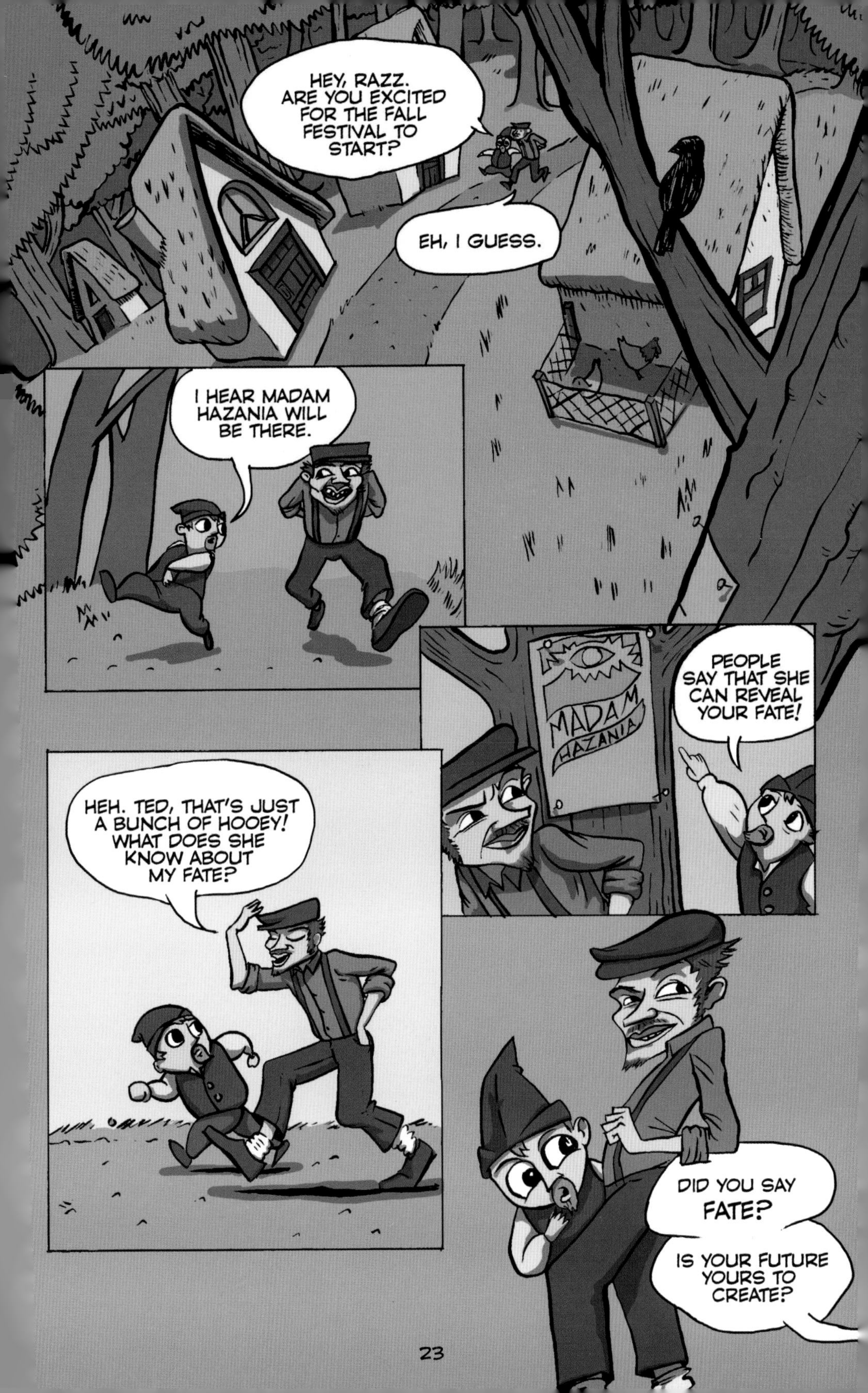
HEY, RAZZ. ARE YOU EXCITED FOR THE FALL FESTIVAL TO START?
EH, I GUESS.
I HEAR MADAM HAZANIA WILL BE THERE.
MADAM HAZANIA
PEOPLE SAY THAT SHE CAN REVEAL YOUR FATE!
HEH. TED, THAT'S JUST A BUNCH OF HOOEY! WHAT DOES SHE KNOW ABOUT MY FATE?
DID YOU SAY FATE?
IS YOUR FUTURE YOURS TO CREATE?

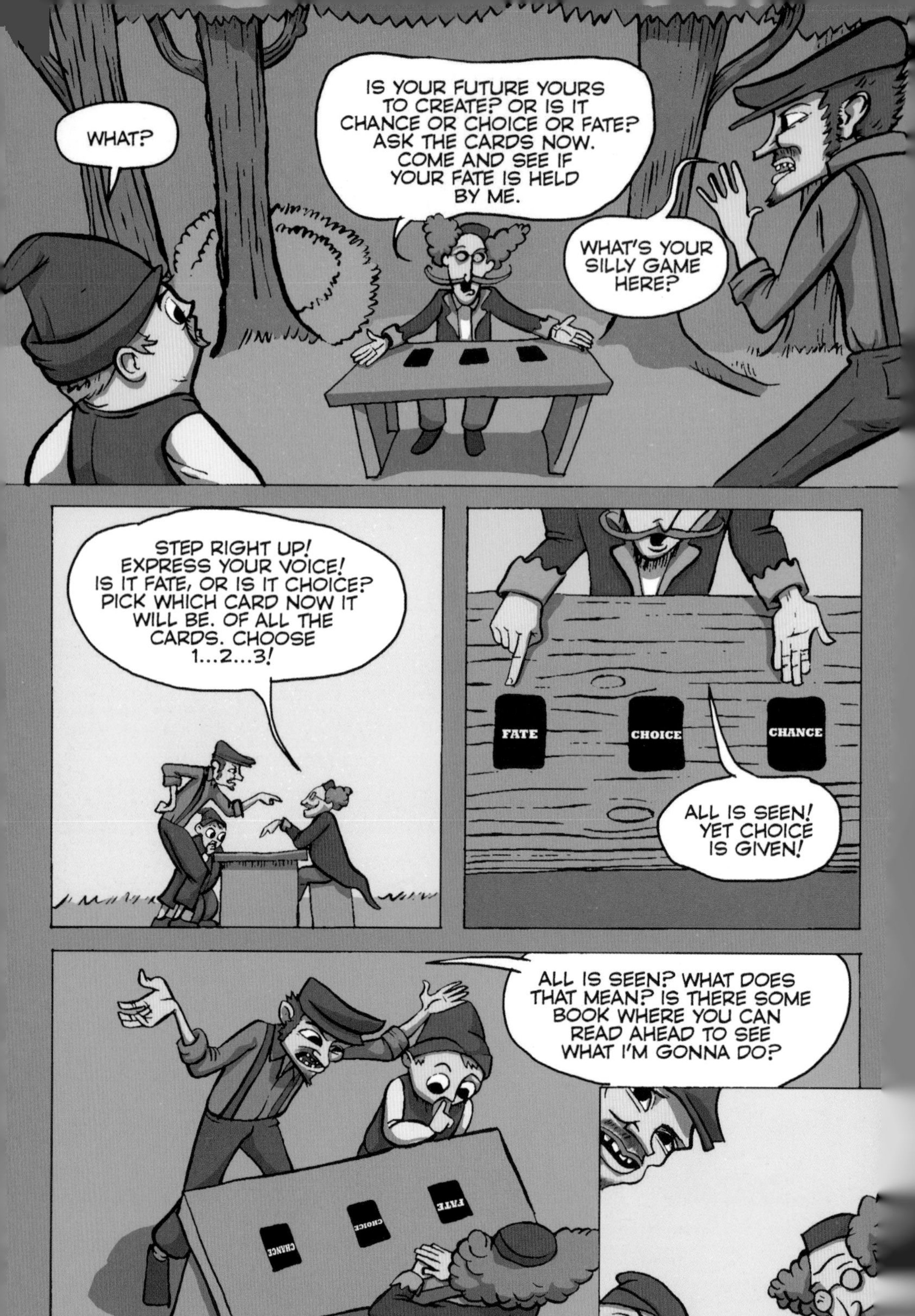
WHAT?
IS YOUR FUTURE YOURS TO CREATE? OR IS IT CHANCE OR CHOICE OR FATE? ASK THE CARDS NOW. COME AND SEE IF YOUR FATE IS HELD BY ME.
WHAT'S YOUR SILLY GAME HERE?
STEP RIGHT UP! EXPRESS YOUR VOICE! IS IT FATE, OR IS IT CHOICE? PICK WHICH CARD NOW IT WILL BE. OF ALL THE CARDS. CHOOSE 1...2...3!
FATE
CHOICE
CHANCE
ALL IS SEEN! YET CHOICE IS GIVEN!
ALL IS SEEN? WHAT DOES THAT MEAN? IS THERE SOME BOOK WHERE YOU CAN READ AHEAD TO SEE WHAT I'M GONNA DO?
CHANCE
CHOICE
FATE

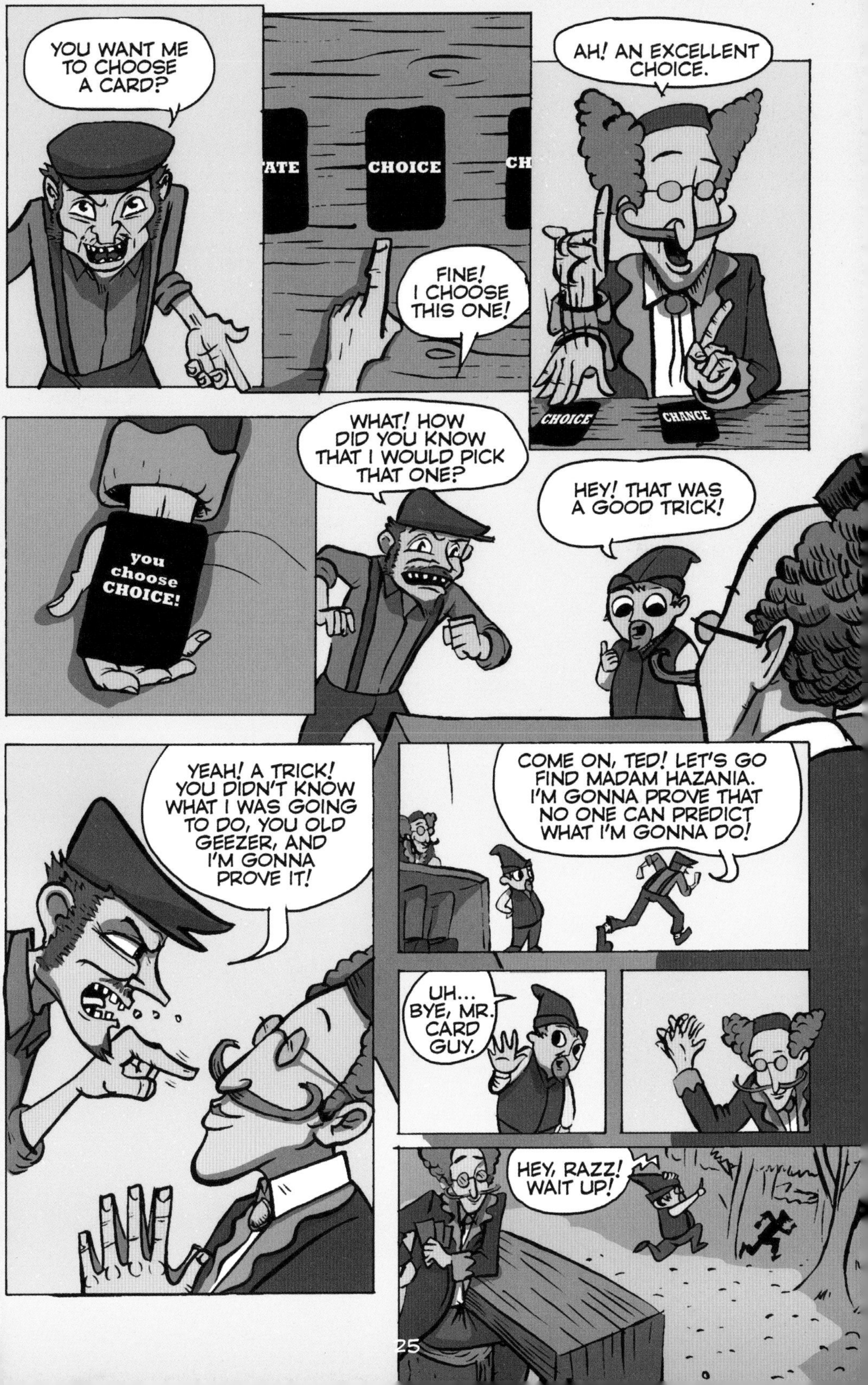
YOU WANT ME TO CHOOSE A CARD?
ATE
CHOICE
CH
FINE! I CHOOSE THIS ONE!
AH! AN EXCELLENT CHOICE.
CHOICE
CHANCE
you choose CHOICE!
WHAT! HOW DID YOU KNOW THAT I WOULD PICK THAT ONE?
HEY! THAT WAS A GOOD TRICK!
YEAH! A TRICK! YOU DIDN'T KNOW WHAT I WAS GOING TO DO, YOU OLD GEEZER, AND I'M GONNA PROVE IT!
COME ON, TED! LET'S GO FIND MADAM HAZANIA. I'M GONNA PROVE THAT NO ONE CAN PREDICT WHAT I'M GONNA DO!
UH... BYE, MR. CARD GUY.
HEY, RAZZ! WAIT UP!

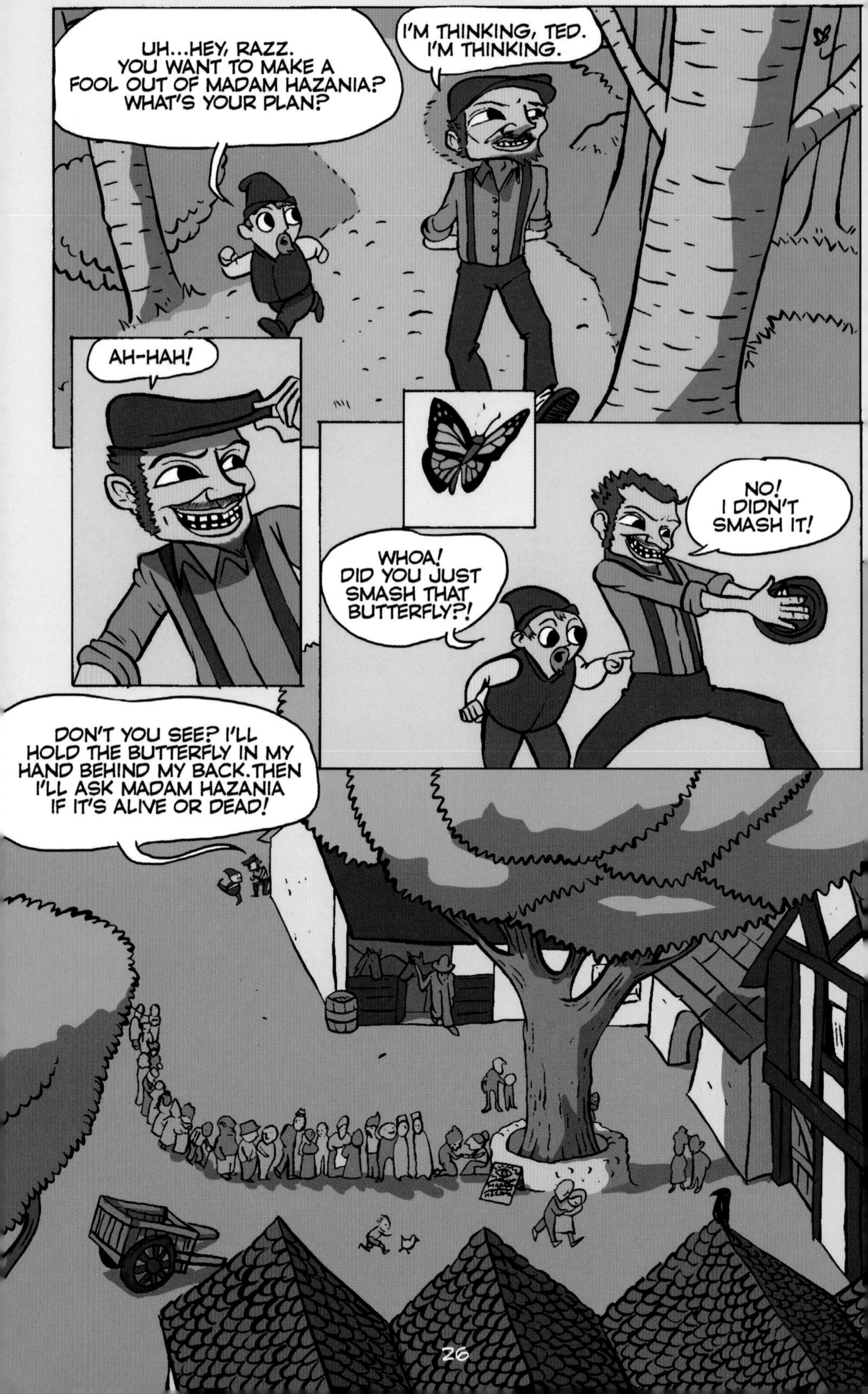

UH...HEY, RAZZ. YOU WANT TO MAKE A FOOL OUT OF MADAM HAZANIA? WHAT'S YOUR PLAN?
I'M THINKING, TED. I'M THINKING.
AH-HAH!
NO! I DIDN'T SMASH IT!
WHOA! DID YOU JUST SMASH THAT BUTTERFLY?!
DON'T YOU SEE? I'LL HOLD THE BUTTERFLY IN MY HAND BEHIND MY BACK. THEN I'LL ASK MADAM HAZANIA IF IT'S ALIVE OR DEAD!

THERE'S NO WAY SHE CAN WIN, RIGHT? IF SHE SAYS THE BUTTERFLY IS DEAD, THEN I'LL LET IT GO, AND IT WILL FLY AWAY!

OH! THAT'S A GOOD PLAN, RAZZ!

BUT... WHAT IF SHE SAYS THAT IT'S ALIVE?

THEN I CRUSH IT IN MY HAND AND SHOW HER THE DEAD BUTTERFLY!

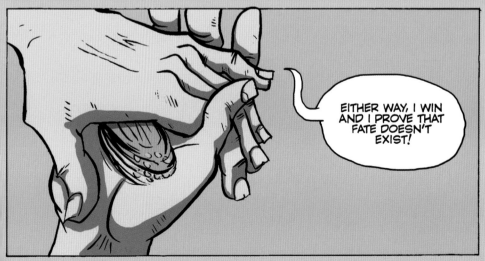

EITHER WAY, I WIN AND I PROVE THAT FATE DOESN'T EXIST!

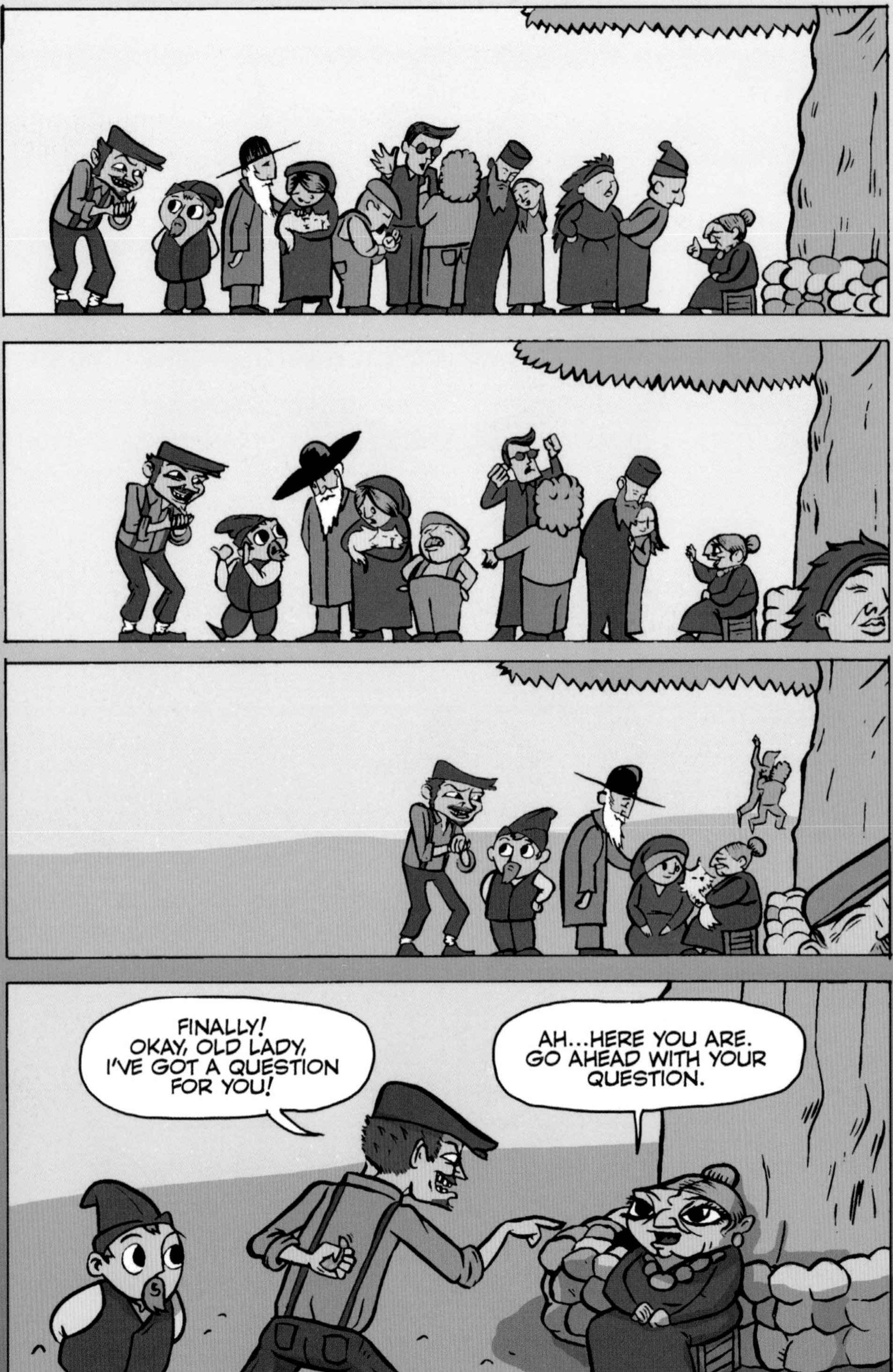
FINALLY!
OKAY, OLD LADY,
I'VE GOT A QUESTION
FOR YOU!
AH...HERE YOU ARE.
GO AHEAD WITH YOUR
QUESTION.

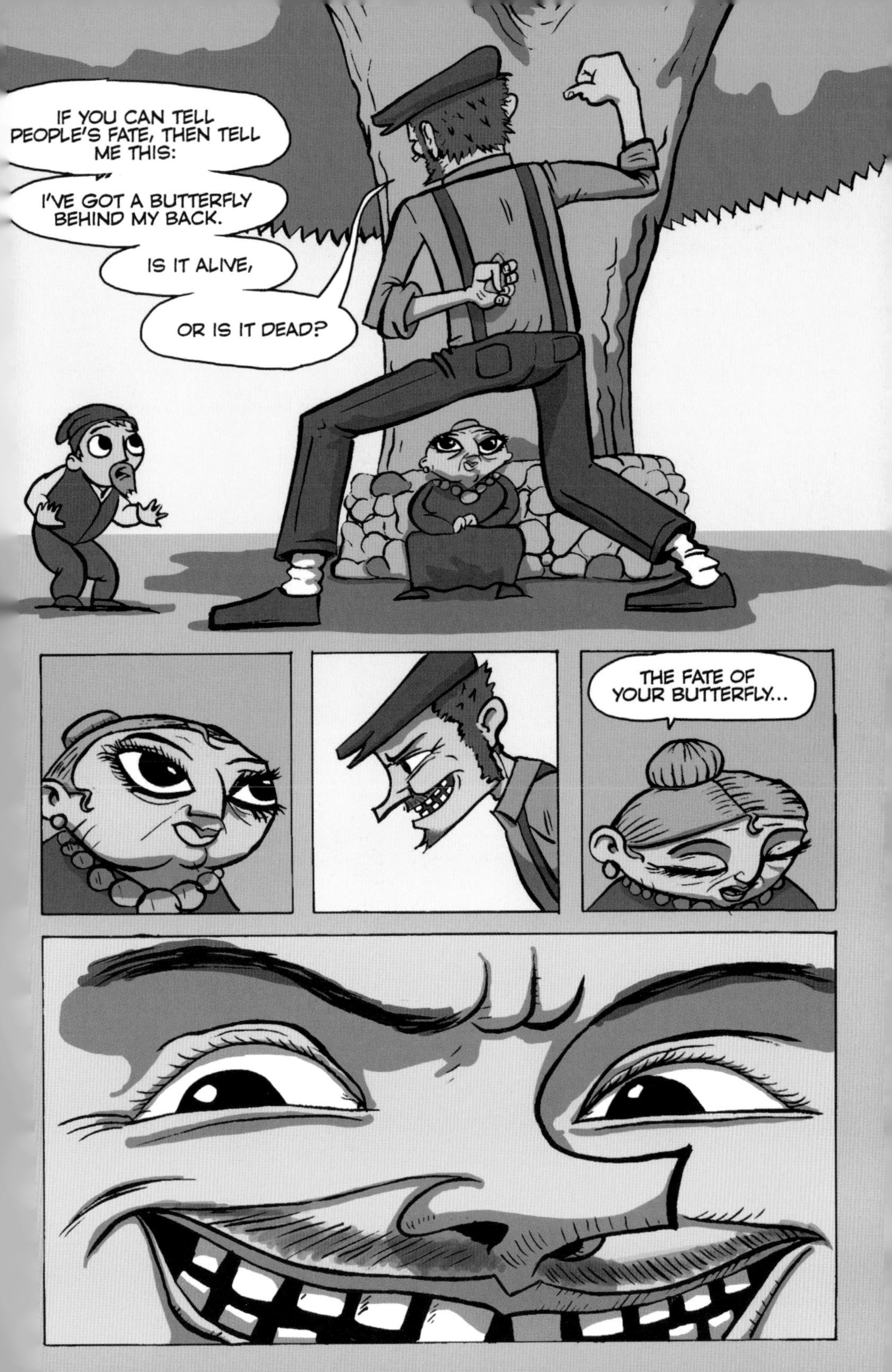
IF YOU CAN TELL PEOPLE'S FATE, THEN TELL ME THIS:
I'VE GOT A BUTTERFLY BEHIND MY BACK.
IS IT ALIVE,
OR IS IT DEAD?
THE FATE OF YOUR BUTTERFLY...

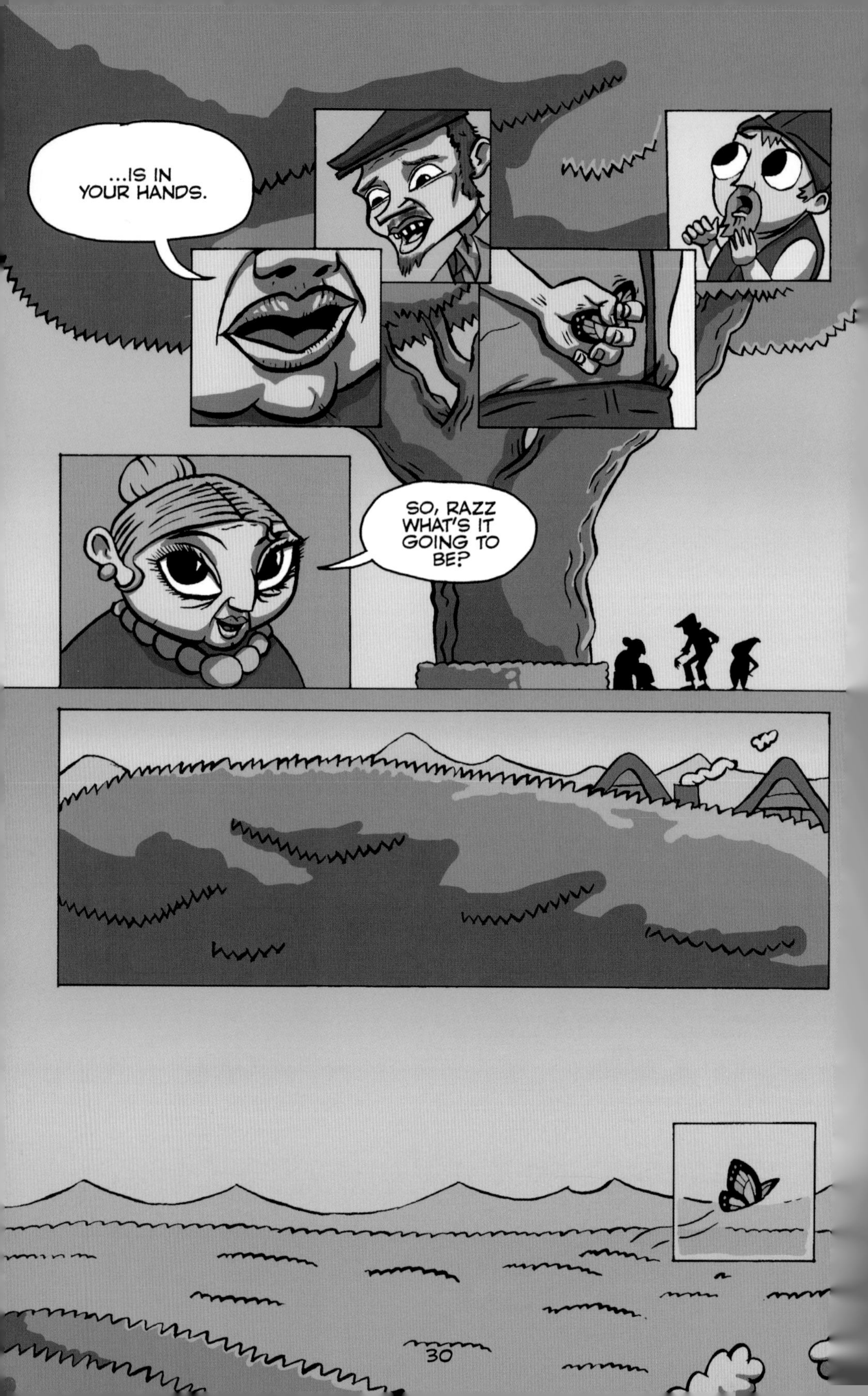

...IS IN YOUR HANDS.
SO, RAZZ WHAT'S IT GOING TO BE?

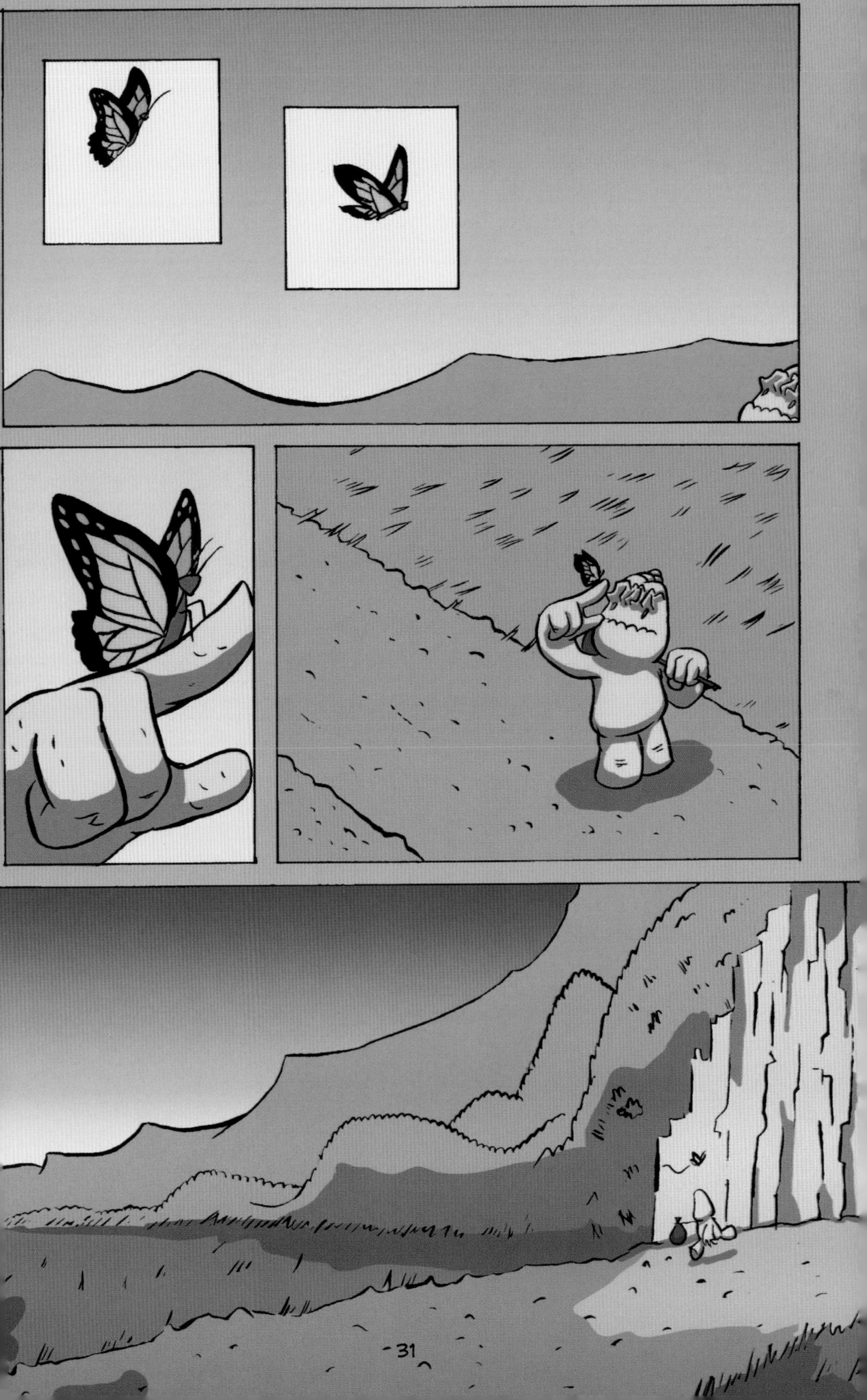

THE SCRIBE AND THE PRINCESS

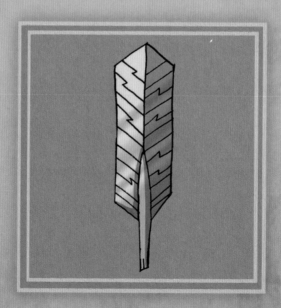

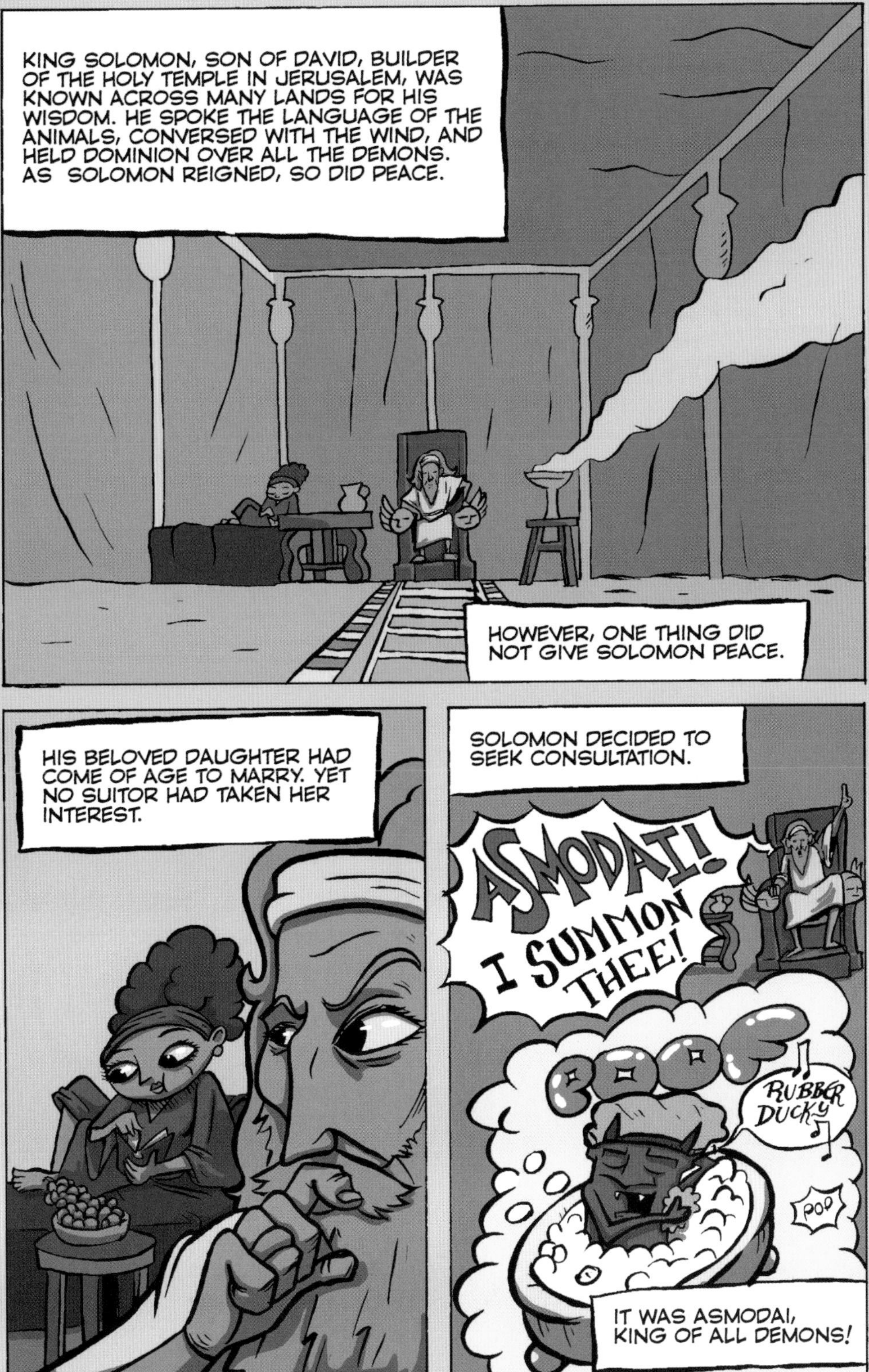
KING SOLOMON, SON OF DAVID, BUILDER OF THE HOLY TEMPLE IN JERUSALEM, WAS KNOWN ACROSS MANY LANDS FOR HIS WISDOM. HE SPOKE THE LANGUAGE OF THE ANIMALS, CONVERSED WITH THE WIND, AND HELD DOMINION OVER ALL THE DEMONS. AS SOLOMON REIGNED, SO DID PEACE.
HOWEVER, ONE THING DID NOT GIVE SOLOMON PEACE.
HIS BELOVED DAUGHTER HAD COME OF AGE TO MARRY. YET NO SUITOR HAD TAKEN HER INTEREST.
SOLOMON DECIDED TO SEEK CONSULTATION.
ASMODAI! I SUMMON THEE!
POOF
RUBBER DUCKY
POP
IT WAS ASMODAI, KING OF ALL DEMONS!

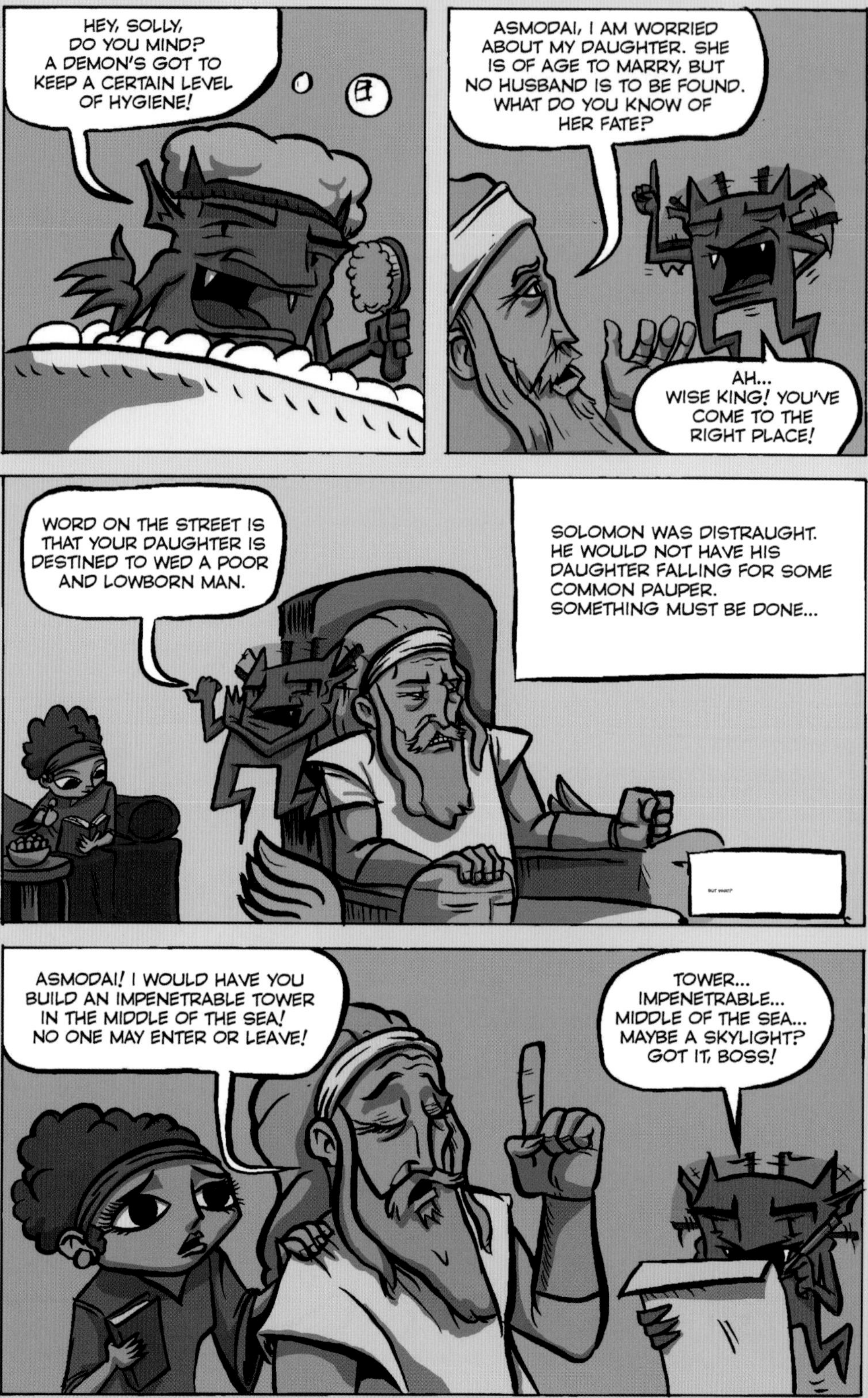
HEY, SOLLY, DO YOU MIND? A DEMON'S GOT TO KEEP A CERTAIN LEVEL OF HYGIENE!
ASMODAI, I AM WORRIED ABOUT MY DAUGHTER. SHE IS OF AGE TO MARRY, BUT NO HUSBAND IS TO BE FOUND. WHAT DO YOU KNOW OF HER FATE?
AH... WISE KING! YOU'VE COME TO THE RIGHT PLACE!
WORD ON THE STREET IS THAT YOUR DAUGHTER IS DESTINED TO WED A POOR AND LOWBORN MAN.
SOLOMON WAS DISTRAUGHT. HE WOULD NOT HAVE HIS DAUGHTER FALLING FOR SOME COMMON PAUPER. SOMETHING MUST BE DONE...
BUT WHAT?
ASMODAI! I WOULD HAVE YOU BUILD AN IMPENETRABLE TOWER IN THE MIDDLE OF THE SEA! NO ONE MAY ENTER OR LEAVE!
TOWER... IMPENETRABLE... MIDDLE OF THE SEA... MAYBE A SKYLIGHT? GOT IT, BOSS!

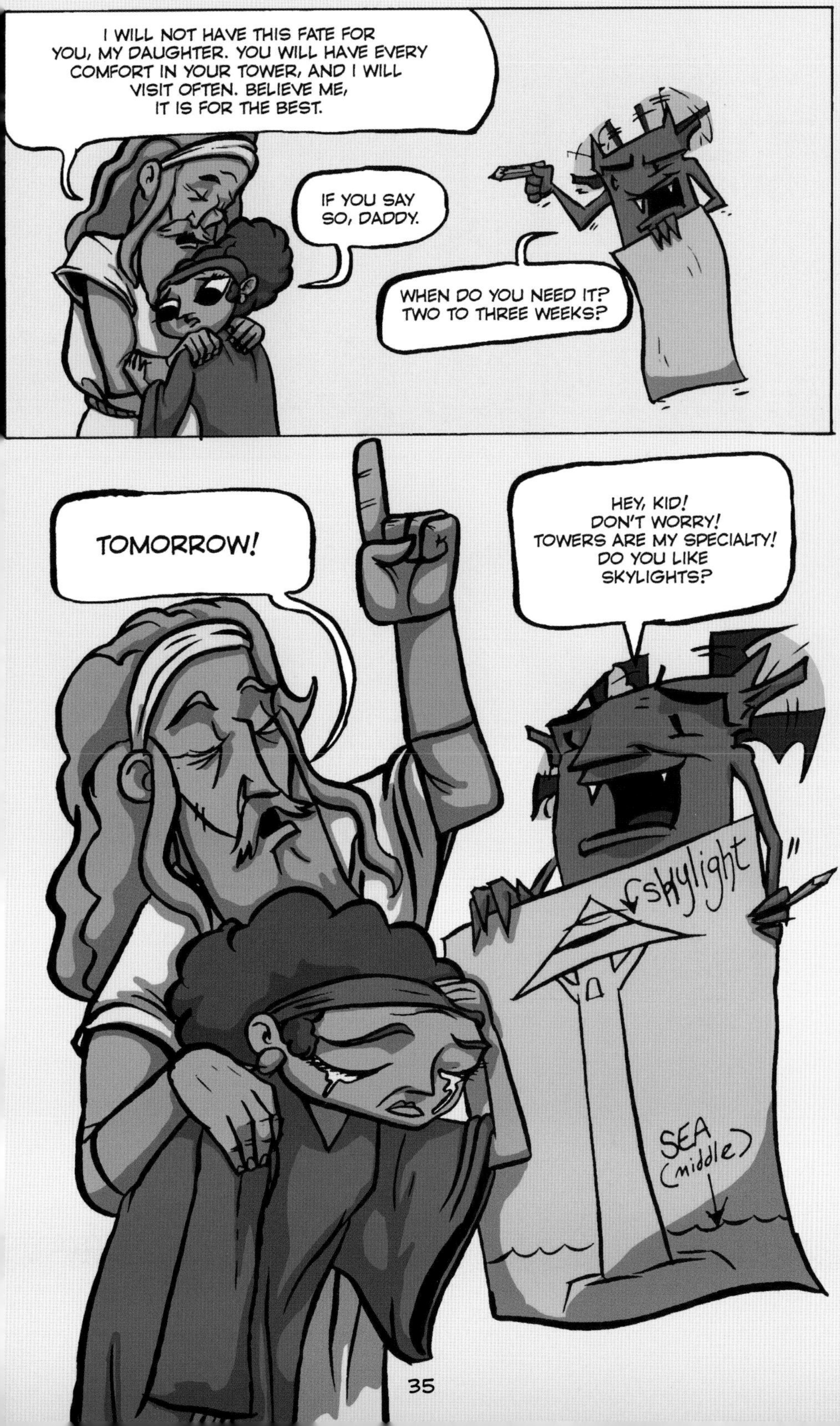
I WILL NOT HAVE THIS FATE FOR YOU, MY DAUGHTER. YOU WILL HAVE EVERY COMFORT IN YOUR TOWER, AND I WILL VISIT OFTEN. BELIEVE ME, IT IS FOR THE BEST.
IF YOU SAY SO, DADDY.
WHEN DO YOU NEED IT? TWO TO THREE WEEKS?
TOMORROW!
HEY, KID! DON'T WORRY! TOWERS ARE MY SPECIALTY! DO YOU LIKE SKYLIGHTS?
skylight
SEA (middle)

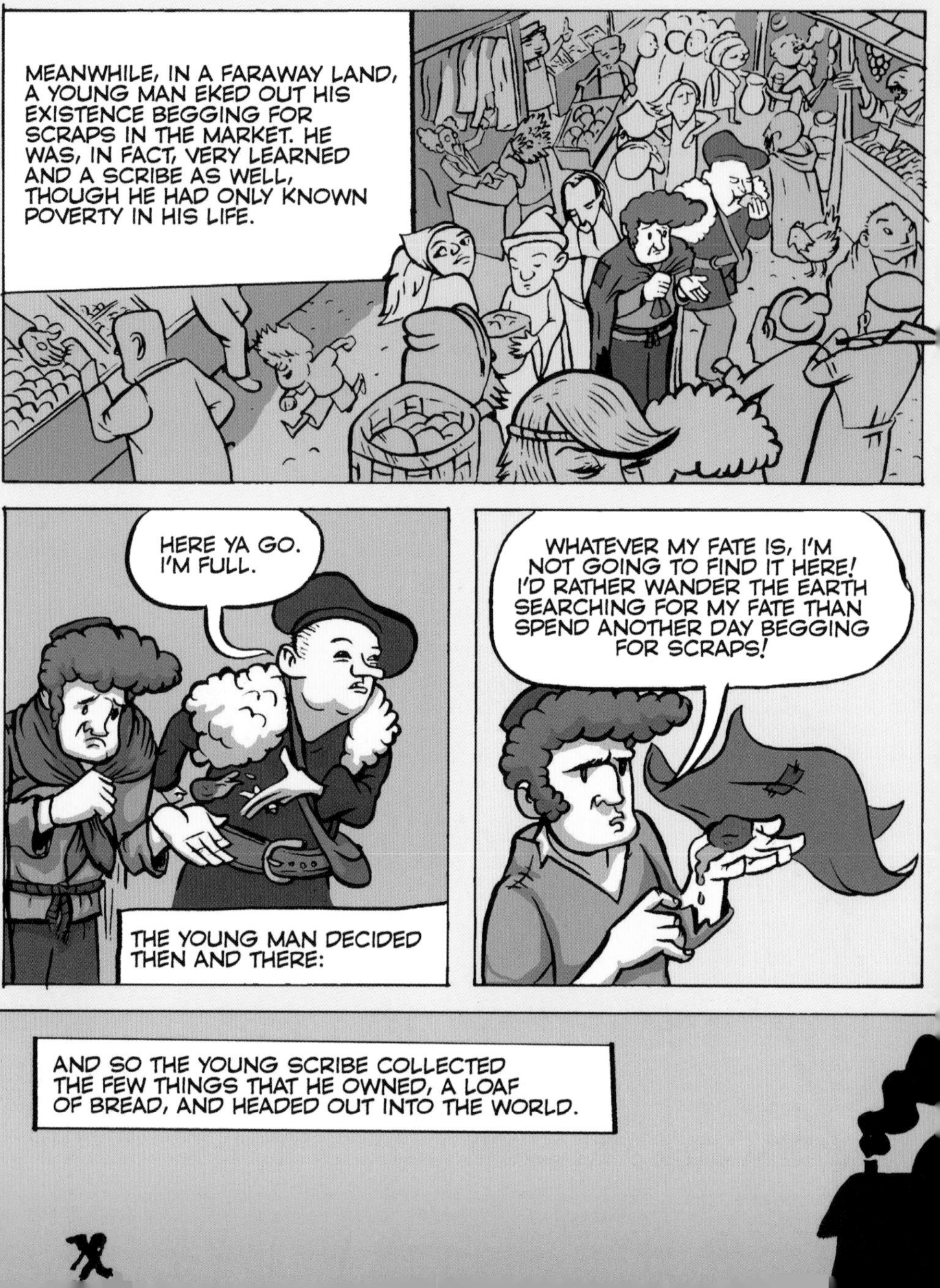
MEANWHILE, IN A FARAWAY LAND, A YOUNG MAN EKED OUT HIS EXISTENCE BEGGING FOR SCRAPS IN THE MARKET. HE WAS, IN FACT, VERY LEARNED AND A SCRIBE AS WELL, THOUGH HE HAD ONLY KNOWN POVERTY IN HIS LIFE.
HERE YA GO. I'M FULL.
THE YOUNG MAN DECIDED THEN AND THERE:
WHATEVER MY FATE IS, I'M NOT GOING TO FIND IT HERE! I'D RATHER WANDER THE EARTH SEARCHING FOR MY FATE THAN SPEND ANOTHER DAY BEGGING FOR SCRAPS!
AND SO THE YOUNG SCRIBE COLLECTED THE FEW THINGS THAT HE OWNED, A LOAF OF BREAD, AND HEADED OUT INTO THE WORLD.

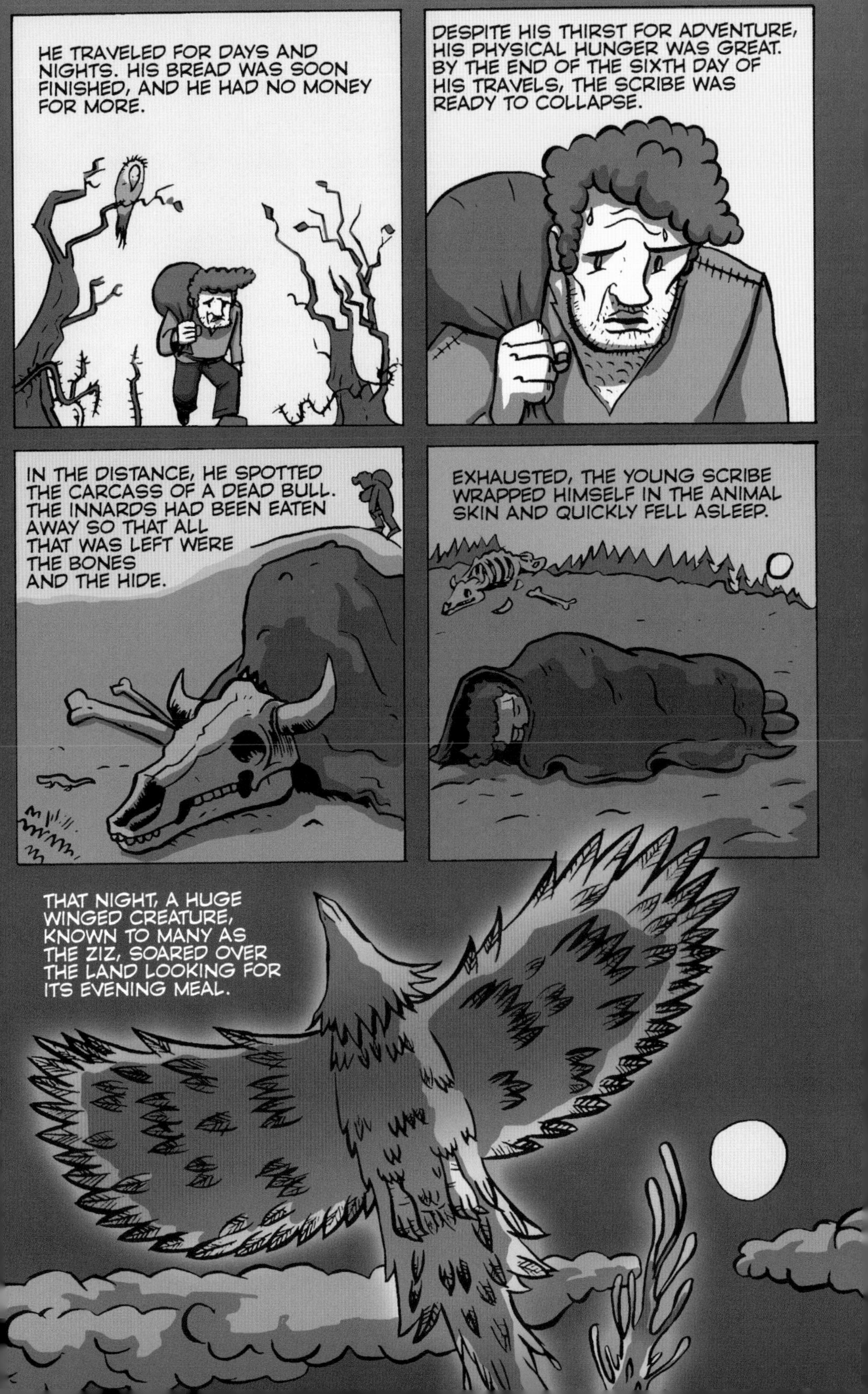
HE TRAVELED FOR DAYS AND NIGHTS. HIS BREAD WAS SOON FINISHED, AND HE HAD NO MONEY FOR MORE.
DESPITE HIS THIRST FOR ADVENTURE, HIS PHYSICAL HUNGER WAS GREAT. BY THE END OF THE SIXTH DAY OF HIS TRAVELS, THE SCRIBE WAS READY TO COLLAPSE.
IN THE DISTANCE, HE SPOTTED THE CARCASS OF A DEAD BULL. THE INNARDS HAD BEEN EATEN AWAY SO THAT ALL THAT WAS LEFT WERE THE BONES AND THE HIDE.
EXHAUSTED, THE YOUNG SCRIBE WRAPPED HIMSELF IN THE ANIMAL SKIN AND QUICKLY FELL ASLEEP.
THAT NIGHT, A HUGE WINGED CREATURE, KNOWN TO MANY AS THE ZIZ, SOARED OVER THE LAND LOOKING FOR ITS EVENING MEAL.

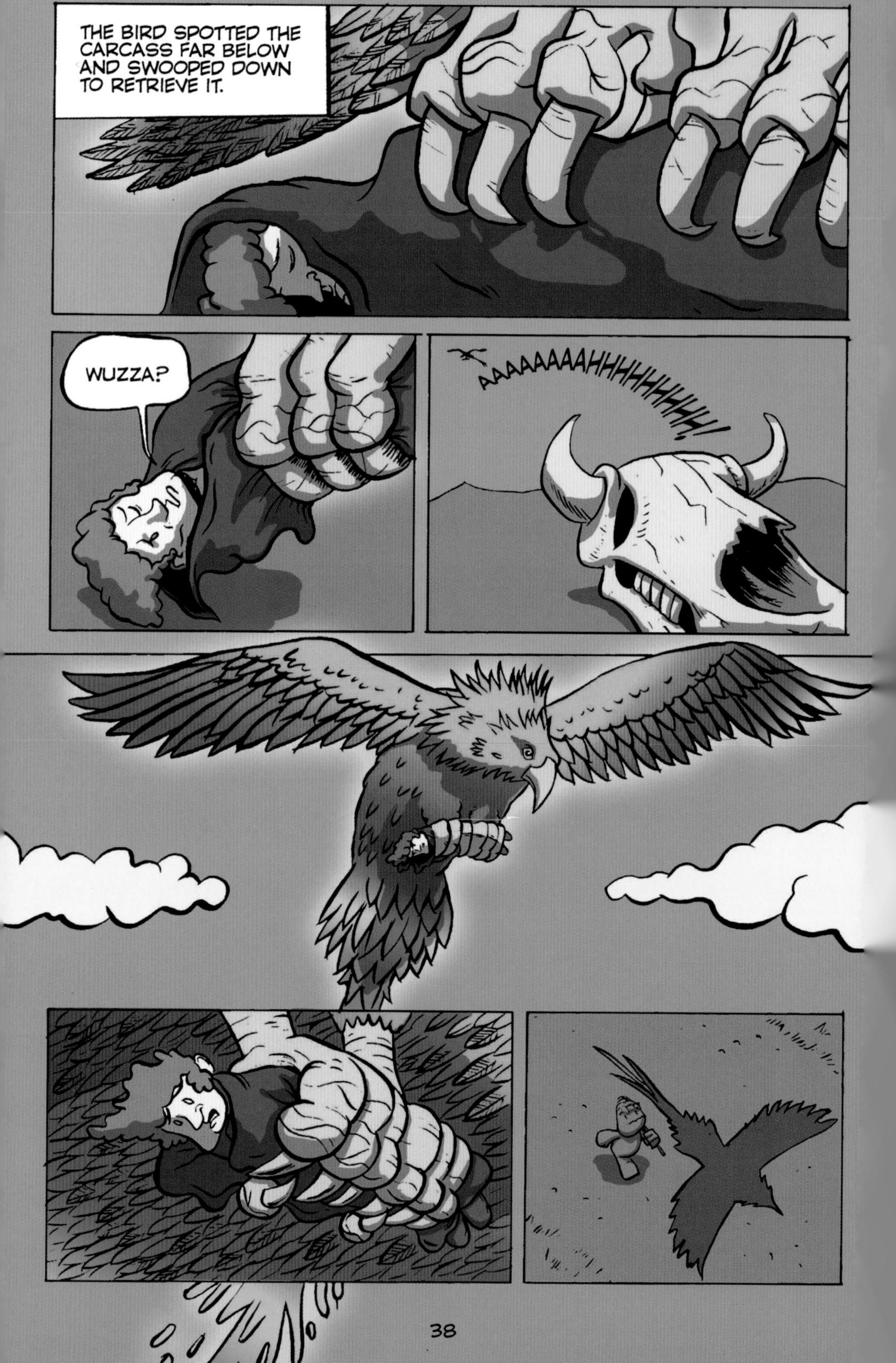
THE BIRD SPOTTED THE CARCASS FAR BELOW AND SWOOPED DOWN TO RETRIEVE IT.
WUZZA?
AAAAAAAAHHHHHHHHH!

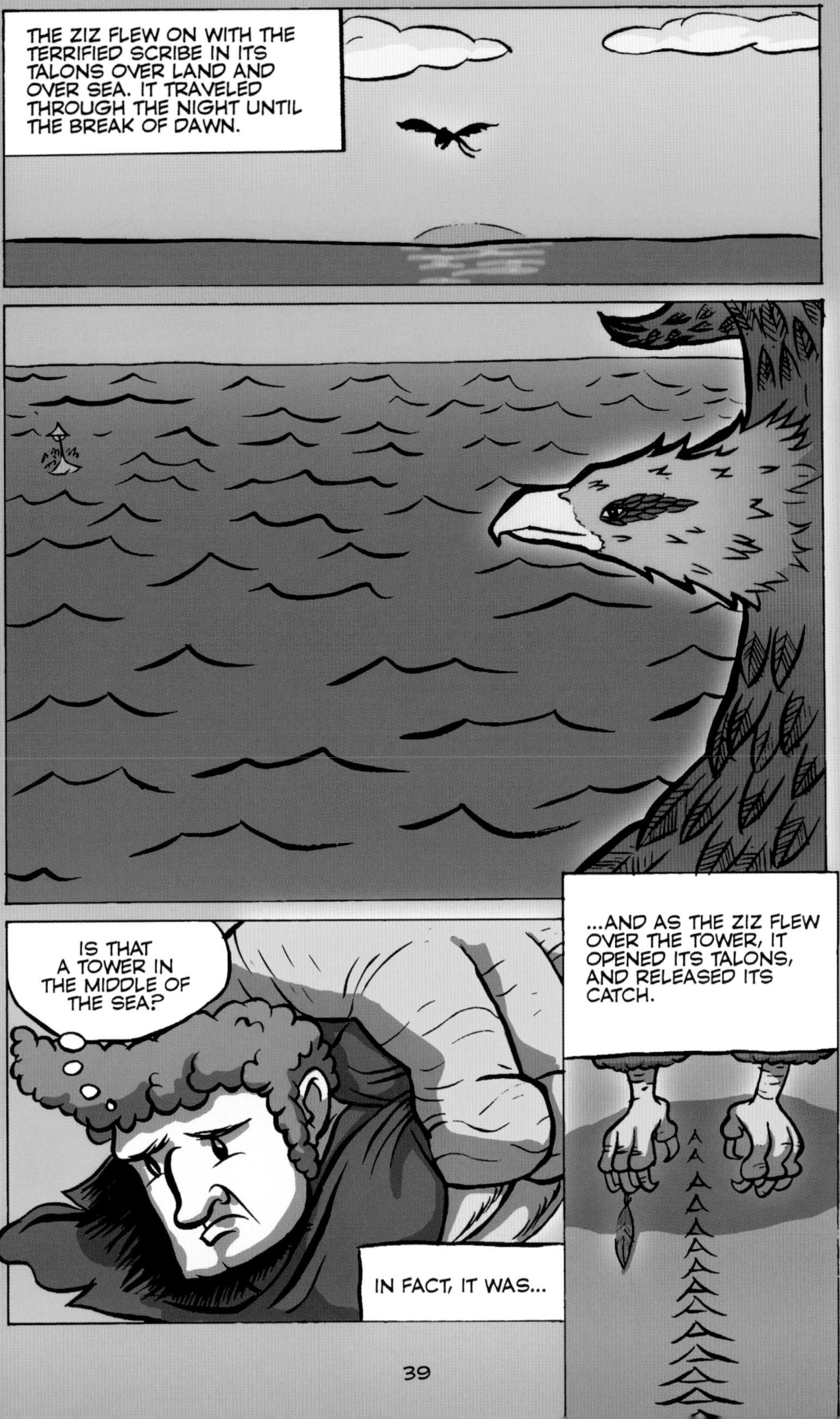
THE ZIZ FLEW ON WITH THE TERRIFIED SCRIBE IN ITS TALONS OVER LAND AND OVER SEA. IT TRAVELED THROUGH THE NIGHT UNTIL THE BREAK OF DAWN.
IS THAT A TOWER IN THE MIDDLE OF THE SEA?
IN FACT, IT WAS...
...AND AS THE ZIZ FLEW OVER THE TOWER, IT OPENED ITS TALONS, AND RELEASED ITS CATCH.
AAAAAAAAAAAAAAAAAA

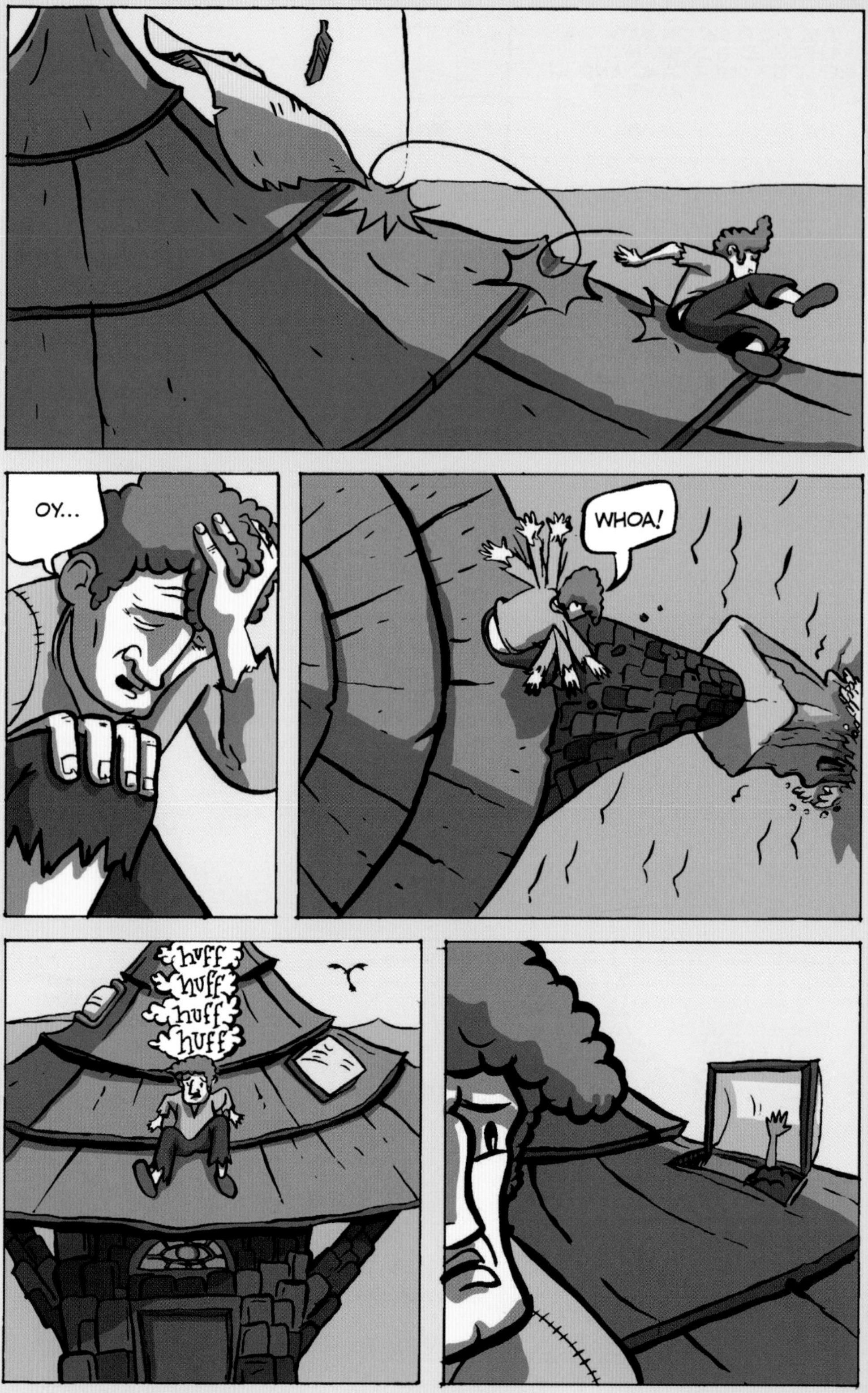
OY...
WHOA!
huff
huff
huff
huff

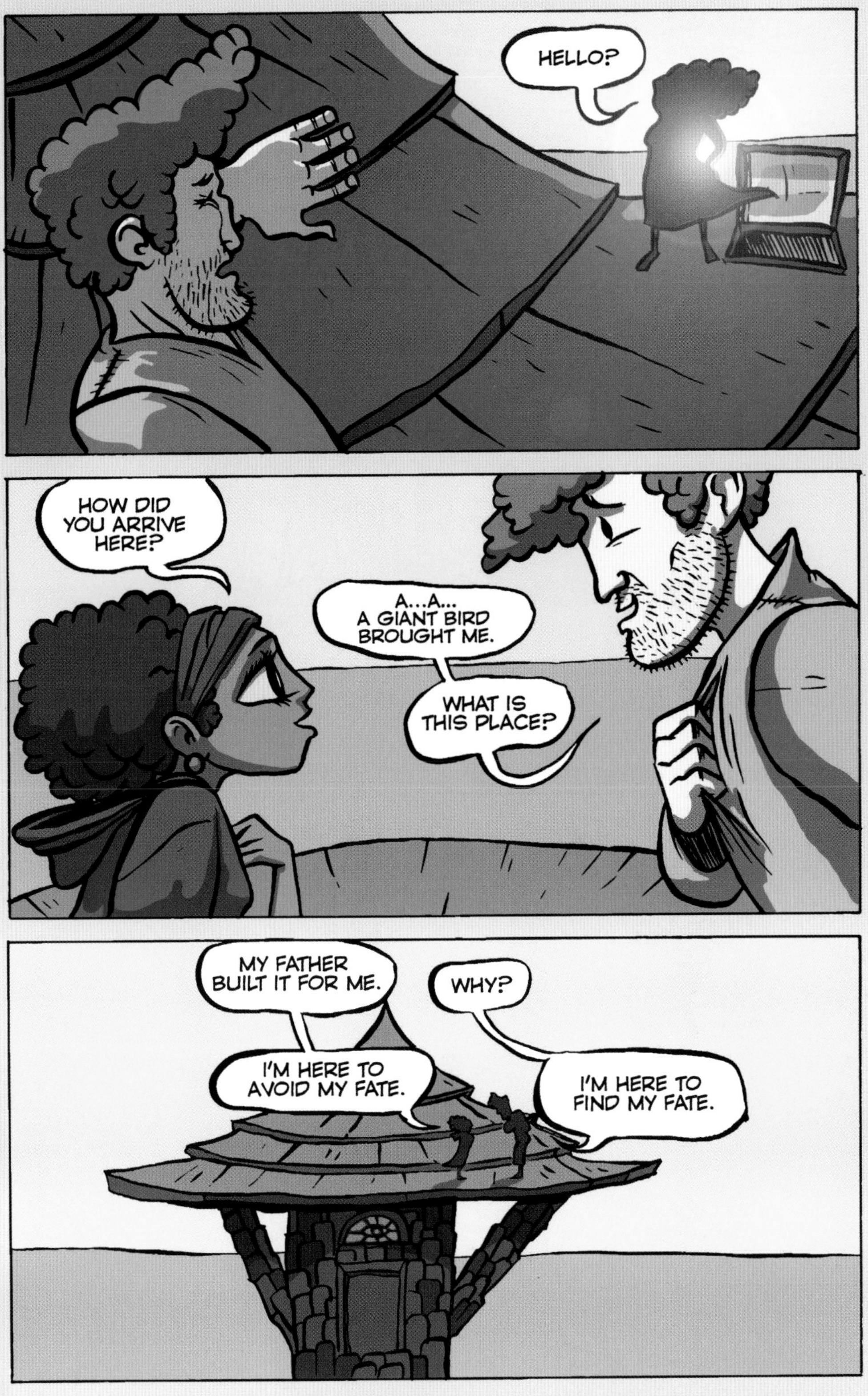
HELLO?
HOW DID YOU ARRIVE HERE?
A...A... A GIANT BIRD BROUGHT ME.
WHAT IS THIS PLACE?
MY FATHER BUILT IT FOR ME.
I'M HERE TO AVOID MY FATE.
WHY?
I'M HERE TO FIND MY FATE.

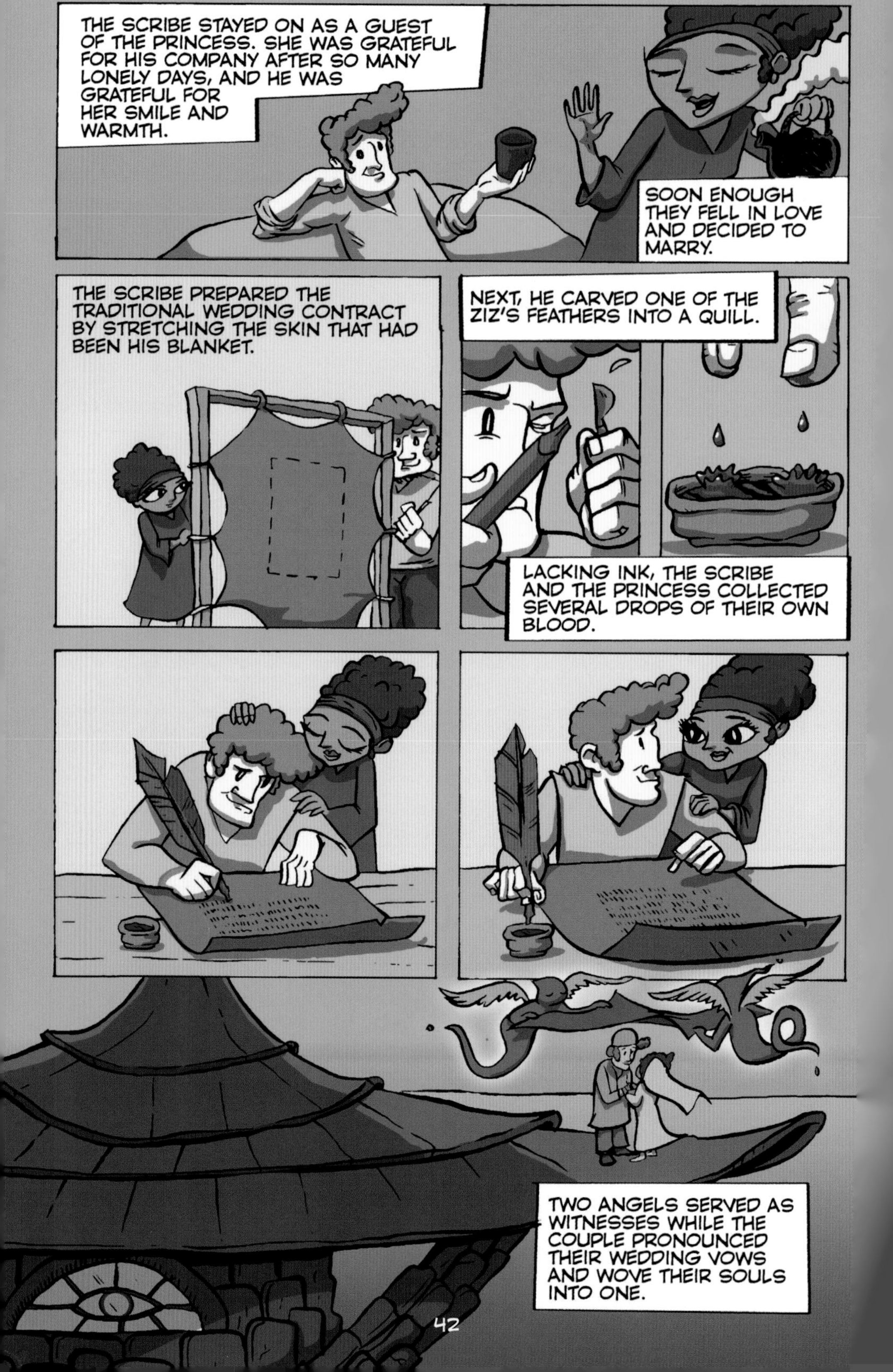
THE SCRIBE STAYED ON AS A GUEST OF THE PRINCESS. SHE WAS GRATEFUL FOR HIS COMPANY AFTER SO MANY LONELY DAYS, AND HE WAS GRATEFUL FOR HER SMILE AND WARMTH.
SOON ENOUGH THEY FELL IN LOVE AND DECIDED TO MARRY.
THE SCRIBE PREPARED THE TRADITIONAL WEDDING CONTRACT BY STRETCHING THE SKIN THAT HAD BEEN HIS BLANKET.
NEXT, HE CARVED ONE OF THE ZIZ'S FEATHERS INTO A QUILL.
LACKING INK, THE SCRIBE AND THE PRINCESS COLLECTED SEVERAL DROPS OF THEIR OWN BLOOD.
TWO ANGELS SERVED AS WITNESSES WHILE THE COUPLE PRONOUNCED THEIR WEDDING VOWS AND WOVE THEIR SOULS INTO ONE.

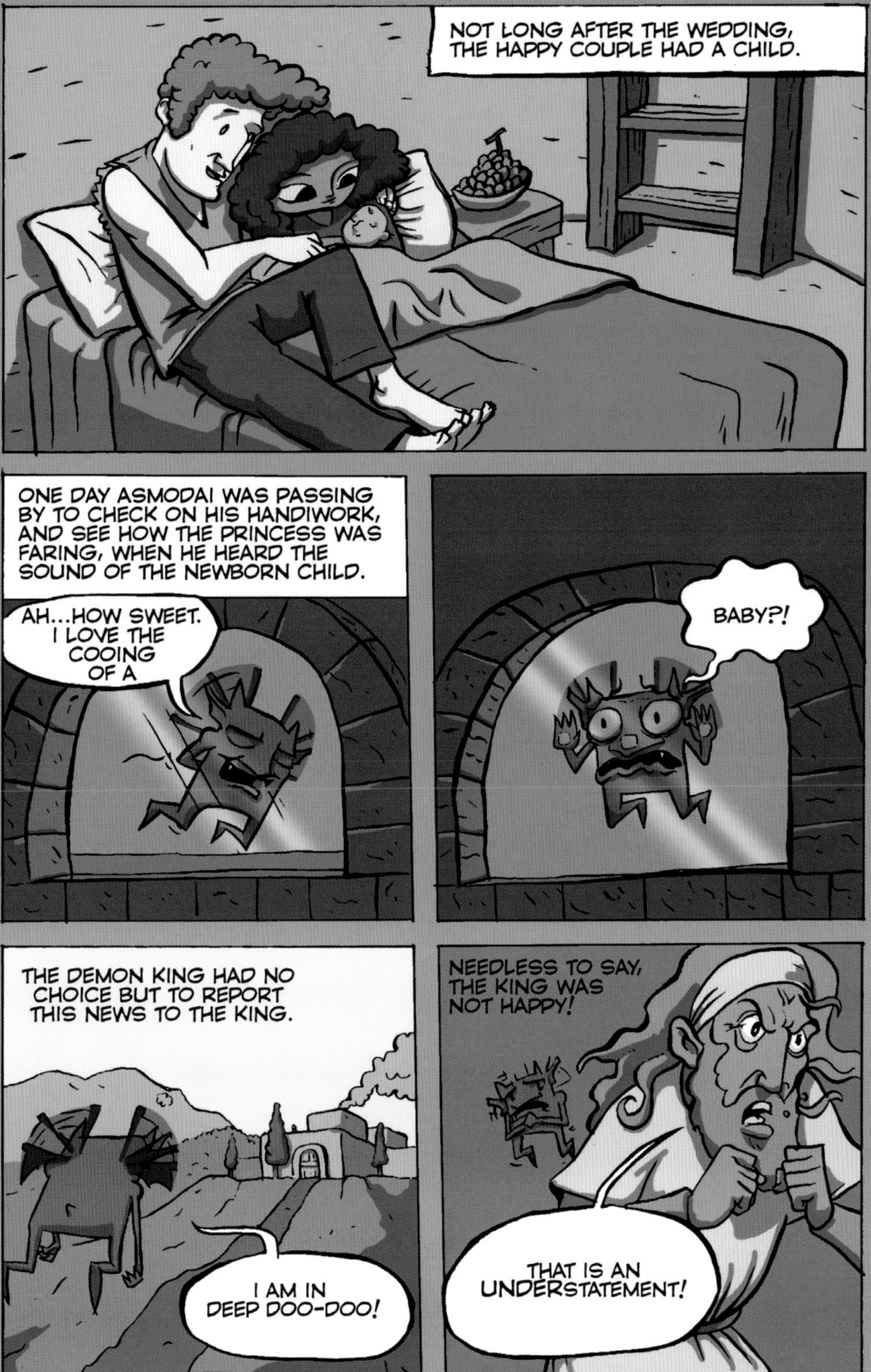
NOT LONG AFTER THE WEDDING, THE HAPPY COUPLE HAD A CHILD.
ONE DAY ASMODAI WAS PASSING BY TO CHECK ON HIS HANDIWORK, AND SEE HOW THE PRINCESS WAS FARING, WHEN HE HEARD THE SOUND OF THE NEWBORN CHILD.
AH...HOW SWEET. I LOVE THE COOING OF A
BABY?!
THE DEMON KING HAD NO CHOICE BUT TO REPORT THIS NEWS TO THE KING.
I AM IN DEEP DOO-DOO!
NEEDLESS TO SAY, THE KING WAS NOT HAPPY!
THAT IS AN UNDERSTATEMENT!

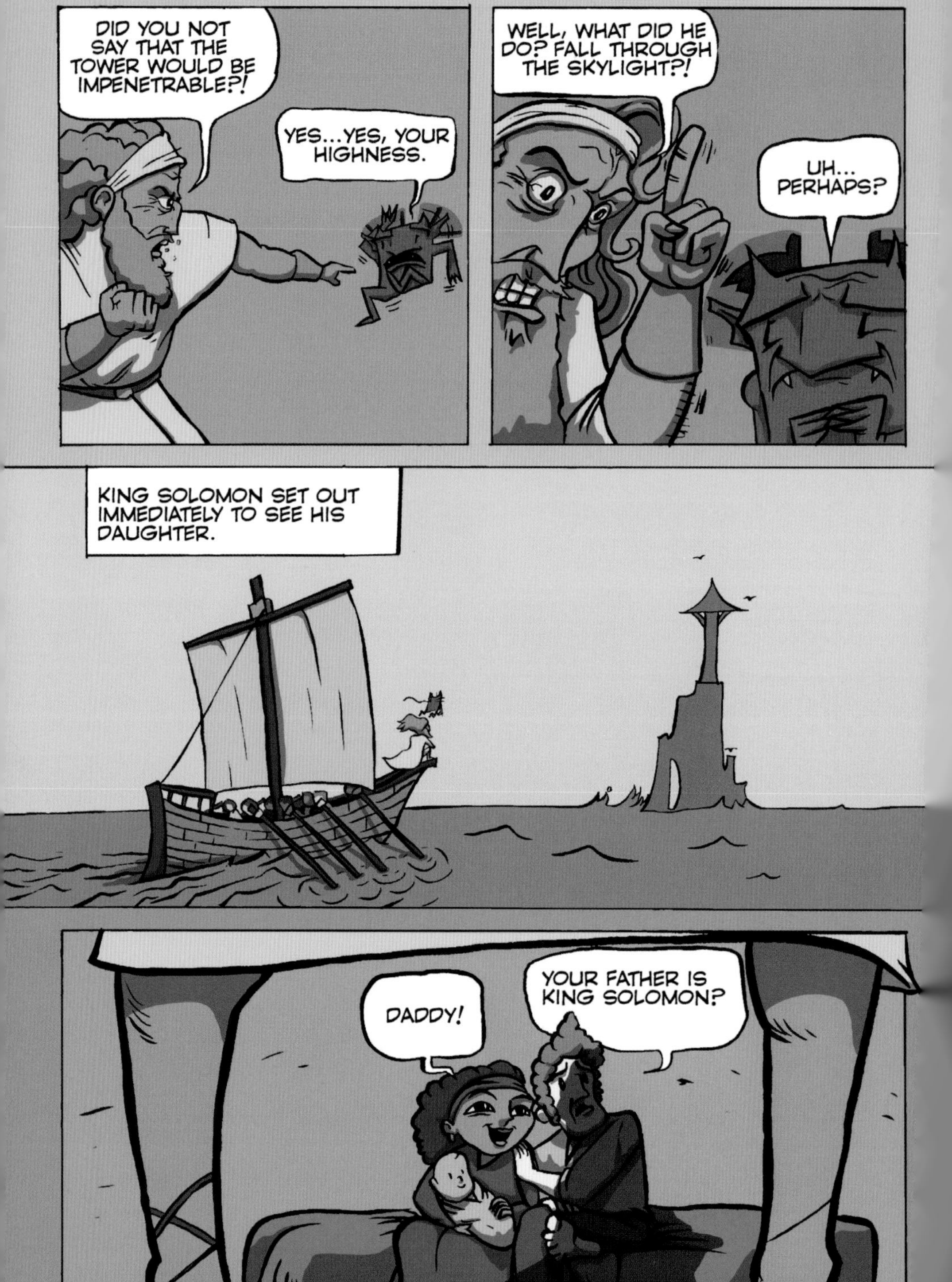
DID YOU NOT SAY THAT THE TOWER WOULD BE IMPENETRABLE?!
YES...YES, YOUR HIGHNESS.
WELL, WHAT DID HE DO? FALL THROUGH THE SKYLIGHT?!
UH... PERHAPS?
KING SOLOMON SET OUT IMMEDIATELY TO SEE HIS DAUGHTER.
DADDY!
YOUR FATHER IS KING SOLOMON?

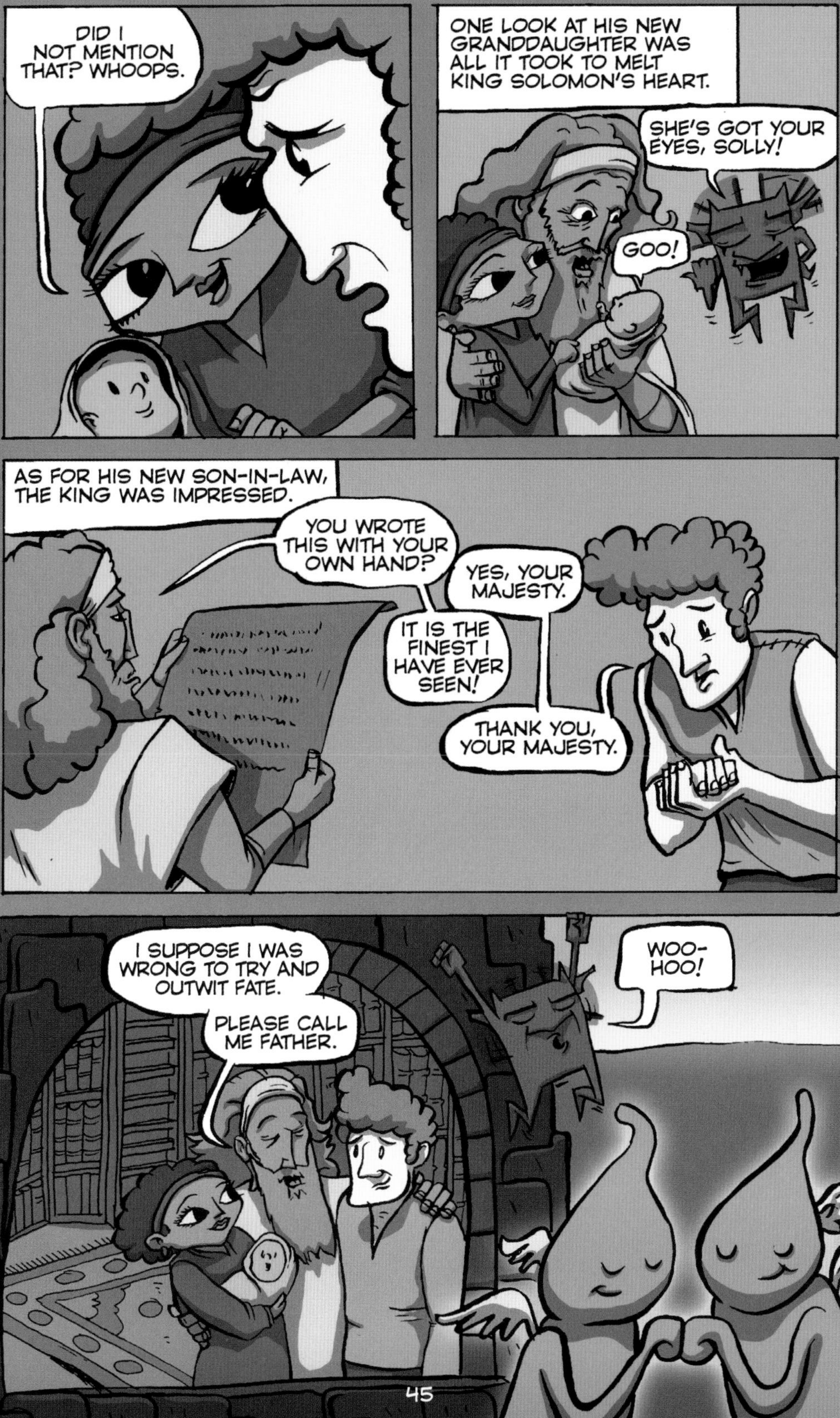
DID I NOT MENTION THAT? WHOOPS.
ONE LOOK AT HIS NEW GRANDDAUGHTER WAS ALL IT TOOK TO MELT KING SOLOMON'S HEART.
SHE'S GOT YOUR EYES, SOLLY!
GOO!
AS FOR HIS NEW SON-IN-LAW, THE KING WAS IMPRESSED.
YOU WROTE THIS WITH YOUR OWN HAND?
YES, YOUR MAJESTY.
IT IS THE FINEST I HAVE EVER SEEN!
THANK YOU, YOUR MAJESTY.
I SUPPOSE I WAS WRONG TO TRY AND OUTWIT FATE.
PLEASE CALL ME FATHER.
WOO-HOO!

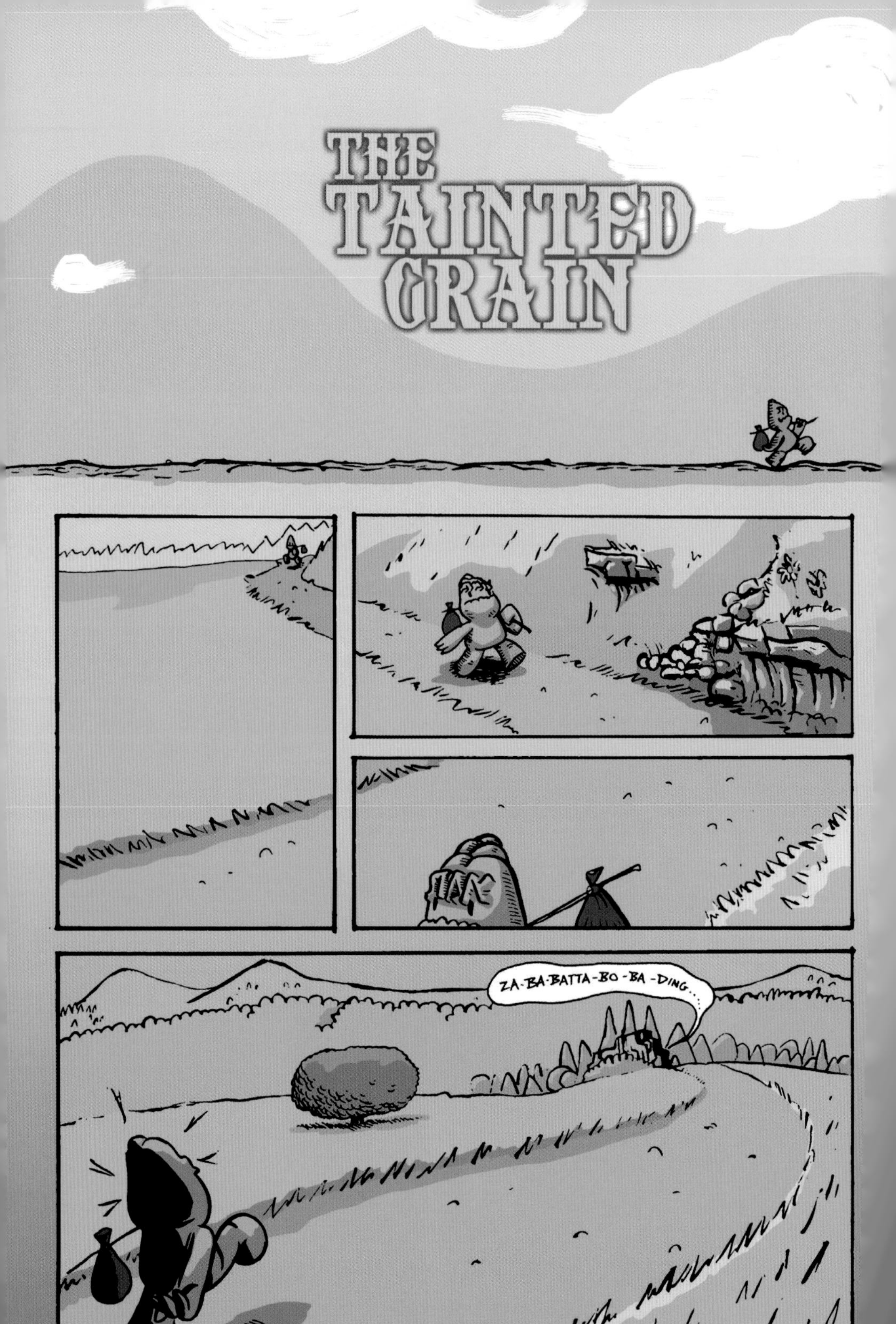
THE TAINTED GRAIN
ZA-BA-BATTA-BO-BA-DING...

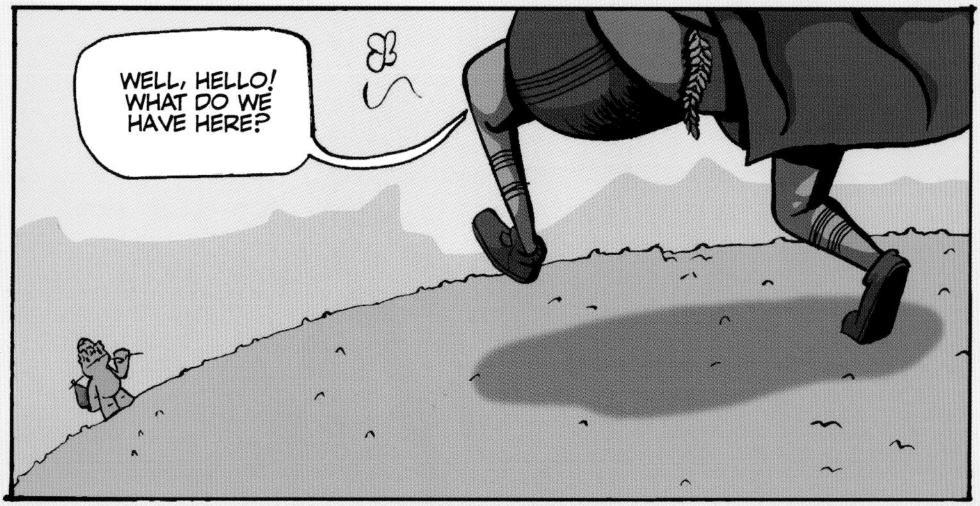
WELL, HELLO! WHAT DO WE HAVE HERE?

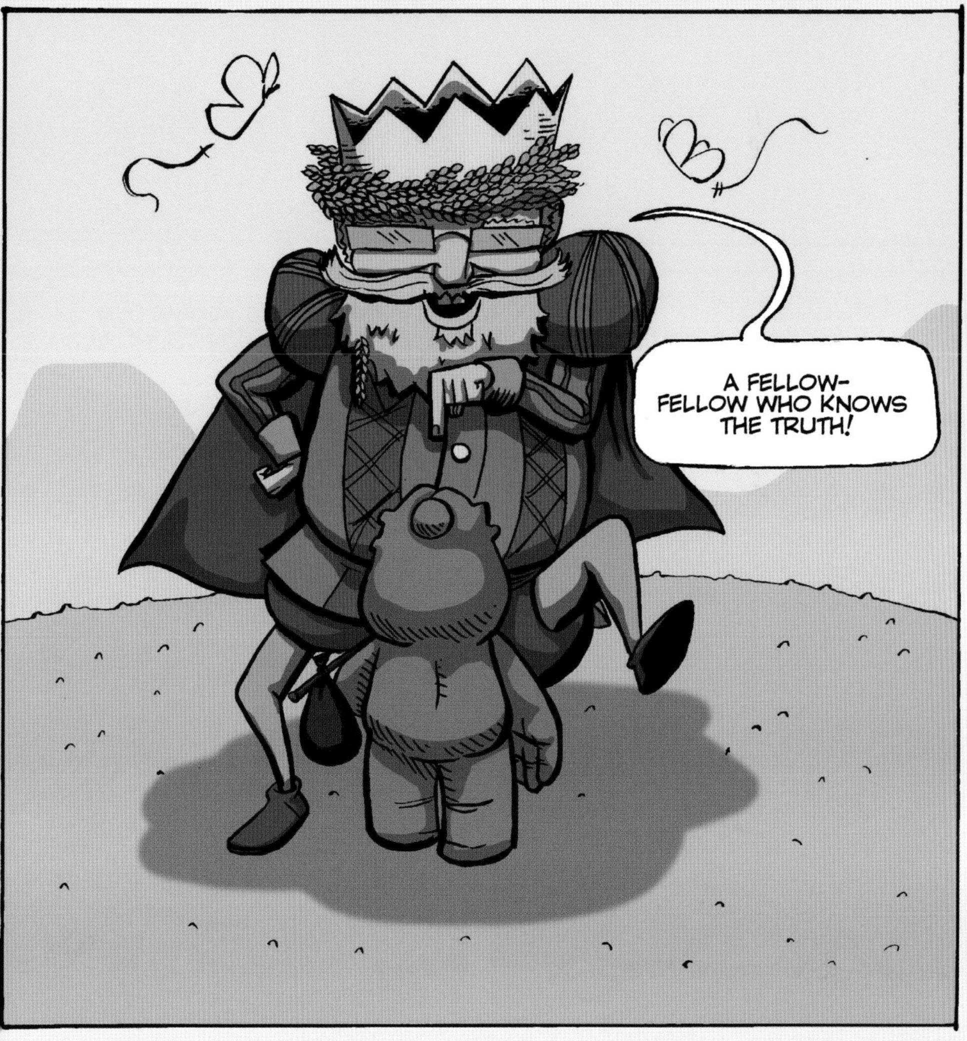
A FELLOW-FELLOW WHO KNOWS THE TRUTH!

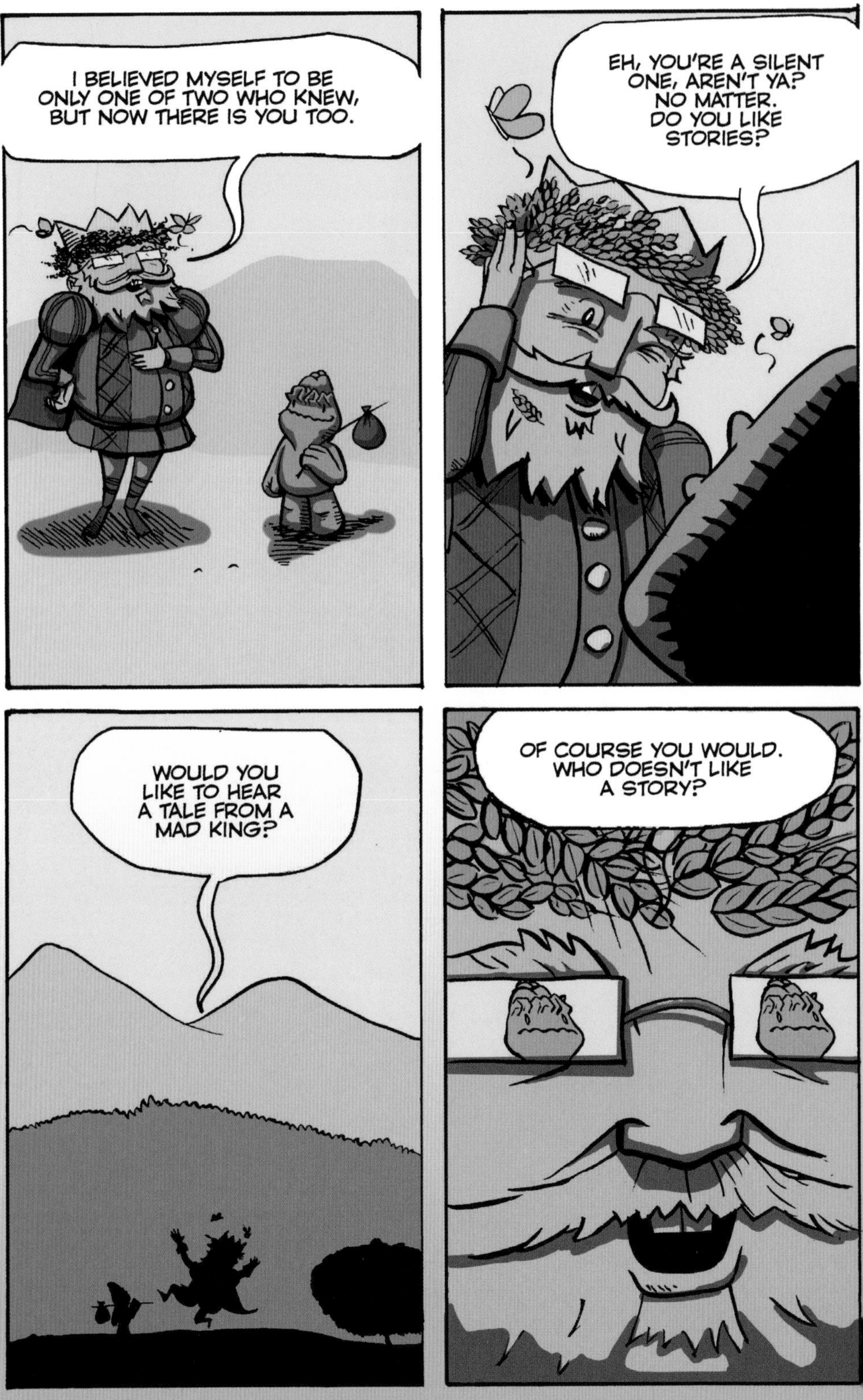
I BELIEVED MYSELF TO BE ONLY ONE OF TWO WHO KNEW, BUT NOW THERE IS YOU TOO.
EH, YOU'RE A SILENT ONE, AREN'T YA? NO MATTER. DO YOU LIKE STORIES?
WOULD YOU LIKE TO HEAR A TALE FROM A MAD KING?
OF COURSE YOU WOULD. WHO DOESN'T LIKE A STORY?

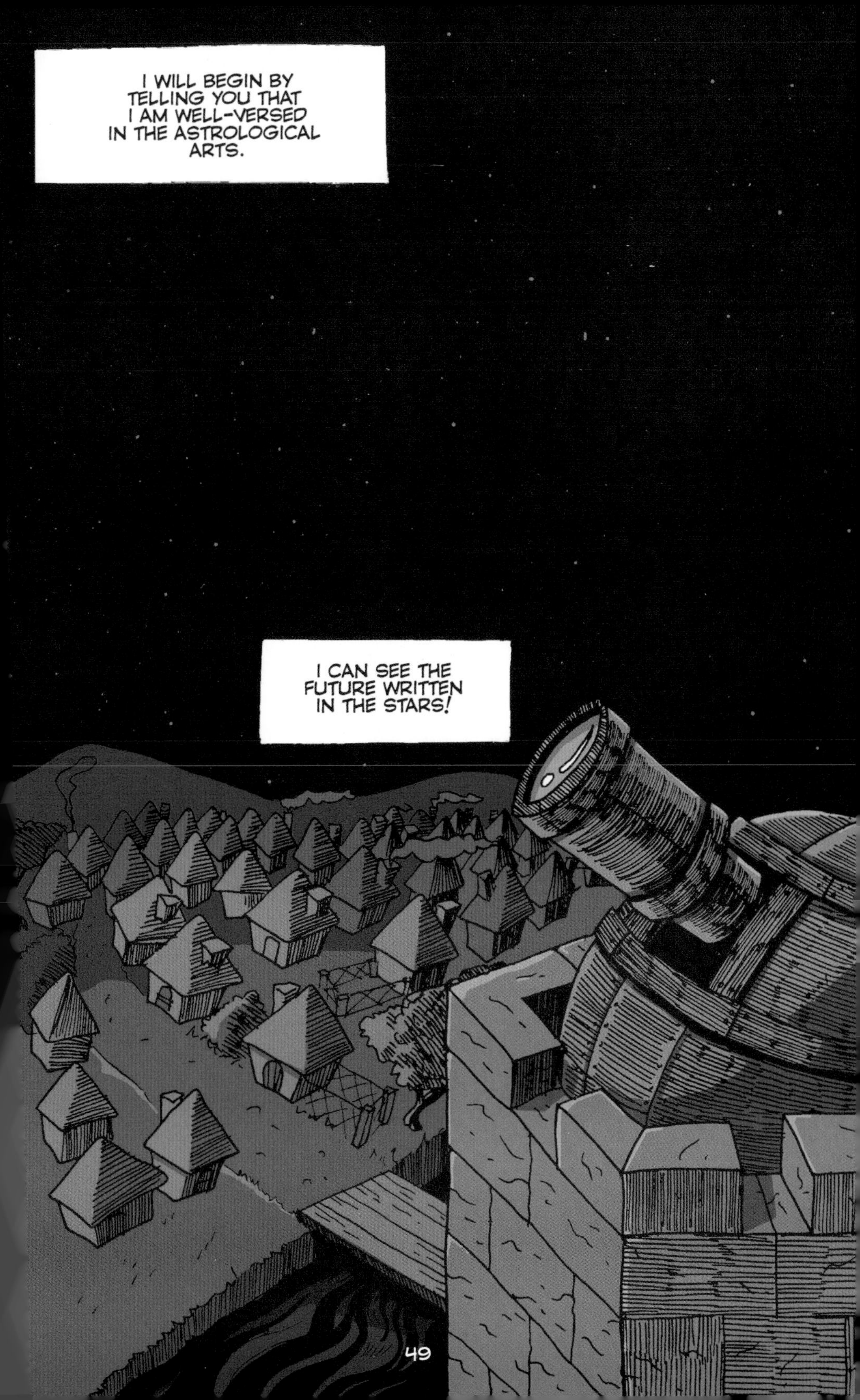
I WILL BEGIN BY TELLING YOU THAT I AM WELL-VERSED IN THE ASTROLOGICAL ARTS.
I CAN SEE THE FUTURE WRITTEN IN THE STARS!

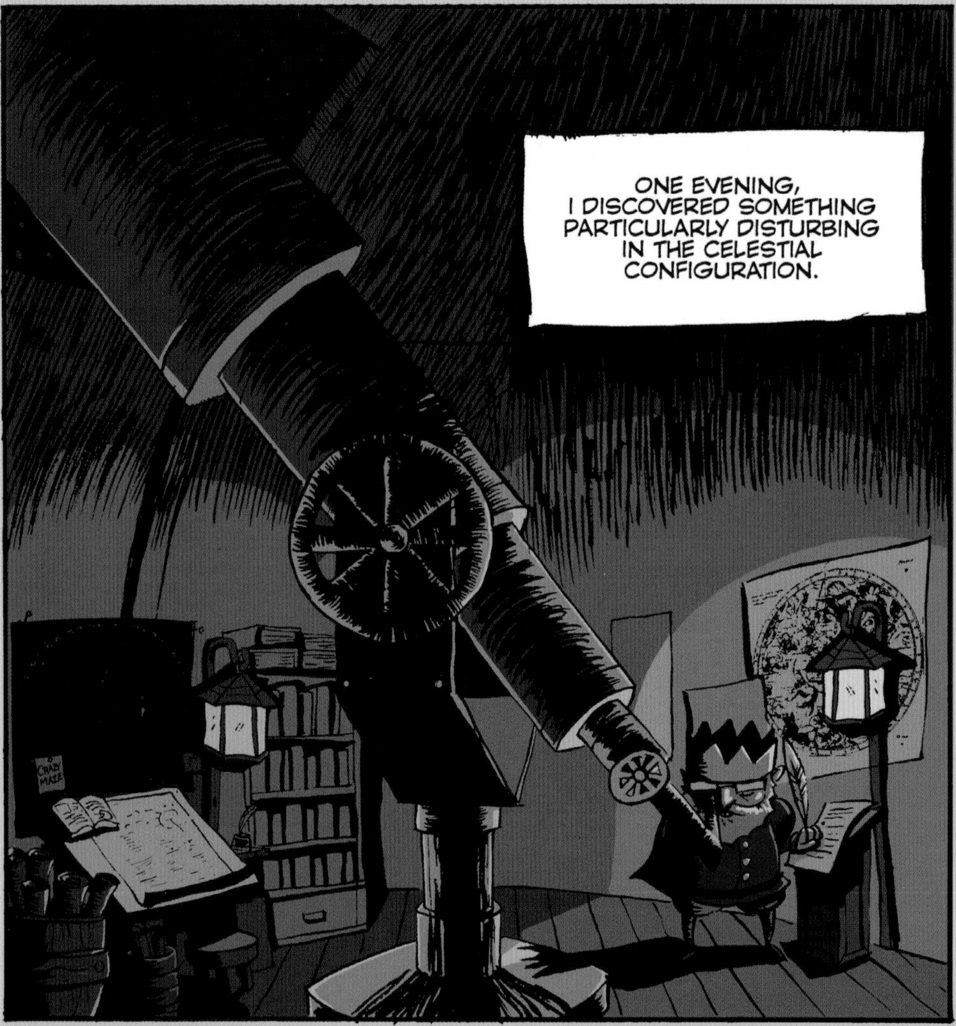
ONE EVENING, I DISCOVERED SOMETHING PARTICULARLY DISTURBING IN THE CELESTIAL CONFIGURATION.

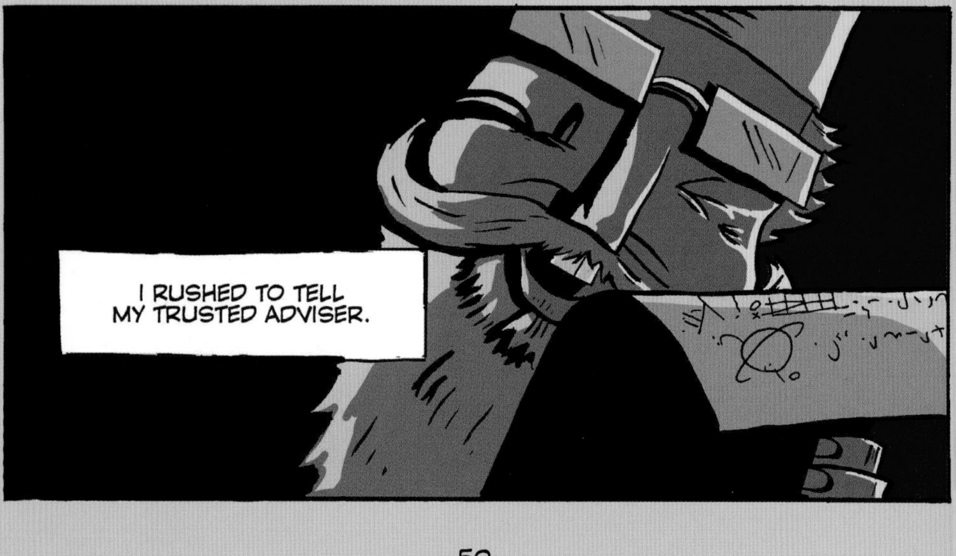
I RUSHED TO TELL MY TRUSTED ADVISER.

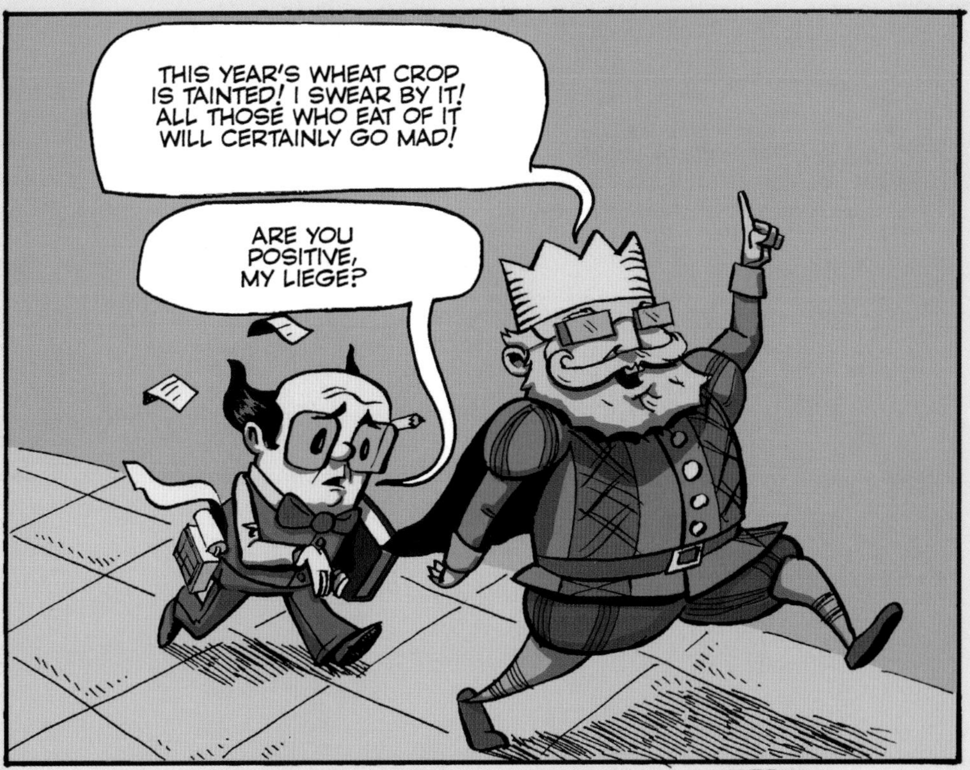
THIS YEAR'S WHEAT CROP IS TAINTED! I SWEAR BY IT! ALL THOSE WHO EAT OF IT WILL CERTAINLY GO MAD!
ARE YOU POSITIVE, MY LIEGE?

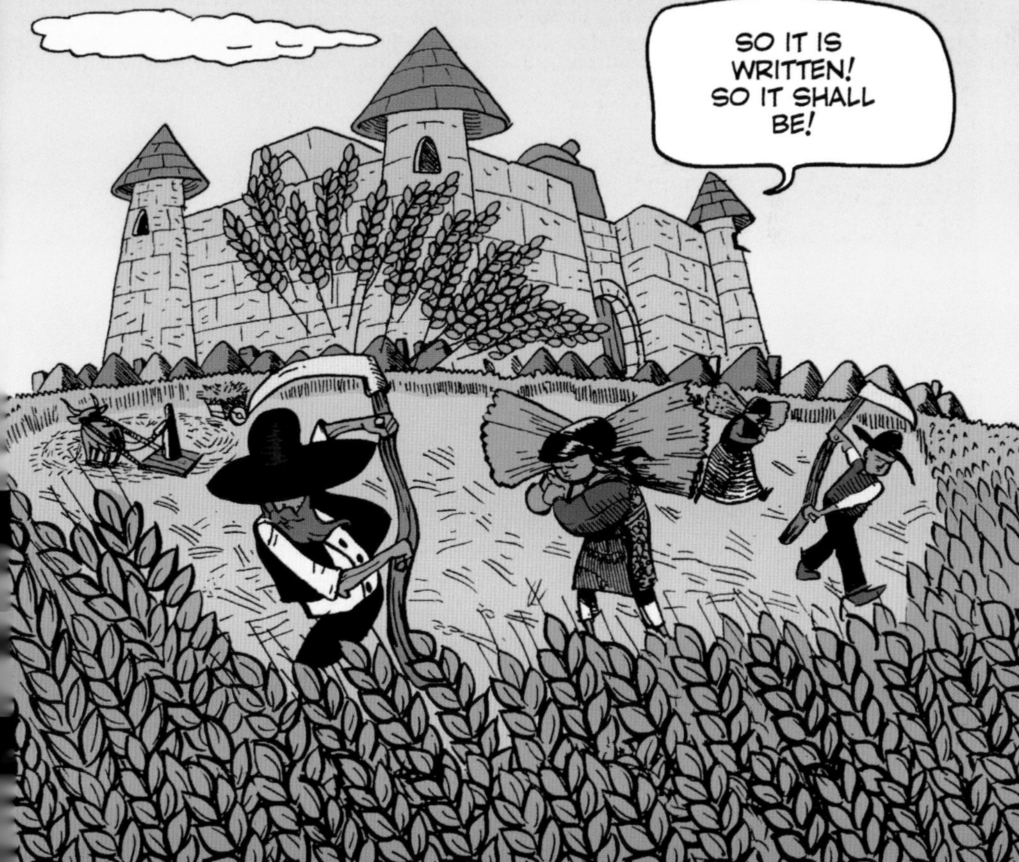
SO IT IS WRITTEN! SO IT SHALL BE!

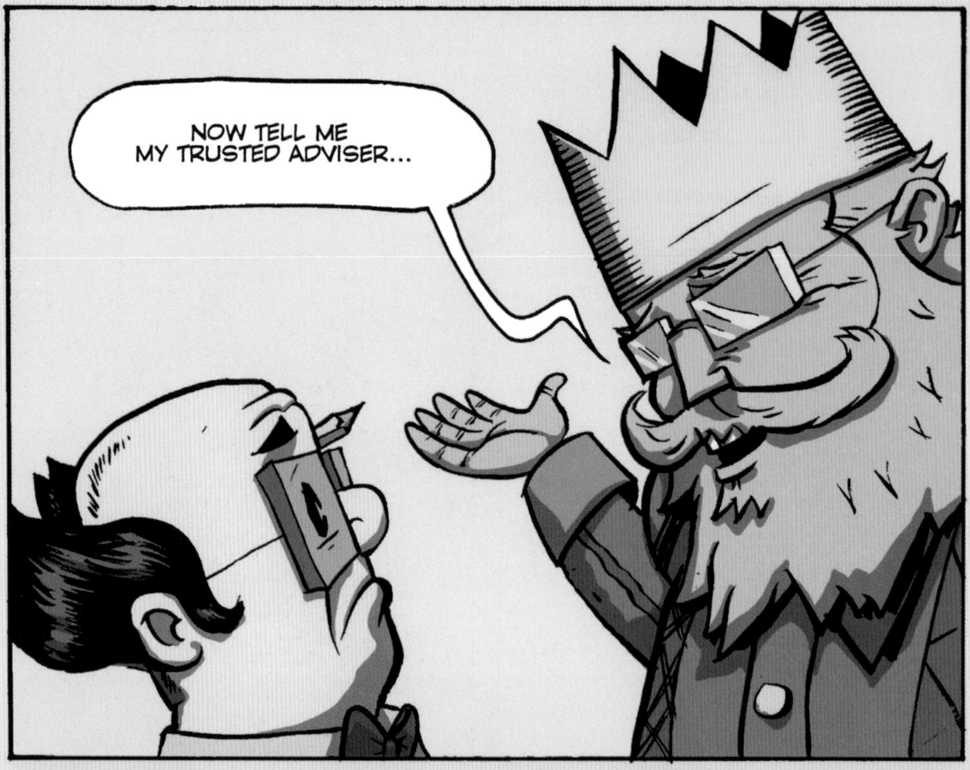
NOW TELL ME MY TRUSTED ADVISER...

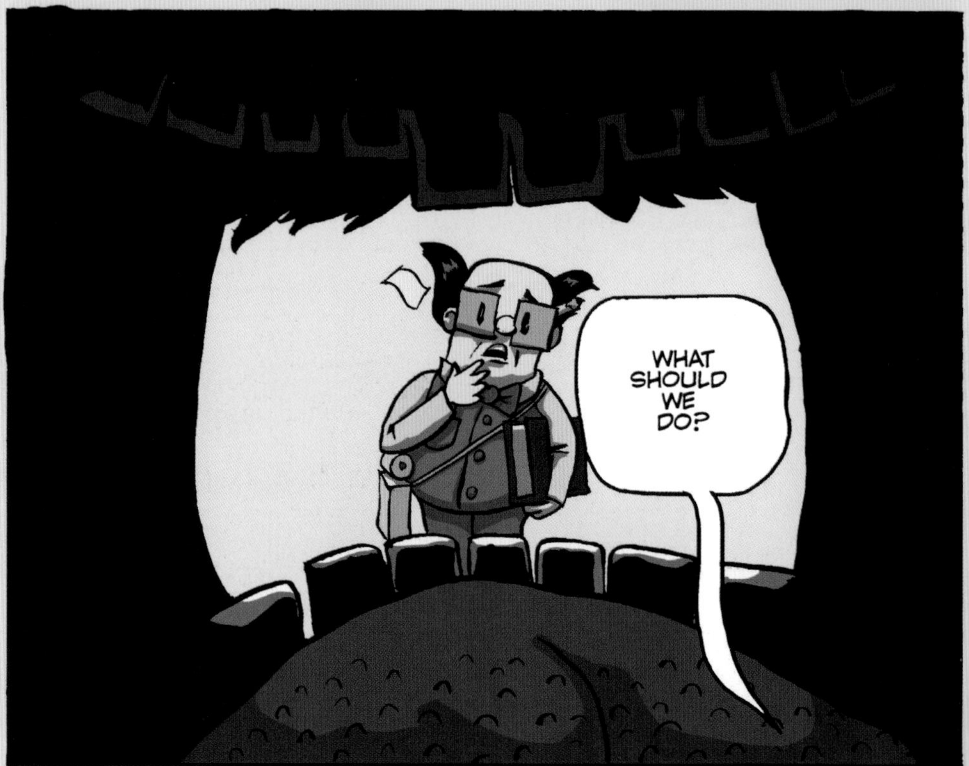
WHAT SHOULD WE DO?

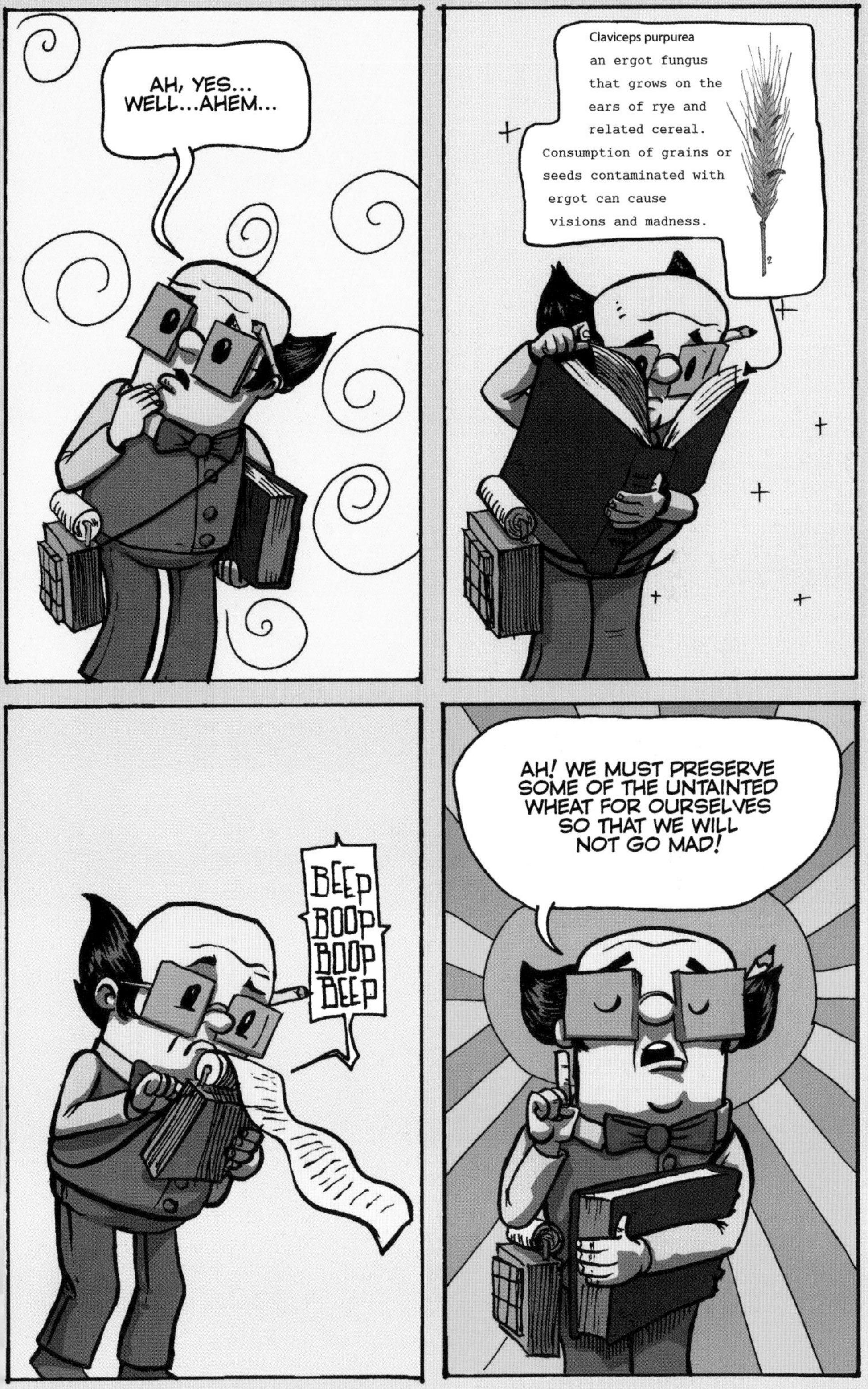
AH, YES...
WELL...AHEM...
Claviceps purpurea
an ergot fungus that grows on the ears of rye and related cereal. Consumption of grains or seeds contaminated with ergot can cause visions and madness.
BEEP BOOP BOOP BEEP
AH! WE MUST PRESERVE SOME OF THE UNTAINTED WHEAT FOR OURSELVES SO THAT WE WILL NOT GO MAD!

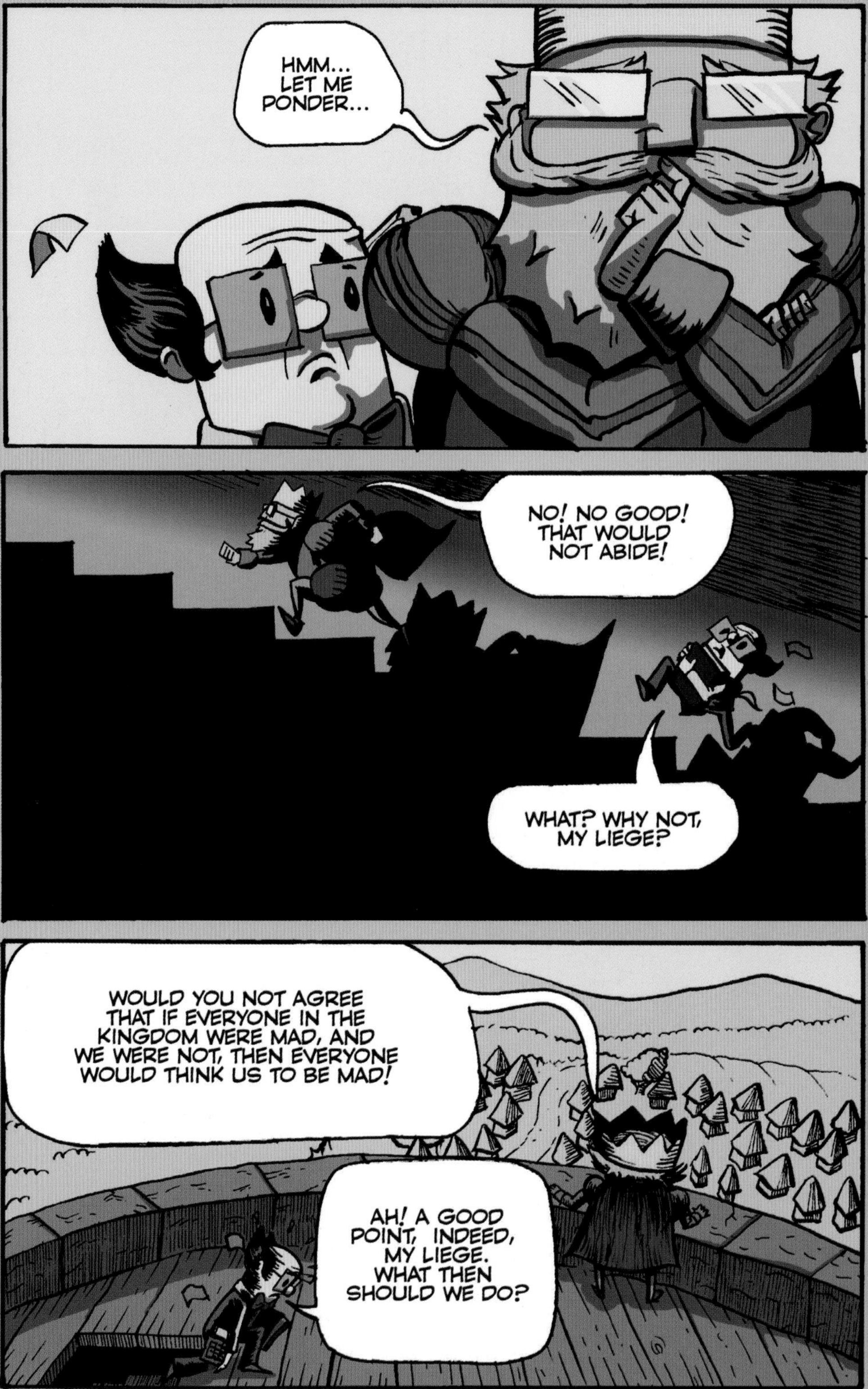
HMM... LET ME PONDER...
NO! NO GOOD! THAT WOULD NOT ABIDE!
WHAT? WHY NOT, MY LIEGE?
WOULD YOU NOT AGREE THAT IF EVERYONE IN THE KINGDOM WERE MAD, AND WE WERE NOT, THEN EVERYONE WOULD THINK US TO BE MAD!
AH! A GOOD POINT, INDEED, MY LIEGE. WHAT THEN SHOULD WE DO?

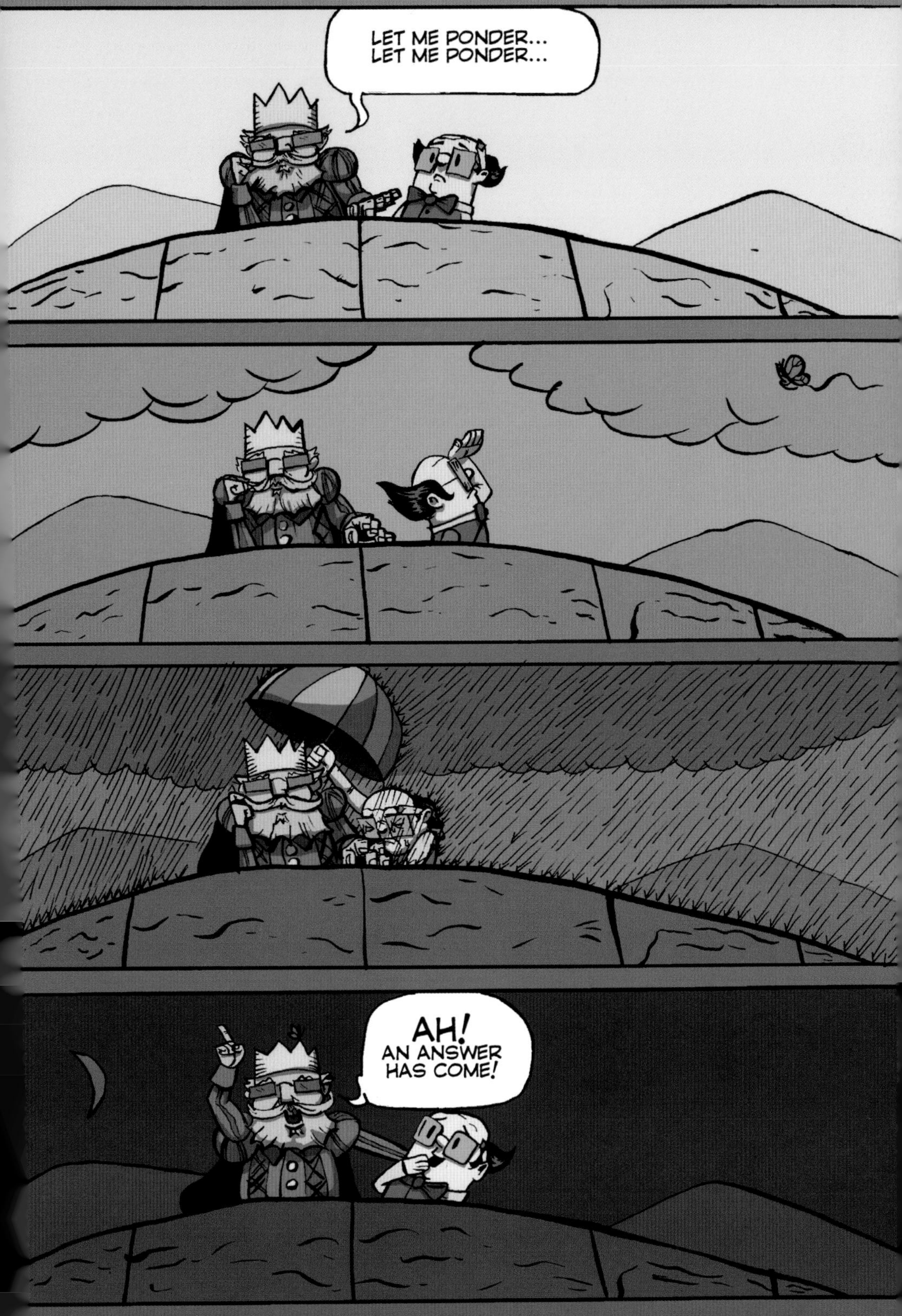
LET ME PONDER...
LET ME PONDER...
AH! AN ANSWER HAS COME!

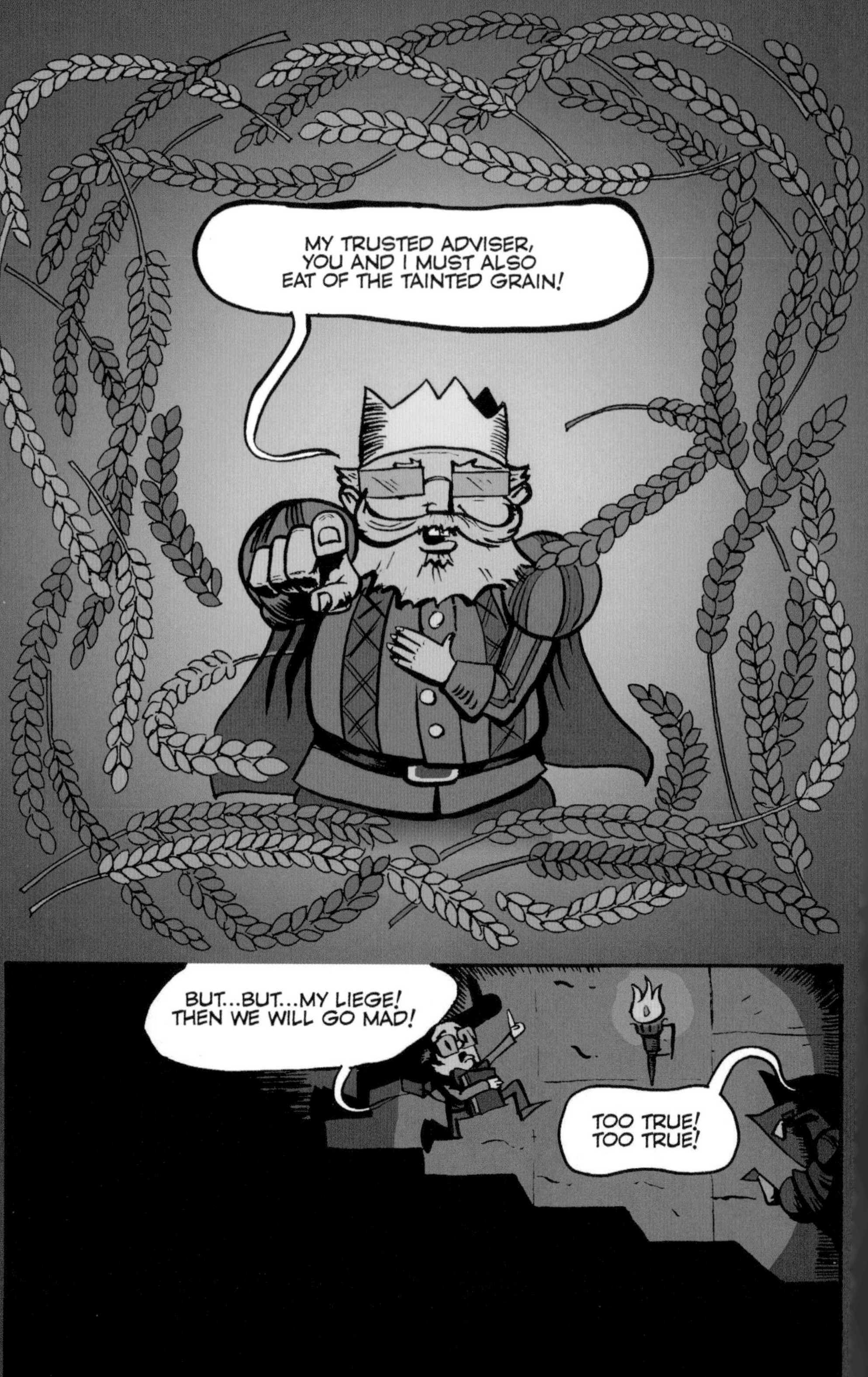
MY TRUSTED ADVISER, YOU AND I MUST ALSO EAT OF THE TAINTED GRAIN!
BUT...BUT...MY LIEGE! THEN WE WILL GO MAD!
TOO TRUE! TOO TRUE!

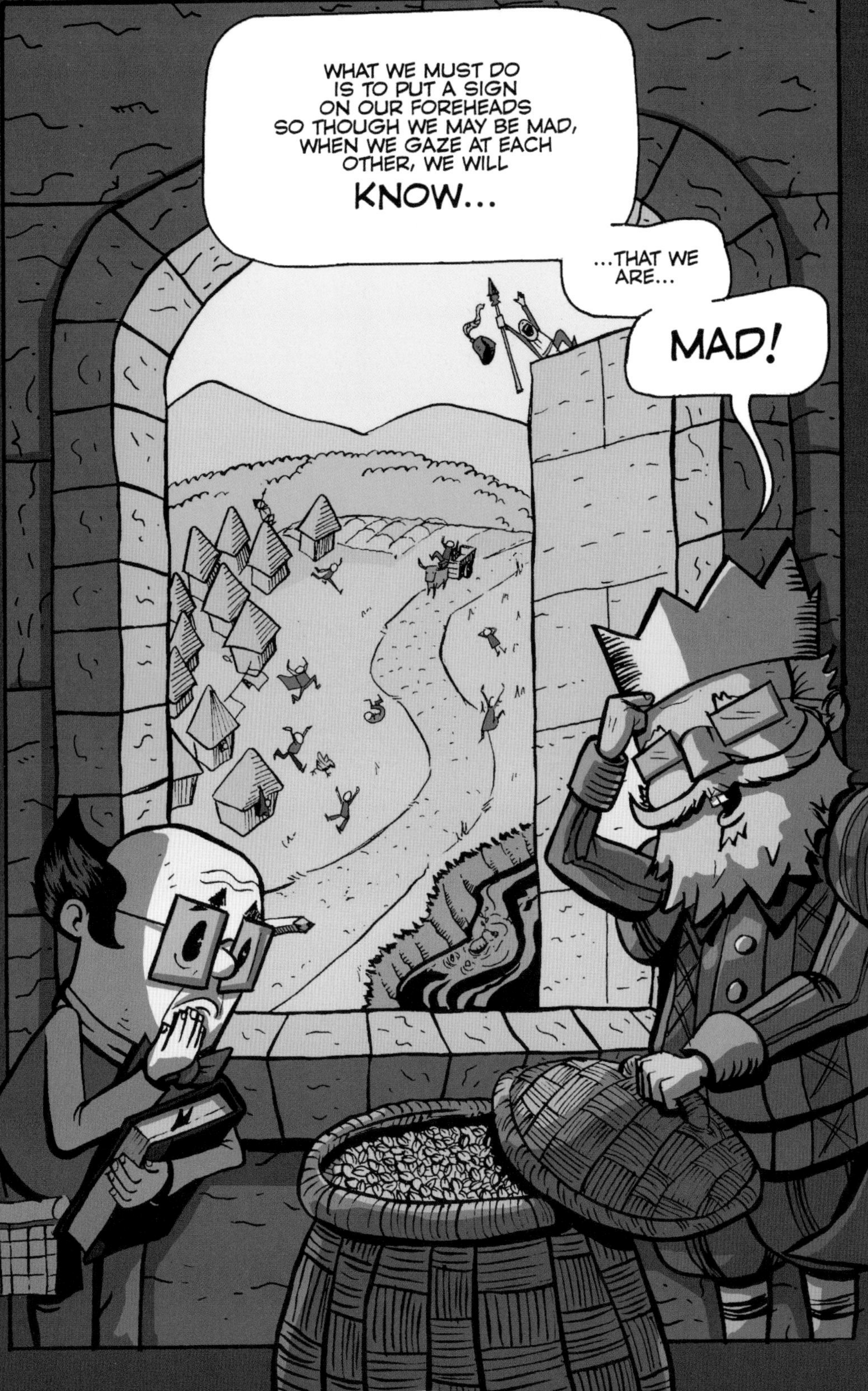
WHAT WE MUST DO IS TO PUT A SIGN ON OUR FOREHEADS SO THOUGH WE MAY BE MAD, WHEN WE GAZE AT EACH OTHER, WE WILL KNOW...
...THAT WE ARE...
MAD!

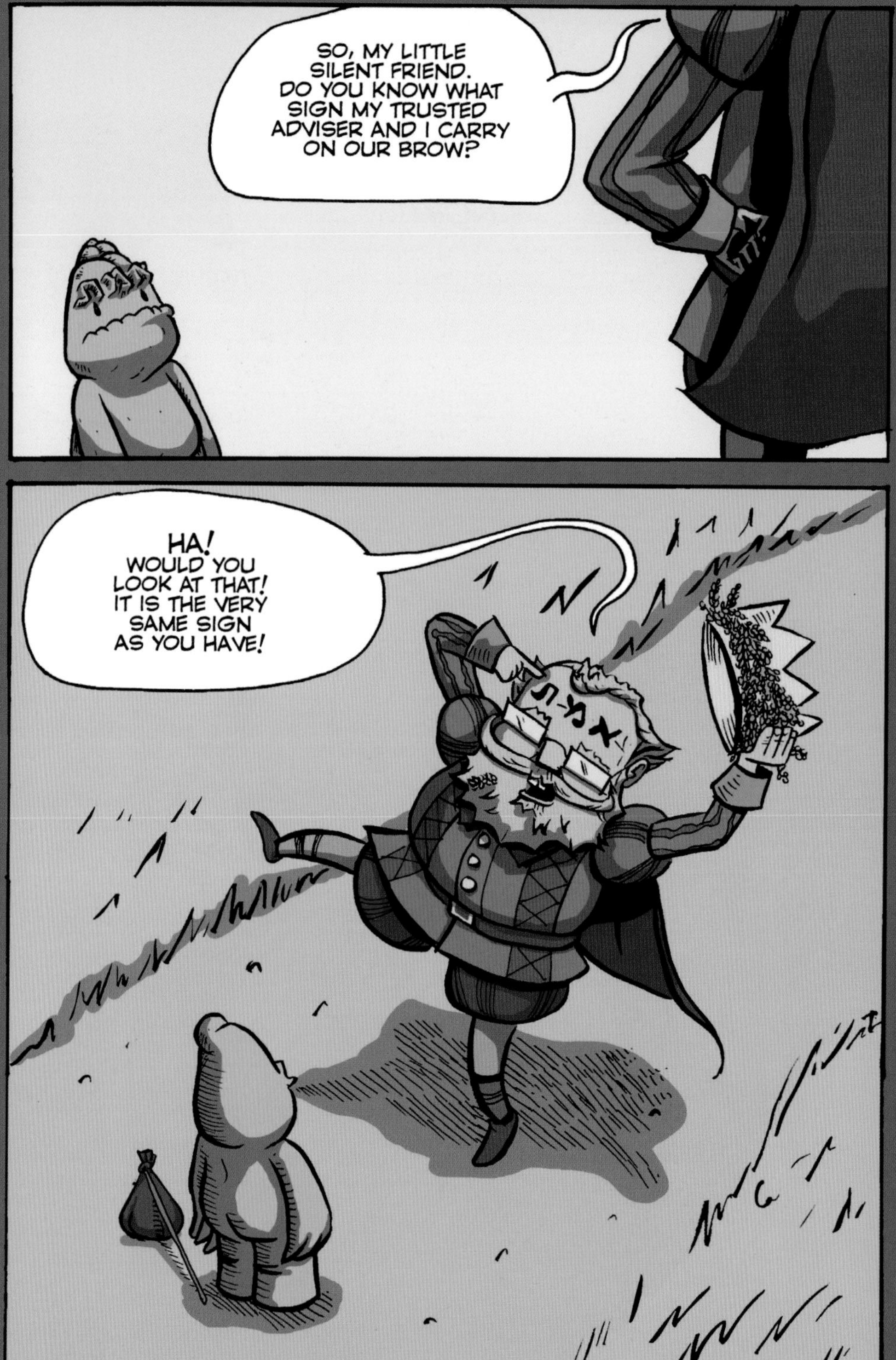
SO, MY LITTLE SILENT FRIEND. DO YOU KNOW WHAT SIGN MY TRUSTED ADVISER AND I CARRY ON OUR BROW?
HA! WOULD YOU LOOK AT THAT! IT IS THE VERY SAME SIGN AS YOU HAVE!

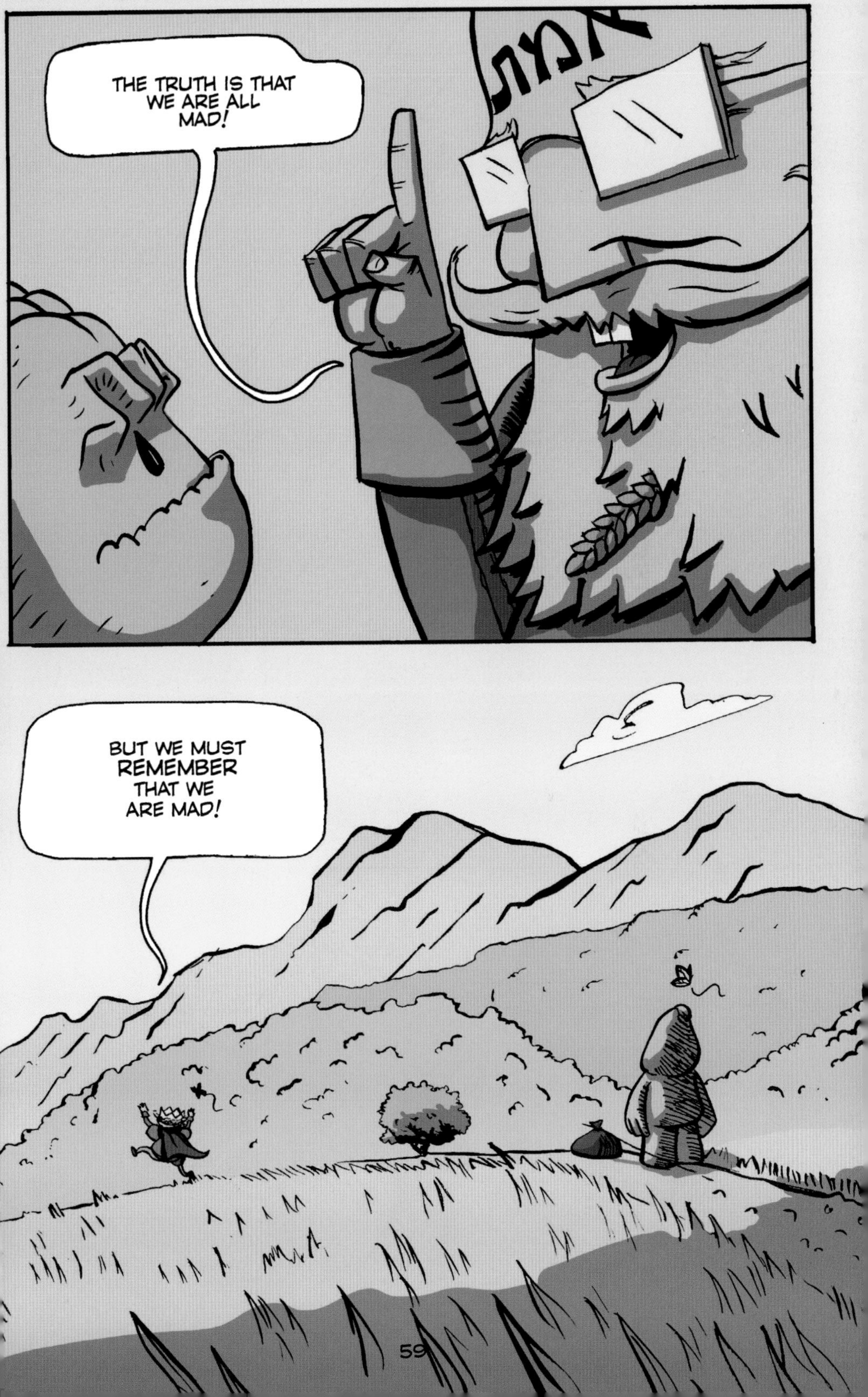
אמת
THE TRUTH IS THAT WE ARE ALL MAD!
BUT WE MUST REMEMBER THAT WE ARE MAD!

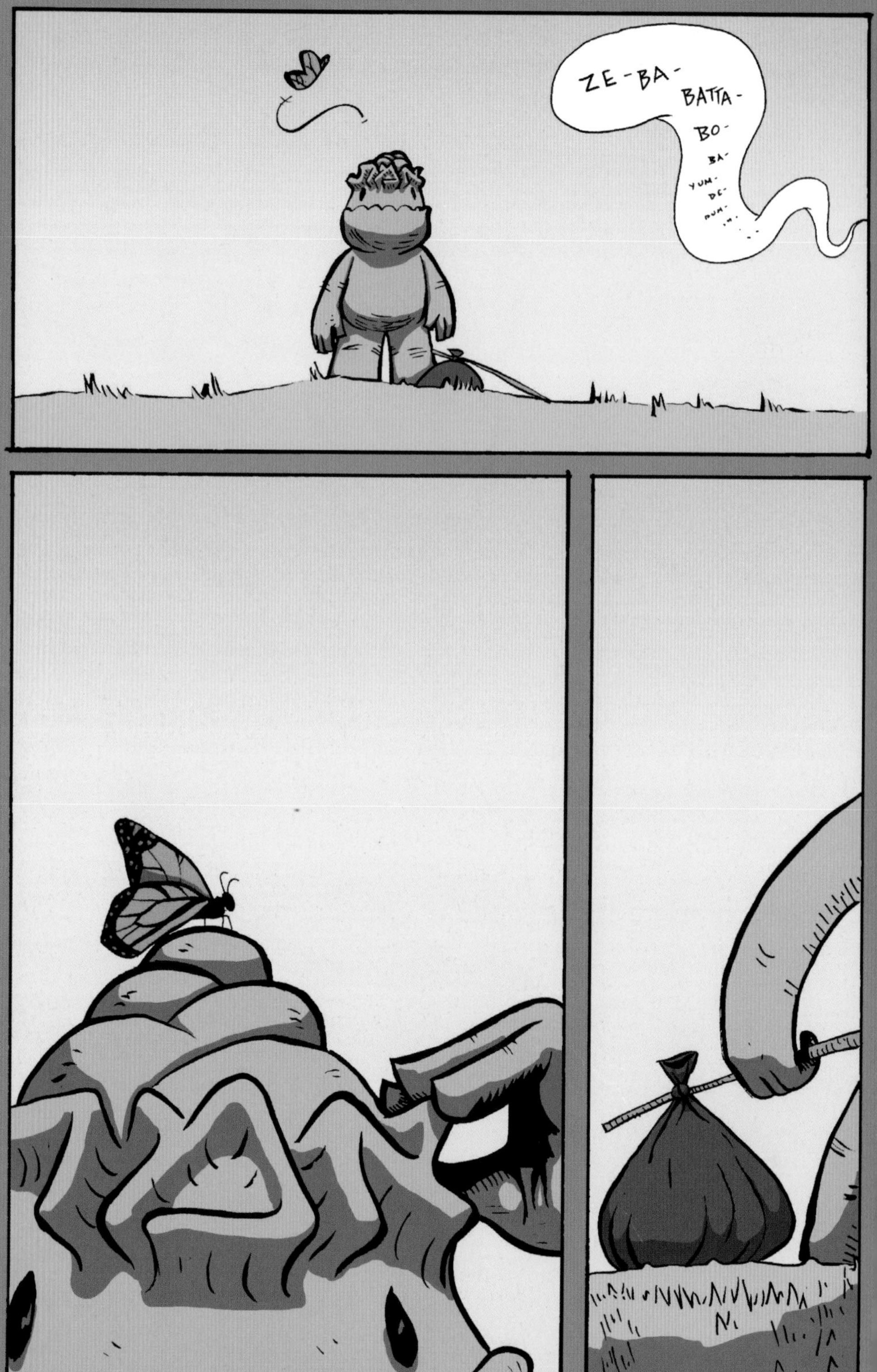
ZE-BA-BATTA-BO-BA-YUM-DE-DUM-

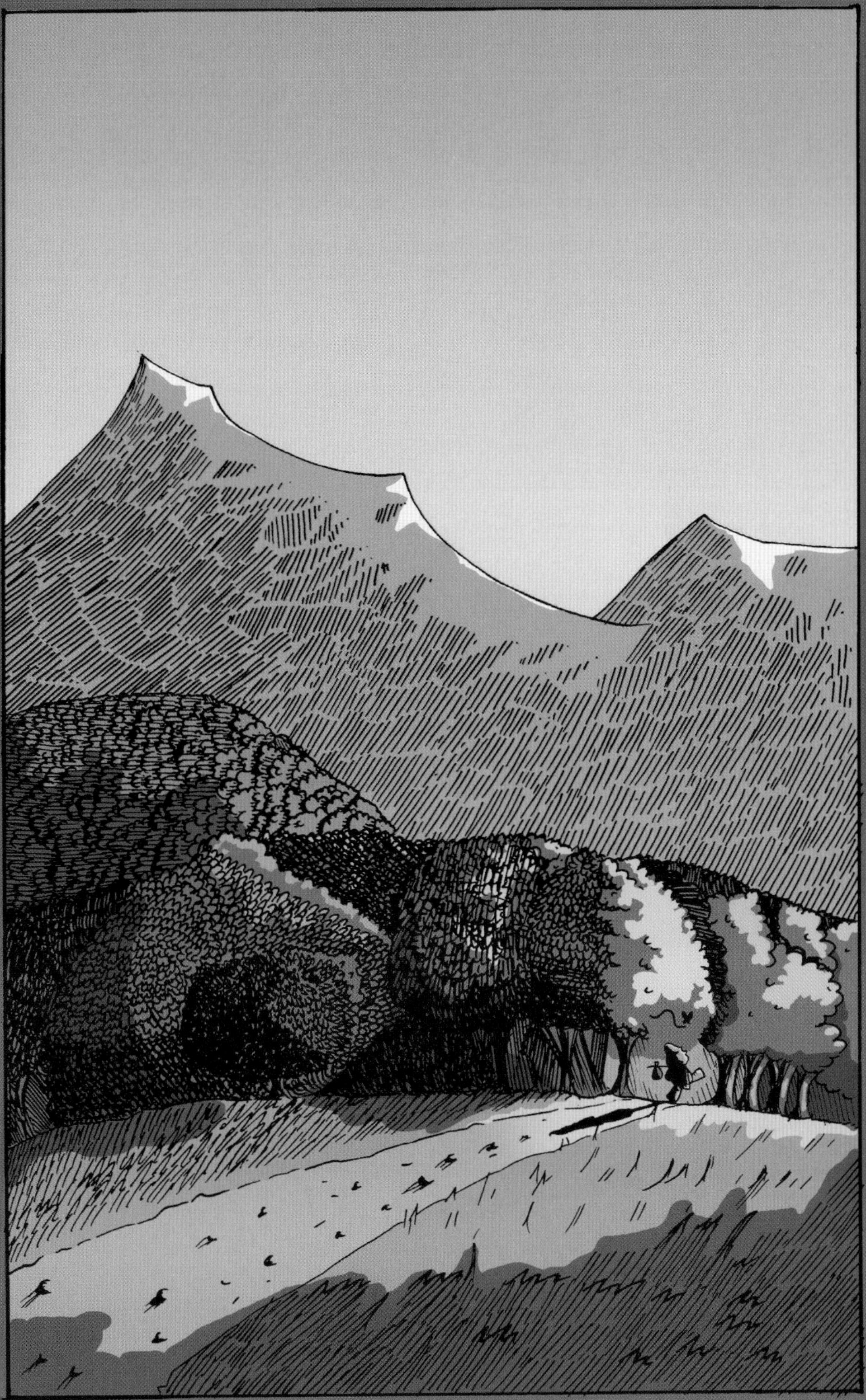

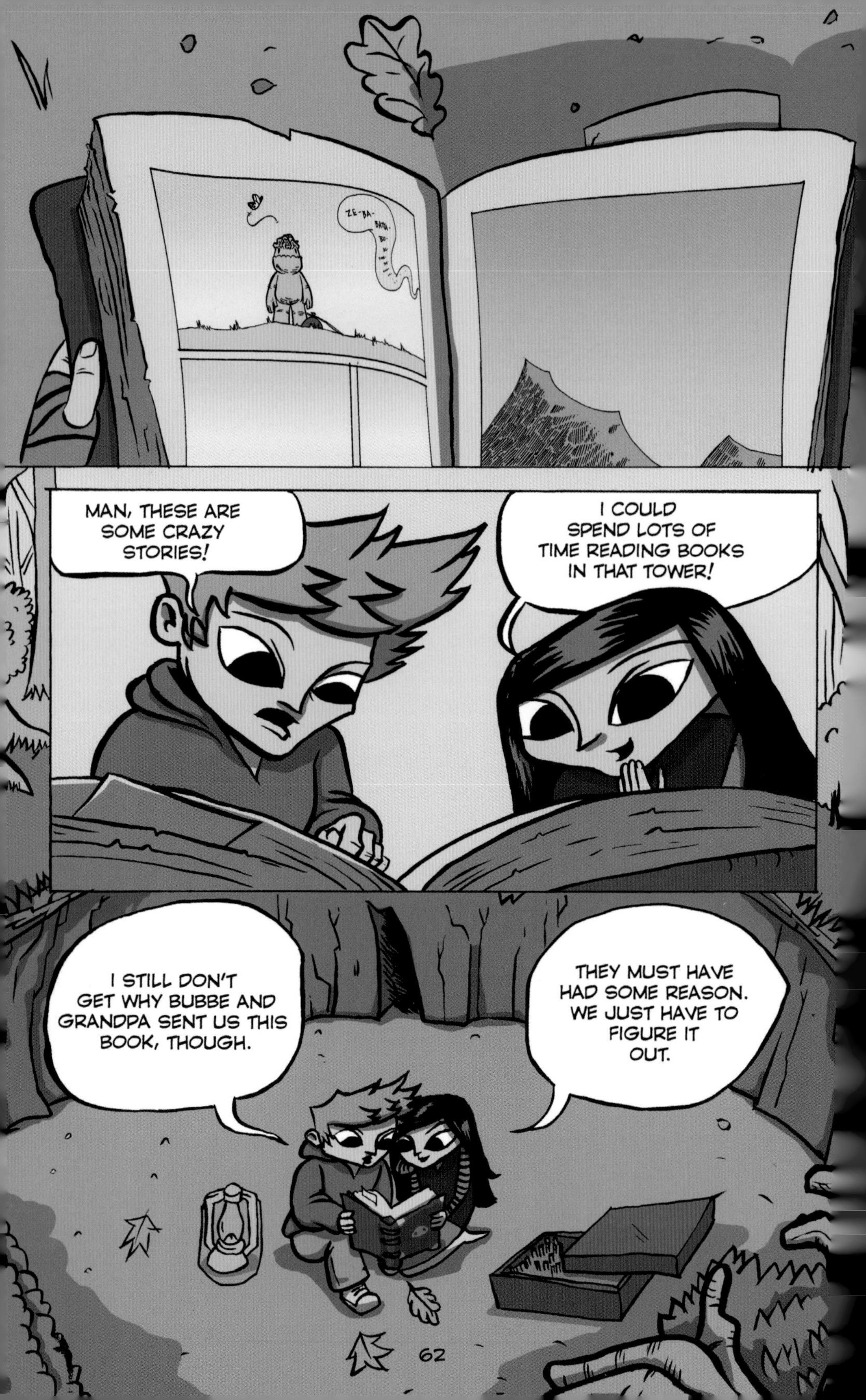
MAN, THESE ARE SOME CRAZY STORIES!
I COULD SPEND LOTS OF TIME READING BOOKS IN THAT TOWER!
I STILL DON'T GET WHY BUBBE AND GRANDPA SENT US THIS BOOK, THOUGH.
THEY MUST HAVE HAD SOME REASON. WE JUST HAVE TO FIGURE IT OUT.

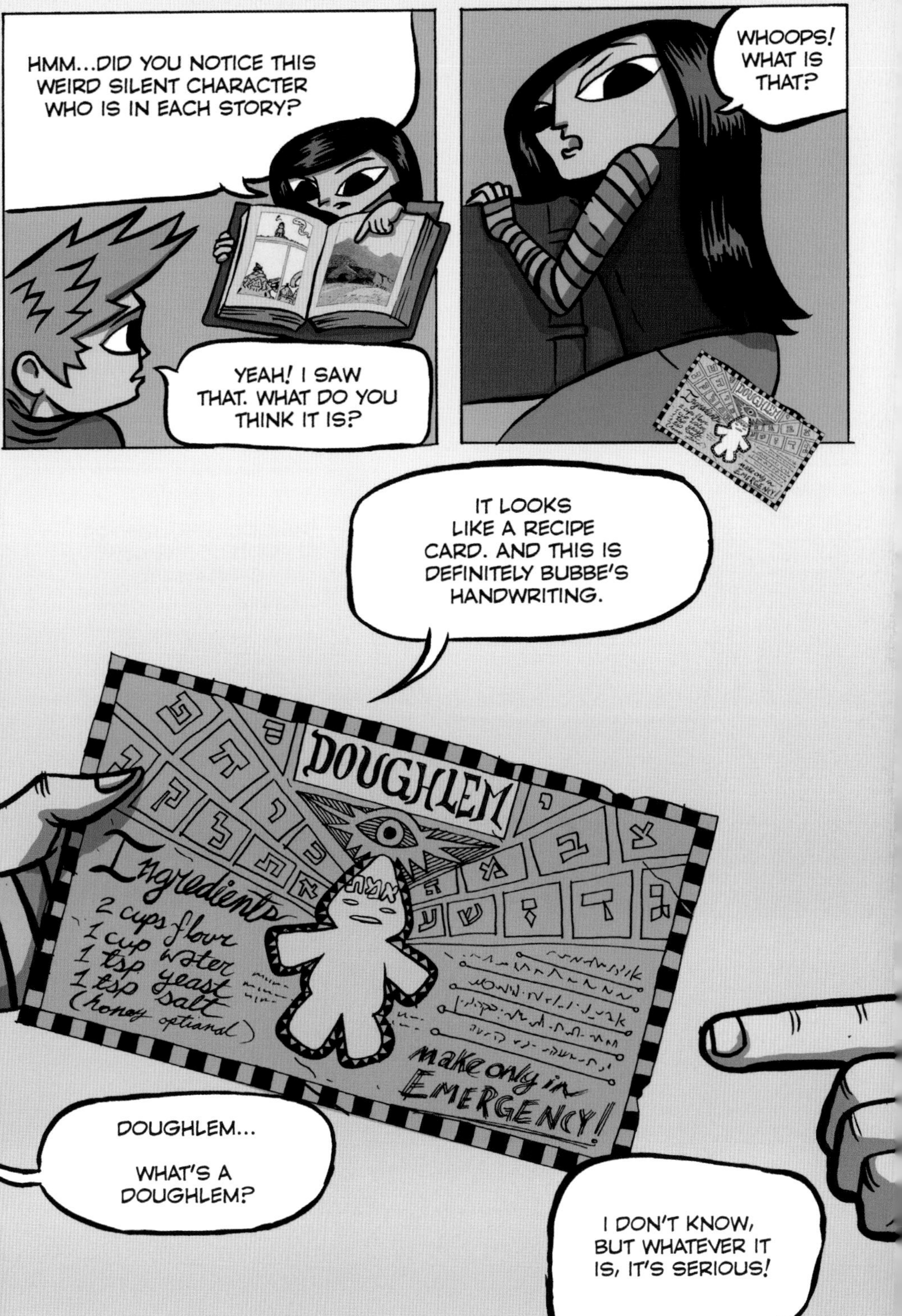
HMM...DID YOU NOTICE THIS WEIRD SILENT CHARACTER WHO IS IN EACH STORY?
YEAH! I SAW THAT. WHAT DO YOU THINK IT IS?
WHOOPS! WHAT IS THAT?
IT LOOKS LIKE A RECIPE CARD. AND THIS IS DEFINITELY BUBBE'S HANDWRITING.
DOUGHLEM
Ingredients
2 cups flour
1 cup water
1 tsp yeast
1 tsp salt
(honey optional)
make only in EMERGENCY!
DOUGHLEM...
WHAT'S A DOUGHLEM?
I DON'T KNOW, BUT WHATEVER IT IS, IT'S SERIOUS!

HMM...

OH...WAIT! I WONDER IF THE DOUGHLEM IS LIKE A GOLEM!

a what?

I READ IN A STORY THAT THE GOLEM WAS A PERSON WHO WAS MADE OUT OF MUD...

...AND THEN A RABBI BROUGHT IT TO LIFE USING SPECIAL PRAYERS.

THE GOLEM'S JOB WAS TO PROTECT THE JEWISH COMMUNITY!

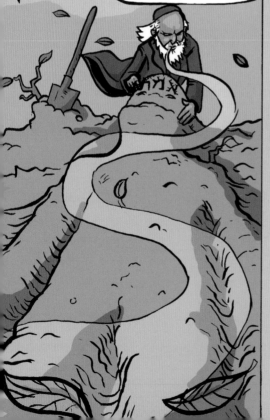

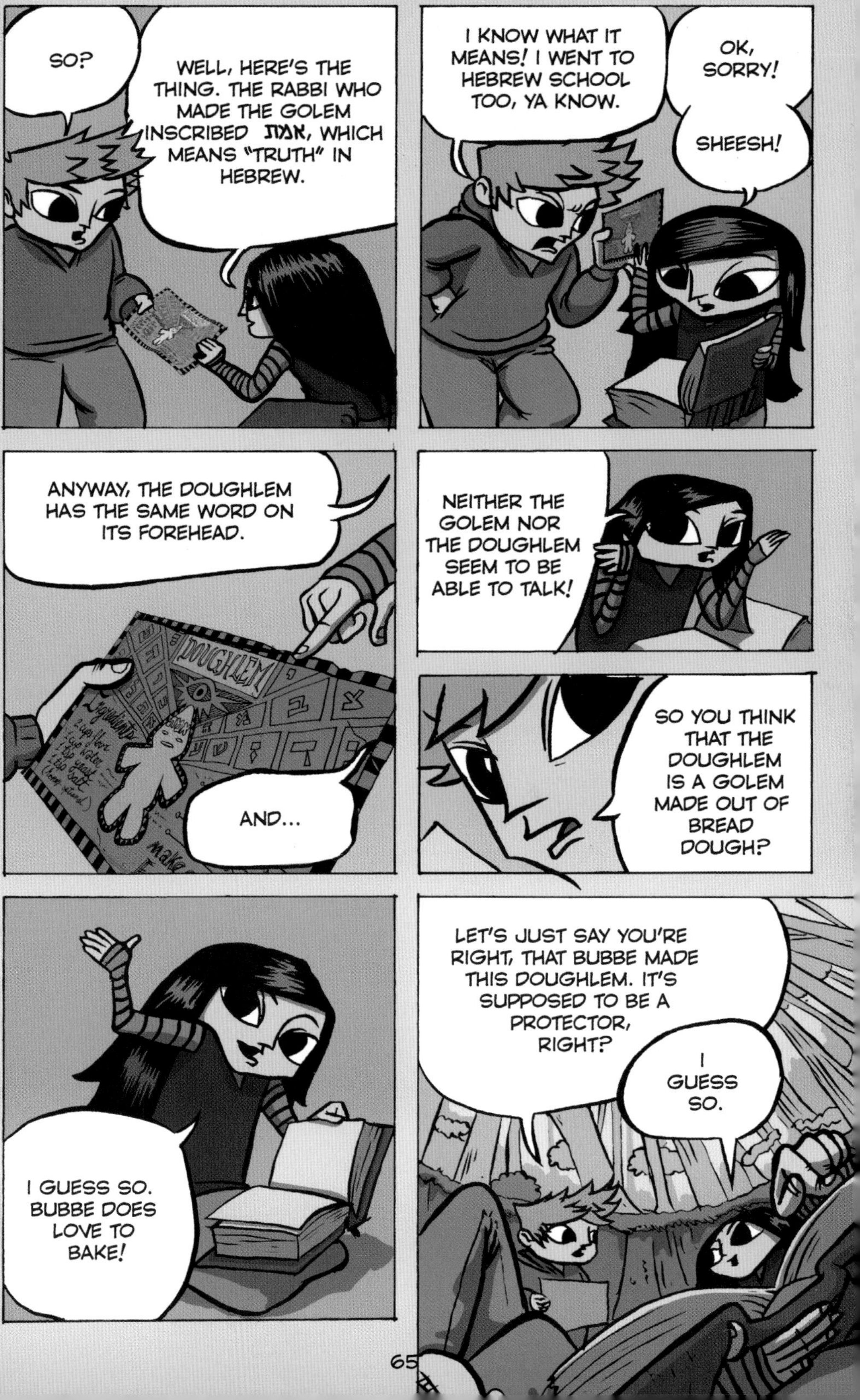
SO?
WELL, HERE'S THE THING. THE RABBI WHO MADE THE GOLEM INSCRIBED אמת, WHICH MEANS "TRUTH" IN HEBREW.
I KNOW WHAT IT MEANS! I WENT TO HEBREW SCHOOL TOO, YA KNOW.
OK, SORRY!
SHEESH!
ANYWAY, THE DOUGHLEM HAS THE SAME WORD ON ITS FOREHEAD.
DOUGHLEM
AND...
NEITHER THE GOLEM NOR THE DOUGHLEM SEEM TO BE ABLE TO TALK!
SO YOU THINK THAT THE DOUGHLEM IS A GOLEM MADE OUT OF BREAD DOUGH?
I GUESS SO. BUBBE DOES LOVE TO BAKE!
LET'S JUST SAY YOU'RE RIGHT, THAT BUBBE MADE THIS DOUGHLEM. IT'S SUPPOSED TO BE A PROTECTOR, RIGHT?
I GUESS SO.

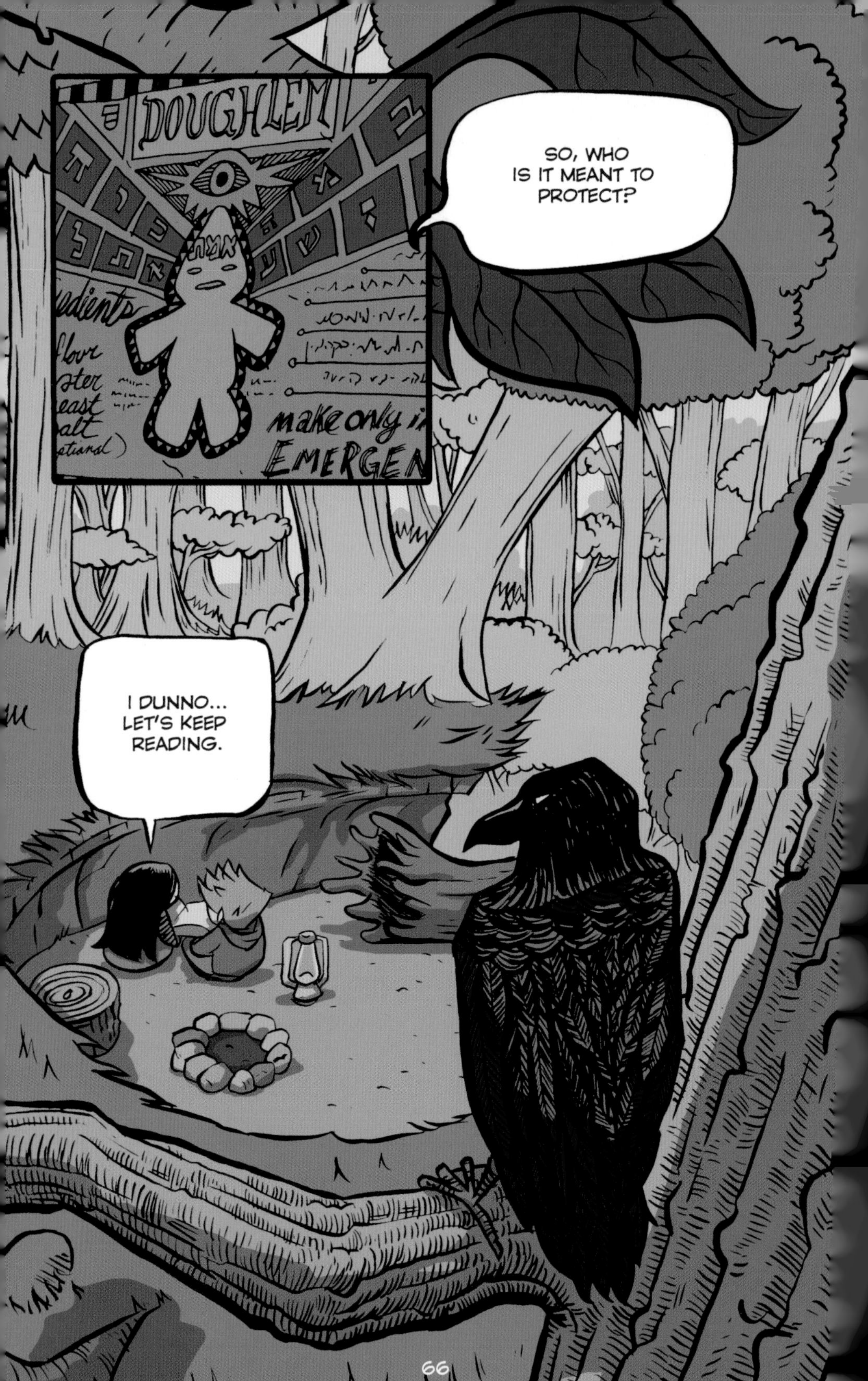
DOUGHLEM
SO, WHO IS IT MEANT TO PROTECT?
I DUNNO... LET'S KEEP READING.

OG
AND THE
TAILOR

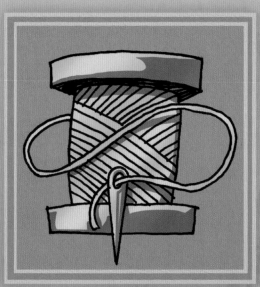

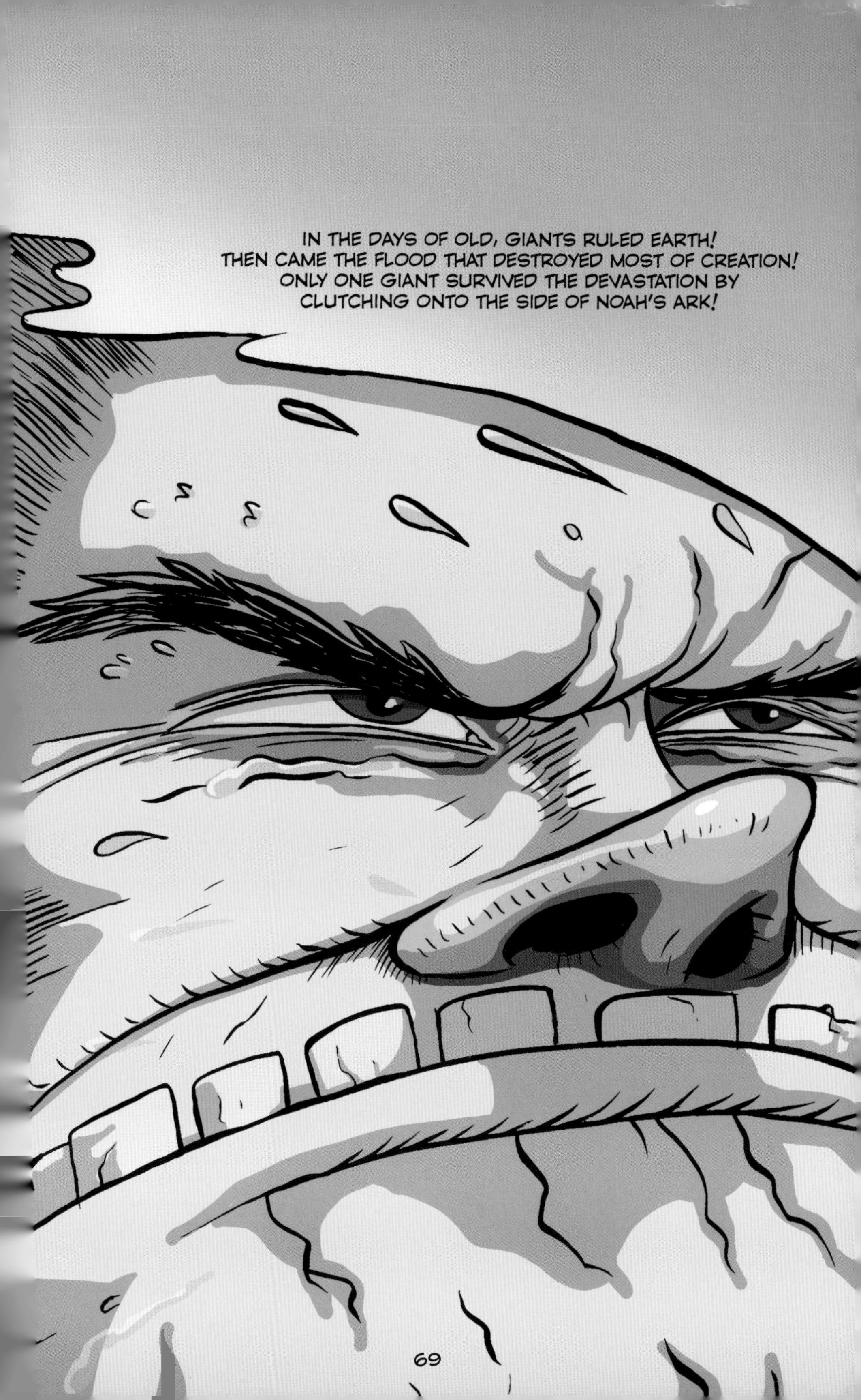
IN THE DAYS OF OLD, GIANTS RULED EARTH!
THEN CAME THE FLOOD THAT DESTROYED MOST OF CREATION!
ONLY ONE GIANT SURVIVED THE DEVASTATION BY
CLUTCHING ONTO THE SIDE OF NOAH'S ARK!

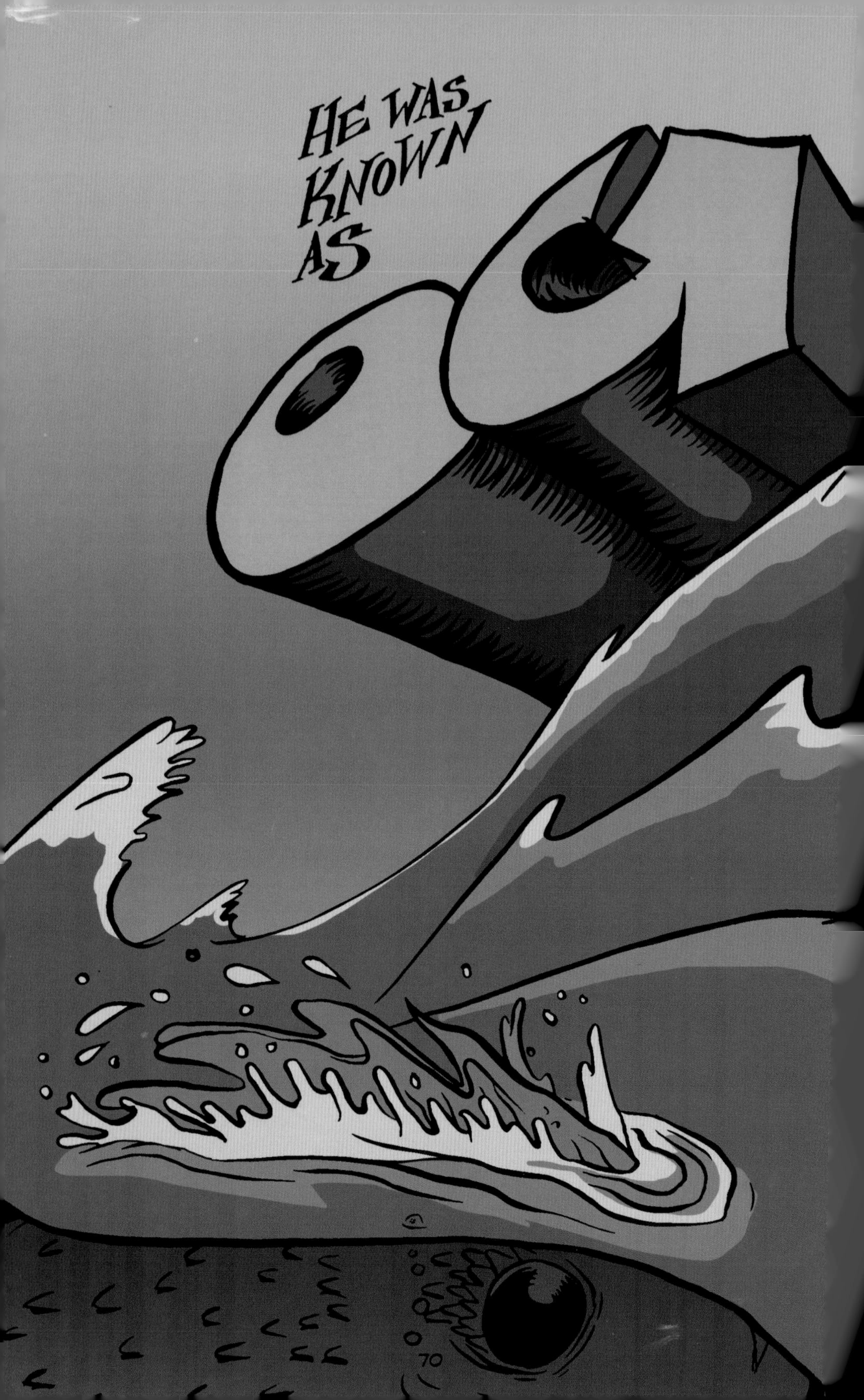
HE WAS KNOWN AS

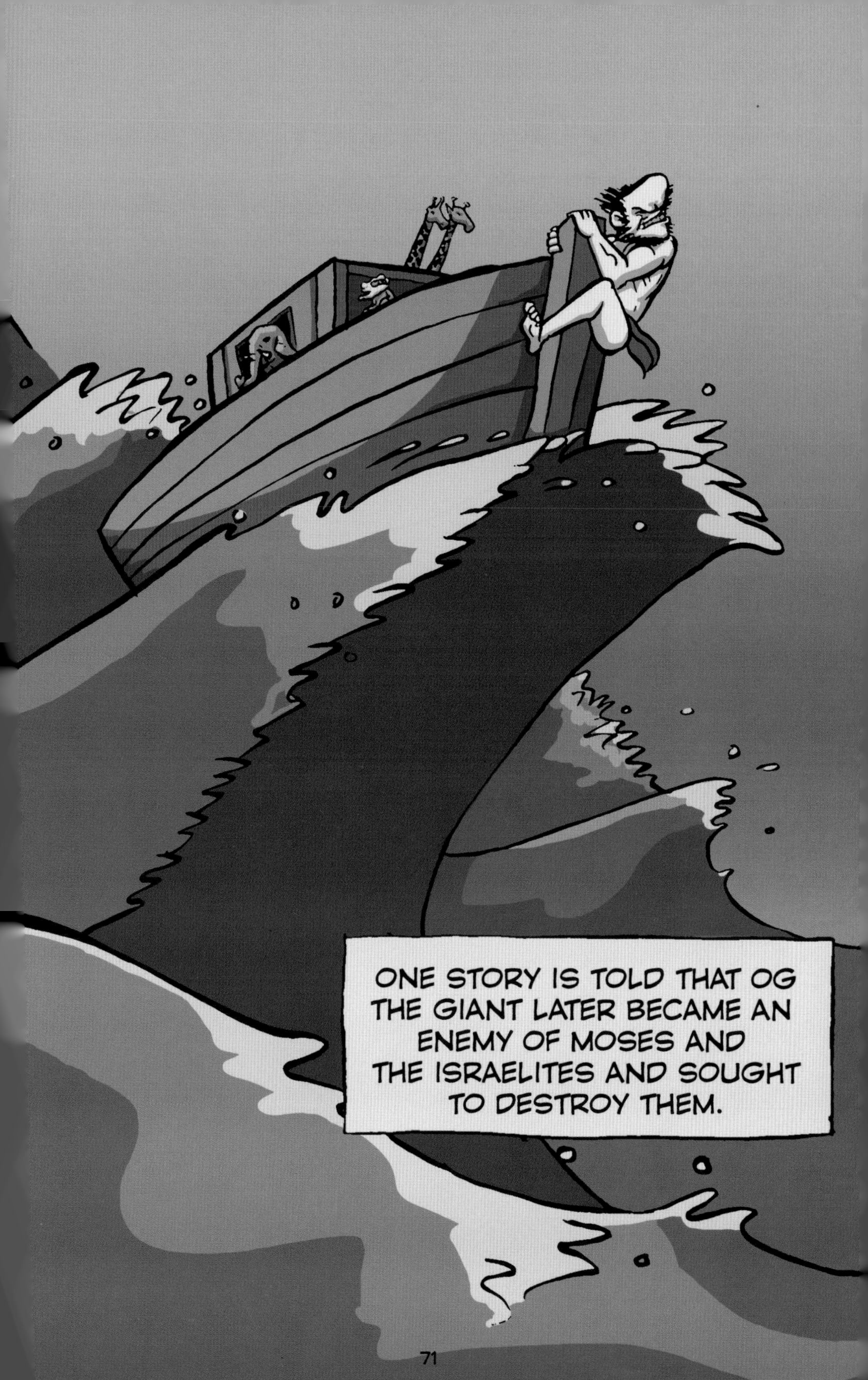
ONE STORY IS TOLD THAT OG THE GIANT LATER BECAME AN ENEMY OF MOSES AND THE ISRAELITES AND SOUGHT TO DESTROY THEM.

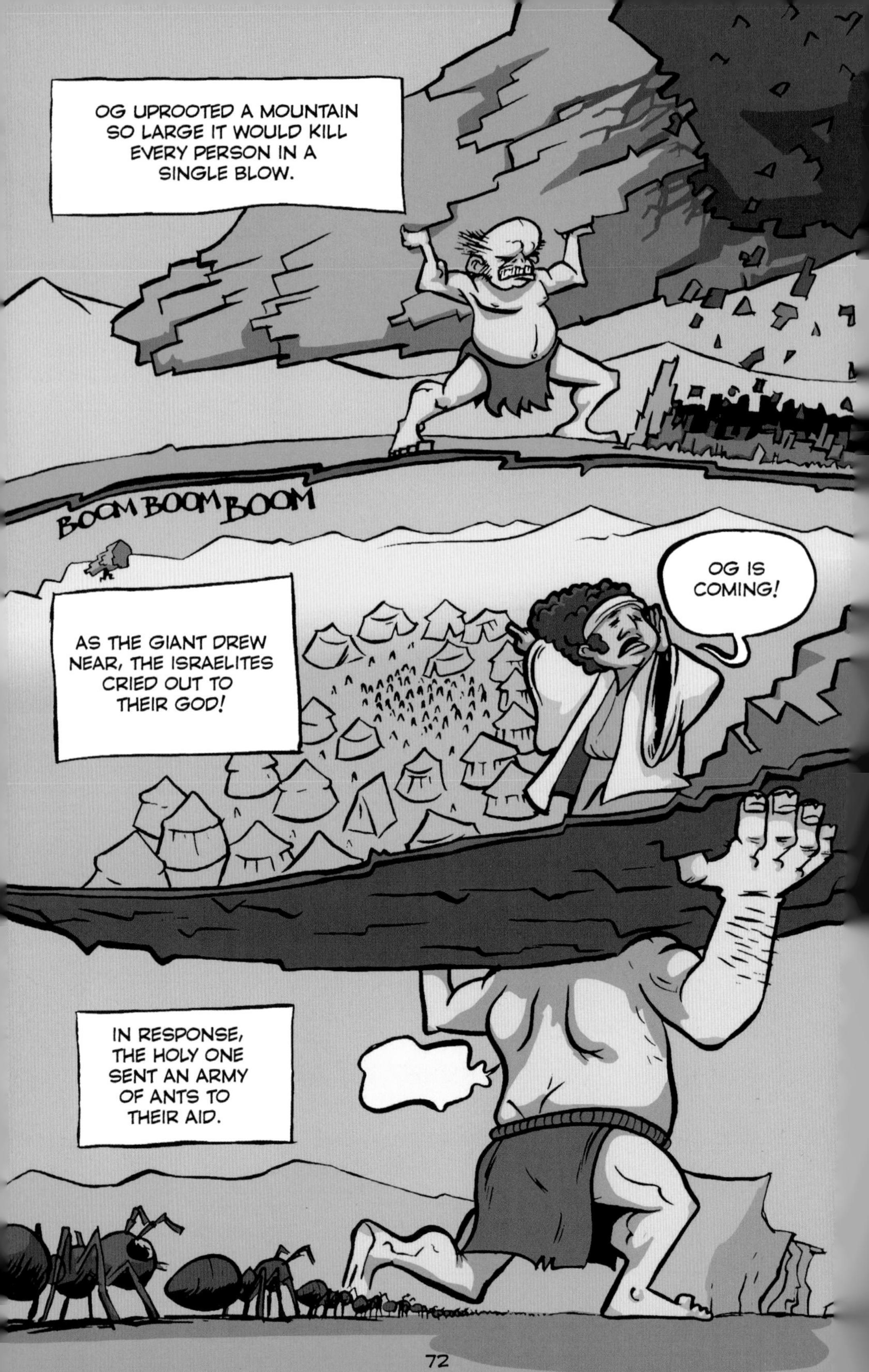

OG UPROOTED A MOUNTAIN SO LARGE IT WOULD KILL EVERY PERSON IN A SINGLE BLOW.
BOOM BOOM BOOM
AS THE GIANT DREW NEAR, THE ISRAELITES CRIED OUT TO THEIR GOD!
OG IS COMING!
IN RESPONSE, THE HOLY ONE SENT AN ARMY OF ANTS TO THEIR AID.

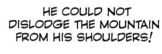
HE COULD NOT DISLODGE THE MOUNTAIN FROM HIS SHOULDERS!

RRRRR...

THE ANTS ATE AWAY AT THE MOUNTAIN UNTIL IT FELL AROUND OG'S HEAD.

AT THAT MOMENT, MOSES, ARMED WITH HIS STAFF, JUMPED UP AND STRUCK OG IN THE ANKLE, KILLING HIM.

BOOM

SOME SAY THAT OG'S BONES CAN STILL BE SEEN RESTING IN THE DESERT.

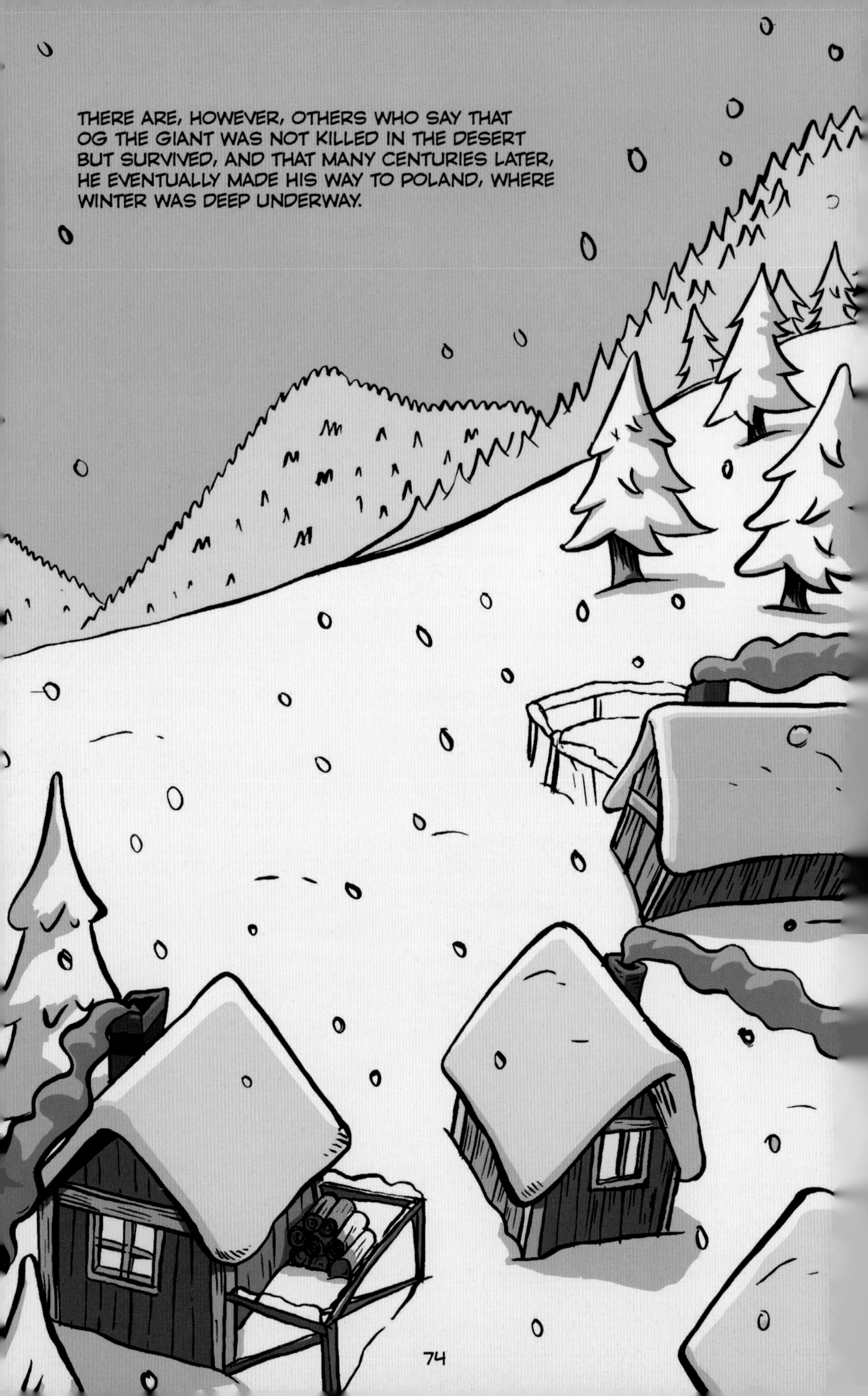
THERE ARE, HOWEVER, OTHERS WHO SAY THAT OG THE GIANT WAS NOT KILLED IN THE DESERT BUT SURVIVED, AND THAT MANY CENTURIES LATER, HE EVENTUALLY MADE HIS WAY TO POLAND, WHERE WINTER WAS DEEP UNDERWAY.

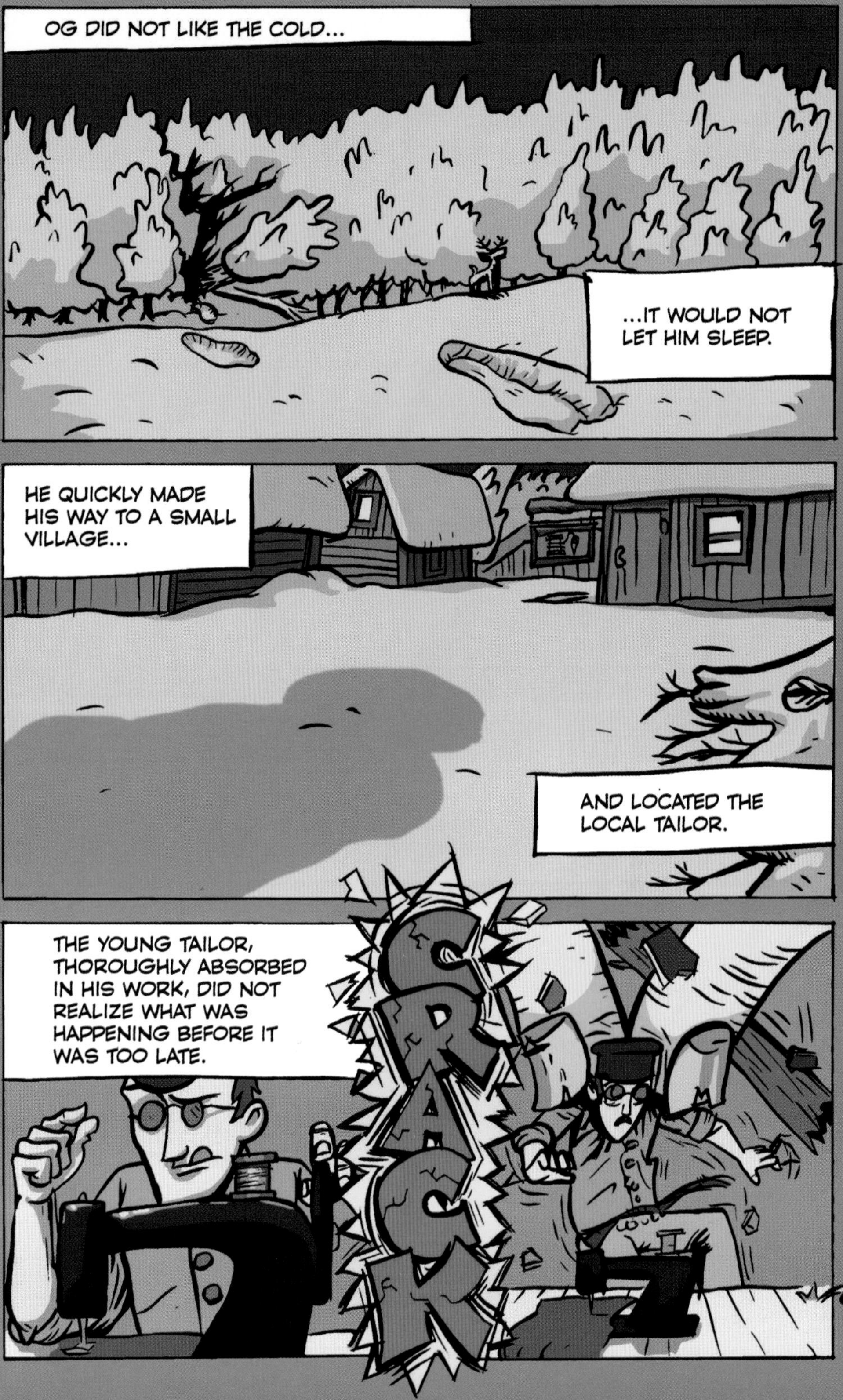
OG DID NOT LIKE THE COLD...
...IT WOULD NOT LET HIM SLEEP.
HE QUICKLY MADE HIS WAY TO A SMALL VILLAGE...
AND LOCATED THE LOCAL TAILOR.
THE YOUNG TAILOR, THOROUGHLY ABSORBED IN HIS WORK, DID NOT REALIZE WHAT WAS HAPPENING BEFORE IT WAS TOO LATE.
CRACK

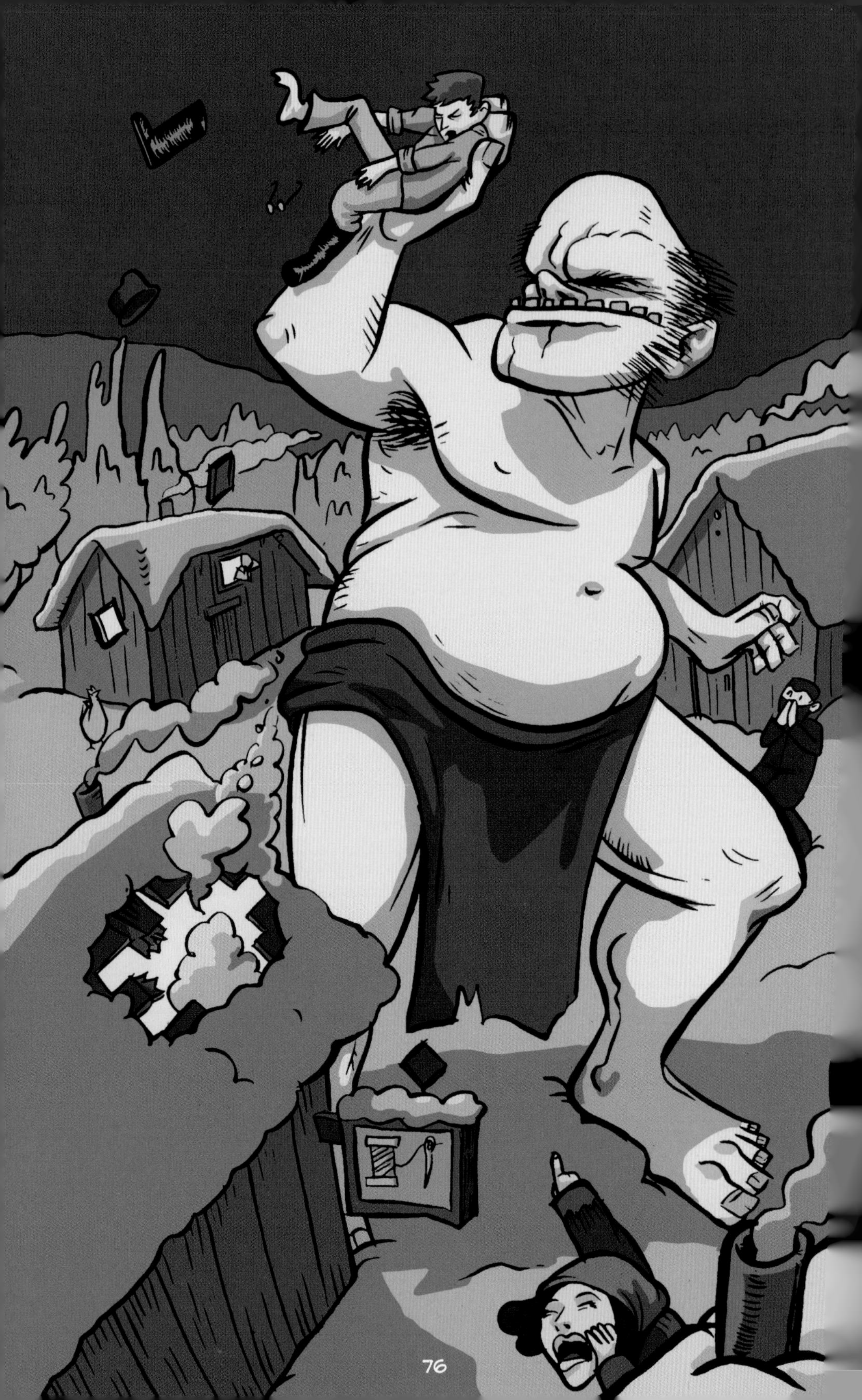

OG COLD! OG NO SLEEP! OG NEED WARM SO HE CAN SLEEP!

WHA?

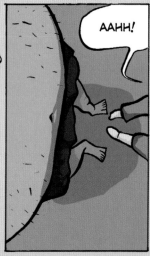
AAHH!

OG WANT COAT! YOU MAKE COAT!

A...A...COAT... YOU WANT A COAT?

LITTLE MAN MAKE COAT FOR OG SO HE CAN SLEEP! NOW!!

IT...IT...IT WILL TAKE TIME...

WHAT TIME!?!

A...A...A...WEEK... I CAN MAKE YOU A COAT IN A WEEK...

OG RETURN IN SEVEN DAYS! MAN MAKE COAT!

OR OG MAKE VILLAGE DUST!

OOF!

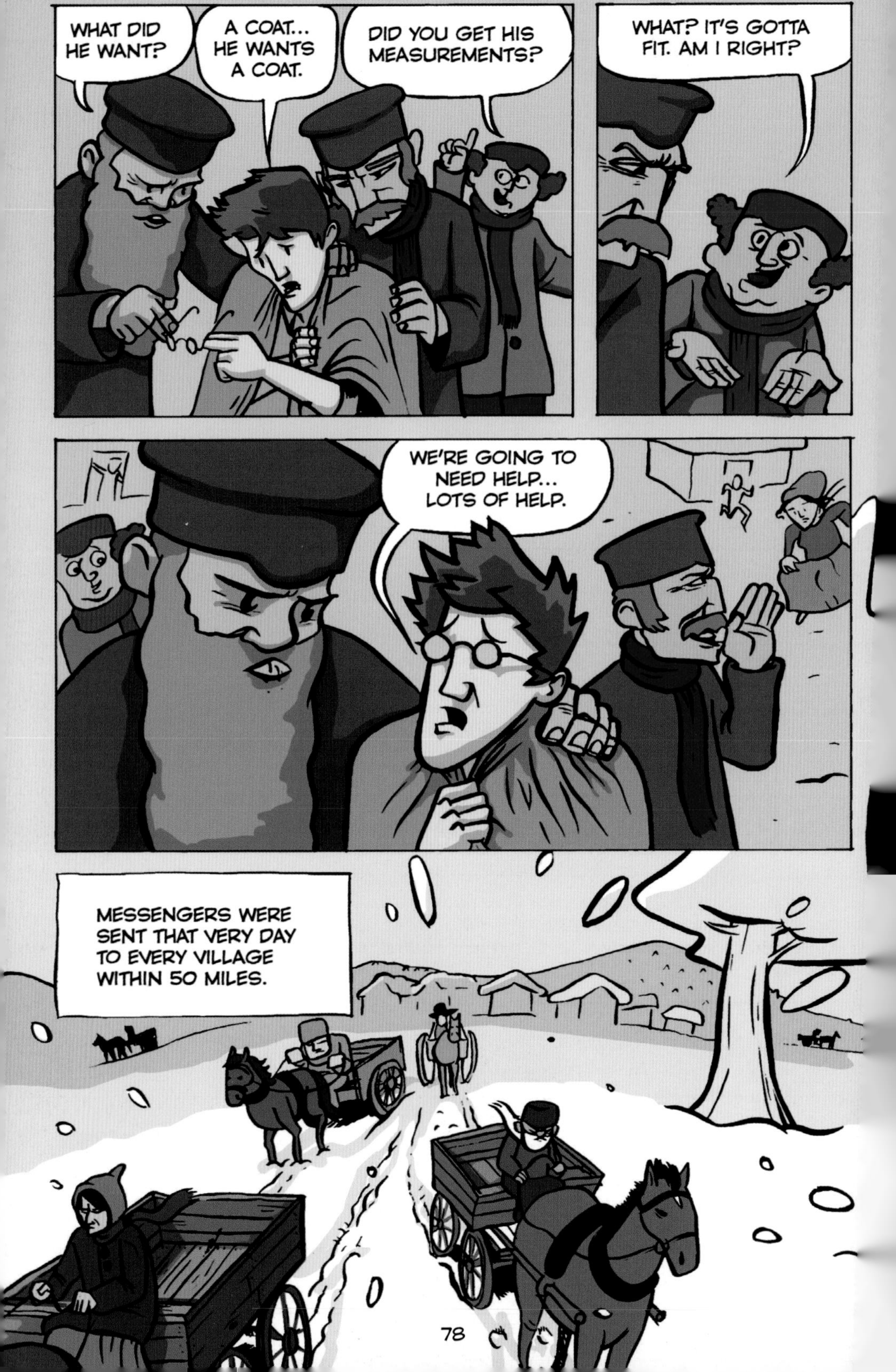
WHAT DID HE WANT?
A COAT... HE WANTS A COAT.
DID YOU GET HIS MEASUREMENTS?
WHAT? IT'S GOTTA FIT. AM I RIGHT?
WE'RE GOING TO NEED HELP... LOTS OF HELP.
MESSENGERS WERE SENT THAT VERY DAY TO EVERY VILLAGE WITHIN 50 MILES.

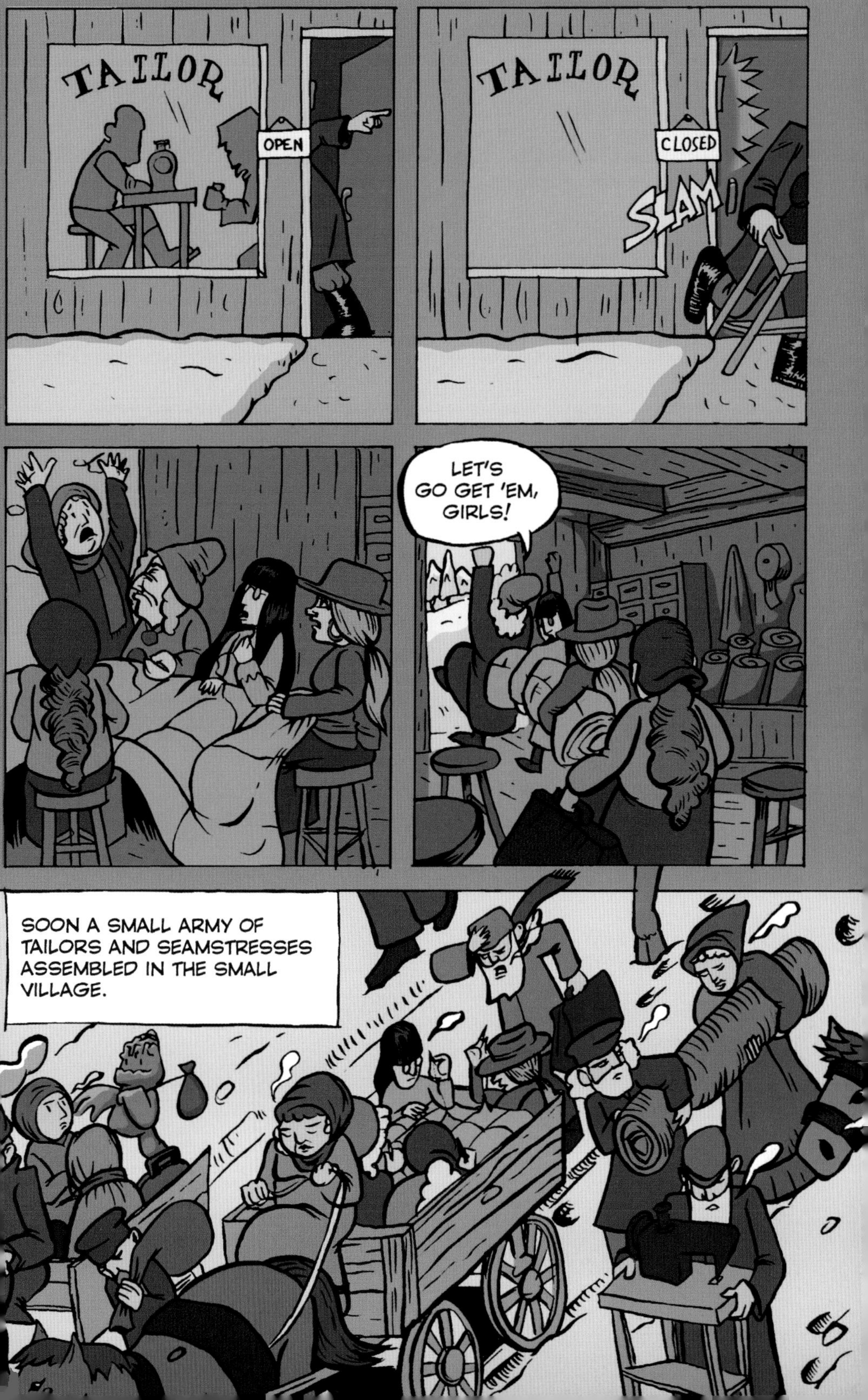
TAILOR
OPEN
TAILOR
CLOSED
SLAM!
LET'S GO GET 'EM, GIRLS!
SOON A SMALL ARMY OF TAILORS AND SEAMSTRESSES ASSEMBLED IN THE SMALL VILLAGE.

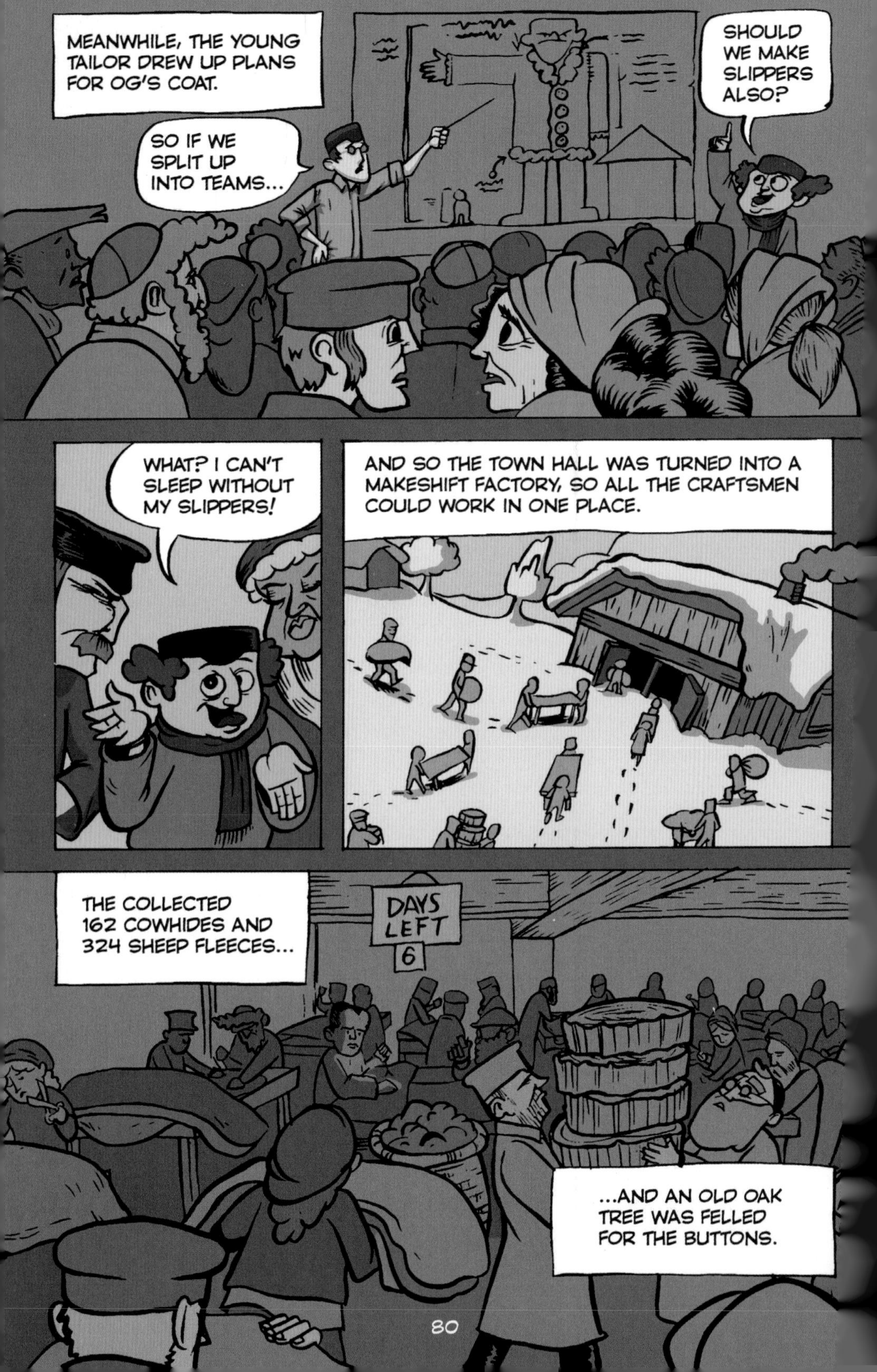
MEANWHILE, THE YOUNG TAILOR DREW UP PLANS FOR OG'S COAT.
SO IF WE SPLIT UP INTO TEAMS...
SHOULD WE MAKE SLIPPERS ALSO?
WHAT? I CAN'T SLEEP WITHOUT MY SLIPPERS!
AND SO THE TOWN HALL WAS TURNED INTO A MAKESHIFT FACTORY, SO ALL THE CRAFTSMEN COULD WORK IN ONE PLACE.
THE COLLECTED 162 COWHIDES AND 324 SHEEP FLEECES...
DAYS LEFT 6
...AND AN OLD OAK TREE WAS FELLED FOR THE BUTTONS.

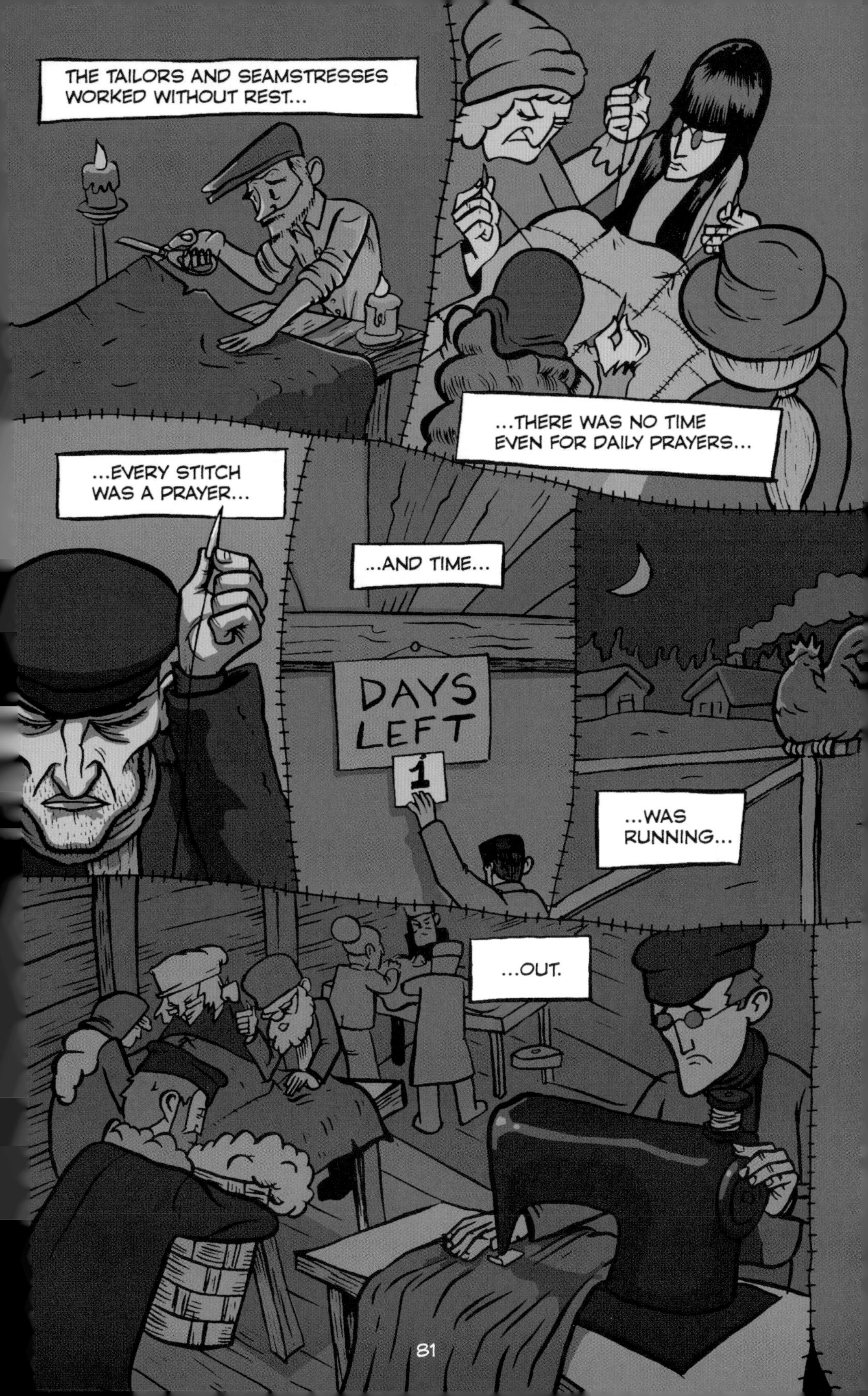
THE TAILORS AND SEAMSTRESSES WORKED WITHOUT REST...
...THERE WAS NO TIME EVEN FOR DAILY PRAYERS...
...EVERY STITCH WAS A PRAYER...
...AND TIME...
DAYS LEFT
1
...WAS RUNNING...
...OUT.

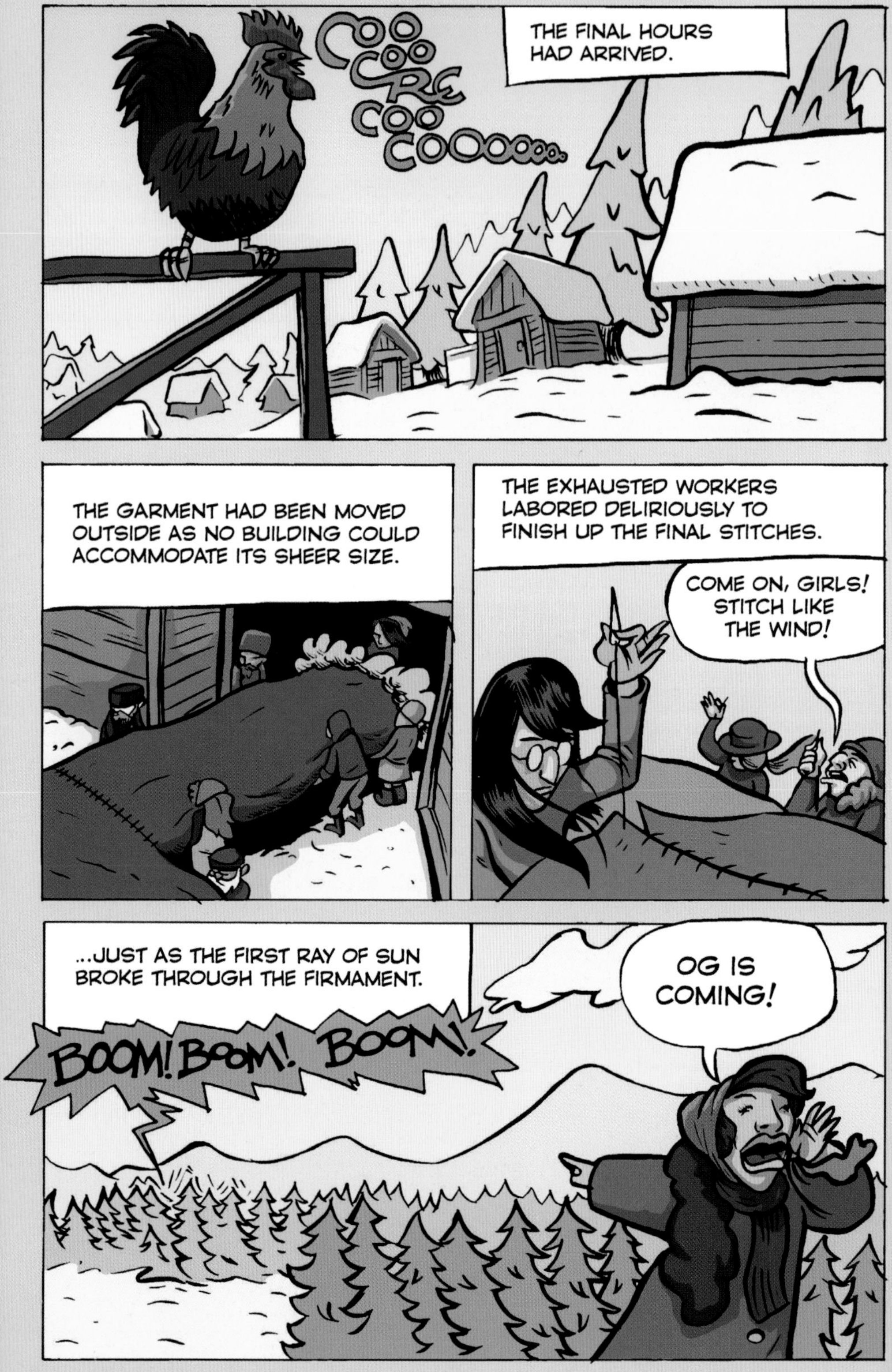
COO COO RE COO COOooooo.
THE FINAL HOURS HAD ARRIVED.
THE GARMENT HAD BEEN MOVED OUTSIDE AS NO BUILDING COULD ACCOMMODATE ITS SHEER SIZE.
THE EXHAUSTED WORKERS LABORED DELIRIOUSLY TO FINISH UP THE FINAL STITCHES.
COME ON, GIRLS! STITCH LIKE THE WIND!
...JUST AS THE FIRST RAY OF SUN BROKE THROUGH THE FIRMAMENT.
BOOM! BOOM! BOOM!
OG IS COMING!

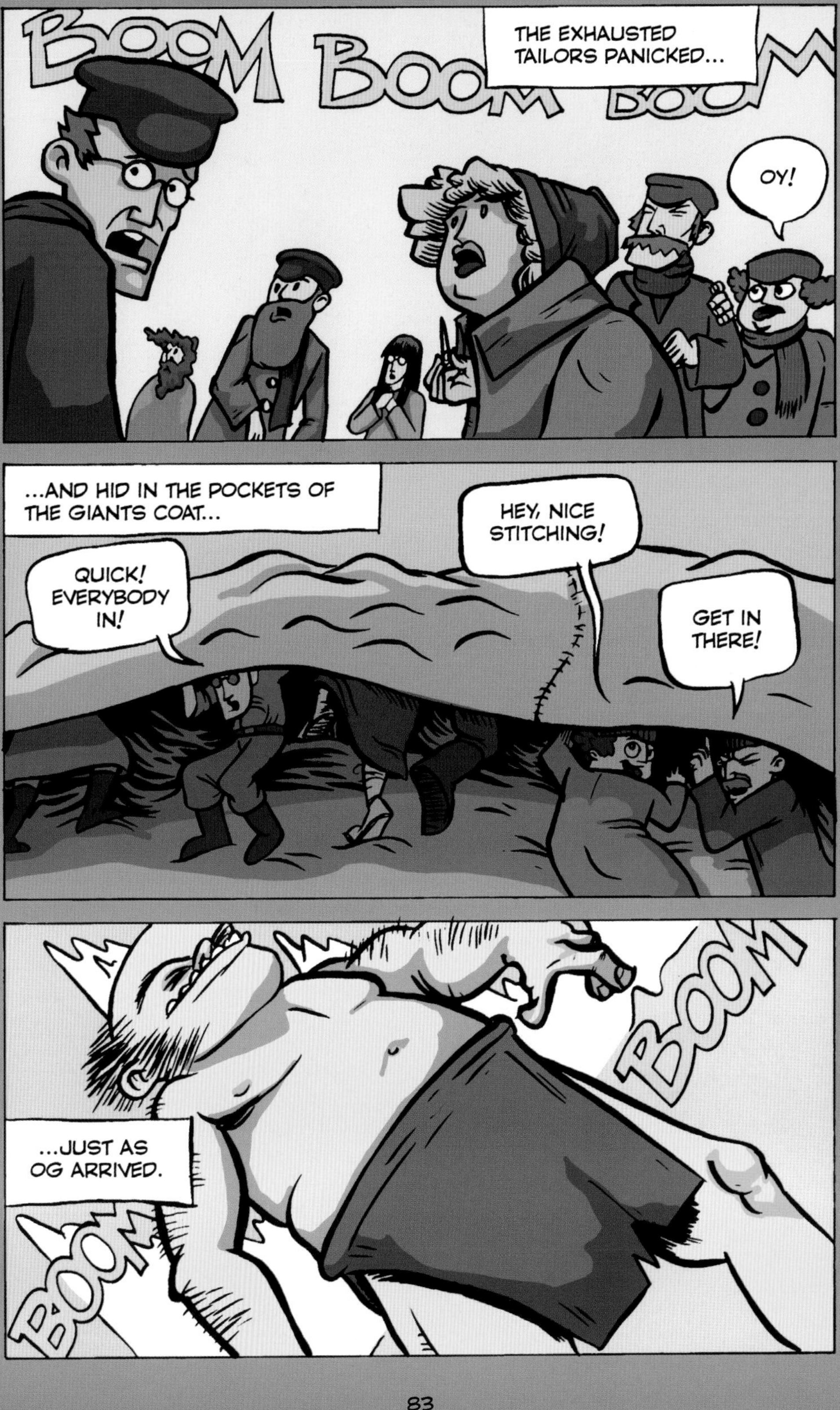
BOOM BOOM BOOM
THE EXHAUSTED TAILORS PANICKED...
OY!
...AND HID IN THE POCKETS OF THE GIANTS COAT...
QUICK! EVERYBODY IN!
HEY, NICE STITCHING!
GET IN THERE!
BOOM
...JUST AS OG ARRIVED.
BOOM

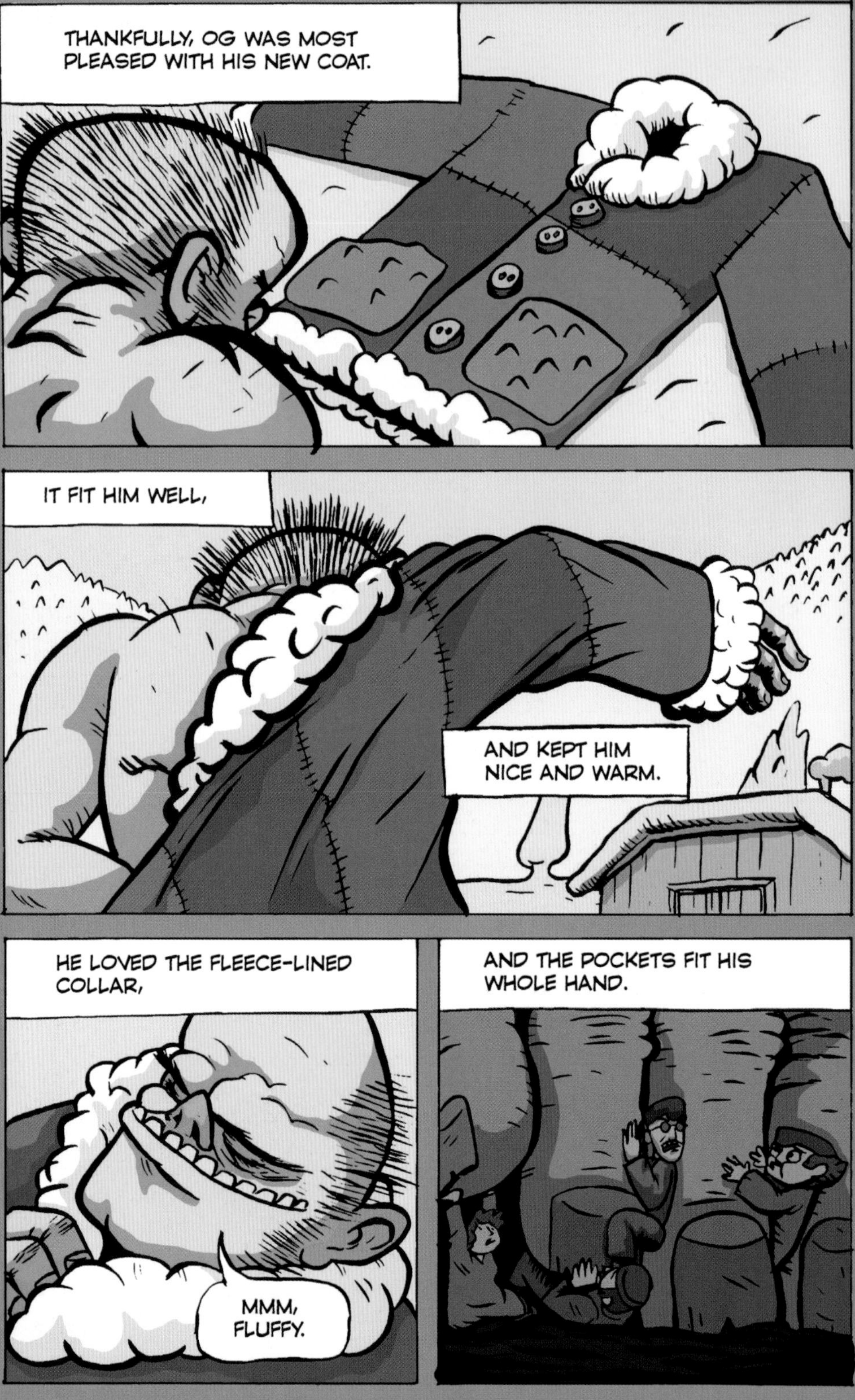
THANKFULLY, OG WAS MOST PLEASED WITH HIS NEW COAT.
IT FIT HIM WELL,
AND KEPT HIM NICE AND WARM.
HE LOVED THE FLEECE-LINED COLLAR,
MMM, FLUFFY.
AND THE POCKETS FIT HIS WHOLE HAND.

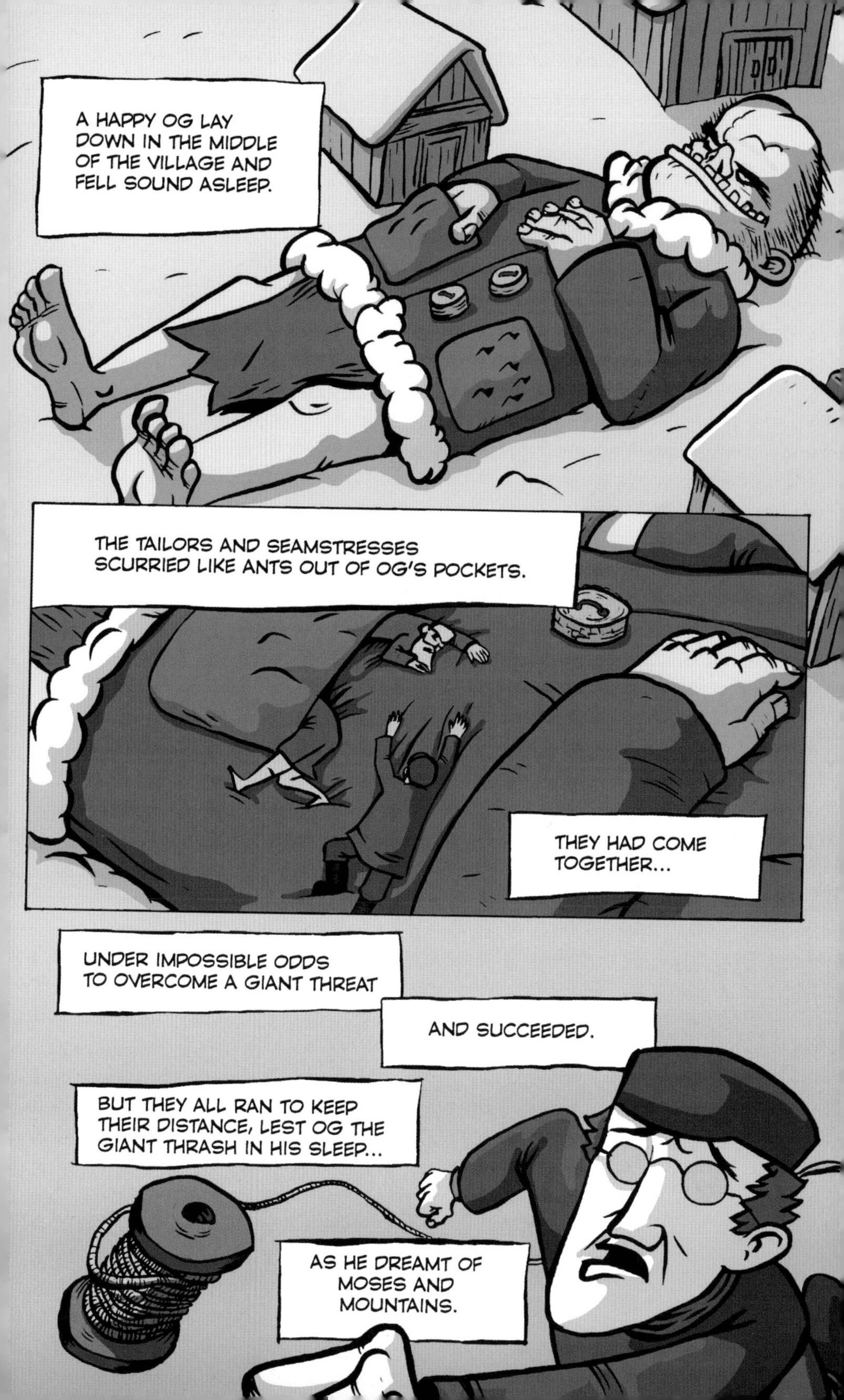
A HAPPY OG LAY DOWN IN THE MIDDLE OF THE VILLAGE AND FELL SOUND ASLEEP.
THE TAILORS AND SEAMSTRESSES SCURRIED LIKE ANTS OUT OF OG'S POCKETS.
THEY HAD COME TOGETHER...
UNDER IMPOSSIBLE ODDS TO OVERCOME A GIANT THREAT
AND SUCCEEDED.
BUT THEY ALL RAN TO KEEP THEIR DISTANCE, LEST OG THE GIANT THRASH IN HIS SLEEP...
AS HE DREAMT OF MOSES AND MOUNTAINS.

UNDER THE BRIDGE

THERE ONCE WAS A CLEVER LASS WHO LIVED IN A SMALL MUSHROOM-SHAPED HUT THAT SHE BUILT WITH HER OWN TWO HANDS.

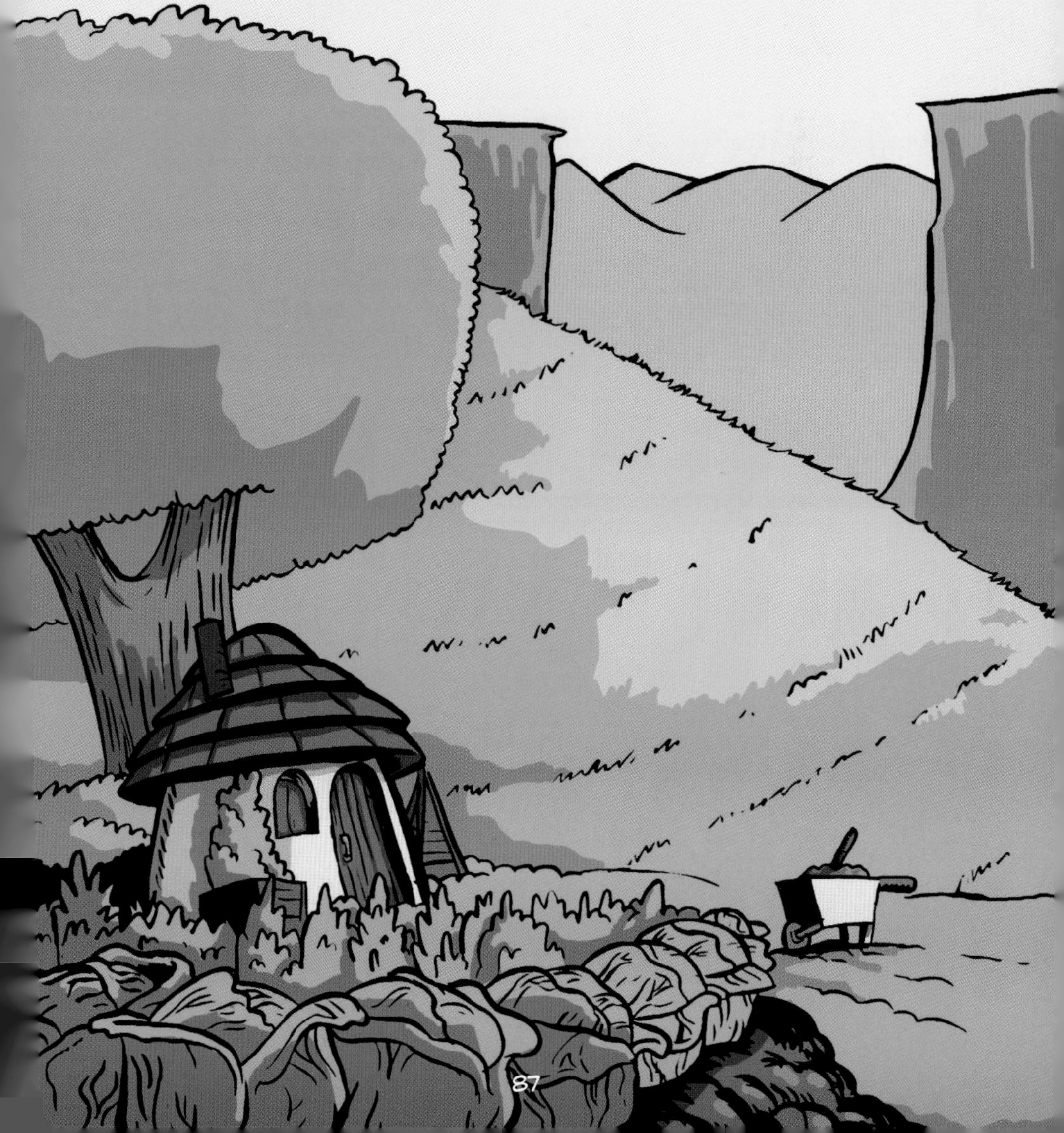

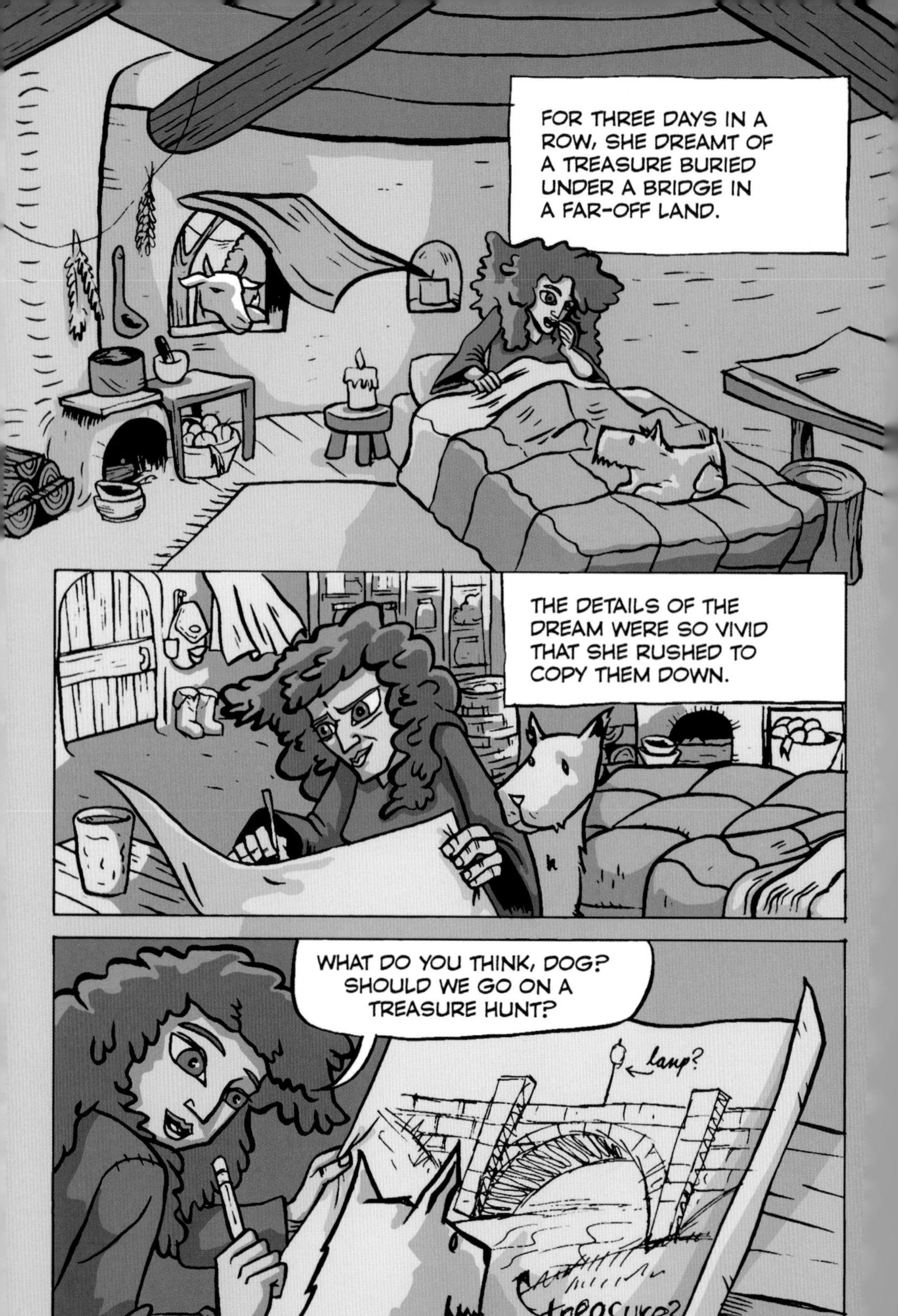
FOR THREE DAYS IN A ROW, SHE DREAMT OF A TREASURE BURIED UNDER A BRIDGE IN A FAR-OFF LAND.
THE DETAILS OF THE DREAM WERE SO VIVID THAT SHE RUSHED TO COPY THEM DOWN.
WHAT DO YOU THINK, DOG? SHOULD WE GO ON A TREASURE HUNT?
lamp?
treasure?

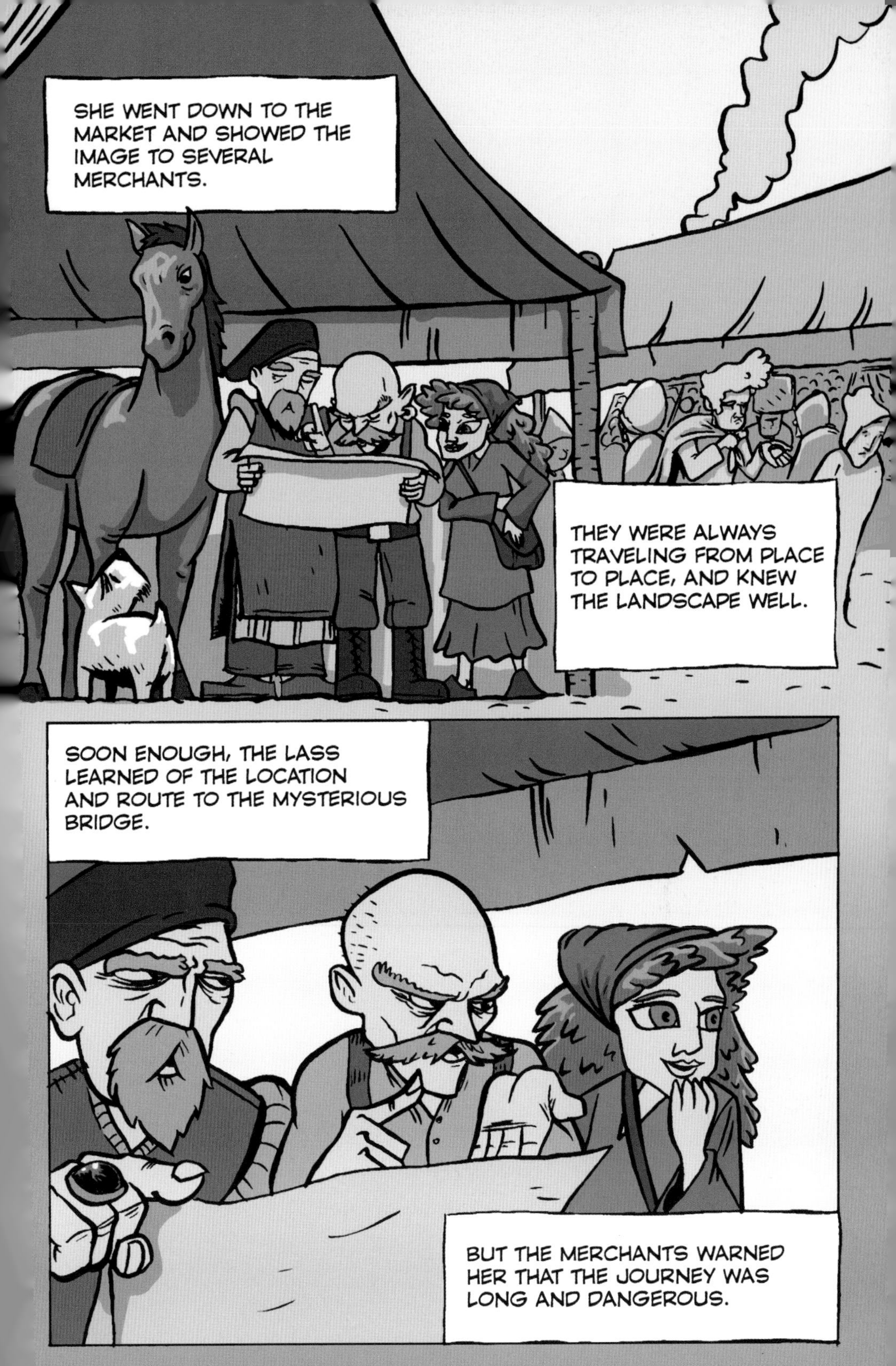
SHE WENT DOWN TO THE MARKET AND SHOWED THE IMAGE TO SEVERAL MERCHANTS.
THEY WERE ALWAYS TRAVELING FROM PLACE TO PLACE, AND KNEW THE LANDSCAPE WELL.
SOON ENOUGH, THE LASS LEARNED OF THE LOCATION AND ROUTE TO THE MYSTERIOUS BRIDGE.
BUT THE MERCHANTS WARNED HER THAT THE JOURNEY WAS LONG AND DANGEROUS.

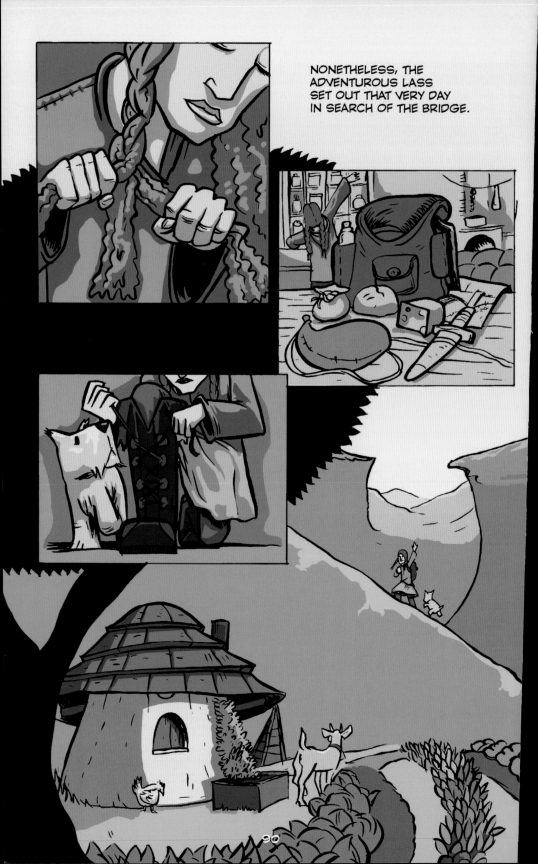

NONETHELESS, THE ADVENTUROUS LASS SET OUT THAT VERY DAY IN SEARCH OF THE BRIDGE.

90

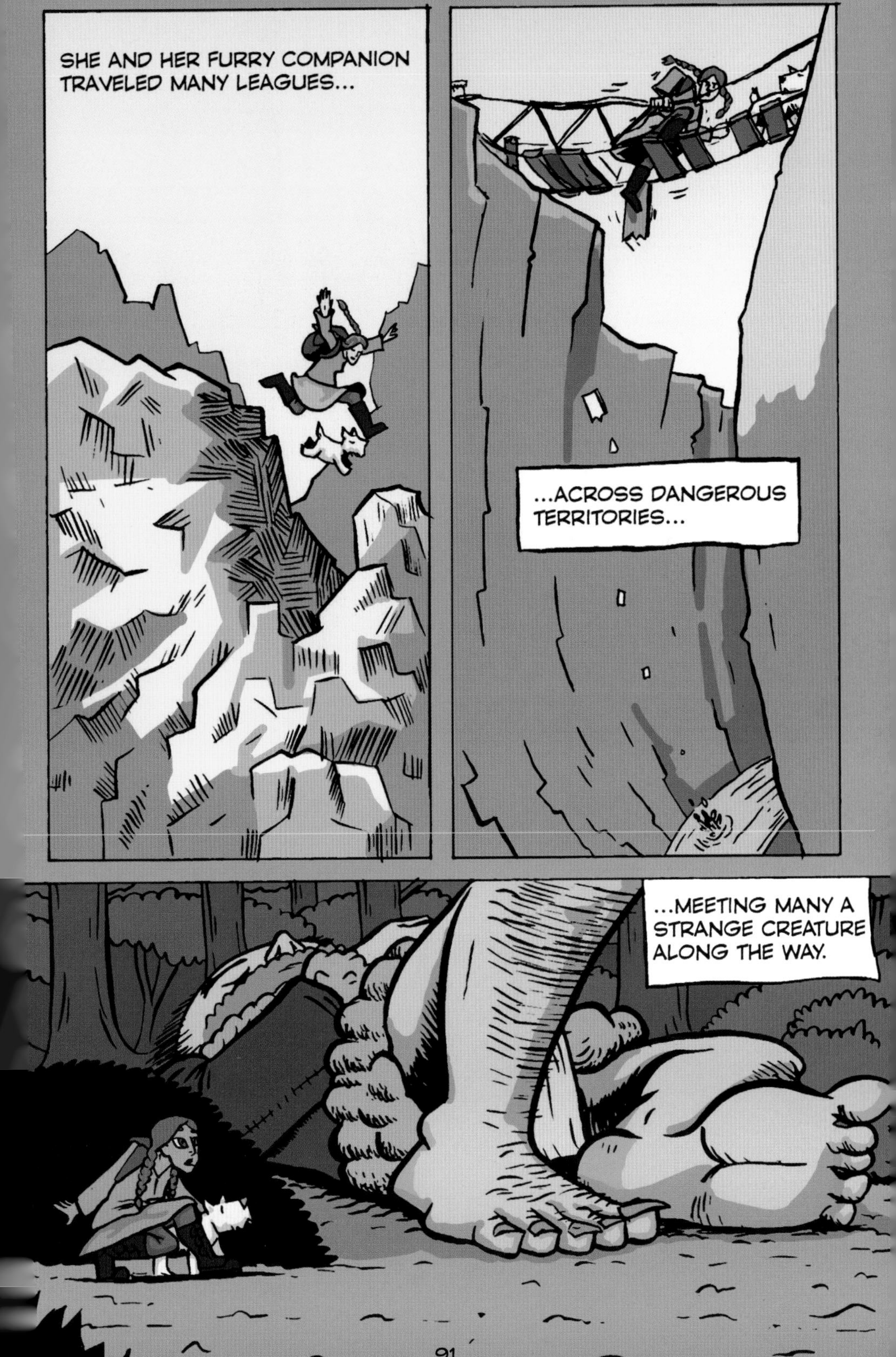
SHE AND HER FURRY COMPANION TRAVELED MANY LEAGUES...
...ACROSS DANGEROUS TERRITORIES...
...MEETING MANY A STRANGE CREATURE ALONG THE WAY.

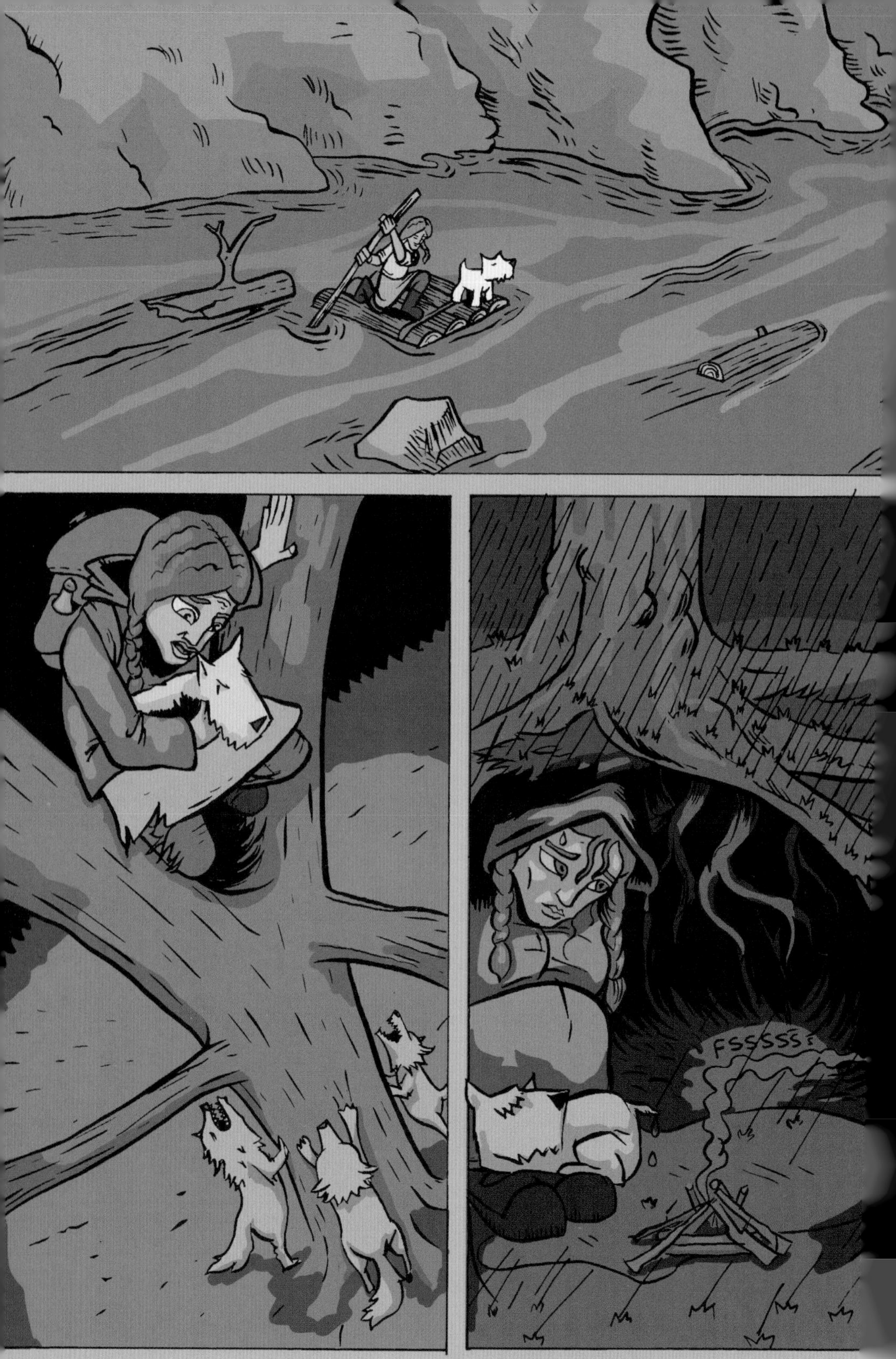
FSSSSSs

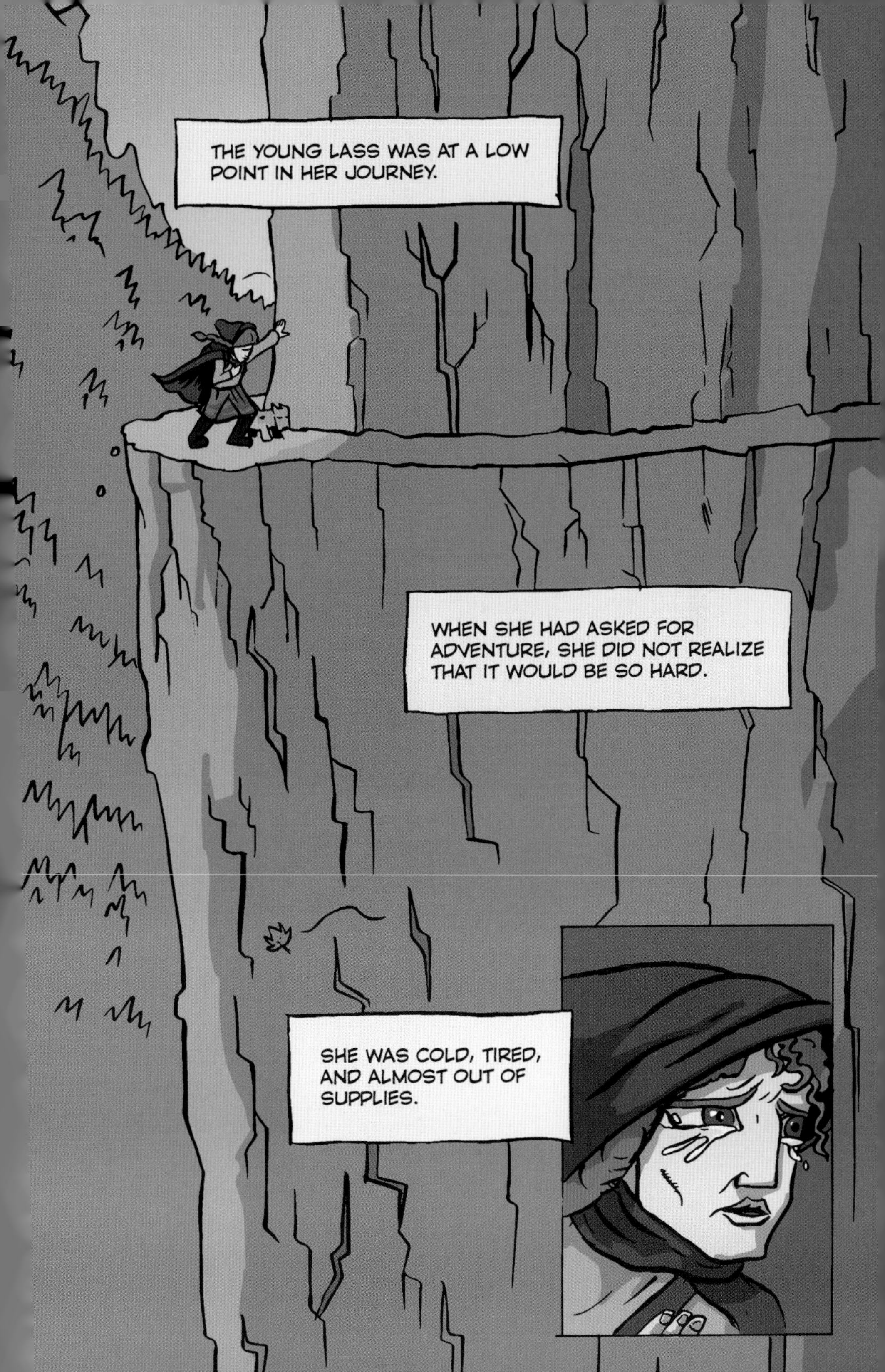
THE YOUNG LASS WAS AT A LOW POINT IN HER JOURNEY.
WHEN SHE HAD ASKED FOR ADVENTURE, SHE DID NOT REALIZE THAT IT WOULD BE SO HARD.
SHE WAS COLD, TIRED, AND ALMOST OUT OF SUPPLIES.

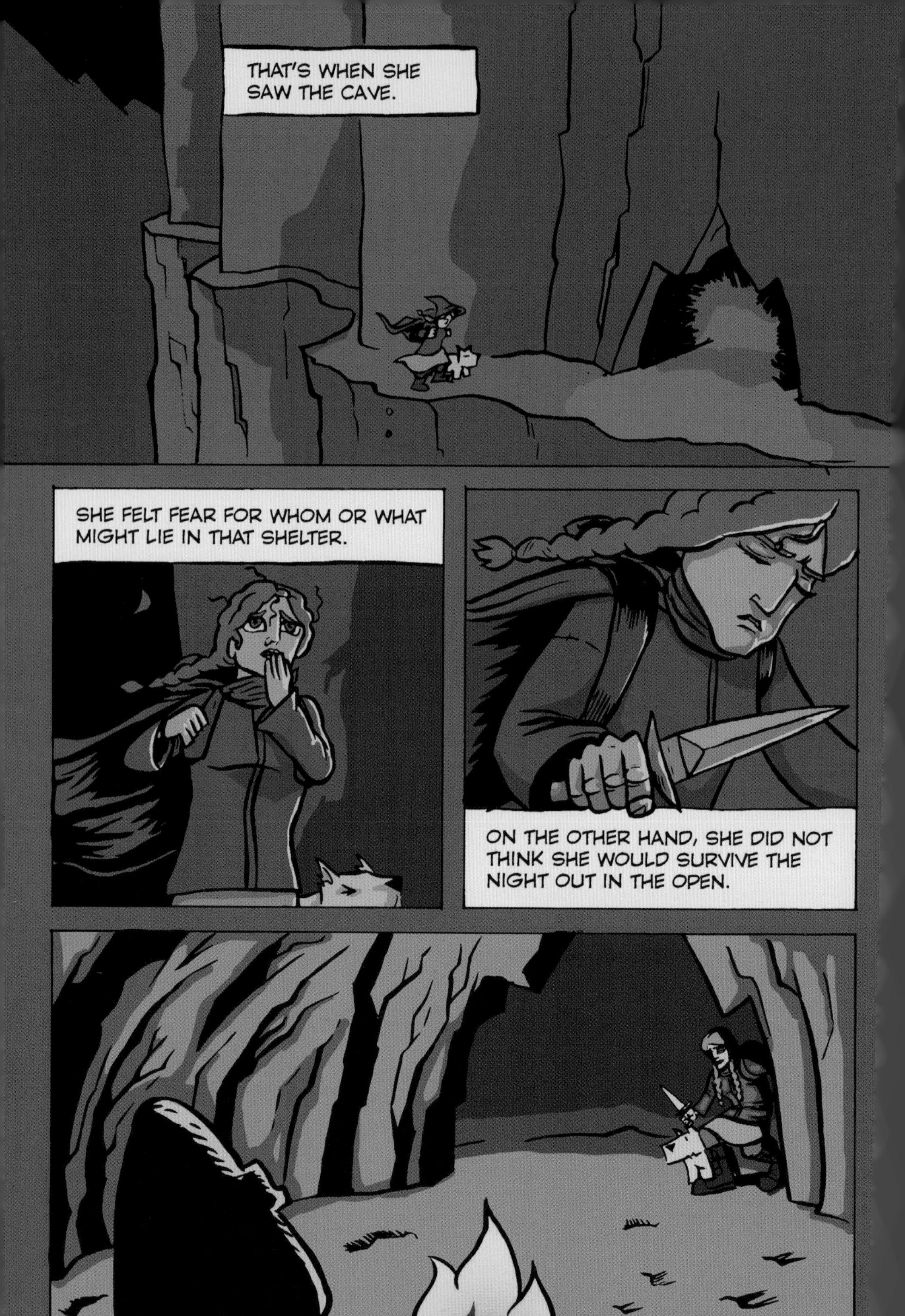
THAT'S WHEN SHE SAW THE CAVE.
SHE FELT FEAR FOR WHOM OR WHAT MIGHT LIE IN THAT SHELTER.
ON THE OTHER HAND, SHE DID NOT THINK SHE WOULD SURVIVE THE NIGHT OUT IN THE OPEN.

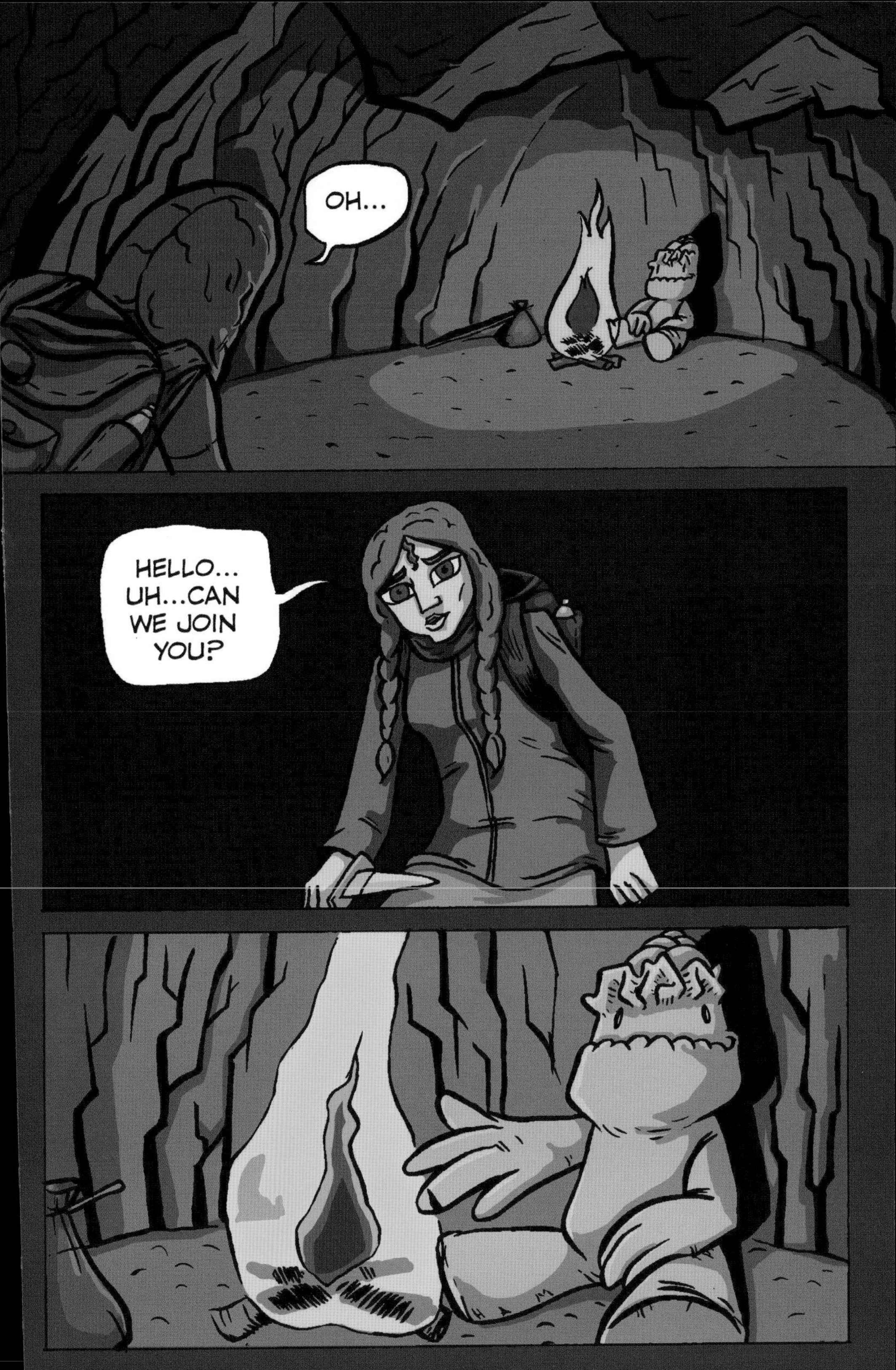

OH...
HELLO... UH...CAN WE JOIN YOU?

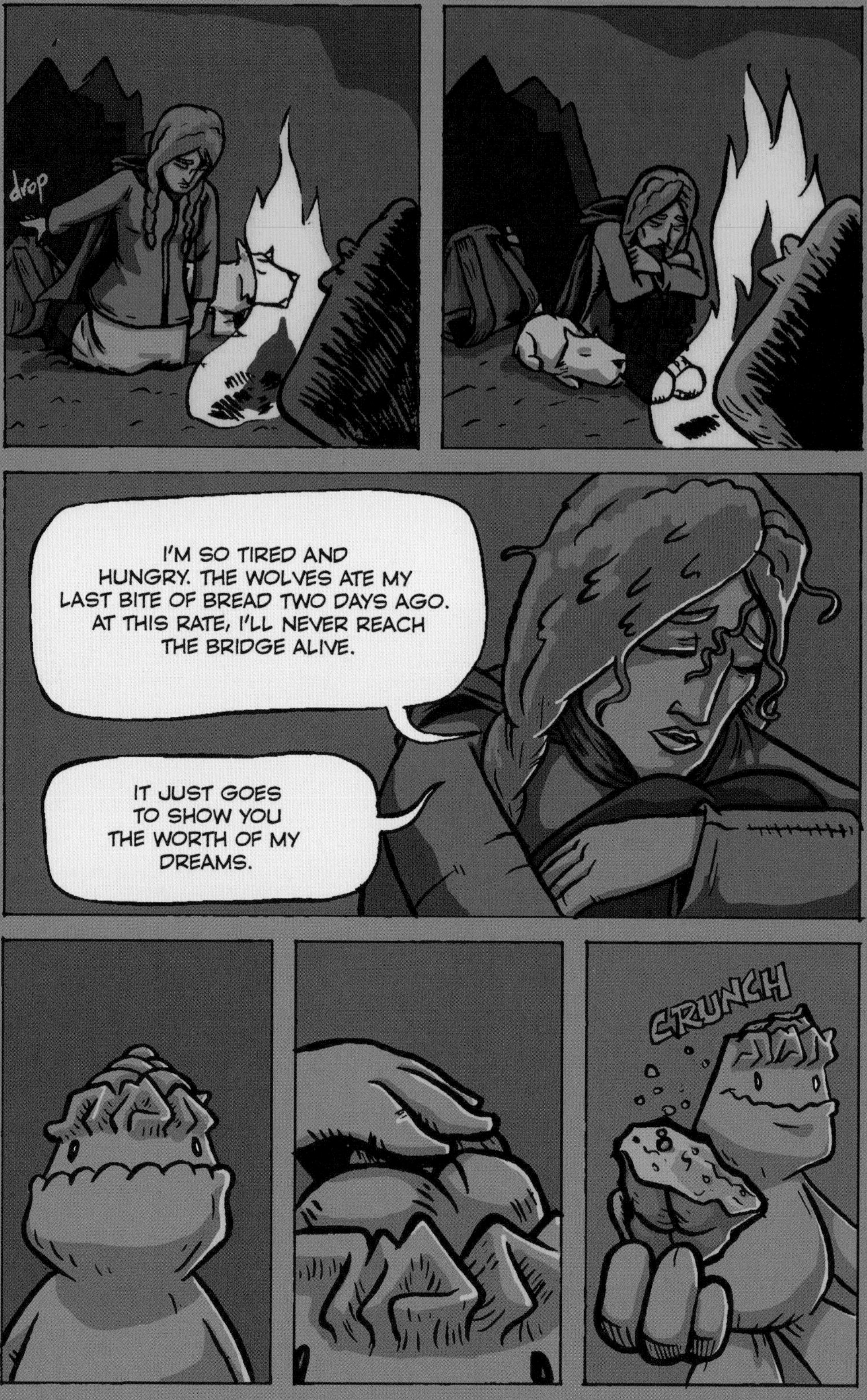
drop
I'M SO TIRED AND HUNGRY. THE WOLVES ATE MY LAST BITE OF BREAD TWO DAYS AGO. AT THIS RATE, I'LL NEVER REACH THE BRIDGE ALIVE.
IT JUST GOES TO SHOW YOU THE WORTH OF MY DREAMS.
CRUNCH

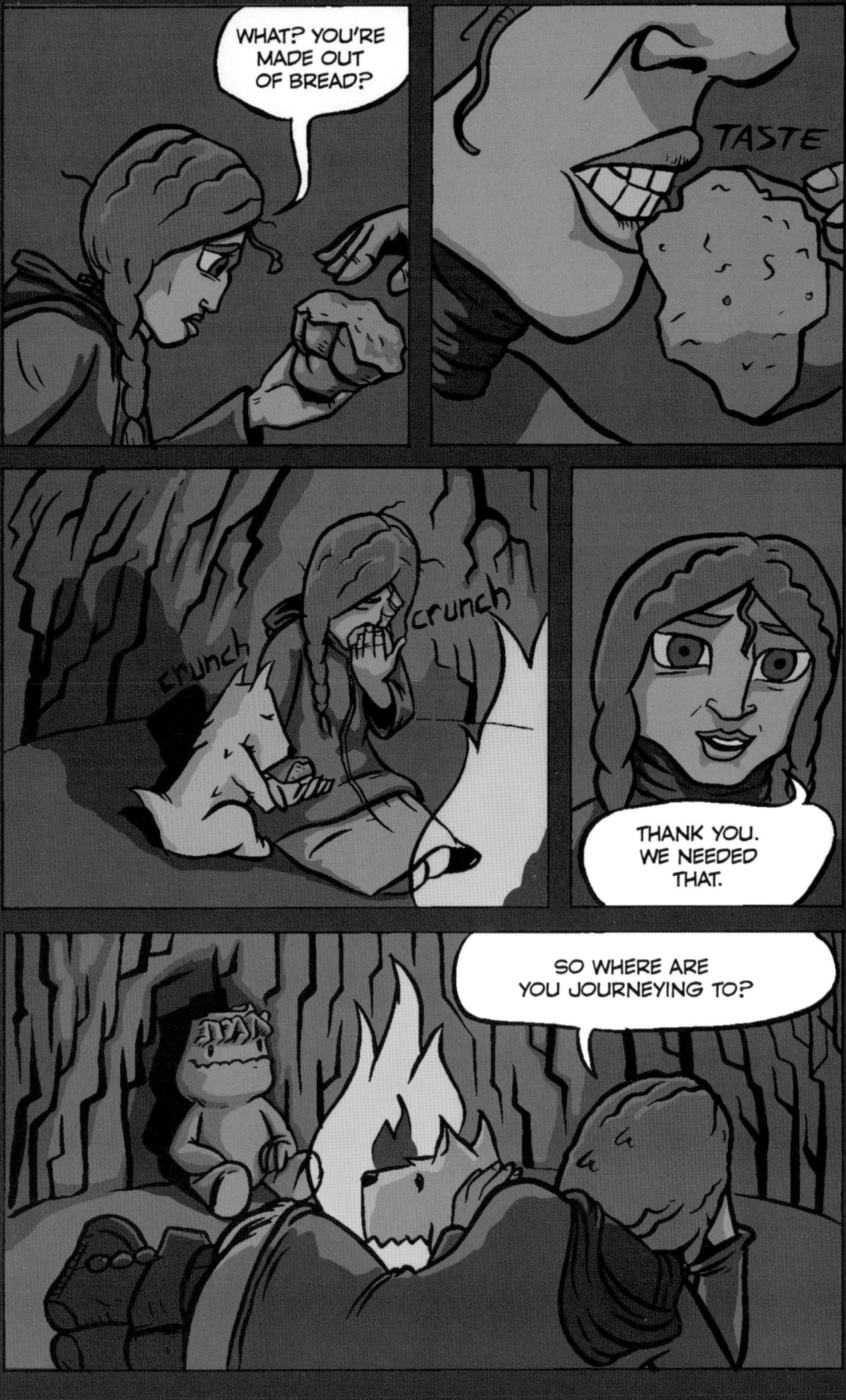
WHAT? YOU'RE MADE OUT OF BREAD?
TASTE
crunch
crunch
THANK YOU. WE NEEDED THAT.
SO WHERE ARE YOU JOURNEYING TO?

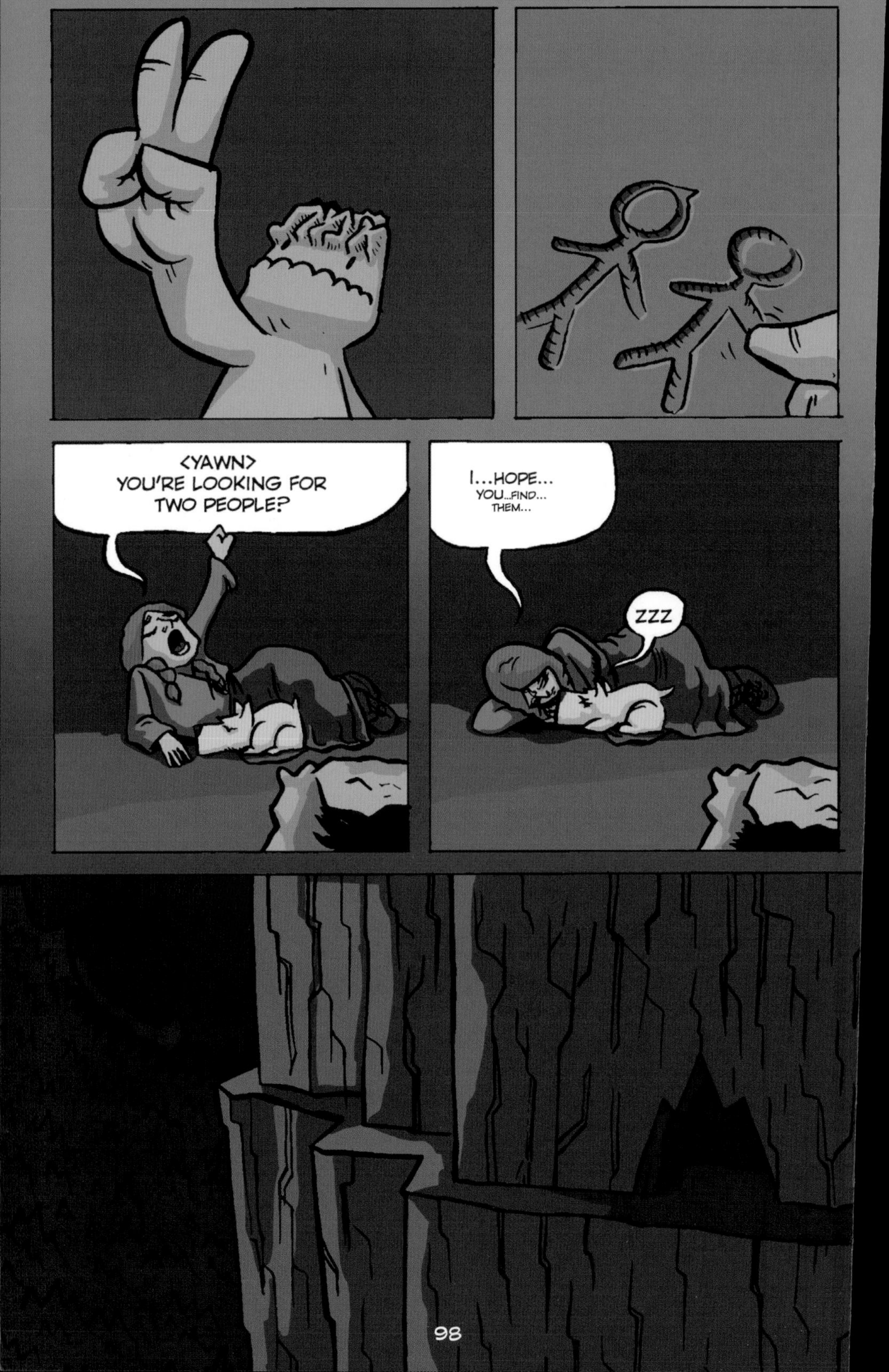
<YAWN> YOU'RE LOOKING FOR TWO PEOPLE?
I...HOPE... YOU...FIND... THEM...
ZZZ

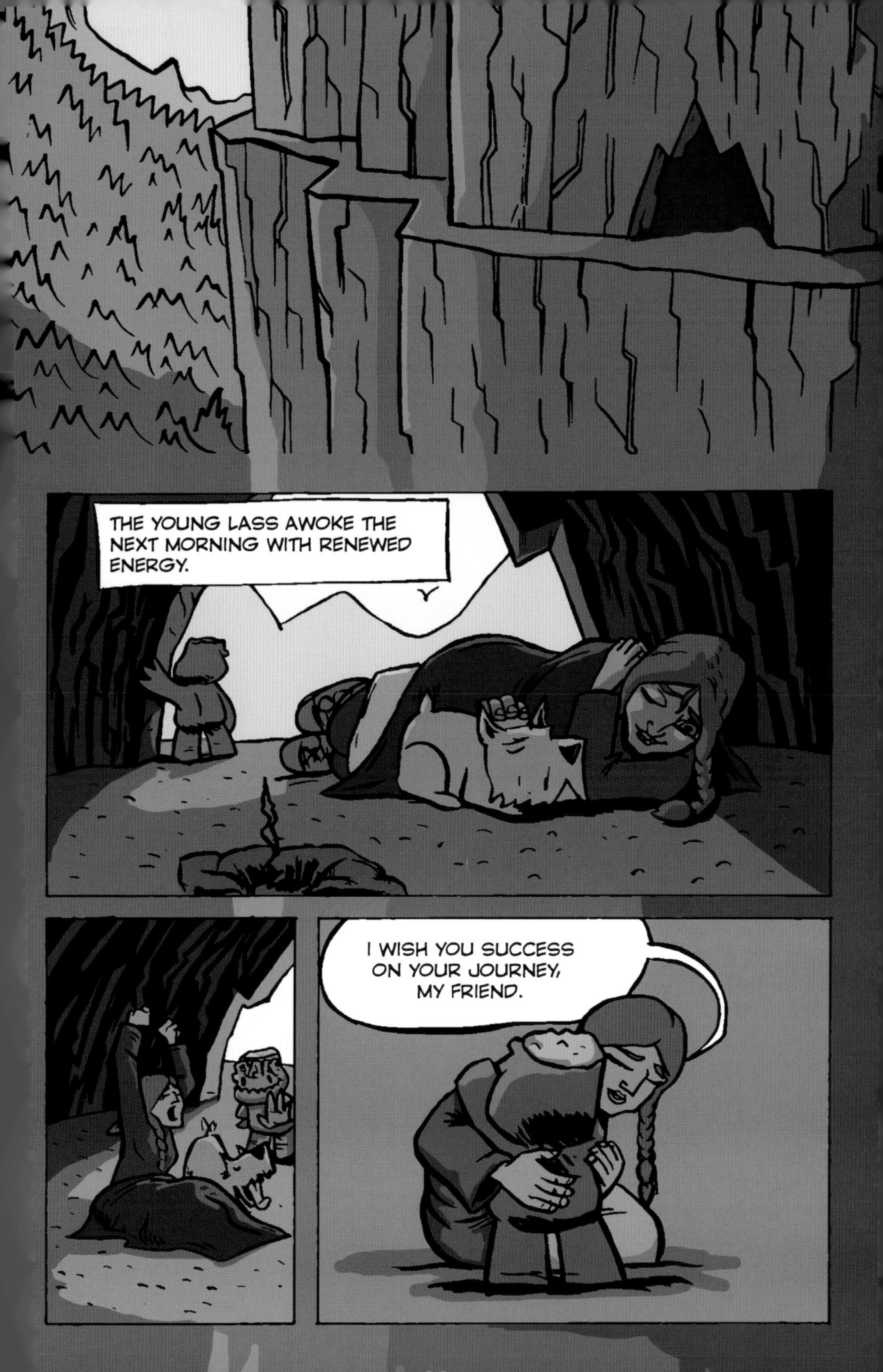
THE YOUNG LASS AWOKE THE NEXT MORNING WITH RENEWED ENERGY.
I WISH YOU SUCCESS ON YOUR JOURNEY, MY FRIEND.

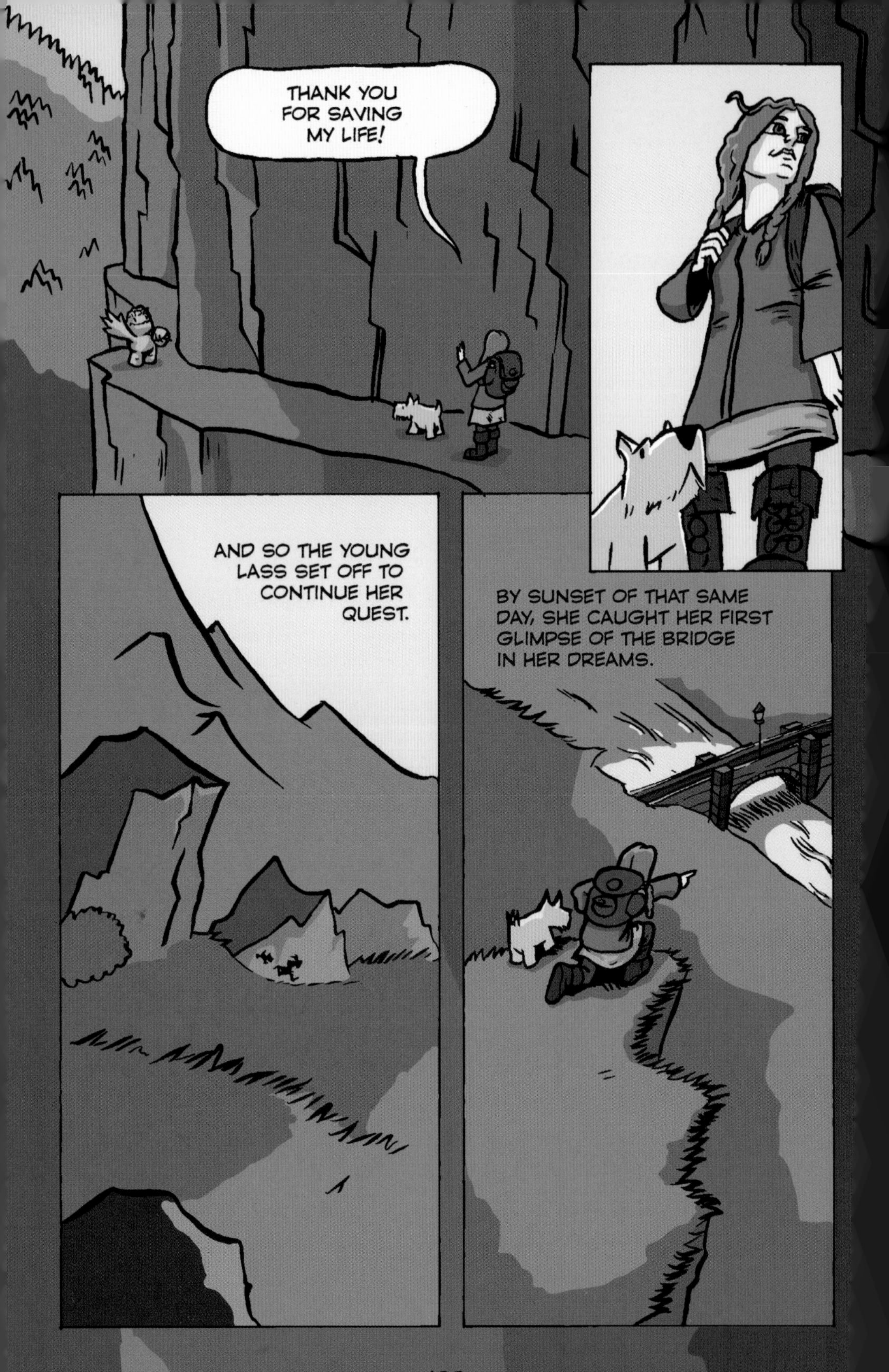
THANK YOU FOR SAVING MY LIFE!
AND SO THE YOUNG LASS SET OFF TO CONTINUE HER QUEST.
BY SUNSET OF THAT SAME DAY, SHE CAUGHT HER FIRST GLIMPSE OF THE BRIDGE IN HER DREAMS.

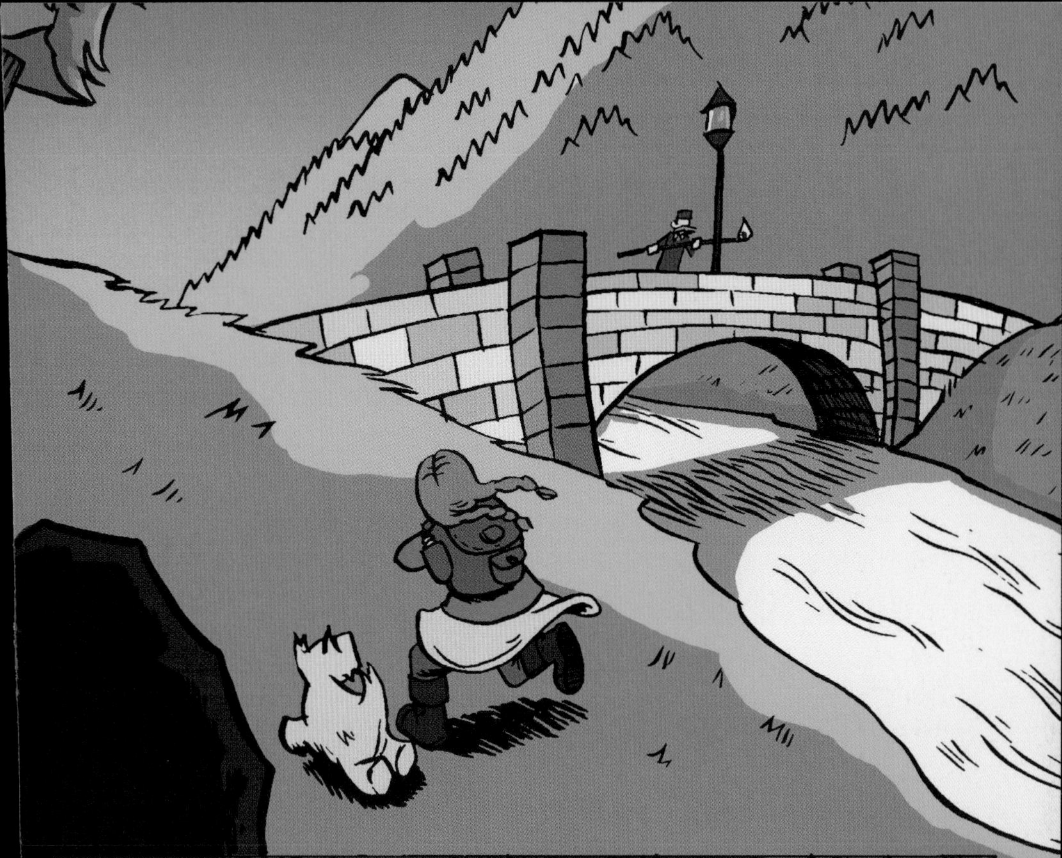

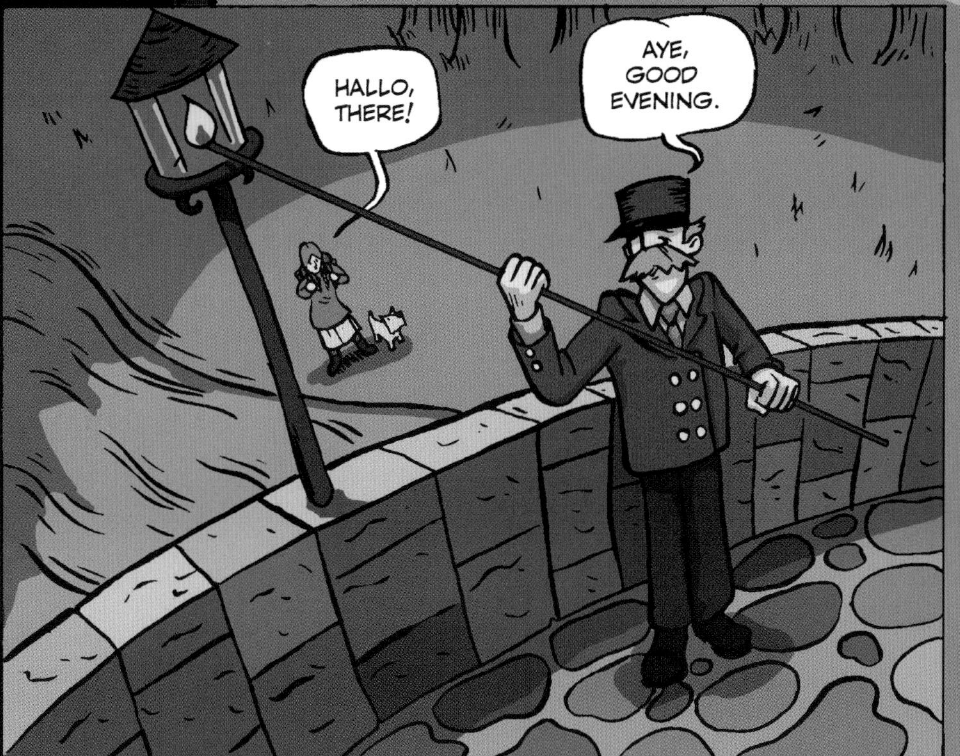
HALLO, THERE!
AYE, GOOD EVENING.

SIR, I'M SURE YOU'RE VERY BUSY, BUT CAN I ASK YOU A QUESTION?

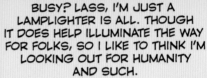

BUSY? LASS, I'M JUST A LAMPLIGHTER IS ALL. THOUGH IT DOES HELP ILLUMINATE THE WAY FOR FOLKS, SO I LIKE TO THINK I'M LOOKING OUT FOR HUMANITY AND SUCH.

ASK YOUR QUESTION.

MIGHT YOU KNOW ABOUT A TREASURE BURIED UNDER THIS BRIDGE?

COME AGAIN?

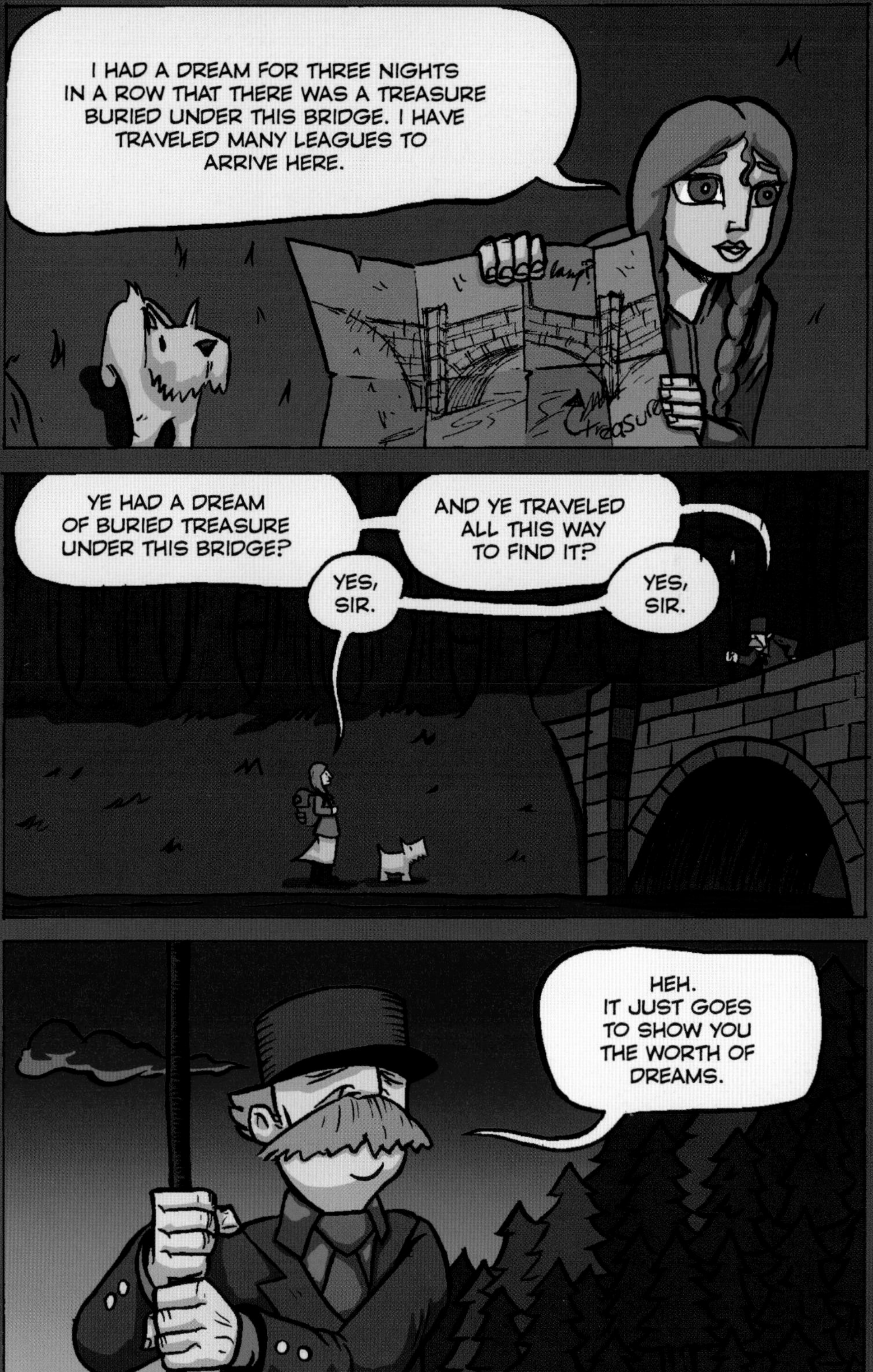
I HAD A DREAM FOR THREE NIGHTS IN A ROW THAT THERE WAS A TREASURE BURIED UNDER THIS BRIDGE. I HAVE TRAVELED MANY LEAGUES TO ARRIVE HERE.
YE HAD A DREAM OF BURIED TREASURE UNDER THIS BRIDGE?
YES, SIR.
AND YE TRAVELED ALL THIS WAY TO FIND IT?
YES, SIR.
HEH. IT JUST GOES TO SHOW YOU THE WORTH OF DREAMS.

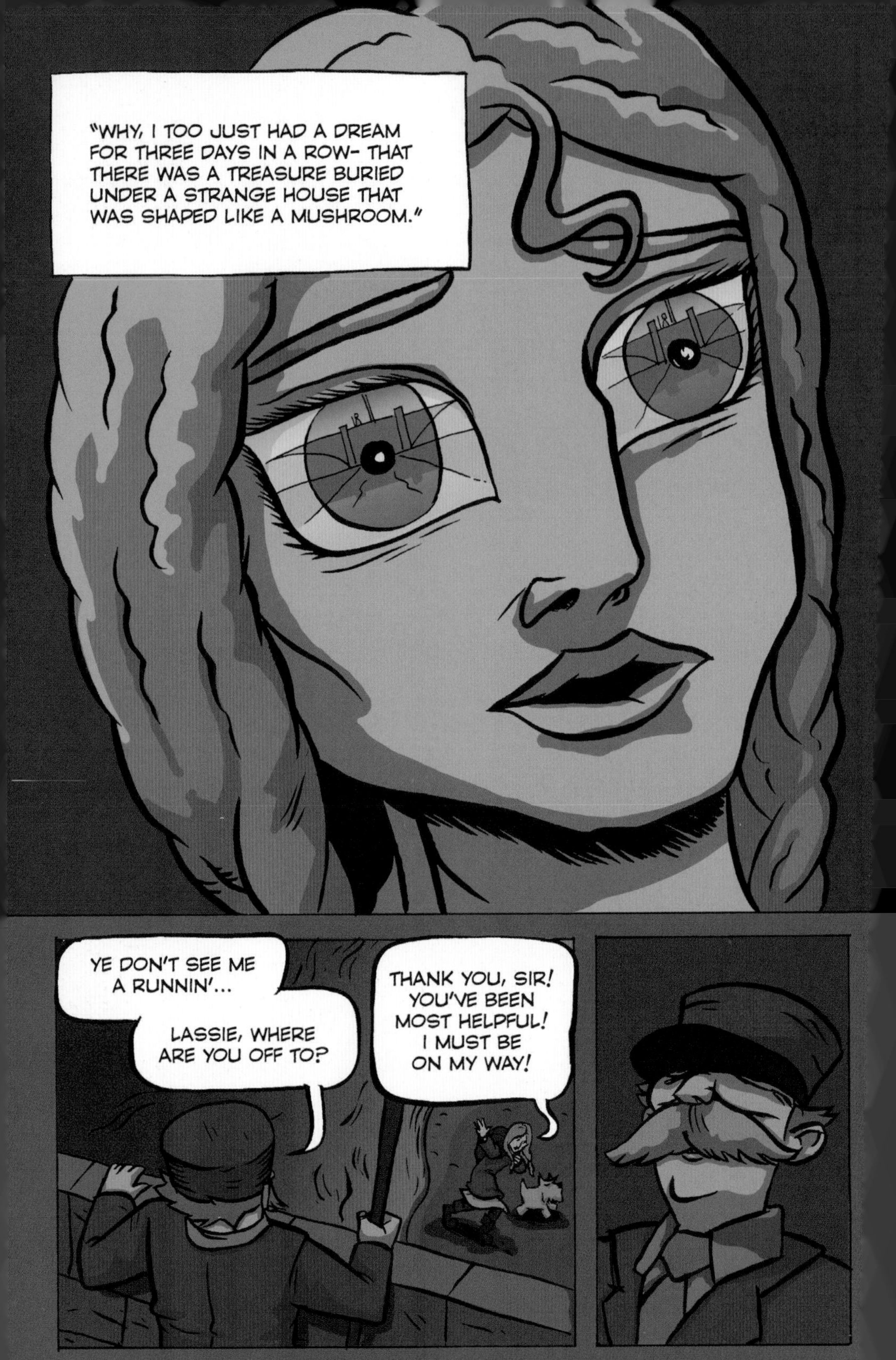
"WHY, I TOO JUST HAD A DREAM FOR THREE DAYS IN A ROW- THAT THERE WAS A TREASURE BURIED UNDER A STRANGE HOUSE THAT WAS SHAPED LIKE A MUSHROOM."
YE DON'T SEE ME A RUNNIN'...
LASSIE, WHERE ARE YOU OFF TO?
THANK YOU, SIR! YOU'VE BEEN MOST HELPFUL! I MUST BE ON MY WAY!

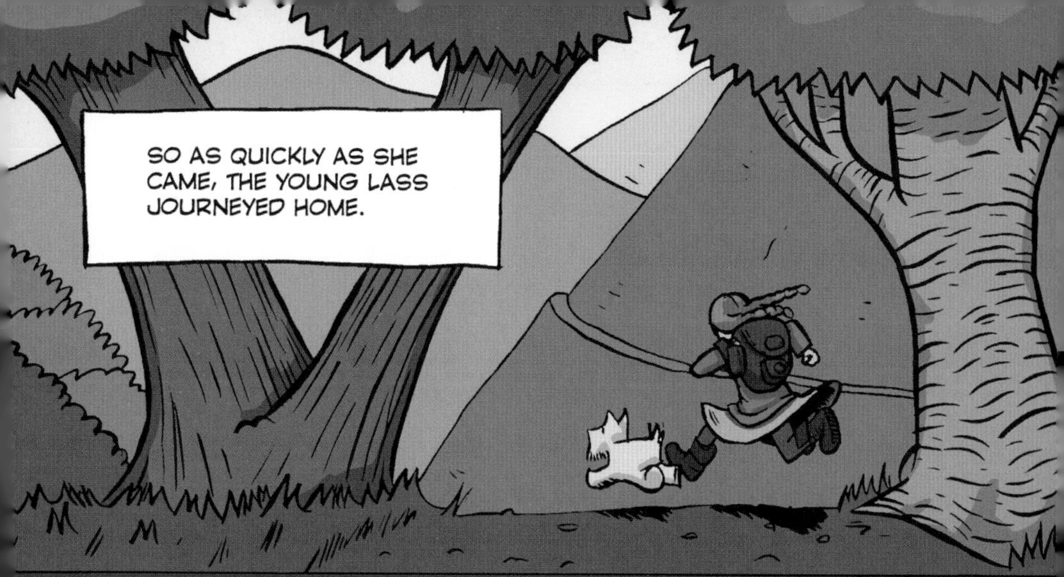
SO AS QUICKLY AS SHE CAME, THE YOUNG LASS JOURNEYED HOME.

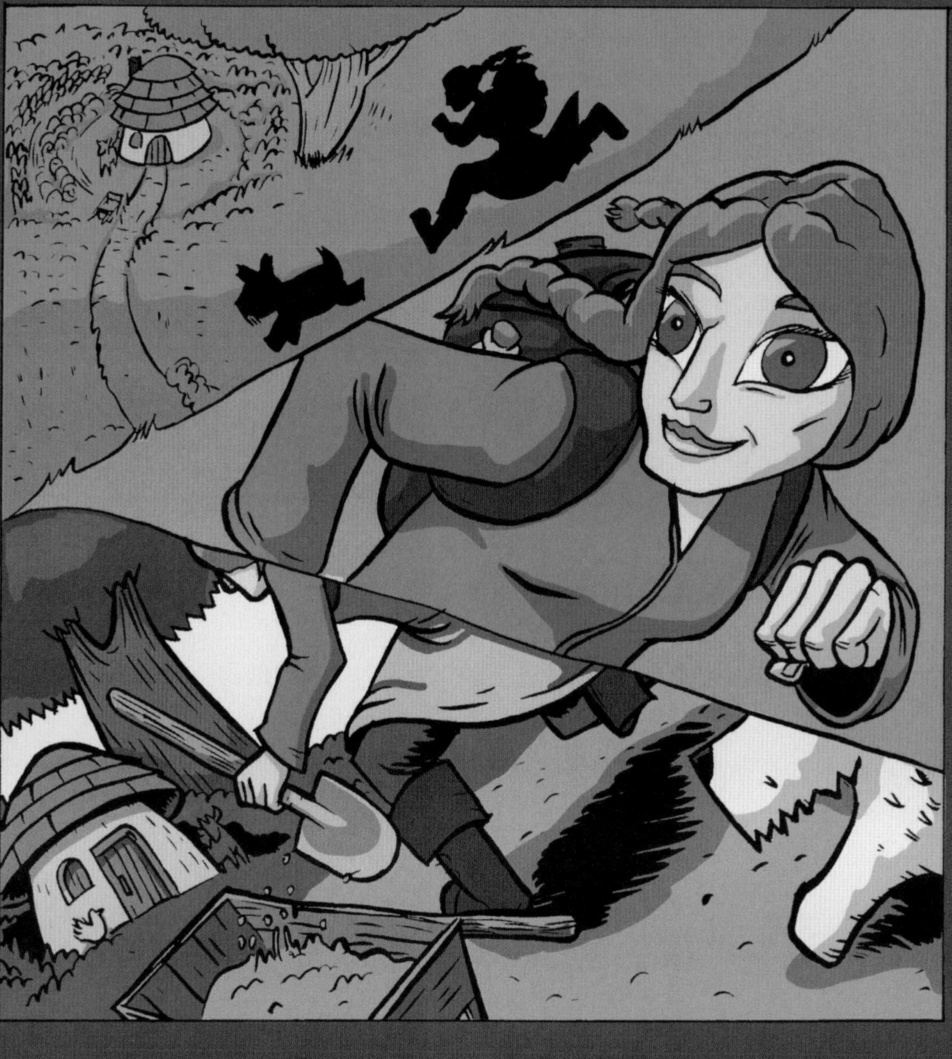

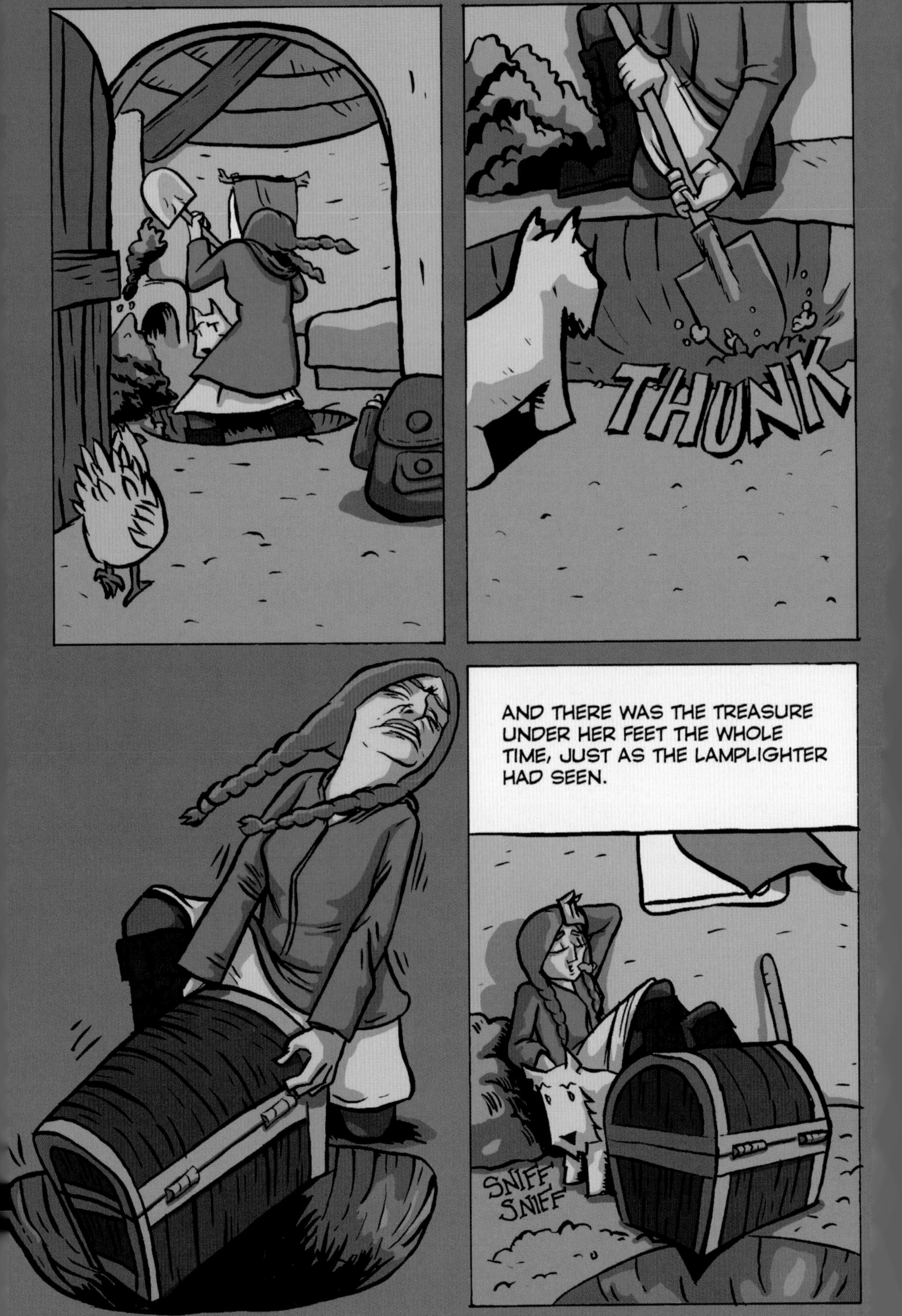
THUNK
AND THERE WAS THE TREASURE UNDER HER FEET THE WHOLE TIME, JUST AS THE LAMPLIGHTER HAD SEEN.
SNIFF SNIFF

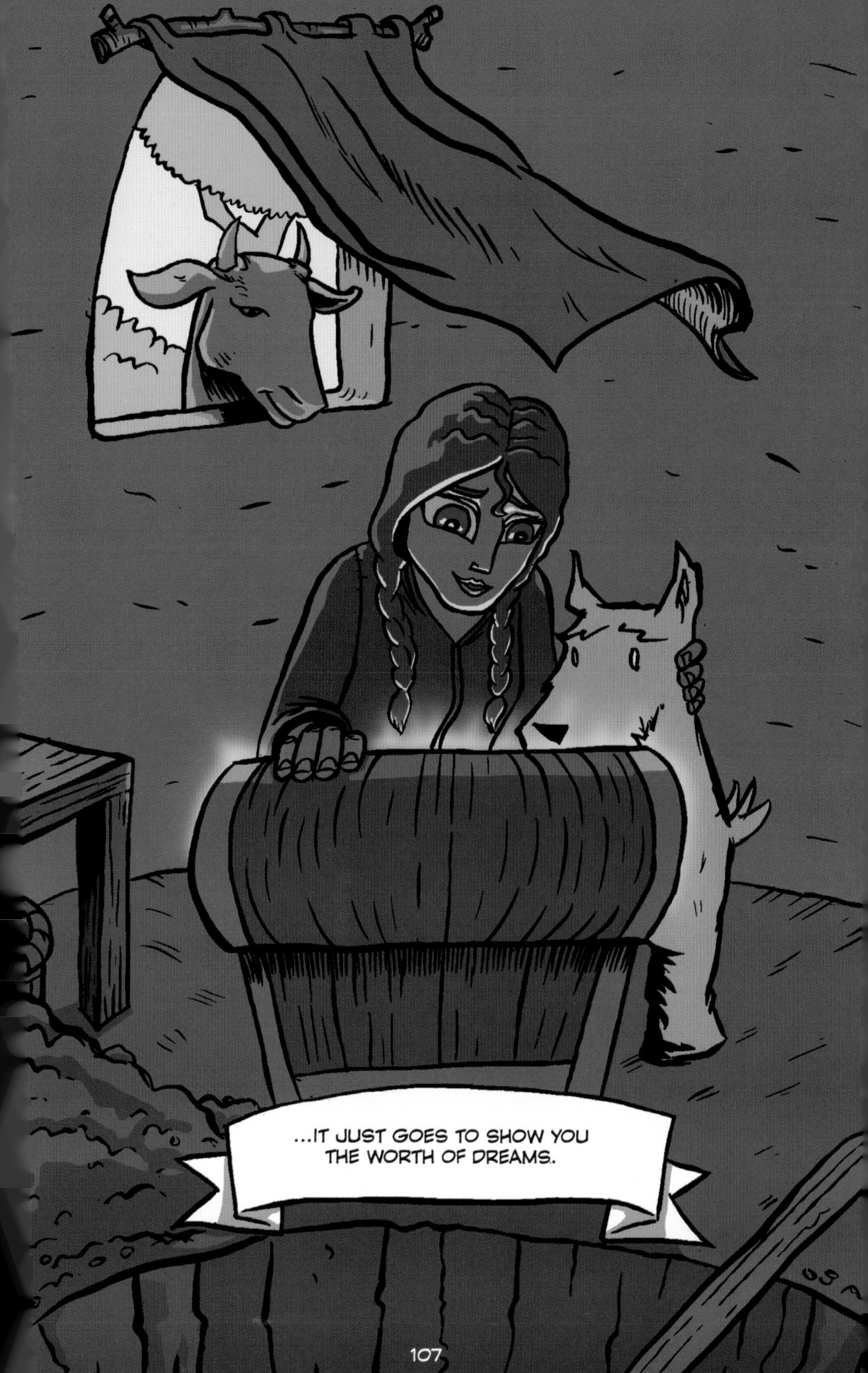
...IT JUST GOES TO SHOW YOU
THE WORTH OF DREAMS.

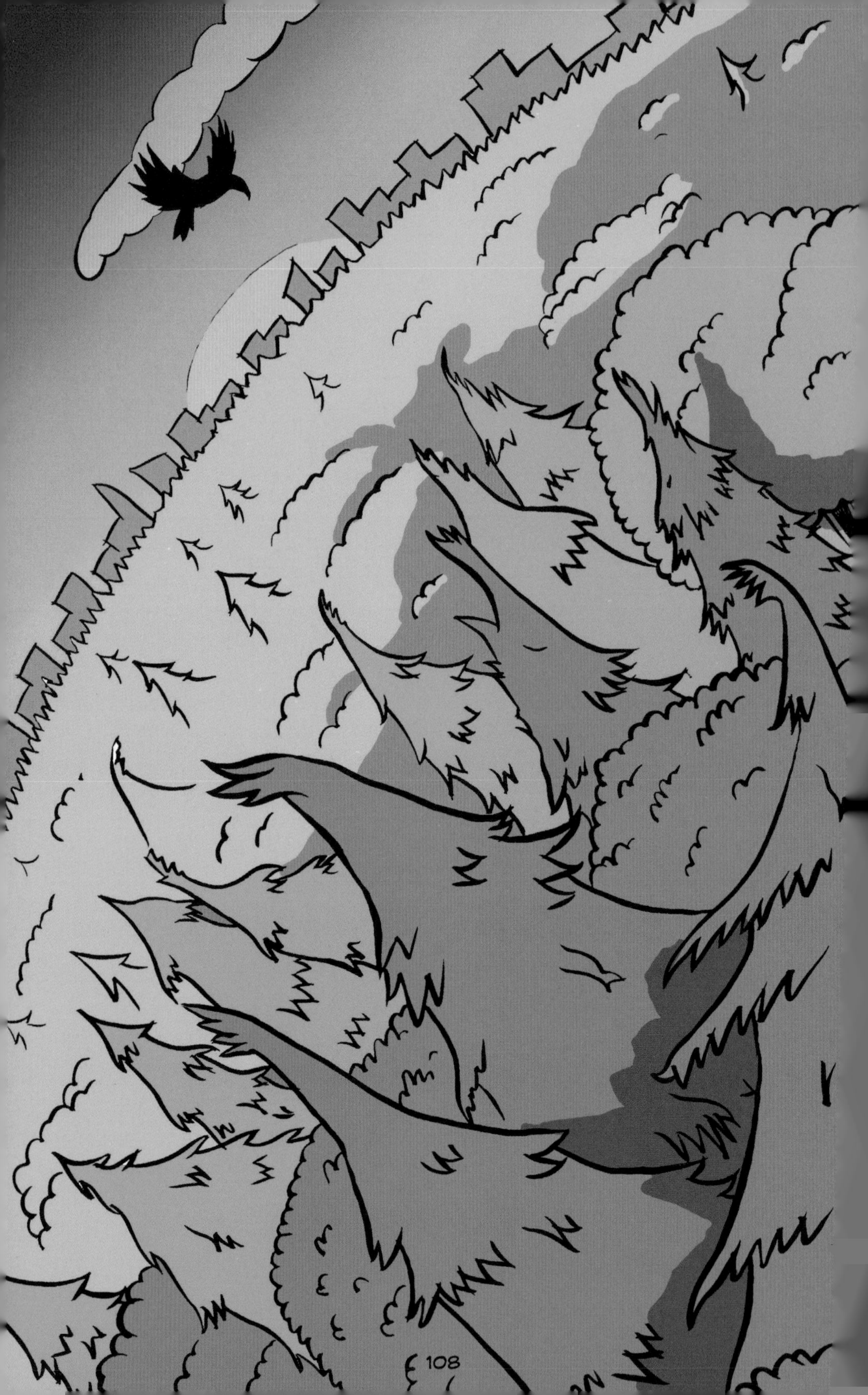

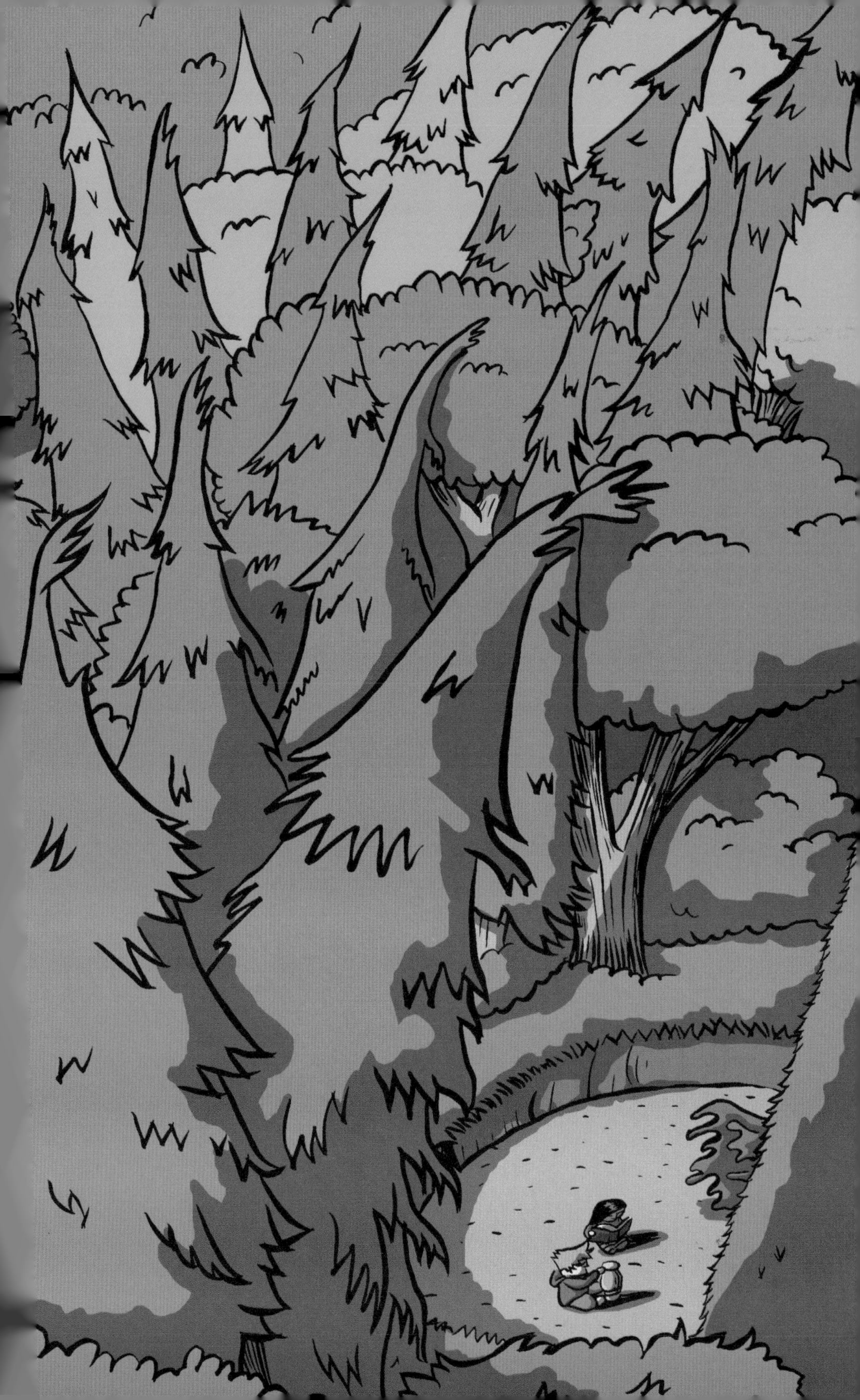

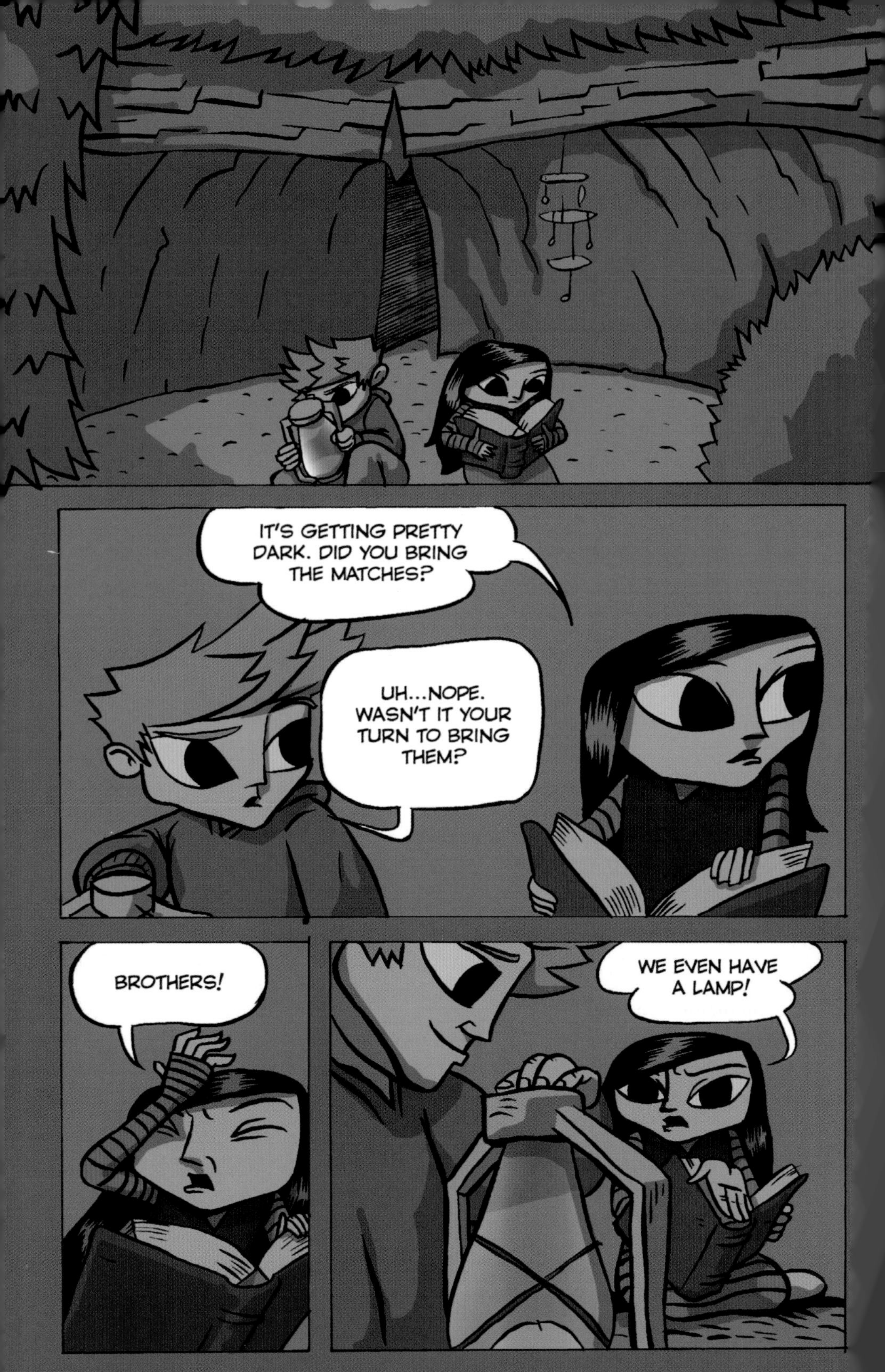
IT'S GETTING PRETTY DARK. DID YOU BRING THE MATCHES?
UH...NOPE. WASN'T IT YOUR TURN TO BRING THEM?
BROTHERS!
WE EVEN HAVE A LAMP!

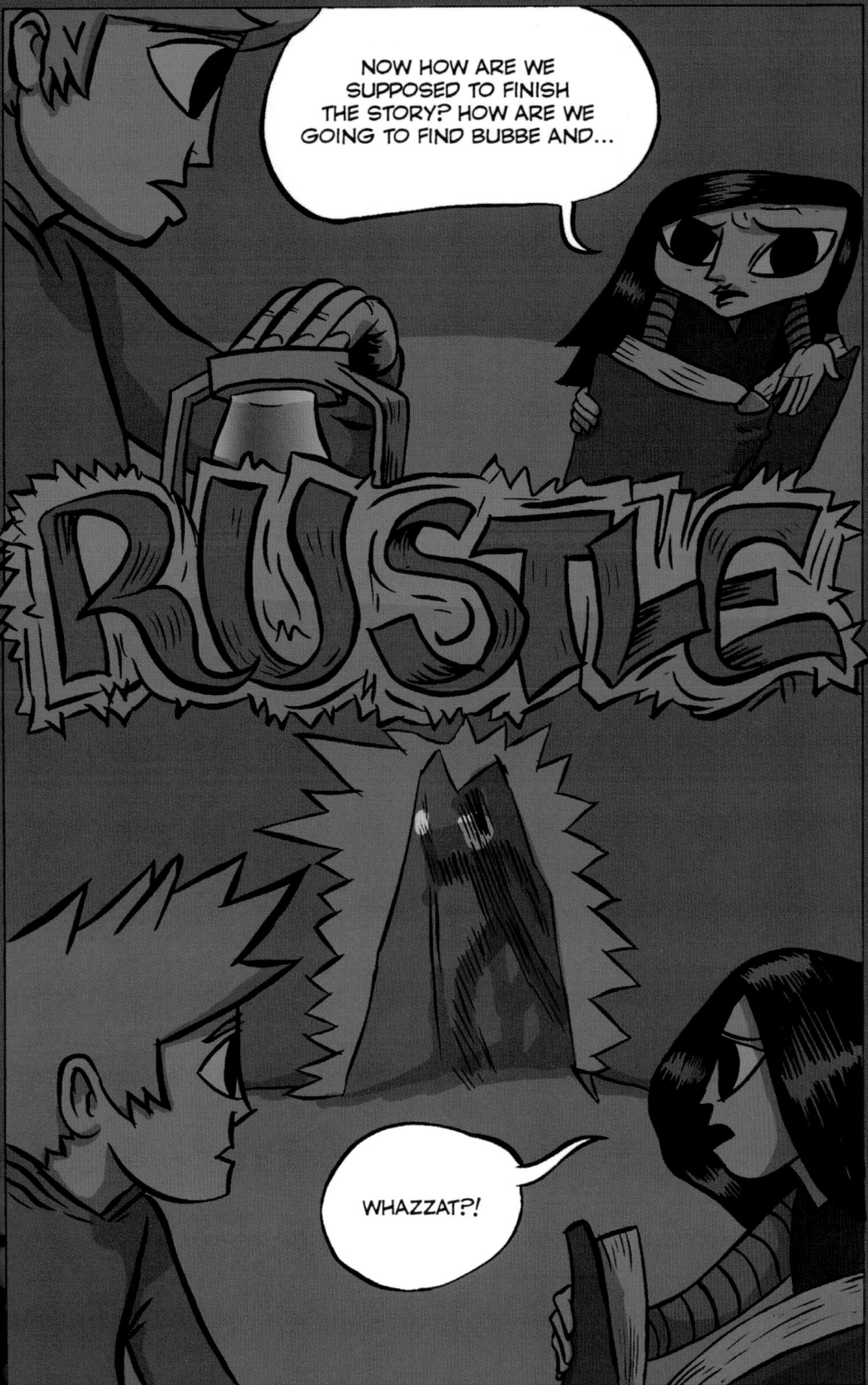
NOW HOW ARE WE SUPPOSED TO FINISH THE STORY? HOW ARE WE GOING TO FIND BUBBE AND...
RUSTLE
WHAZZAT?!

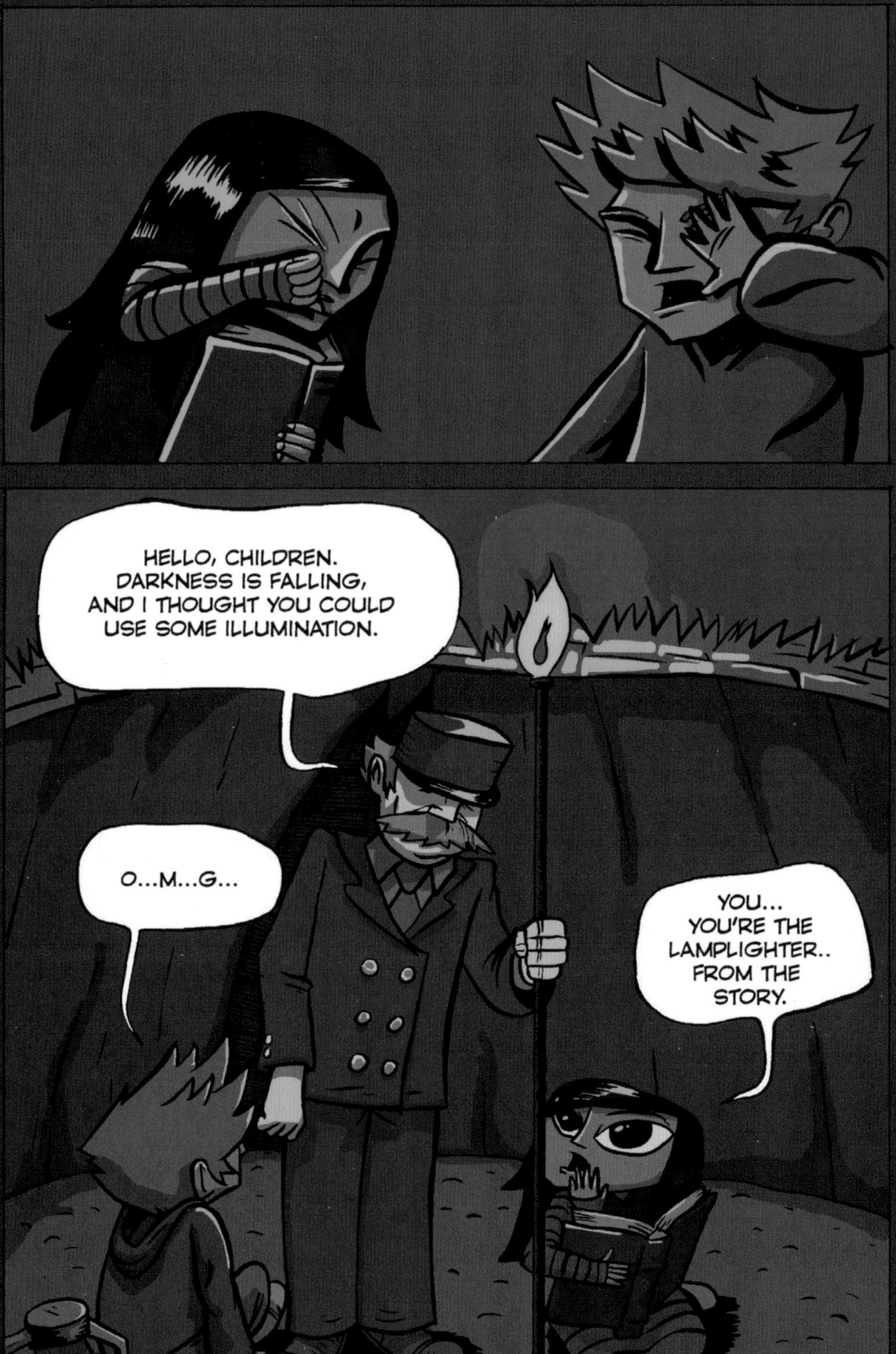
HELLO, CHILDREN. DARKNESS IS FALLING, AND I THOUGHT YOU COULD USE SOME ILLUMINATION.
O...M...G...
YOU... YOU'RE THE LAMPLIGHTER.. FROM THE STORY.

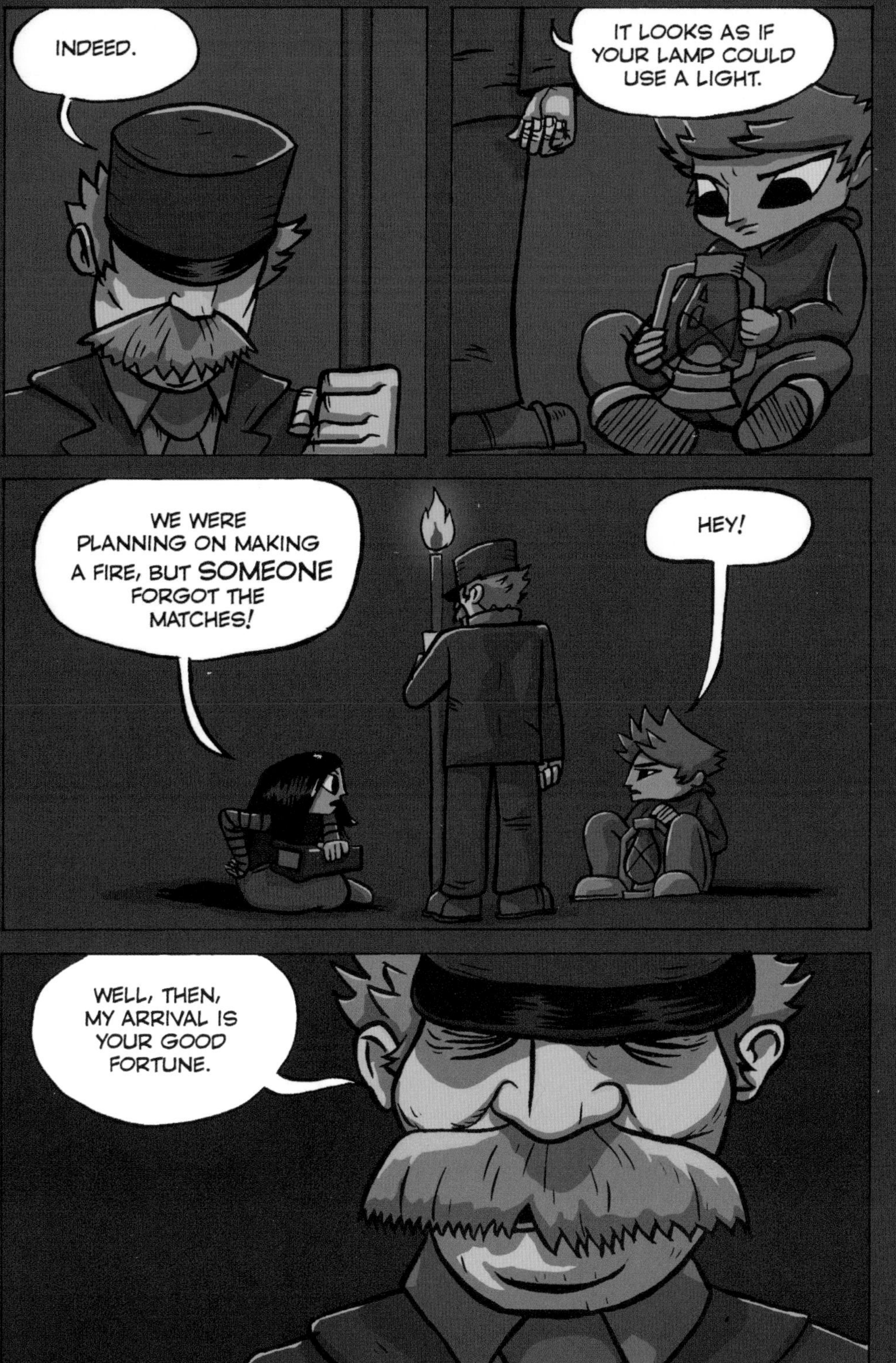
INDEED.
IT LOOKS AS IF YOUR LAMP COULD USE A LIGHT.
WE WERE PLANNING ON MAKING A FIRE, BUT SOMEONE FORGOT THE MATCHES!
HEY!
WELL, THEN, MY ARRIVAL IS YOUR GOOD FORTUNE.

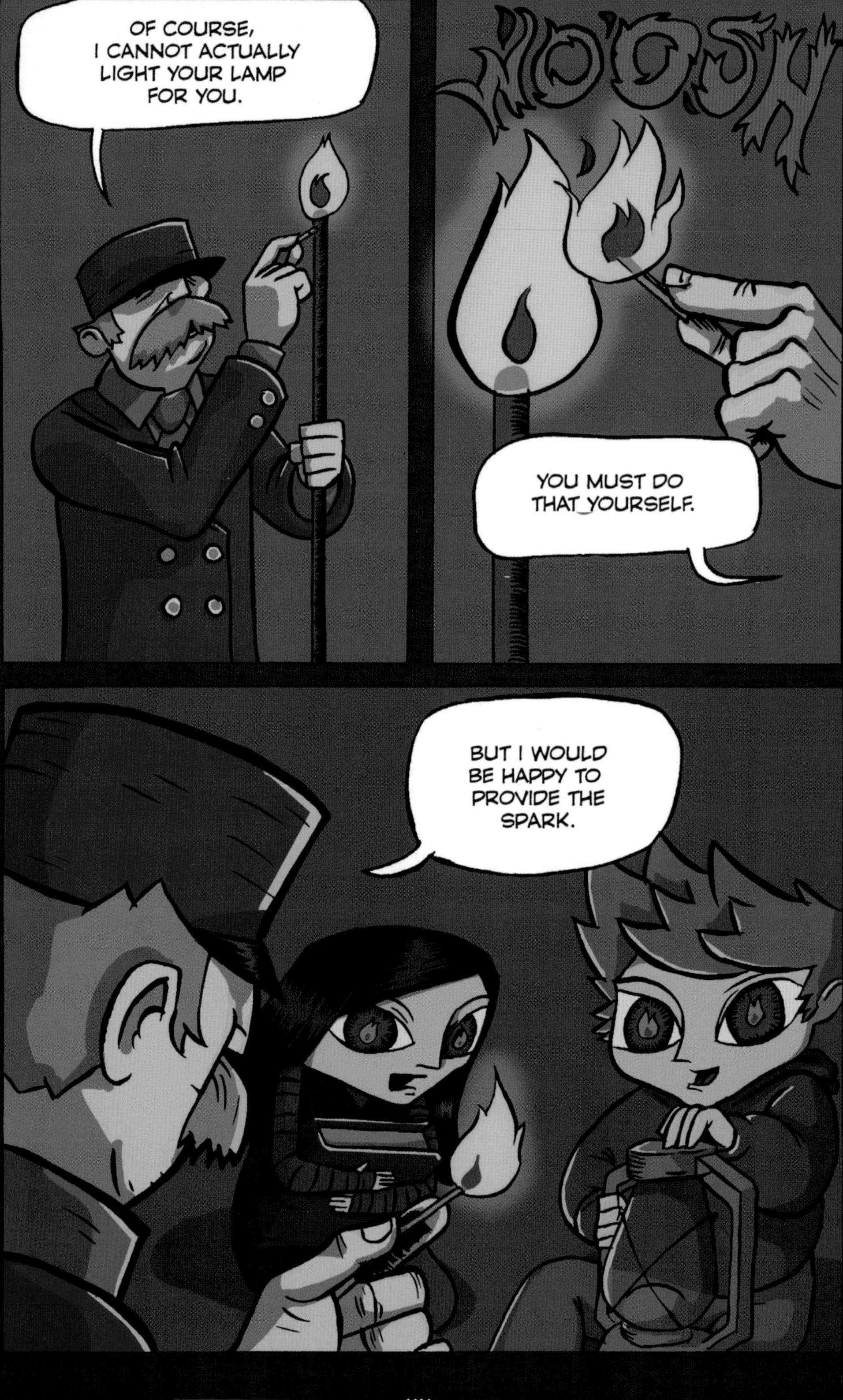

OF COURSE, I CANNOT ACTUALLY LIGHT YOUR LAMP FOR YOU.
WHOOSH
YOU MUST DO THAT YOURSELF.
BUT I WOULD BE HAPPY TO PROVIDE THE SPARK.

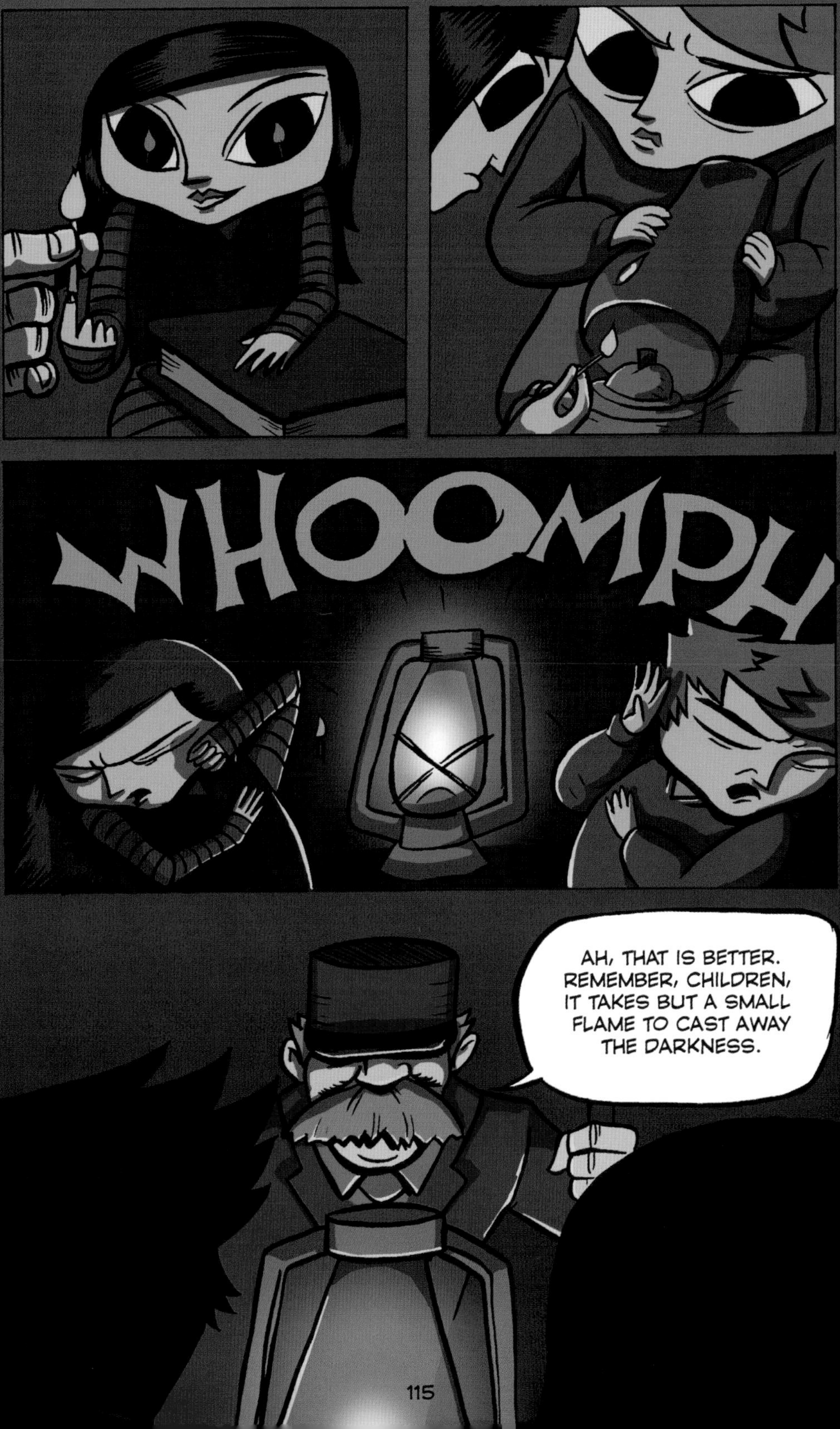
WHOOMPH
AH, THAT IS BETTER. REMEMBER, CHILDREN, IT TAKES BUT A SMALL FLAME TO CAST AWAY THE DARKNESS.

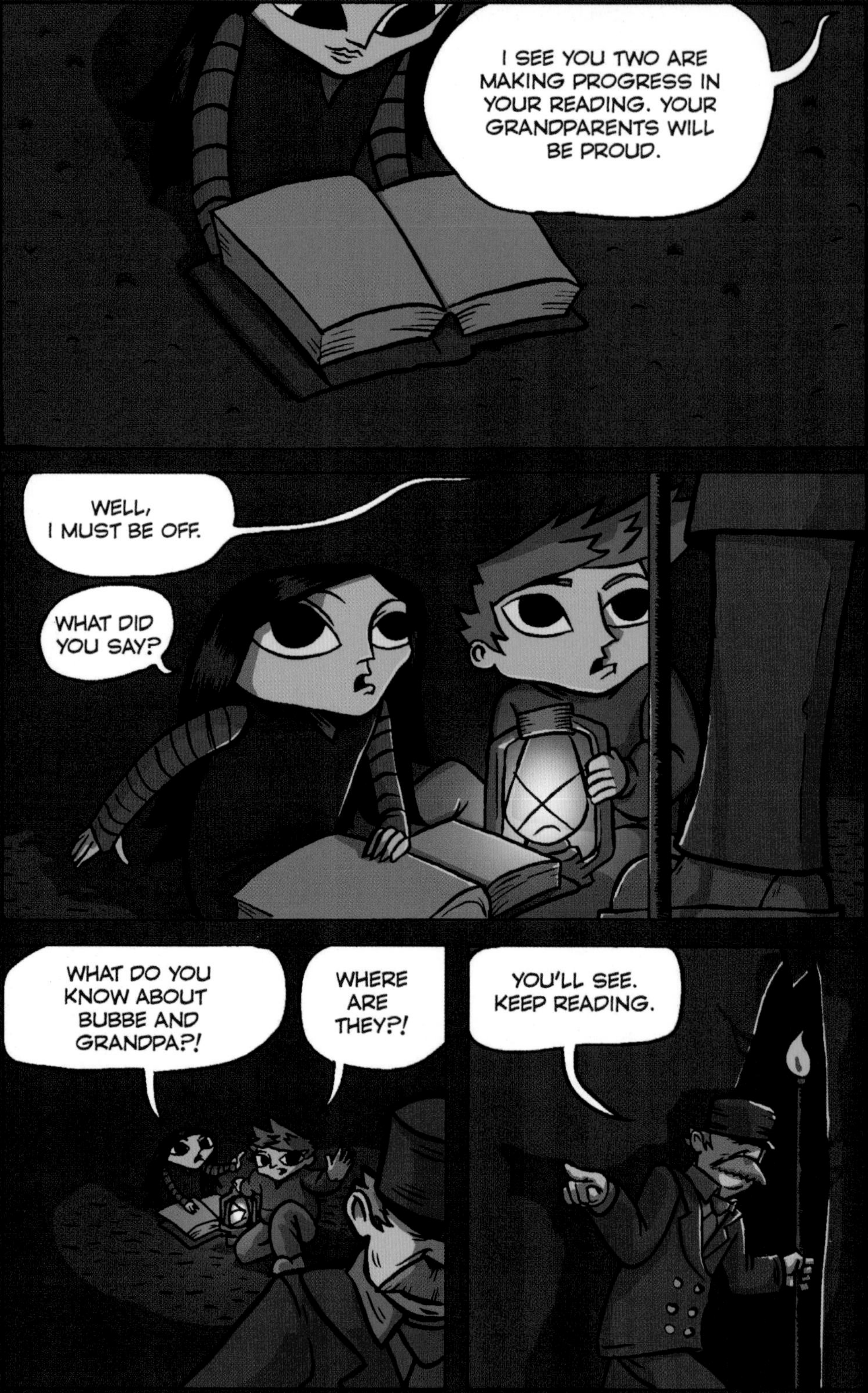
I SEE YOU TWO ARE MAKING PROGRESS IN YOUR READING. YOUR GRANDPARENTS WILL BE PROUD.
WELL, I MUST BE OFF.
WHAT DID YOU SAY?
WHAT DO YOU KNOW ABOUT BUBBE AND GRANDPA?!
WHERE ARE THEY?!
YOU'LL SEE. KEEP READING.

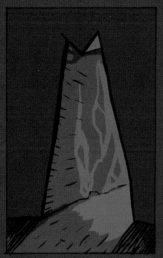
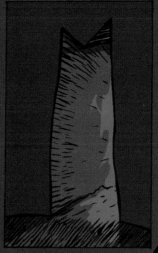

THIS IS GETTING WEIRDER AND WEIRDER.

YOU CAN SAY THAT AGAIN.

DO YOU WANT TO FIND BUBBE AND GRANDPA?

OF COURSE! DUH!

WELL, YOU HEARD THE MAN. LET'S KEEP READING.

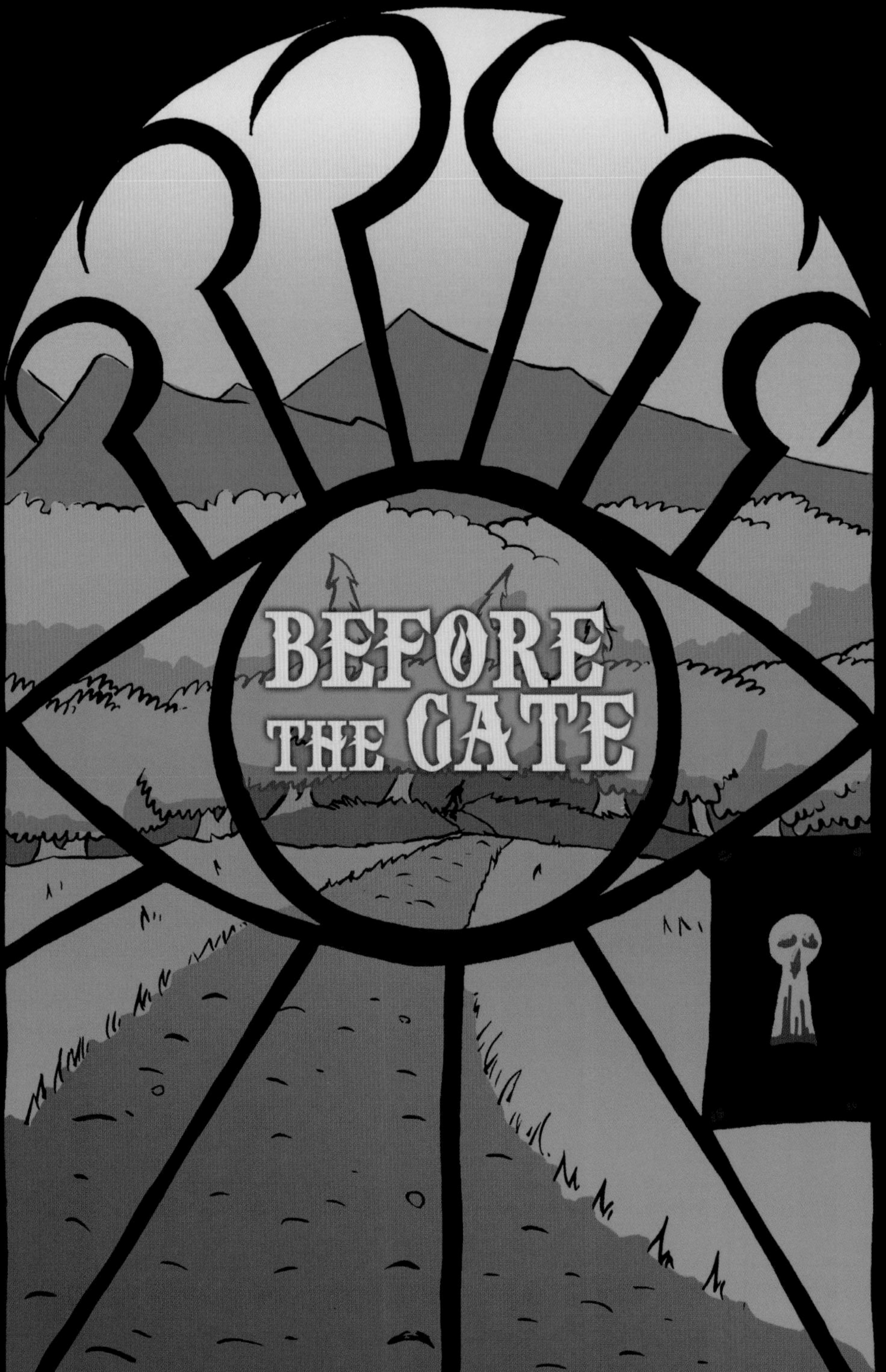
BEFORE
THE GATE

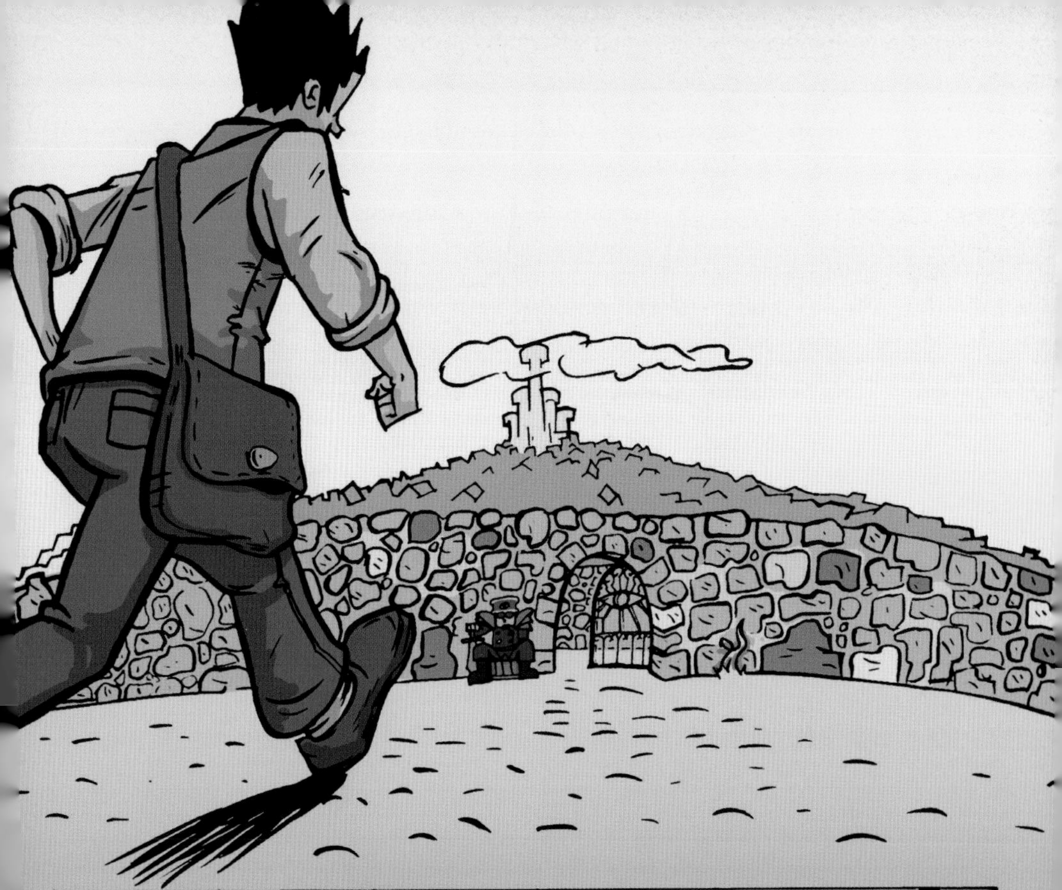

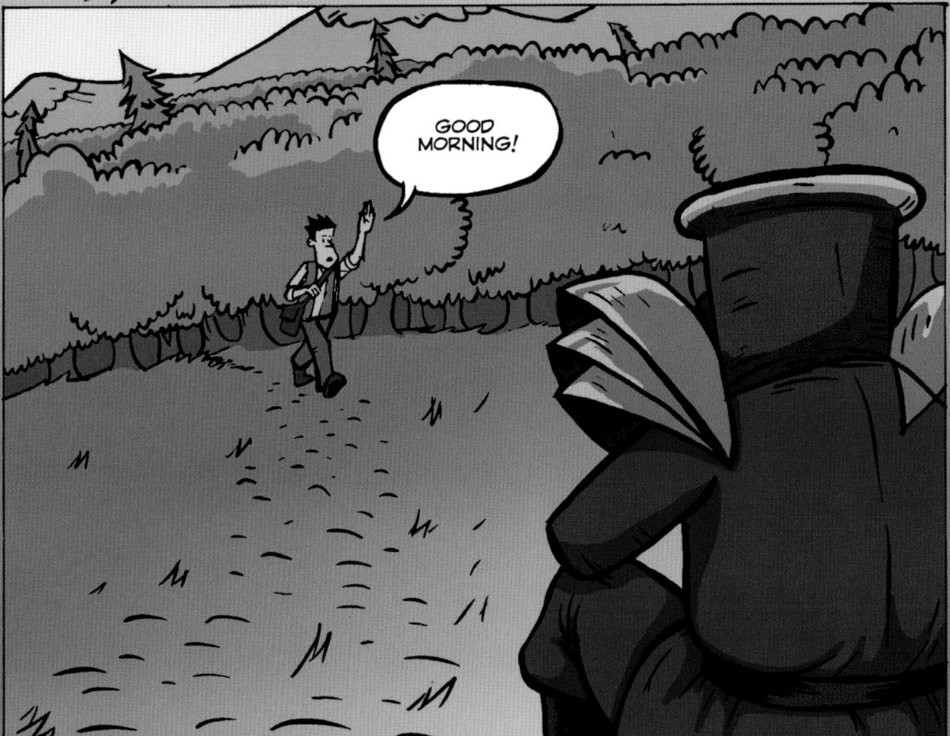
GOOD MORNING!

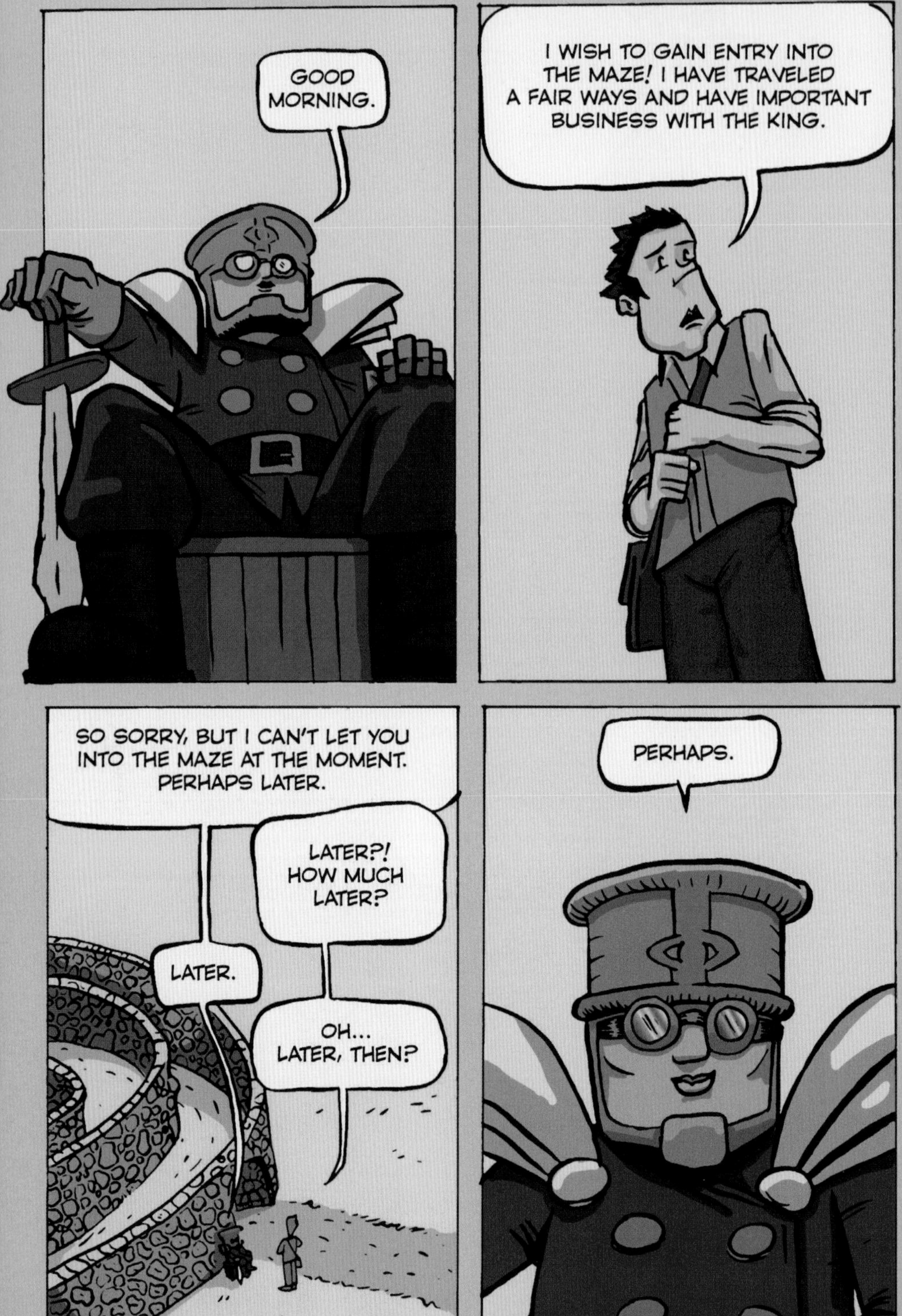
GOOD MORNING.
I WISH TO GAIN ENTRY INTO THE MAZE! I HAVE TRAVELED A FAIR WAYS AND HAVE IMPORTANT BUSINESS WITH THE KING.
SO SORRY, BUT I CAN'T LET YOU INTO THE MAZE AT THE MOMENT. PERHAPS LATER.
LATER?! HOW MUCH LATER?
LATER.
OH... LATER, THEN?
PERHAPS.

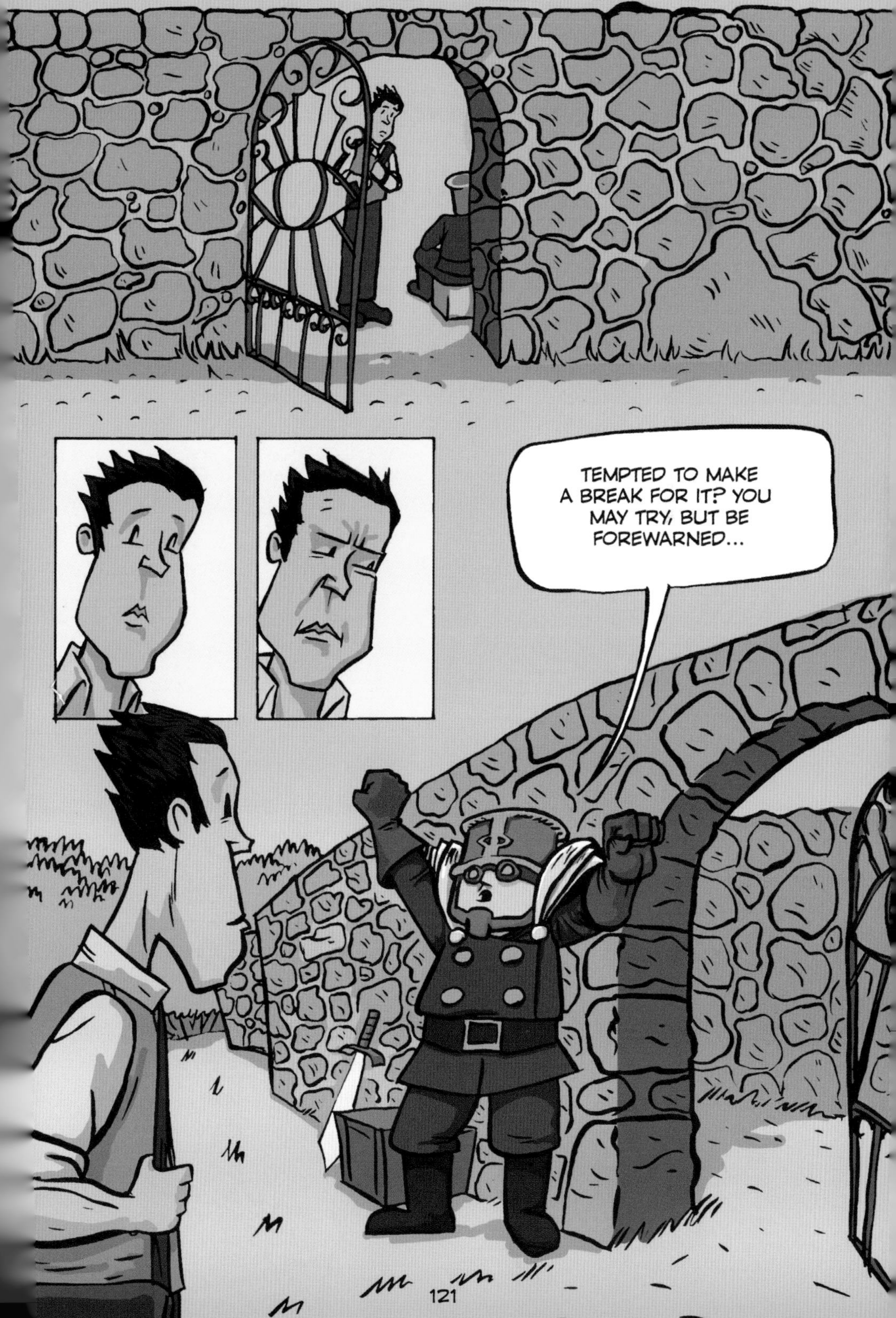
TEMPTED TO MAKE A BREAK FOR IT? YOU MAY TRY, BUT BE FOREWARNED...

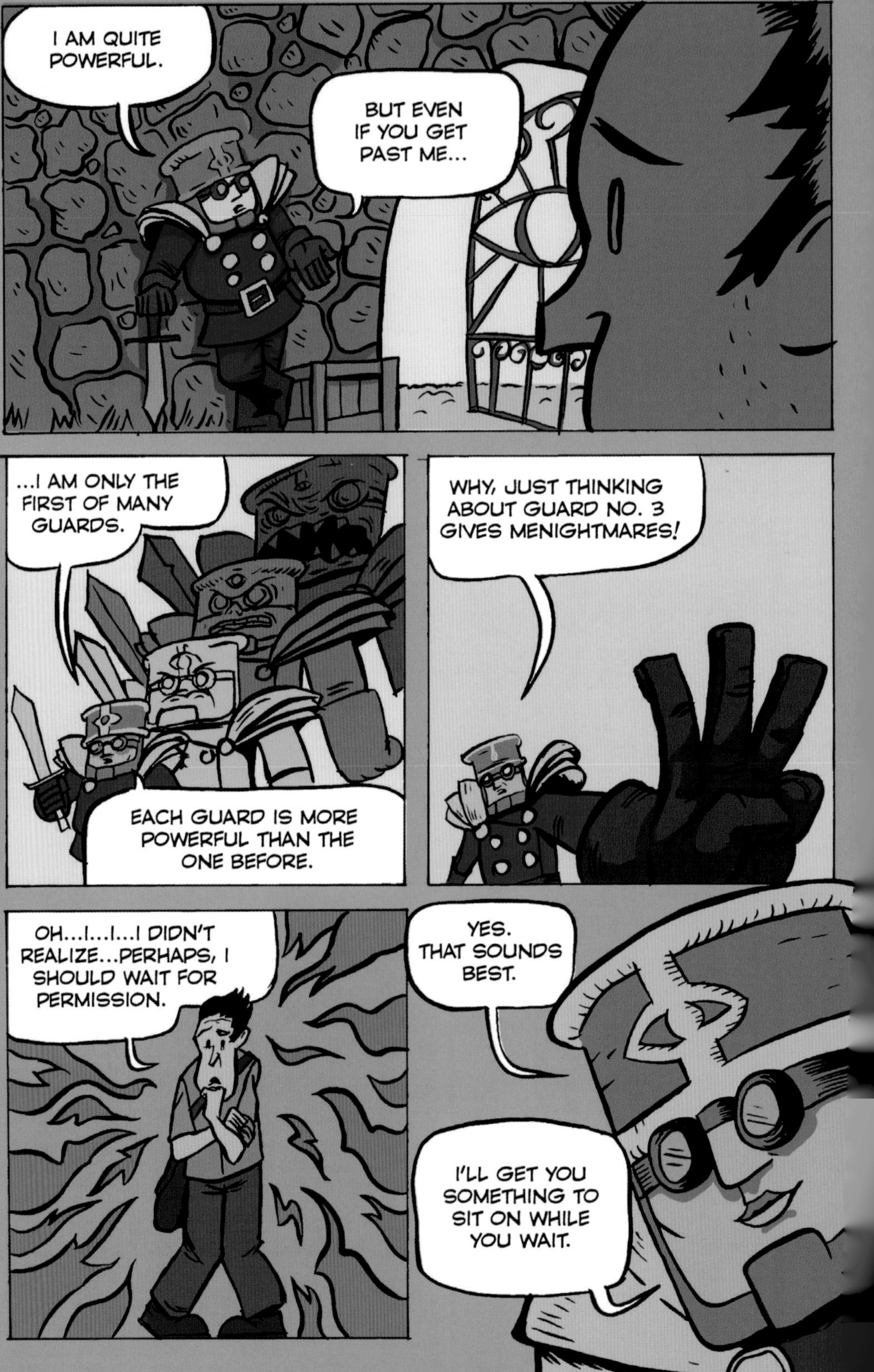
I AM QUITE POWERFUL.
BUT EVEN IF YOU GET PAST ME...
...I AM ONLY THE FIRST OF MANY GUARDS.
EACH GUARD IS MORE POWERFUL THAN THE ONE BEFORE.
WHY, JUST THINKING ABOUT GUARD NO. 3 GIVES MENIGHTMARES!
OH...I...I...I DIDN'T REALIZE...PERHAPS, I SHOULD WAIT FOR PERMISSION.
YES. THAT SOUNDS BEST.
I'LL GET YOU SOMETHING TO SIT ON WHILE YOU WAIT.

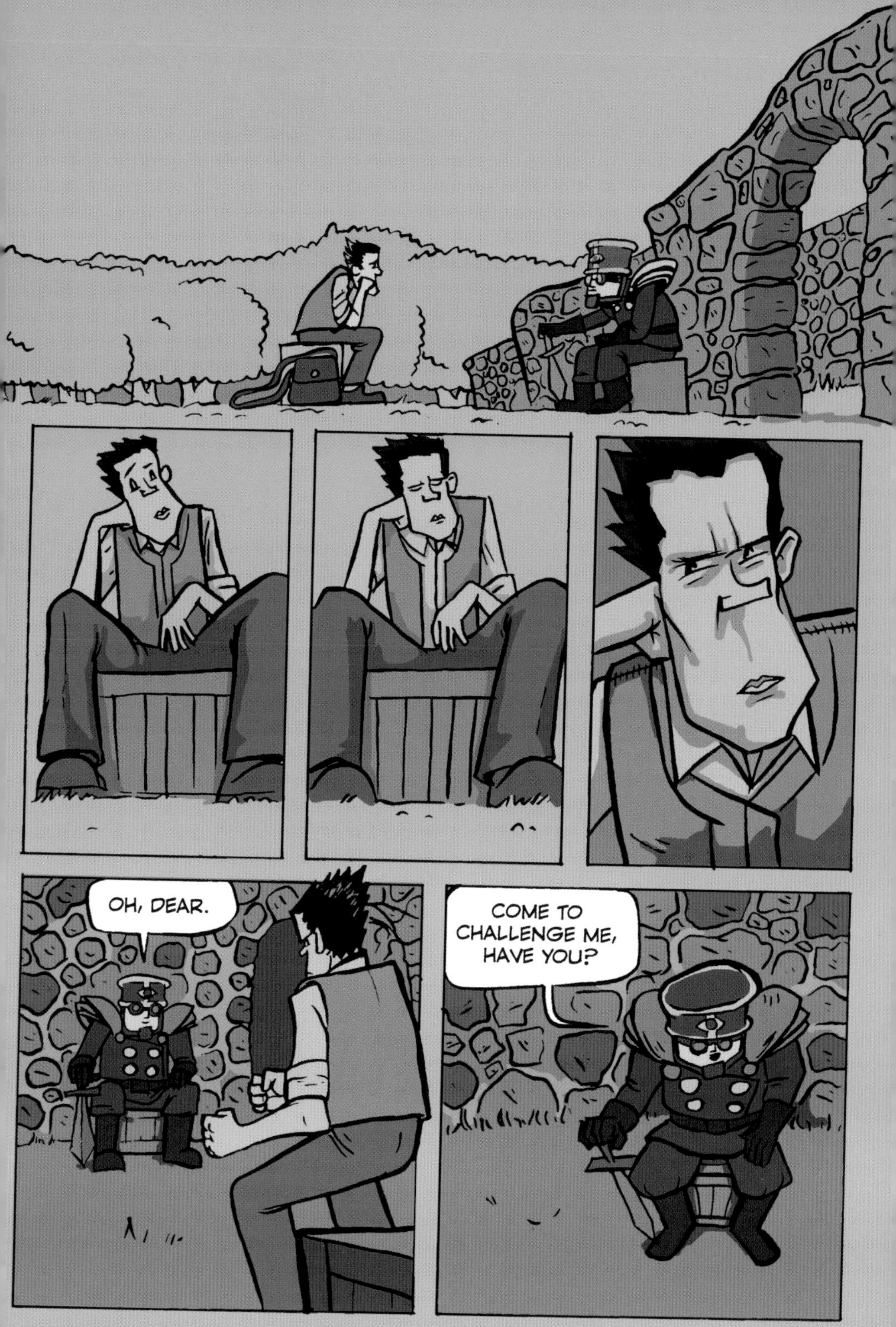
OH, DEAR.
COME TO CHALLENGE ME, HAVE YOU?

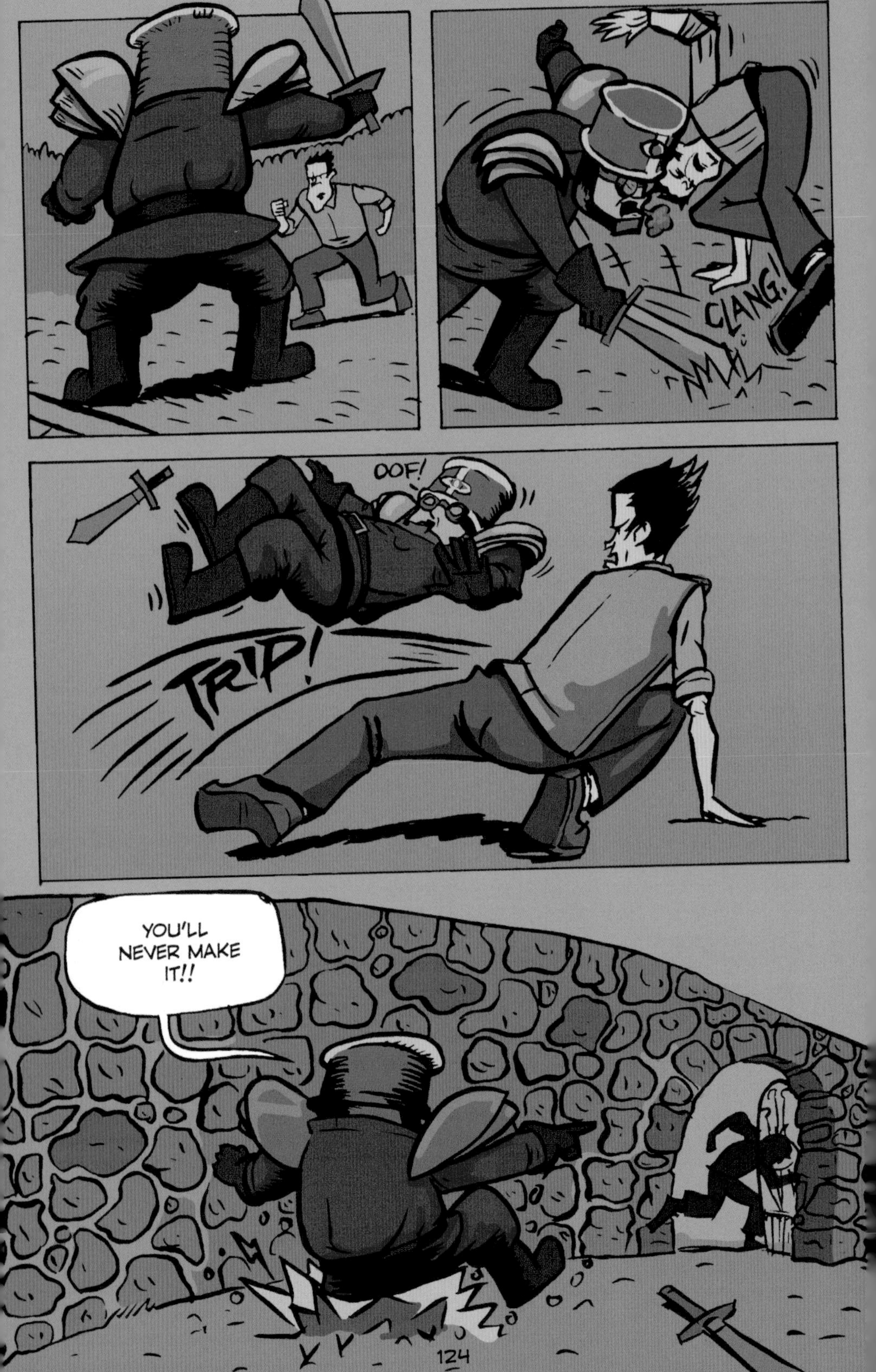
CLANG!
OOF!
TRIP!
YOU'LL NEVER MAKE IT!!

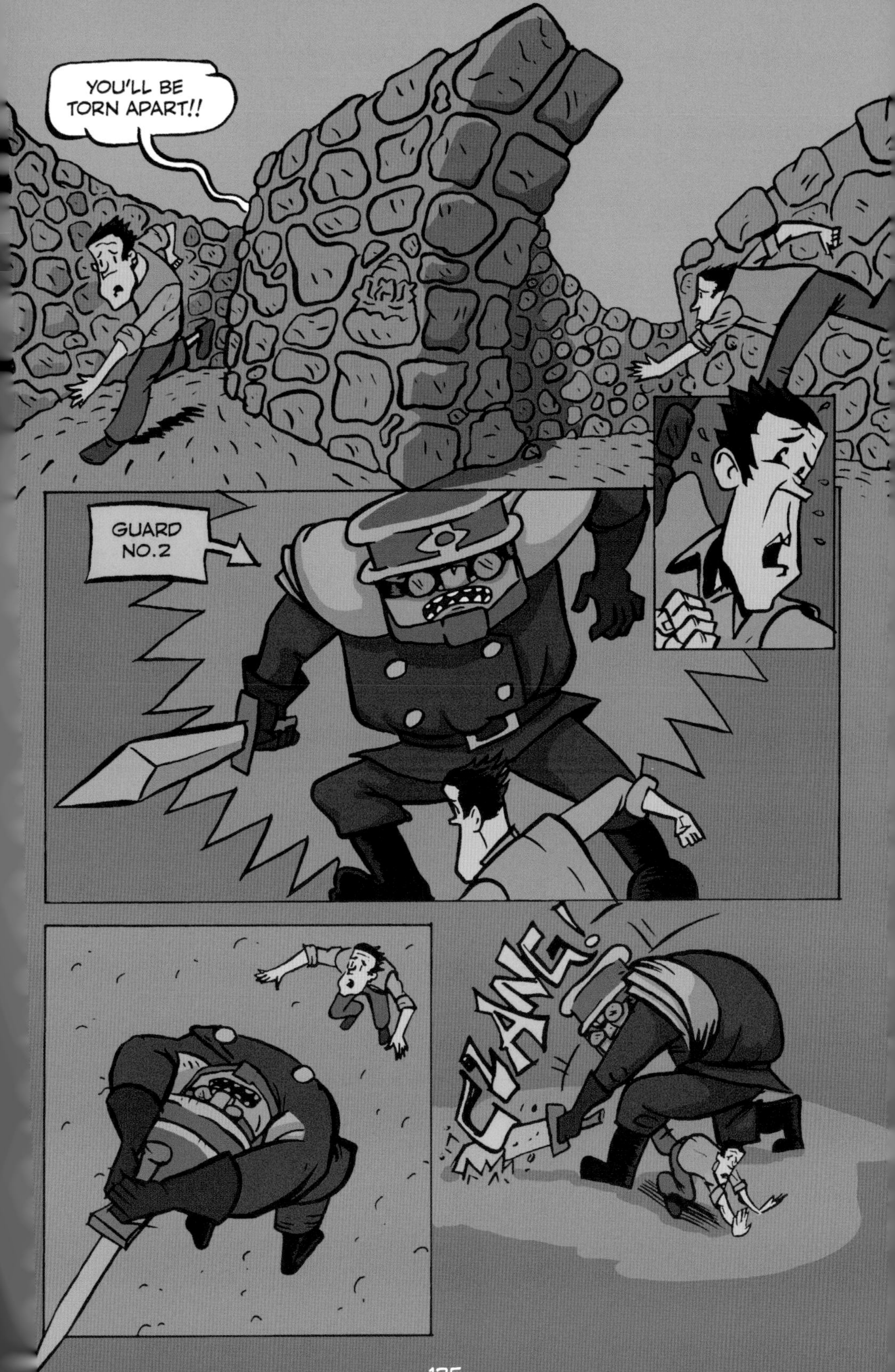

YOU'LL BE TORN APART!!
GUARD NO.2
CLANG!

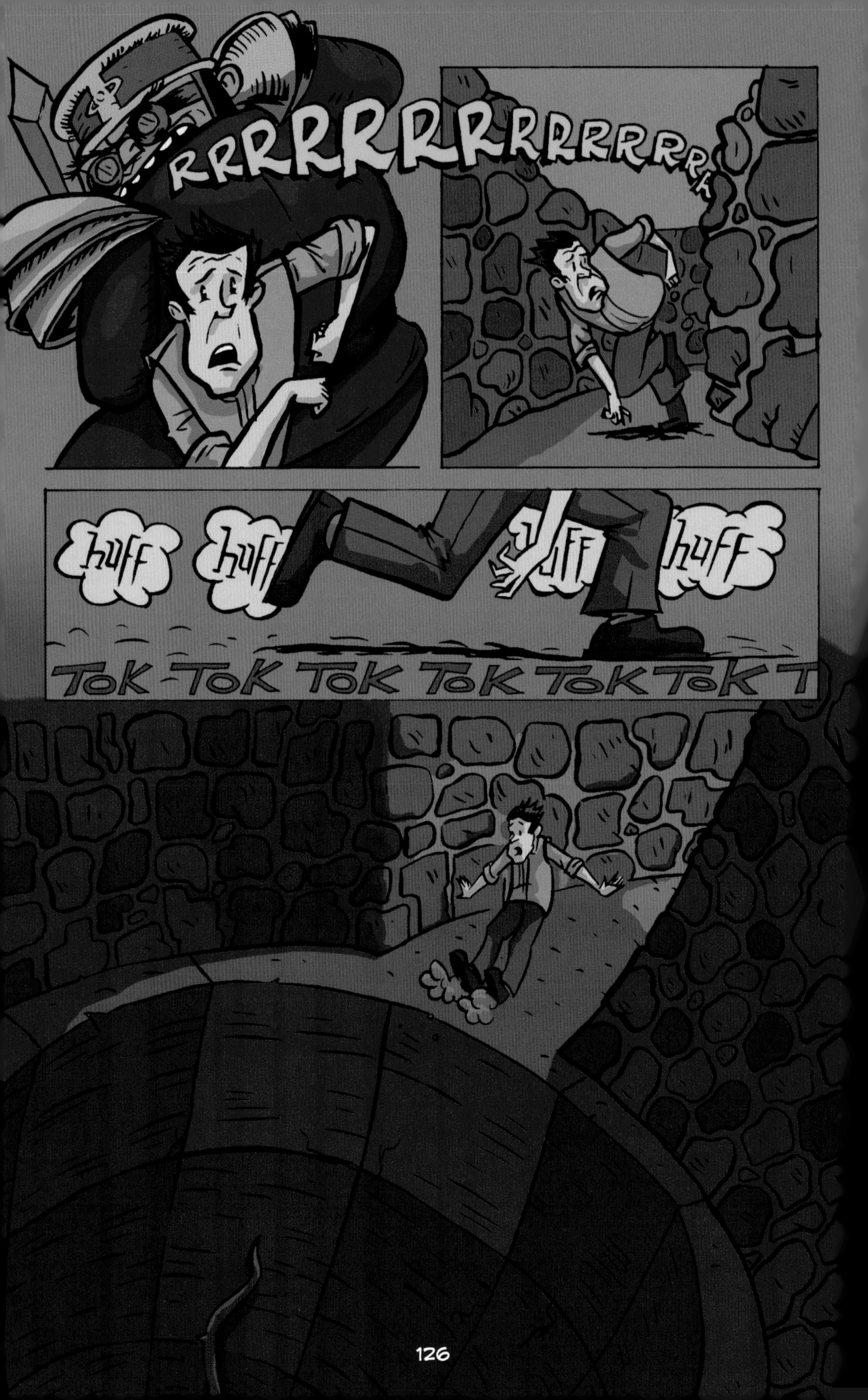
RRRRRRRRRRRRRRRR
huff huff huff huff
TOK TOK TOK TOK TOK TOK T

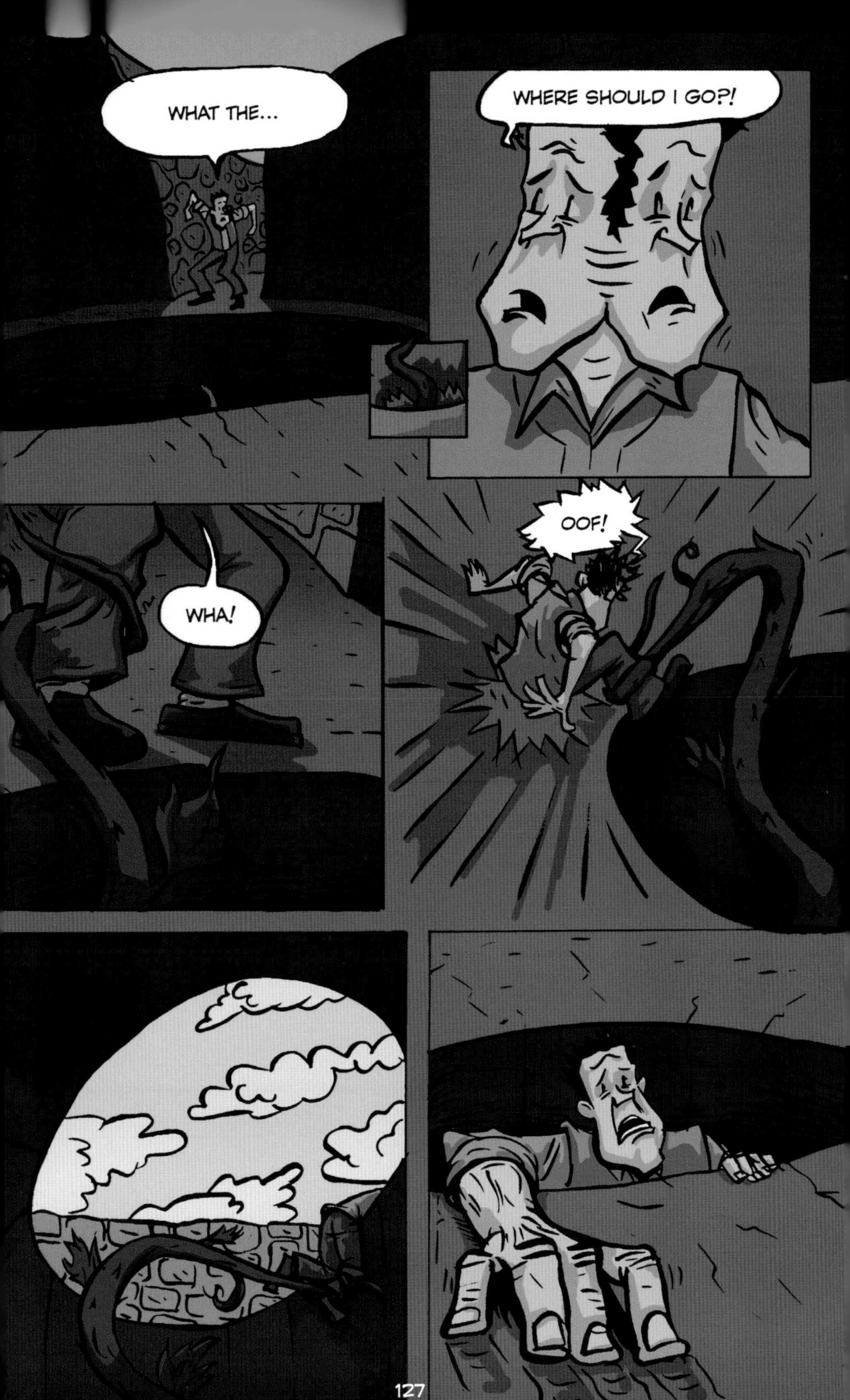
WHAT THE...
WHERE SHOULD I GO?!
WHA!
OOF!

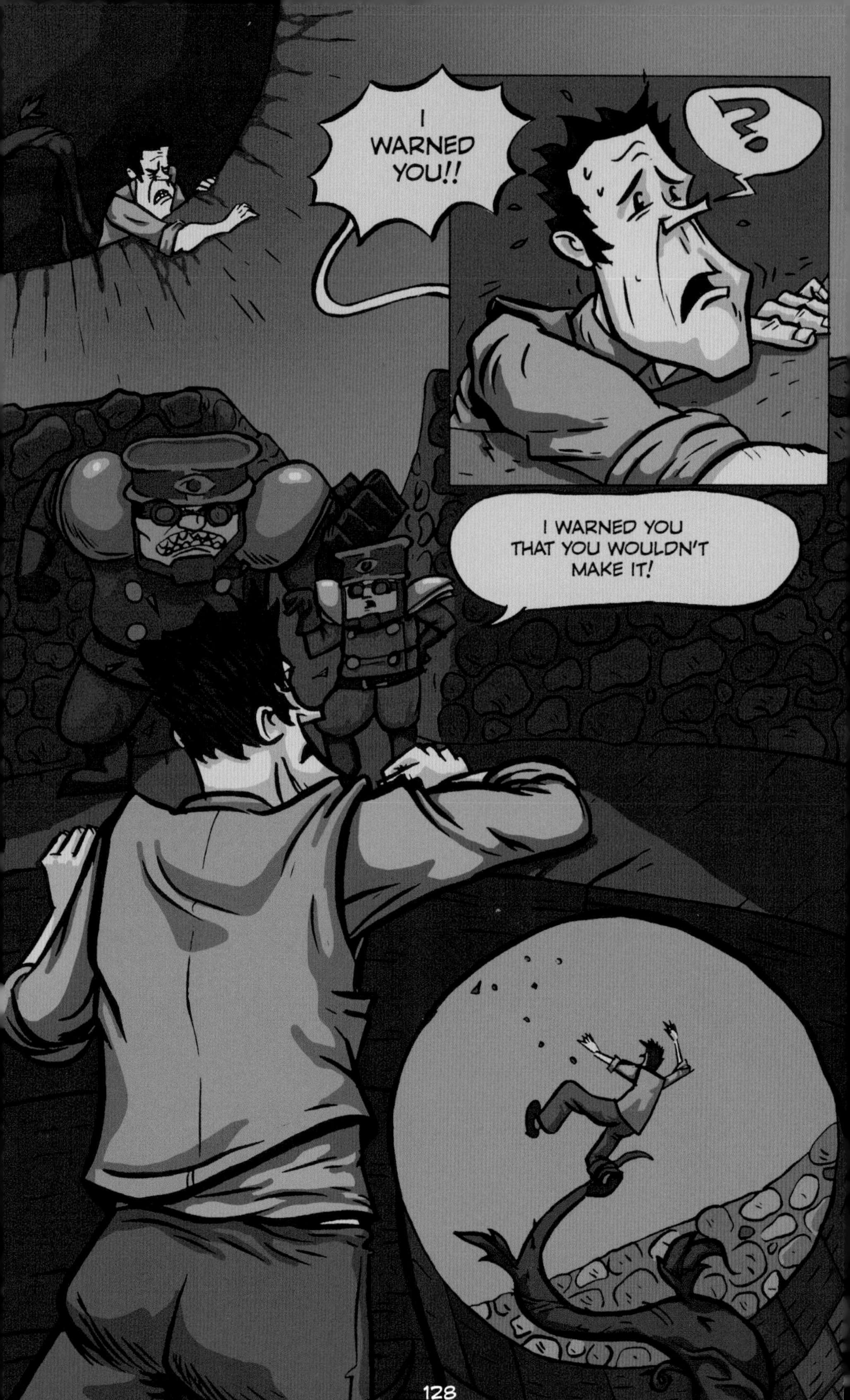
I WARNED YOU!!
?
I WARNED YOU THAT YOU WOULDN'T MAKE IT!

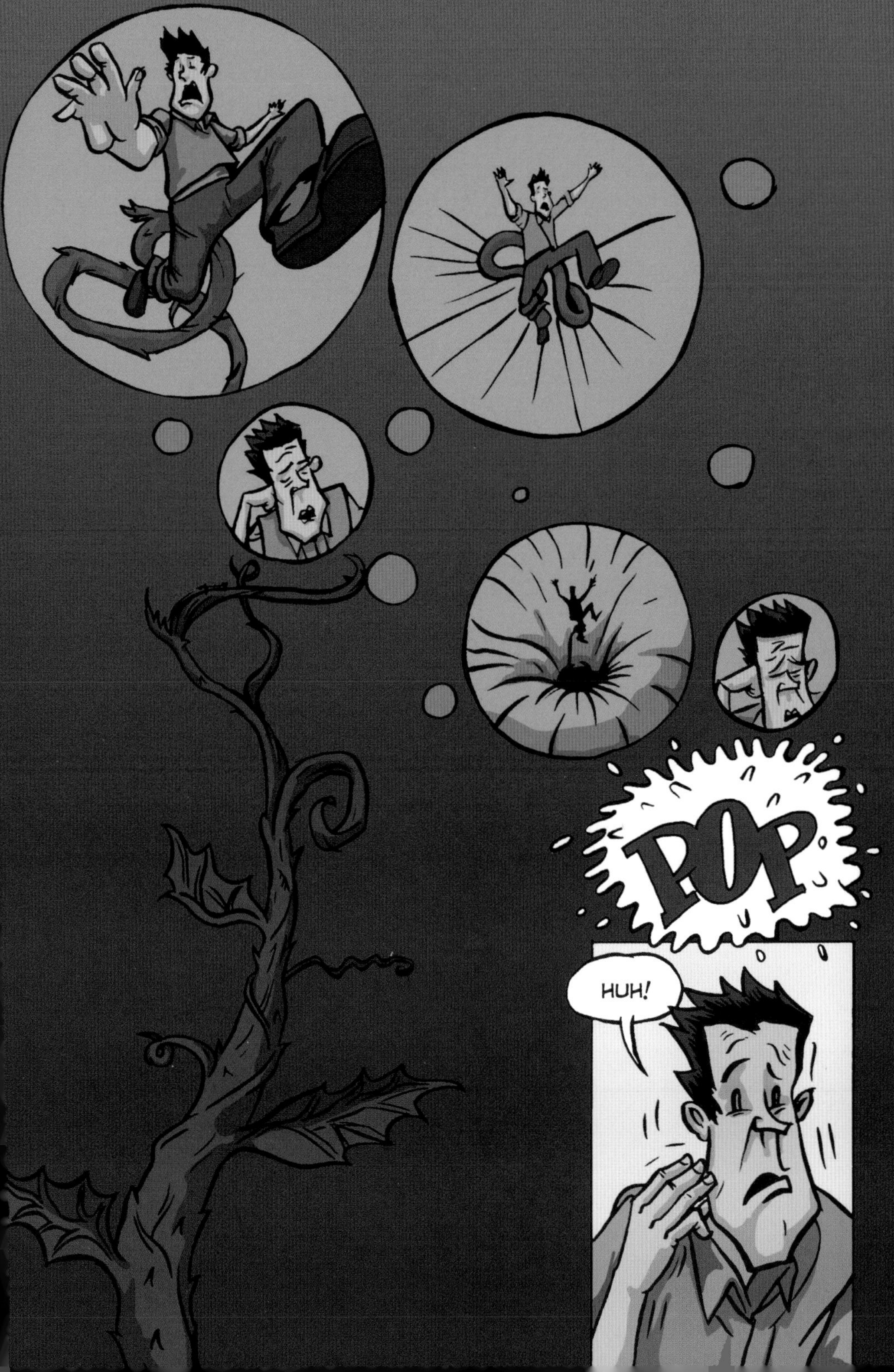
POP
HUH!

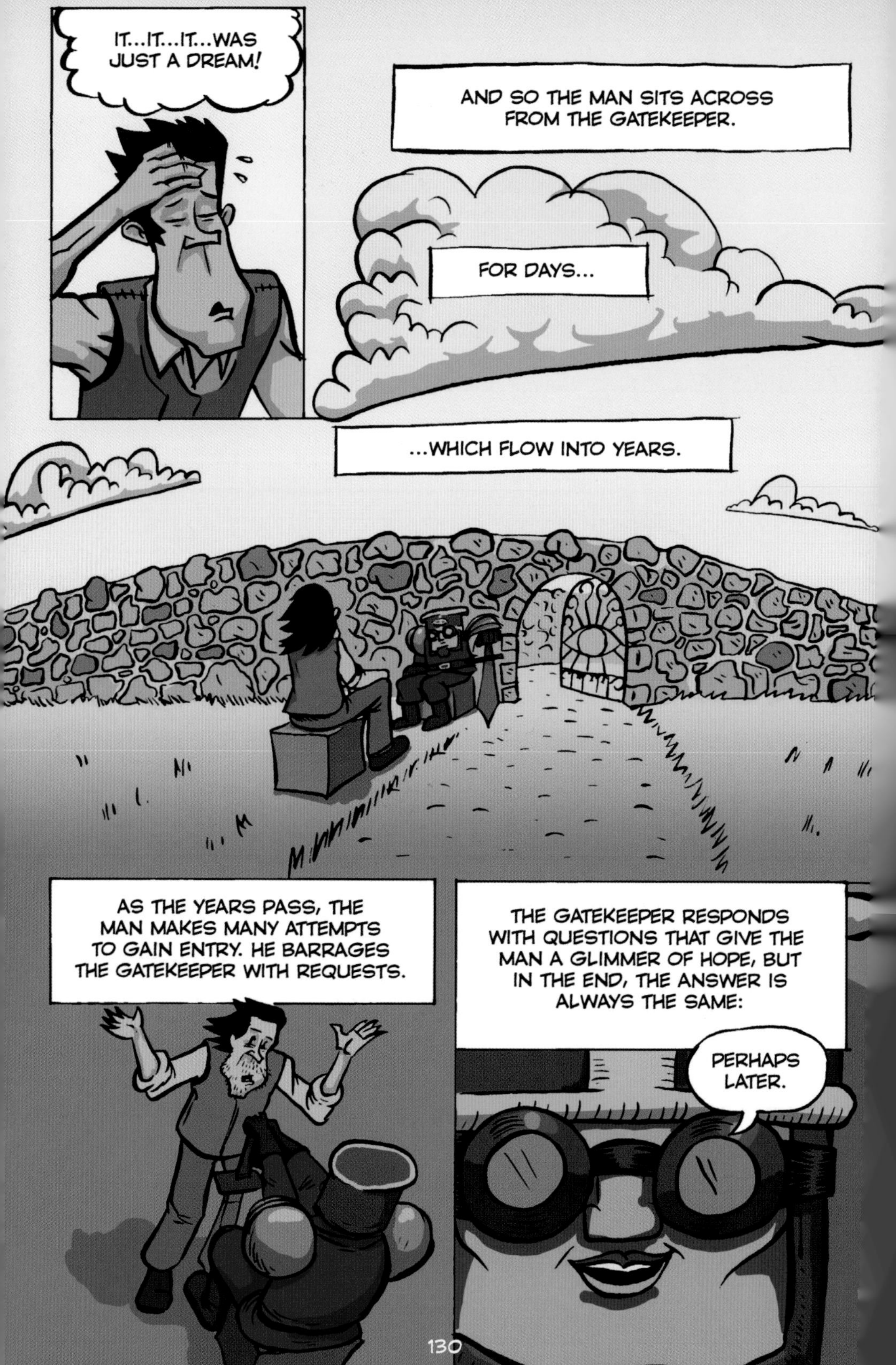
IT...IT...IT...WAS JUST A DREAM!
AND SO THE MAN SITS ACROSS FROM THE GATEKEEPER.
FOR DAYS...
...WHICH FLOW INTO YEARS.
AS THE YEARS PASS, THE MAN MAKES MANY ATTEMPTS TO GAIN ENTRY. HE BARRAGES THE GATEKEEPER WITH REQUESTS.
THE GATEKEEPER RESPONDS WITH QUESTIONS THAT GIVE THE MAN A GLIMMER OF HOPE, BUT IN THE END, THE ANSWER IS ALWAYS THE SAME:
PERHAPS LATER.

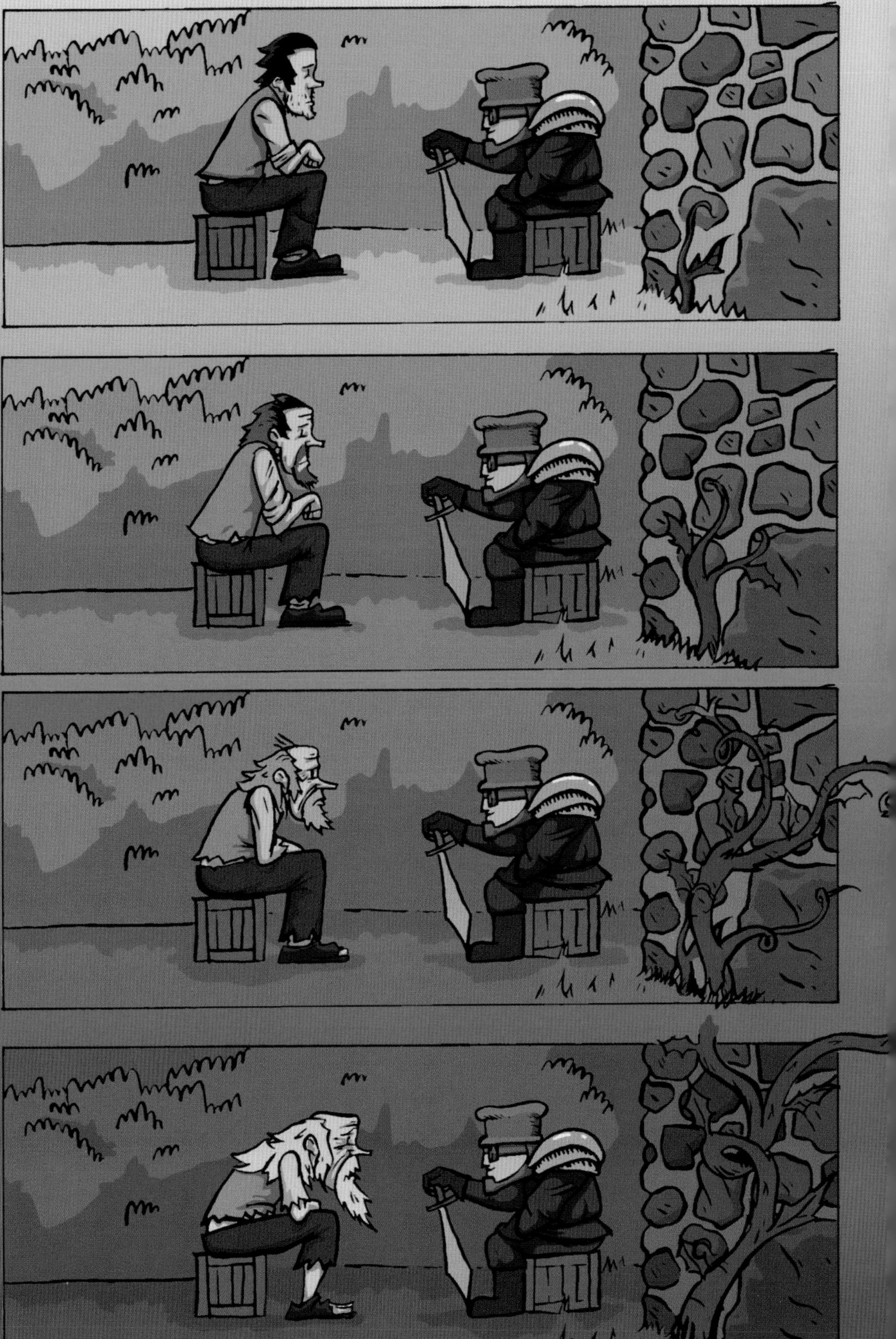

THE MAN'S EYES GROW DIM.

THE LAST DAY APPROACHES.

HE GROWS FEEBLE.

HE MUMBLES TO HIMSELF.

THE GATEKEEPER HAS BEEN THE FOCUS OF HIS LIFE FOR SO MANY YEARS, HE HAS LONG FORGOTTEN HIS BUSINESS WITH THE KING.

YOU ARE PERSISTENT, GOOD SIR. HOW CAN I HELP YOU TODAY?

I...I...HAVE A QUESTION.

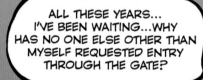

ALL THESE YEARS... I'VE BEEN WAITING...WHY HAS NO ONE ELSE OTHER THAN MYSELF REQUESTED ENTRY THROUGH THE GATE?

AH!

YOU'VE FINALLY ASKED THE IMPORTANT QUESTION!

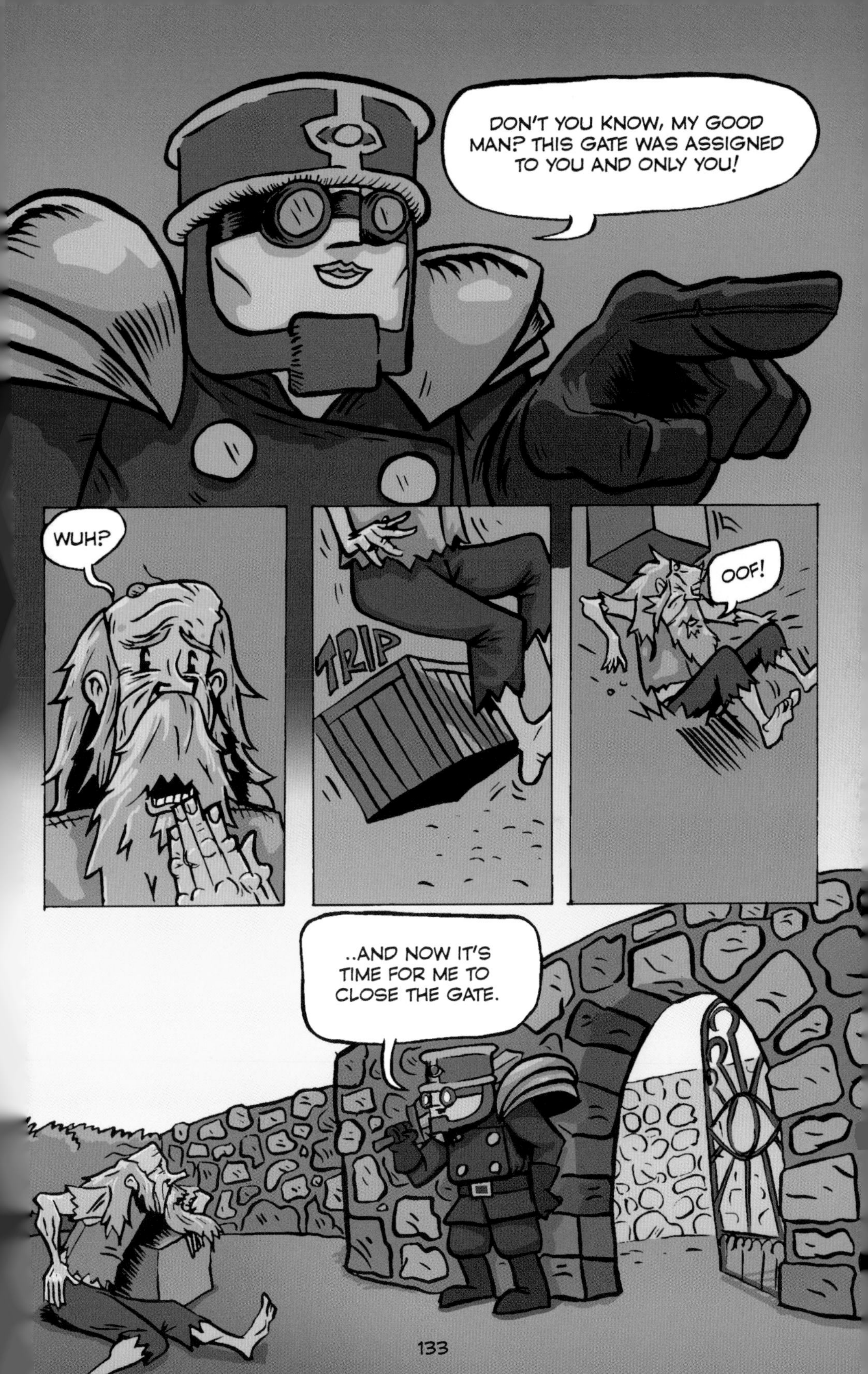
DON'T YOU KNOW, MY GOOD MAN? THIS GATE WAS ASSIGNED TO YOU AND ONLY YOU!
WUH?
TRIP
OOF!
..AND NOW IT'S TIME FOR ME TO CLOSE THE GATE.

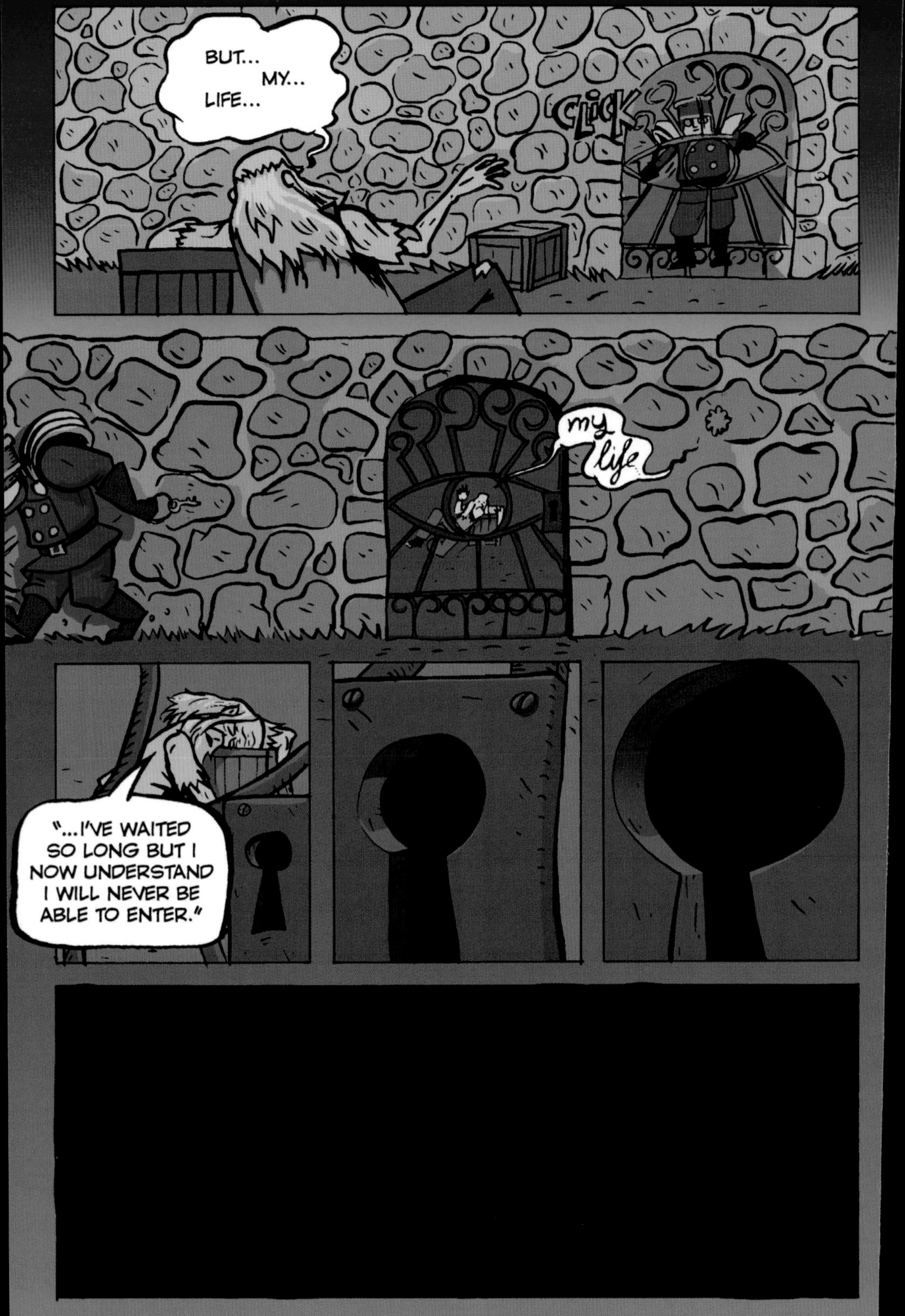
BUT... MY... LIFE...
CLICK
my life
"...I'VE WAITED SO LONG BUT I NOW UNDERSTAND I WILL NEVER BE ABLE TO ENTER."

AND THE STORY WAS ENOUGH

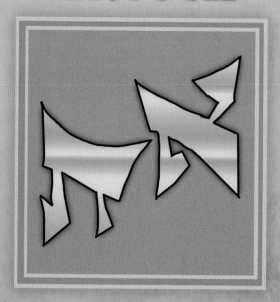

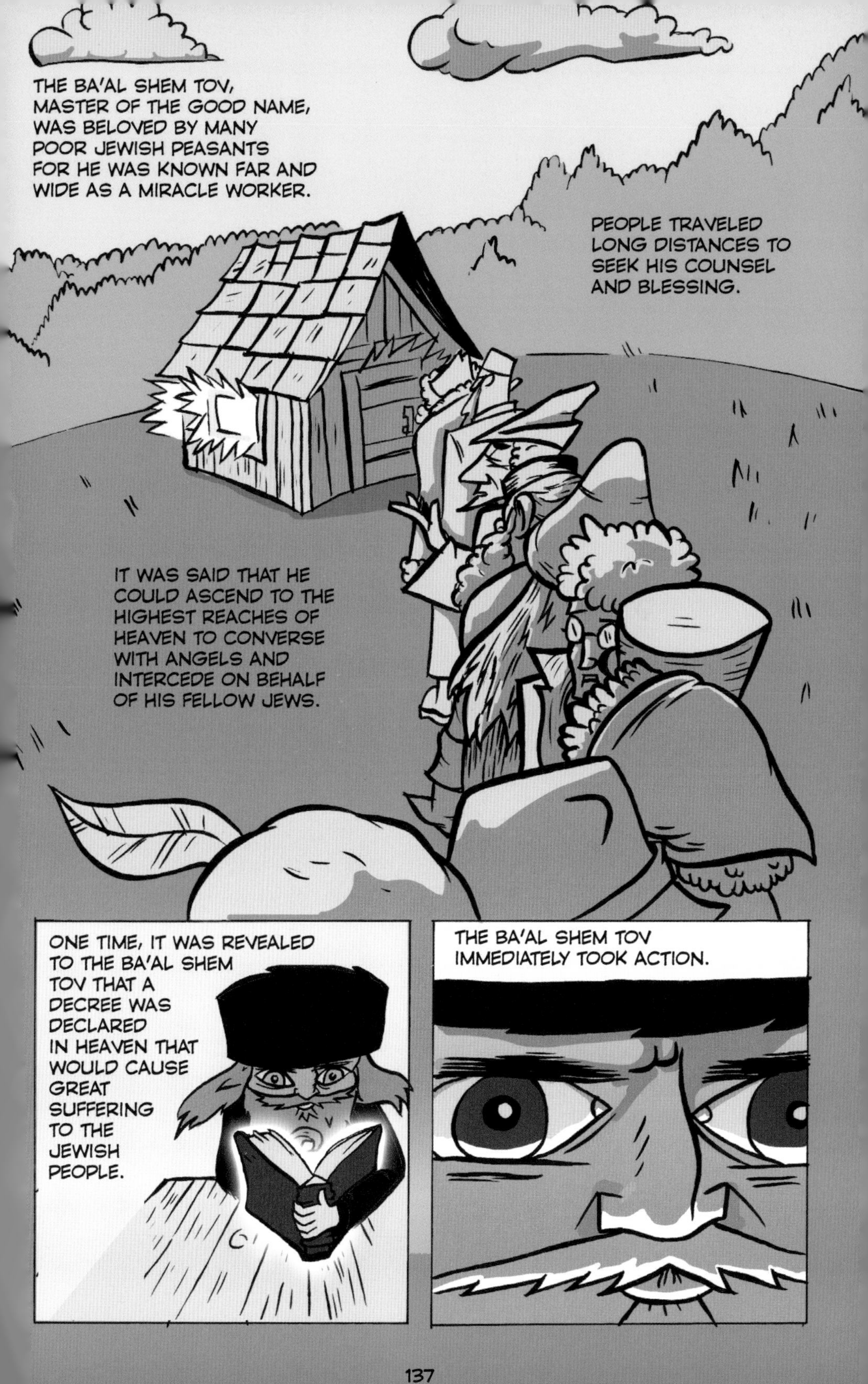
THE BA'AL SHEM TOV, MASTER OF THE GOOD NAME, WAS BELOVED BY MANY POOR JEWISH PEASANTS FOR HE WAS KNOWN FAR AND WIDE AS A MIRACLE WORKER.
PEOPLE TRAVELED LONG DISTANCES TO SEEK HIS COUNSEL AND BLESSING.
IT WAS SAID THAT HE COULD ASCEND TO THE HIGHEST REACHES OF HEAVEN TO CONVERSE WITH ANGELS AND INTERCEDE ON BEHALF OF HIS FELLOW JEWS.
ONE TIME, IT WAS REVEALED TO THE BA'AL SHEM TOV THAT A DECREE WAS DECLARED IN HEAVEN THAT WOULD CAUSE GREAT SUFFERING TO THE JEWISH PEOPLE.
THE BA'AL SHEM TOV IMMEDIATELY TOOK ACTION.

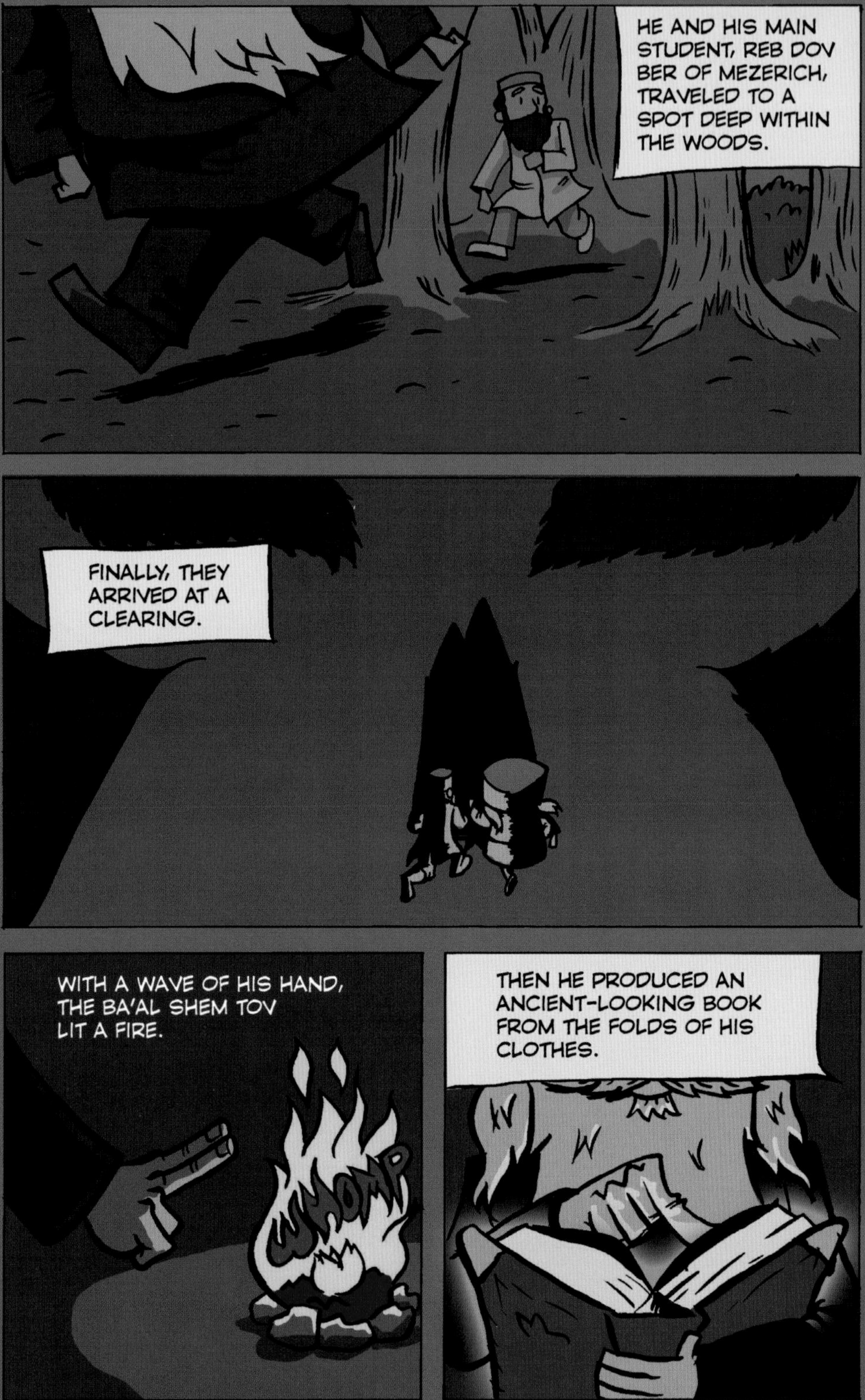
HE AND HIS MAIN STUDENT, REB DOV BER OF MEZERICH, TRAVELED TO A SPOT DEEP WITHIN THE WOODS.
FINALLY, THEY ARRIVED AT A CLEARING.
WITH A WAVE OF HIS HAND, THE BA'AL SHEM TOV LIT A FIRE.
WHOMP
THEN HE PRODUCED AN ANCIENT-LOOKING BOOK FROM THE FOLDS OF HIS CLOTHES.

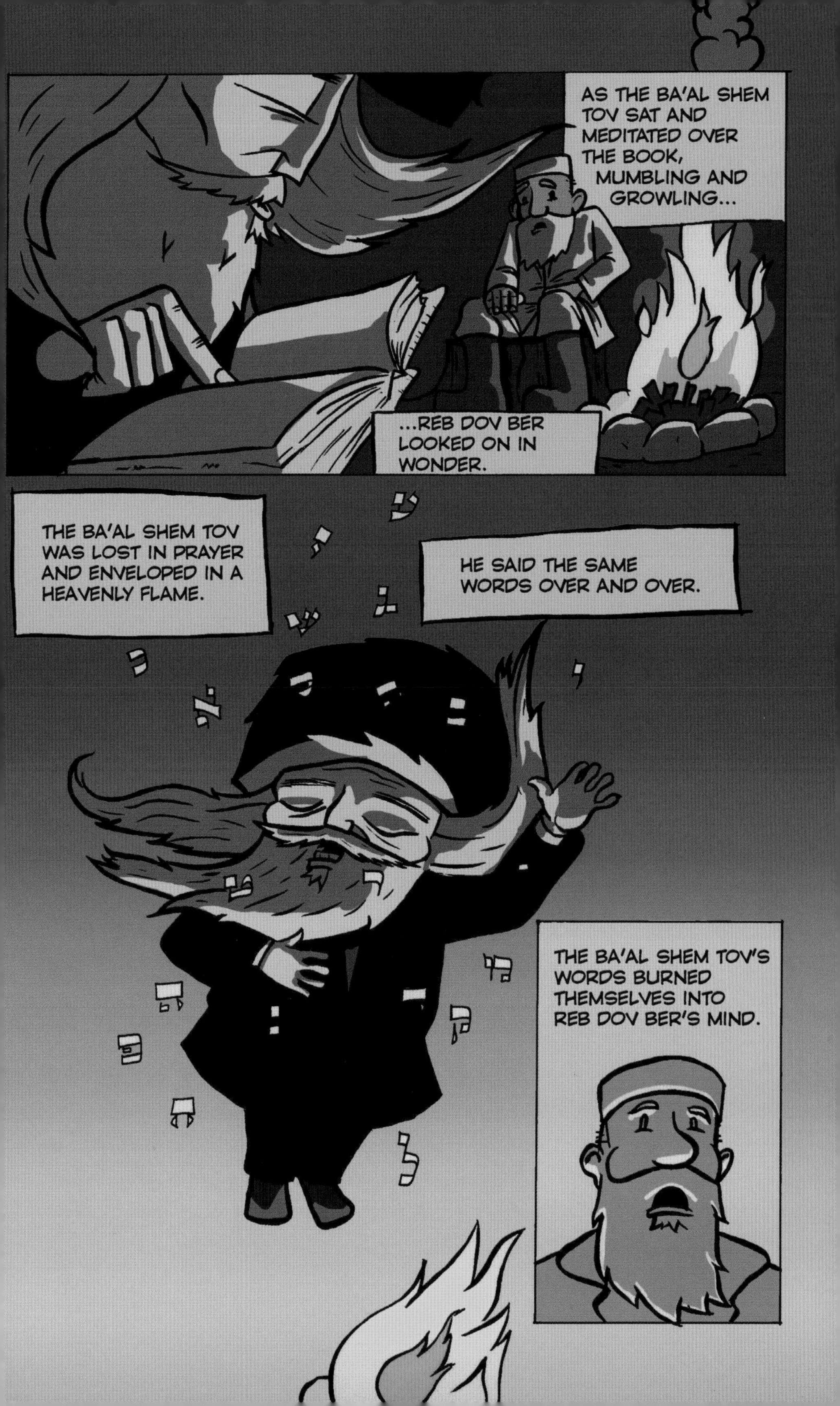
AS THE BA'AL SHEM TOV SAT AND MEDITATED OVER THE BOOK, MUMBLING AND GROWLING...
...REB DOV BER LOOKED ON IN WONDER.
THE BA'AL SHEM TOV WAS LOST IN PRAYER AND ENVELOPED IN A HEAVENLY FLAME.
HE SAID THE SAME WORDS OVER AND OVER.
THE BA'AL SHEM TOV'S WORDS BURNED THEMSELVES INTO REB DOV BER'S MIND.

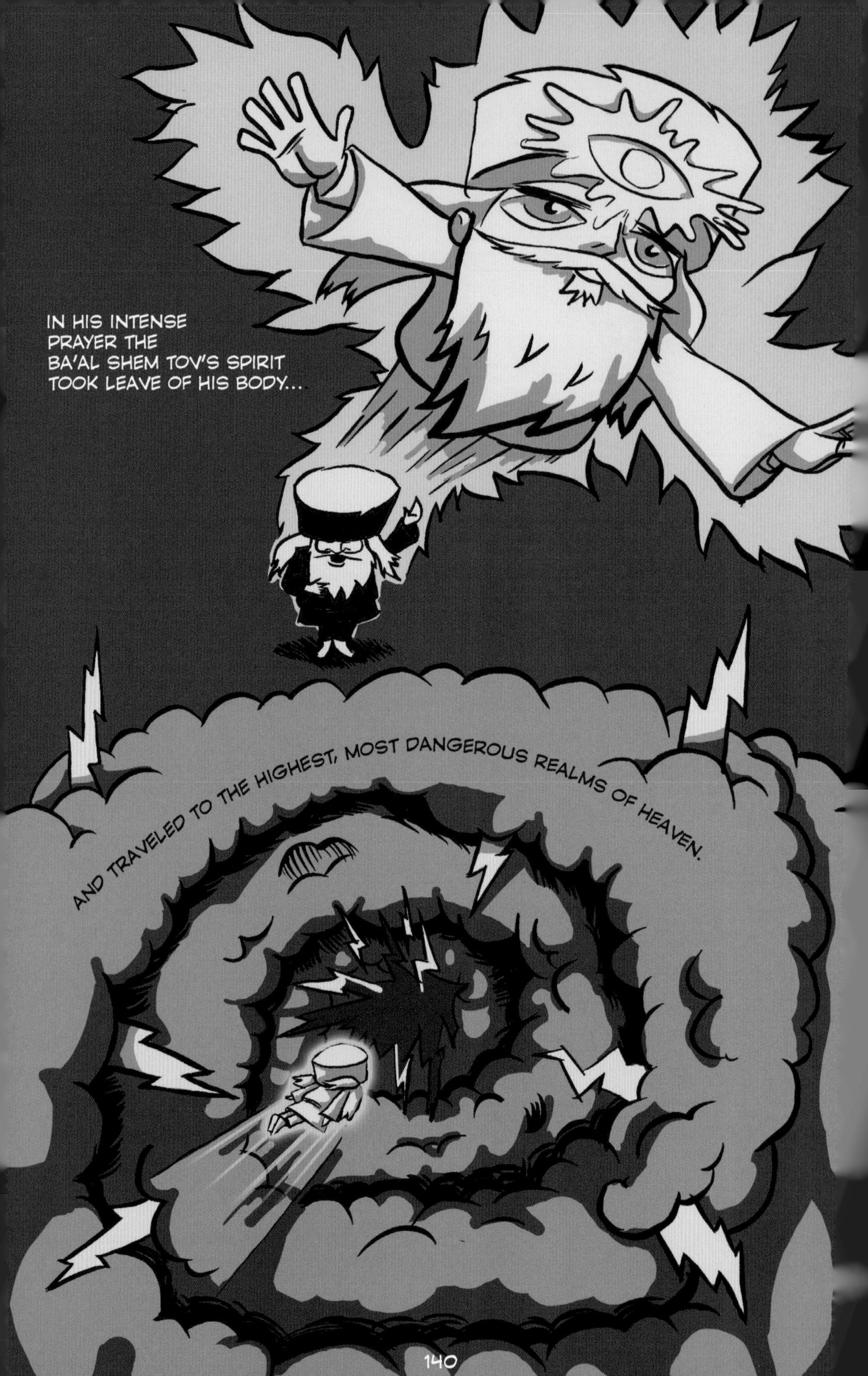
IN HIS INTENSE PRAYER THE BA'AL SHEM TOV'S SPIRIT TOOK LEAVE OF HIS BODY...
AND TRAVELED TO THE HIGHEST, MOST DANGEROUS REALMS OF HEAVEN.

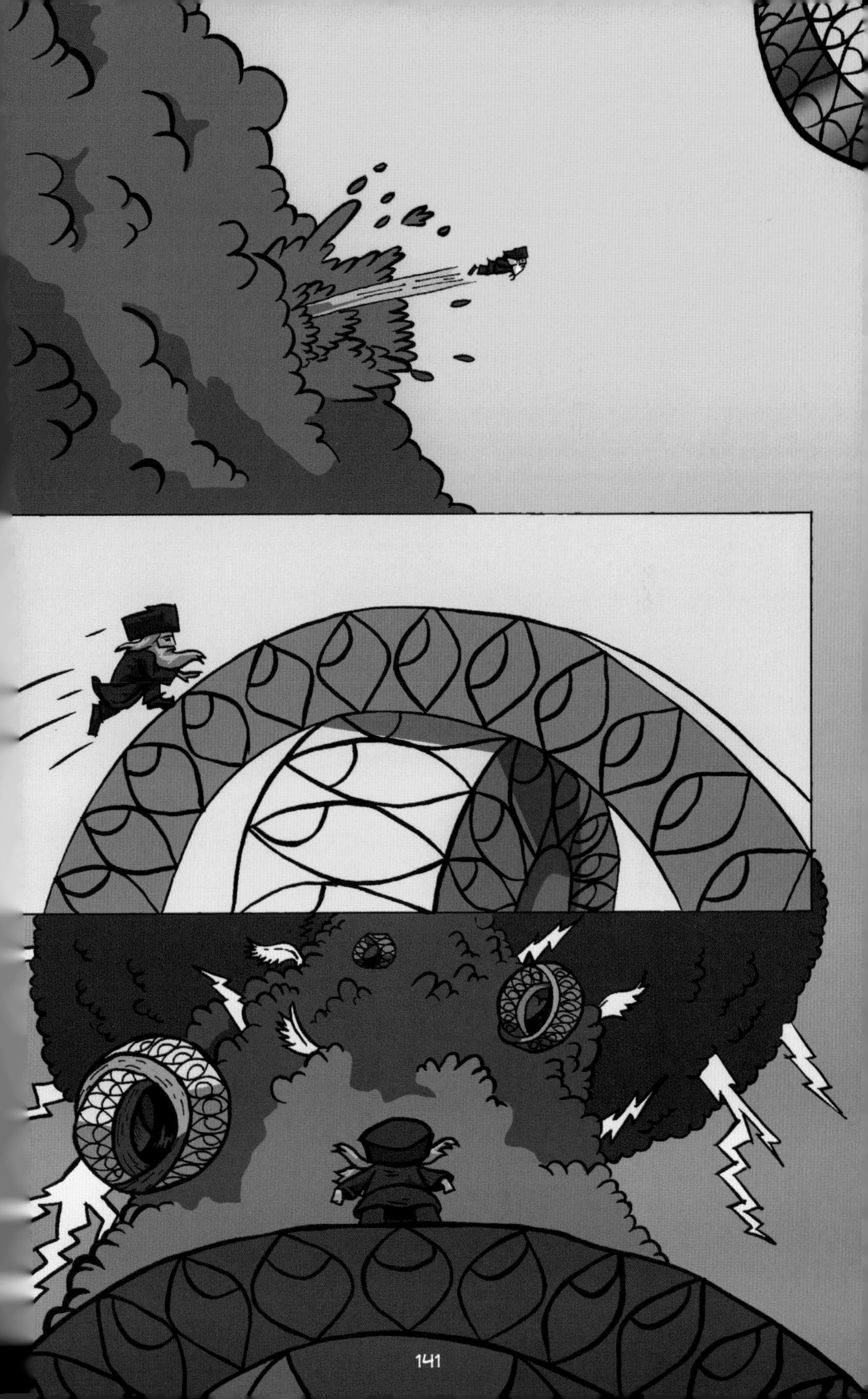

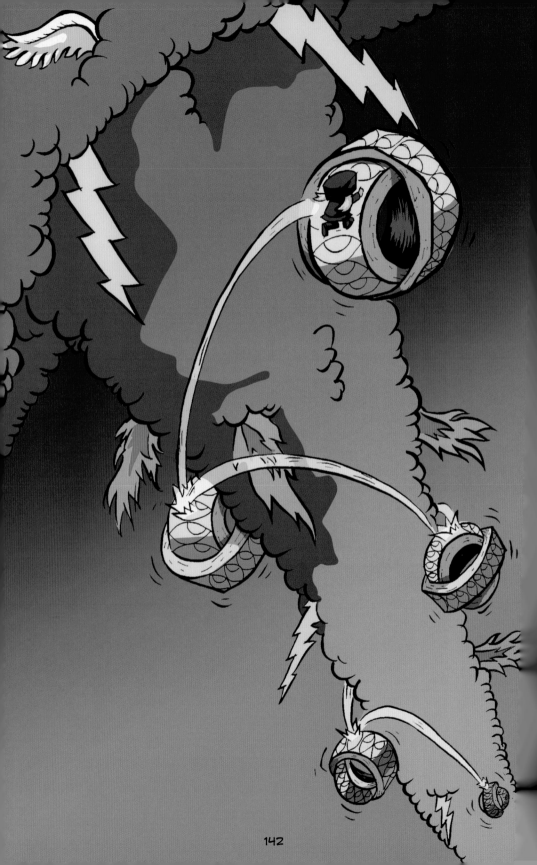

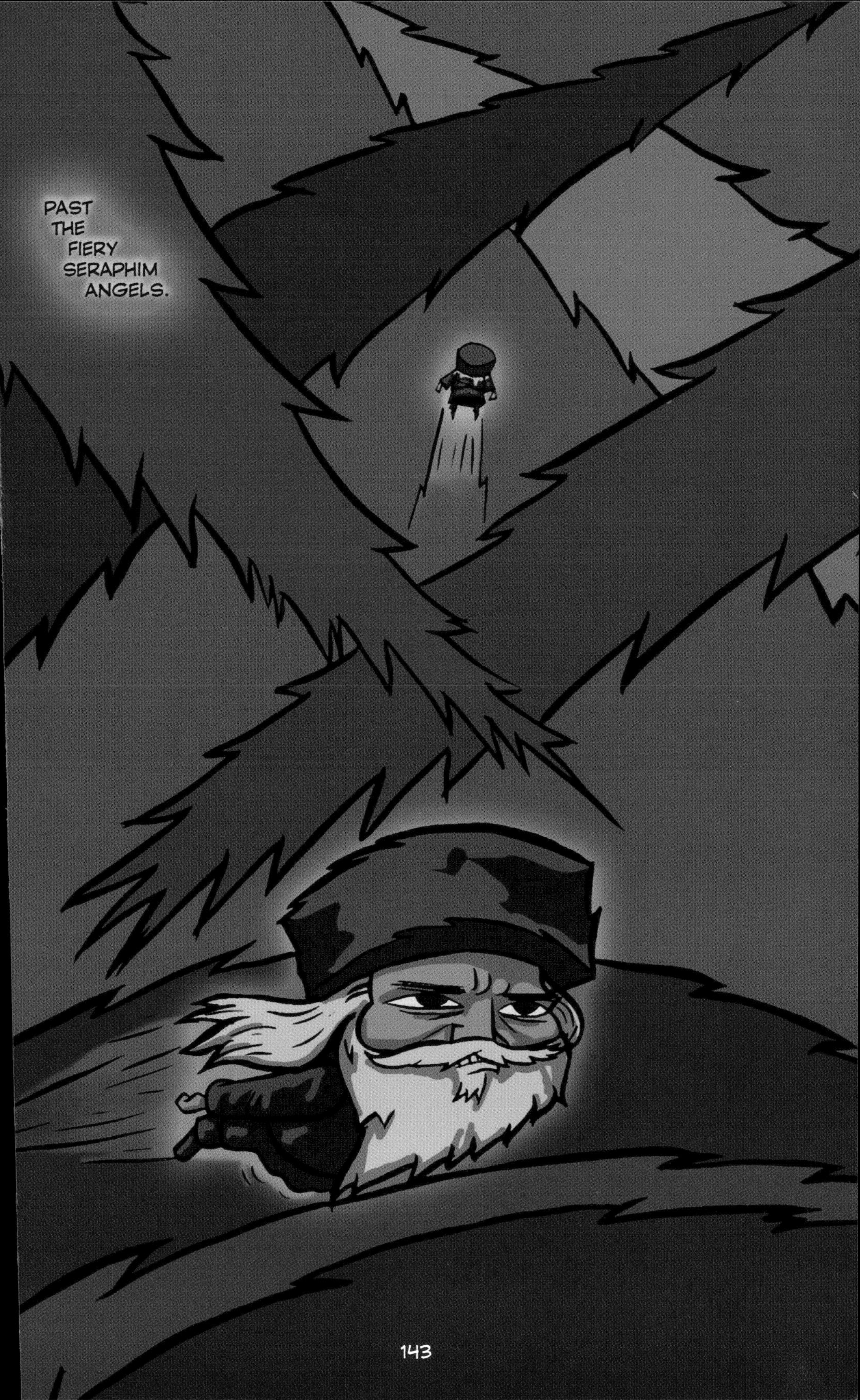
PAST THE FIERY SERAPHIM ANGELS.

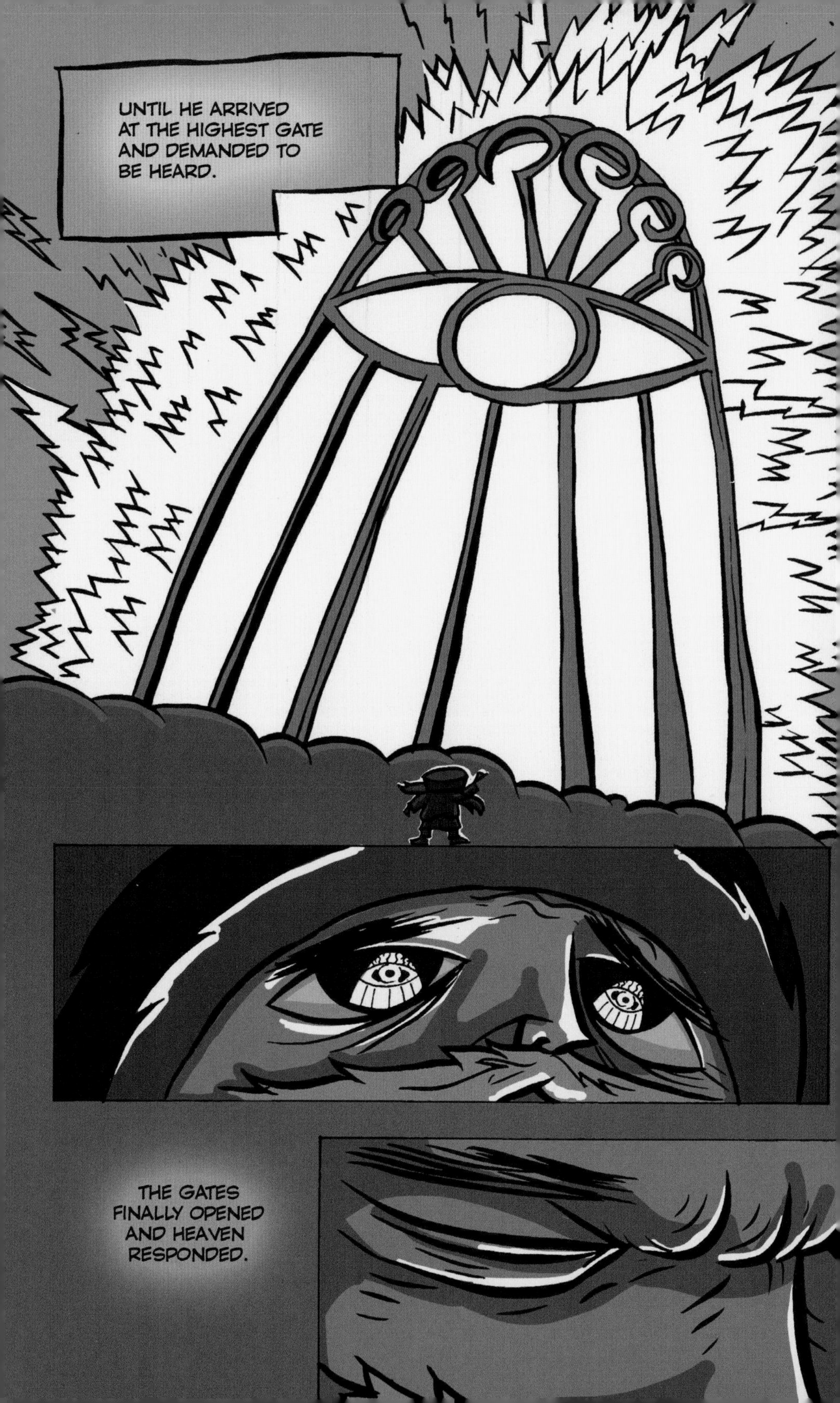
UNTIL HE ARRIVED AT THE HIGHEST GATE AND DEMANDED TO BE HEARD.
THE GATES FINALLY OPENED AND HEAVEN RESPONDED.

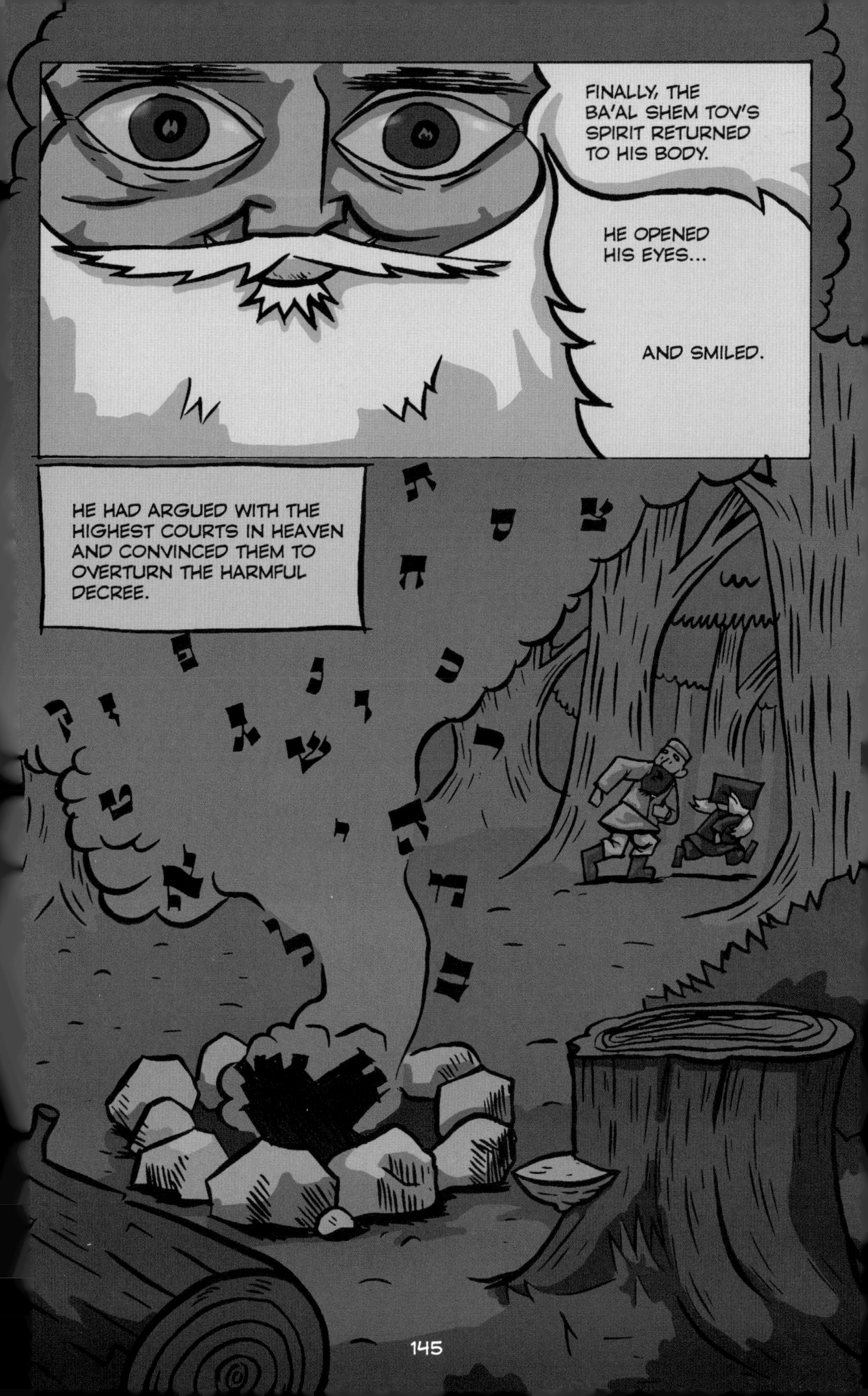
FINALLY, THE BA'AL SHEM TOV'S SPIRIT RETURNED TO HIS BODY.
HE OPENED HIS EYES...
AND SMILED.
HE HAD ARGUED WITH THE HIGHEST COURTS IN HEAVEN AND CONVINCED THEM TO OVERTURN THE HARMFUL DECREE.

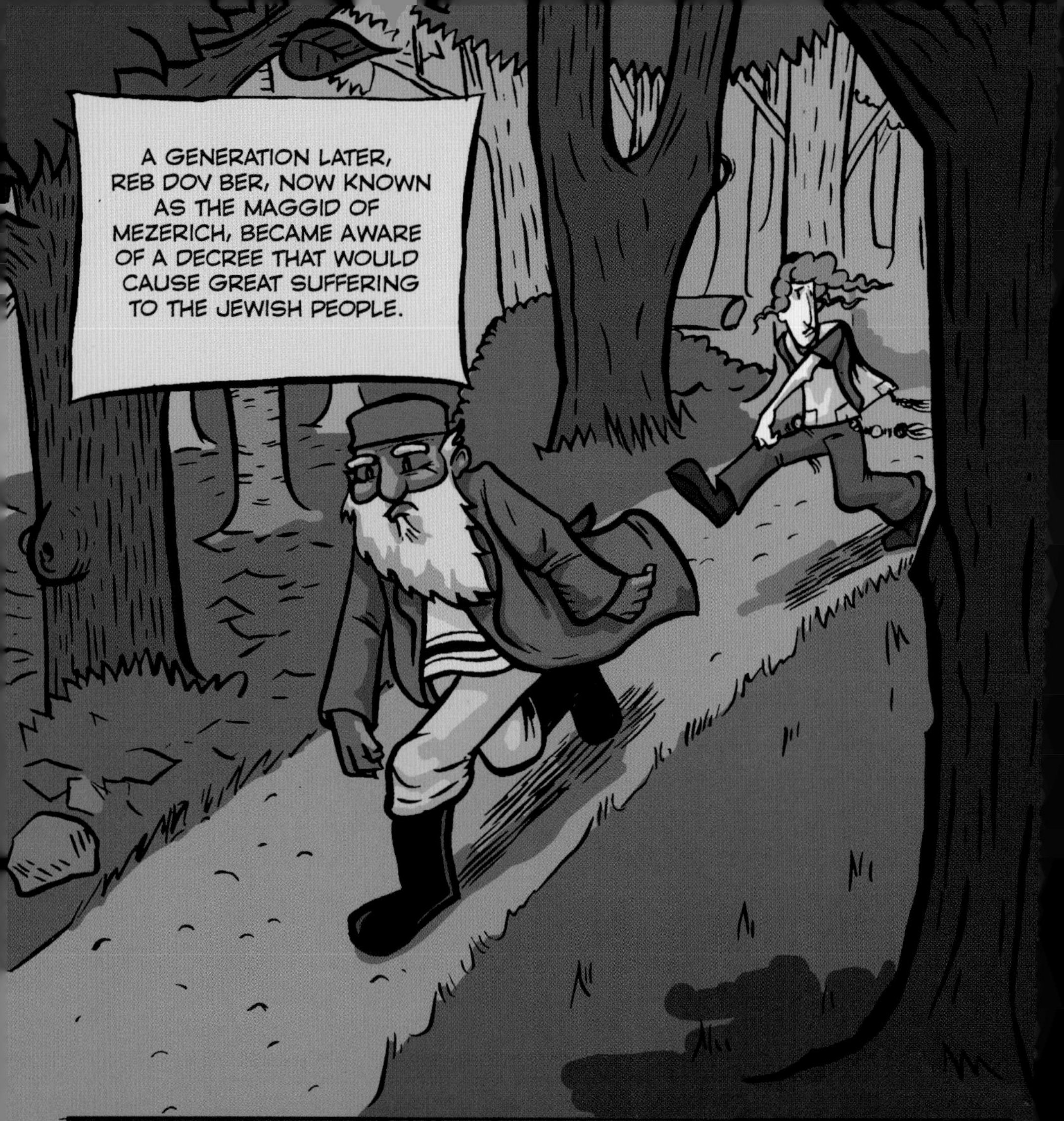
A GENERATION LATER, REB DOV BER, NOW KNOWN AS THE MAGGID OF MEZERICH, BECAME AWARE OF A DECREE THAT WOULD CAUSE GREAT SUFFERING TO THE JEWISH PEOPLE.

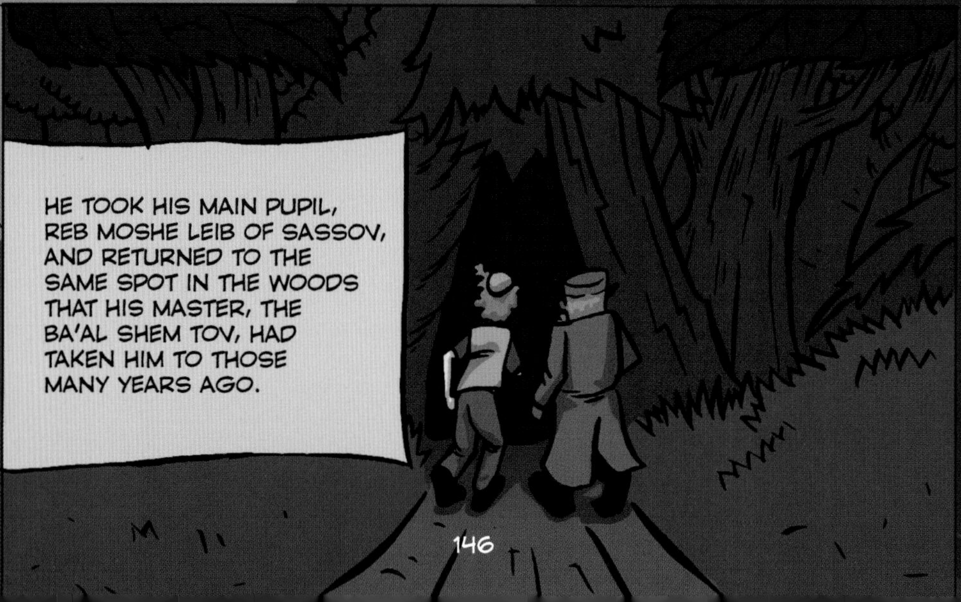
HE TOOK HIS MAIN PUPIL, REB MOSHE LEIB OF SASSOV, AND RETURNED TO THE SAME SPOT IN THE WOODS THAT HIS MASTER, THE BA'AL SHEM TOV, HAD TAKEN HIM TO THOSE MANY YEARS AGO.

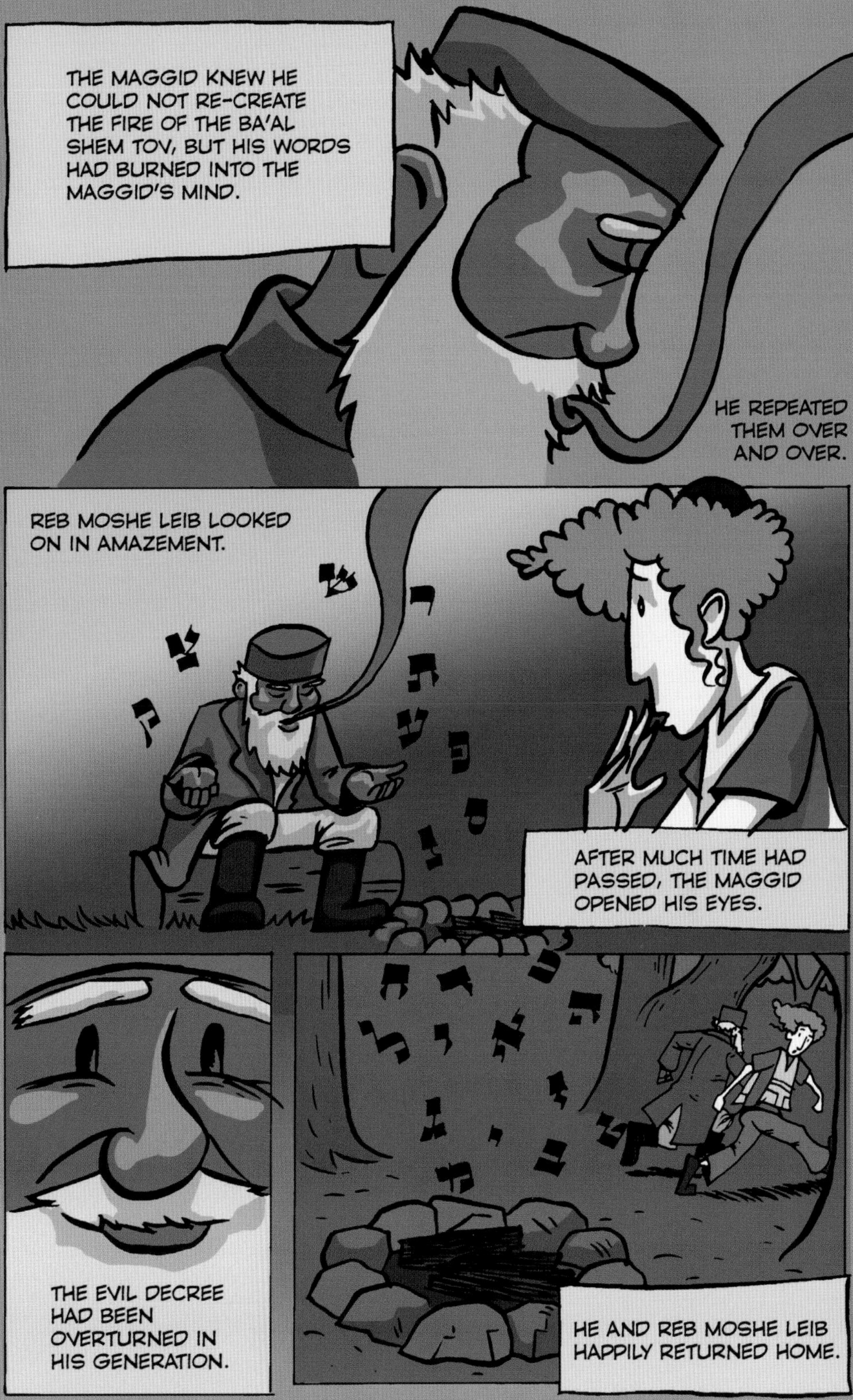
THE MAGGID KNEW HE COULD NOT RE-CREATE THE FIRE OF THE BA'AL SHEM TOV, BUT HIS WORDS HAD BURNED INTO THE MAGGID'S MIND.
HE REPEATED THEM OVER AND OVER.
REB MOSHE LEIB LOOKED ON IN AMAZEMENT.
AFTER MUCH TIME HAD PASSED, THE MAGGID OPENED HIS EYES.
THE EVIL DECREE HAD BEEN OVERTURNED IN HIS GENERATION.
HE AND REB MOSHE LEIB HAPPILY RETURNED HOME.

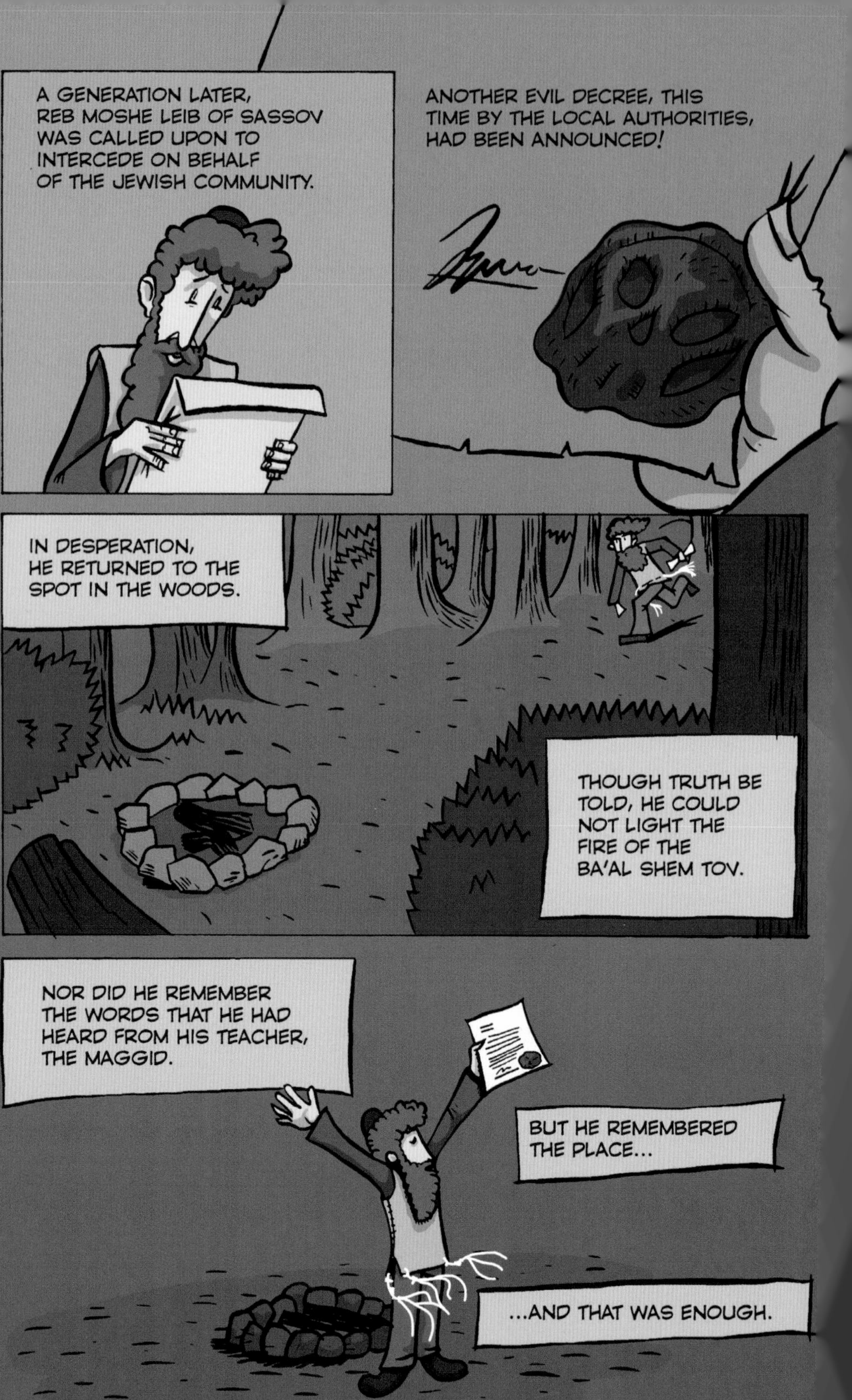
A GENERATION LATER, REB MOSHE LEIB OF SASSOV WAS CALLED UPON TO INTERCEDE ON BEHALF OF THE JEWISH COMMUNITY.
ANOTHER EVIL DECREE, THIS TIME BY THE LOCAL AUTHORITIES, HAD BEEN ANNOUNCED!
IN DESPERATION, HE RETURNED TO THE SPOT IN THE WOODS.
THOUGH TRUTH BE TOLD, HE COULD NOT LIGHT THE FIRE OF THE BA'AL SHEM TOV.
NOR DID HE REMEMBER THE WORDS THAT HE HAD HEARD FROM HIS TEACHER, THE MAGGID.
BUT HE REMEMBERED THE PLACE...
...AND THAT WAS ENOUGH.

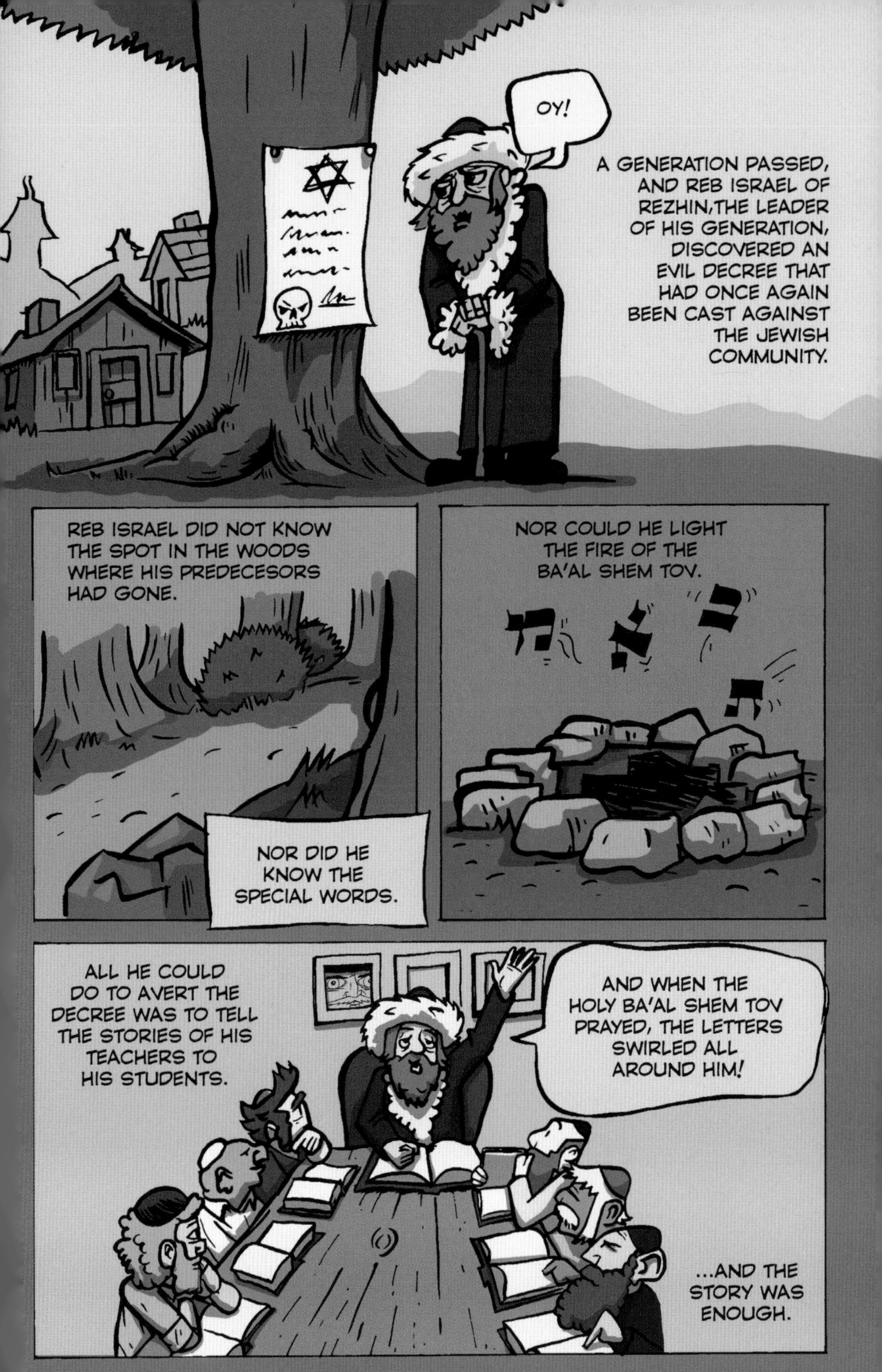
OY!
A GENERATION PASSED, AND REB ISRAEL OF REZHIN,THE LEADER OF HIS GENERATION, DISCOVERED AN EVIL DECREE THAT HAD ONCE AGAIN BEEN CAST AGAINST THE JEWISH COMMUNITY.
REB ISRAEL DID NOT KNOW THE SPOT IN THE WOODS WHERE HIS PREDECESORS HAD GONE.
NOR DID HE KNOW THE SPECIAL WORDS.
NOR COULD HE LIGHT THE FIRE OF THE BA'AL SHEM TOV.
ALL HE COULD DO TO AVERT THE DECREE WAS TO TELL THE STORIES OF HIS TEACHERS TO HIS STUDENTS.
AND WHEN THE HOLY BA'AL SHEM TOV PRAYED, THE LETTERS SWIRLED ALL AROUND HIM!
...AND THE STORY WAS ENOUGH.

THE
BOOK
OF
SECRETS

There is a story...

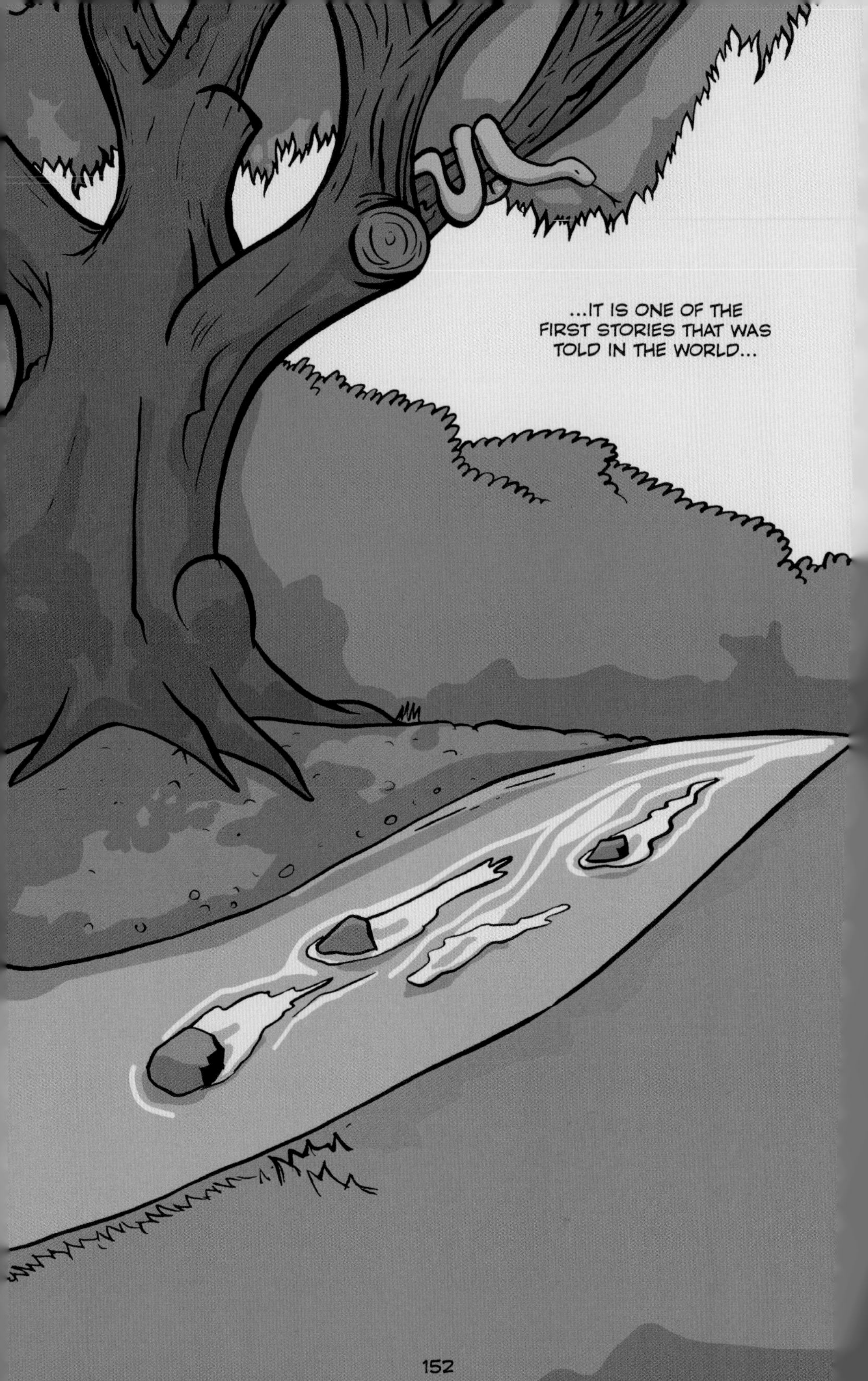
...IT IS ONE OF THE FIRST STORIES THAT WAS TOLD IN THE WORLD...

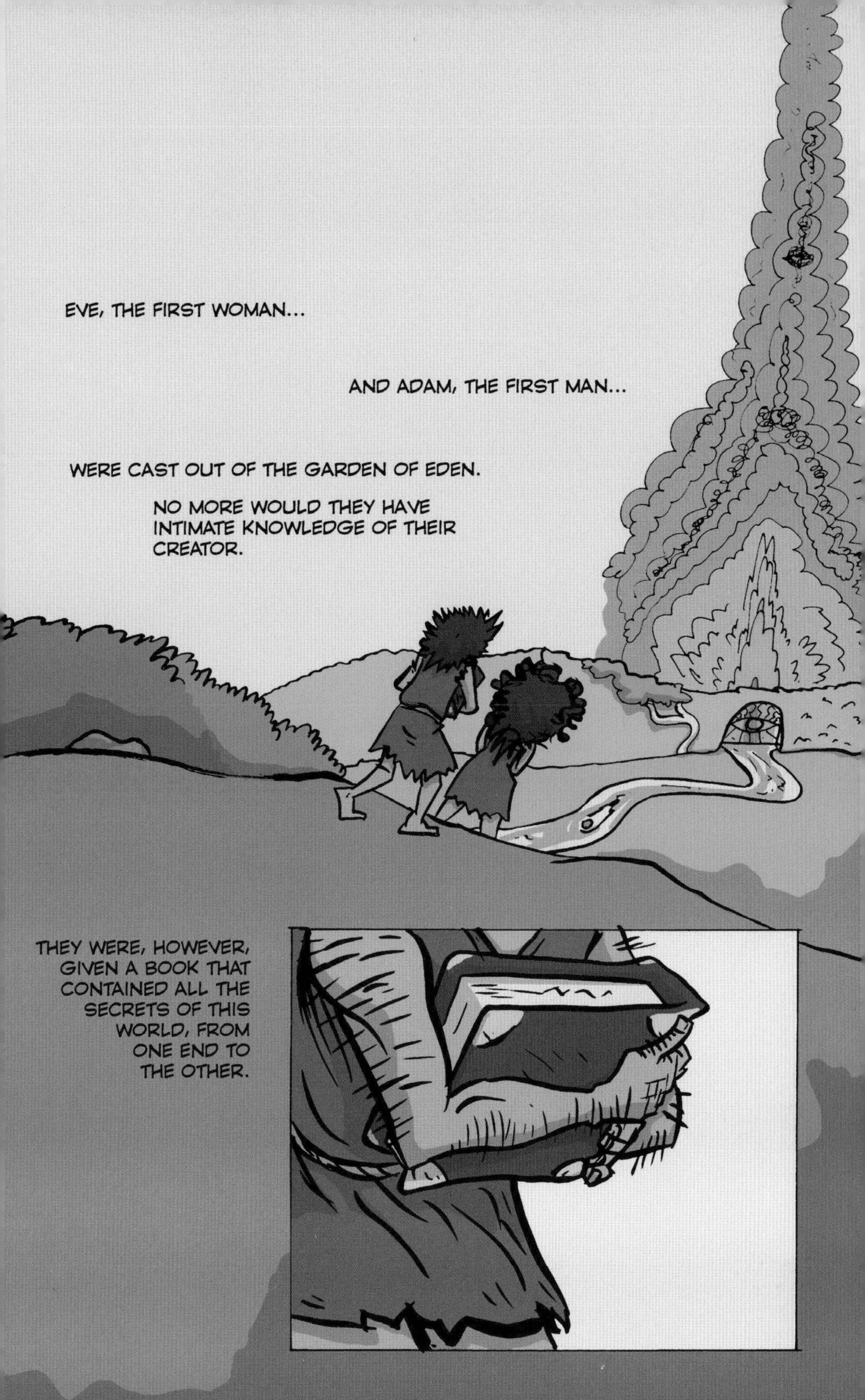
EVE, THE FIRST WOMAN...
AND ADAM, THE FIRST MAN...
WERE CAST OUT OF THE GARDEN OF EDEN.
NO MORE WOULD THEY HAVE INTIMATE KNOWLEDGE OF THEIR CREATOR.
THEY WERE, HOWEVER, GIVEN A BOOK THAT CONTAINED ALL THE SECRETS OF THIS WORLD, FROM ONE END TO THE OTHER.

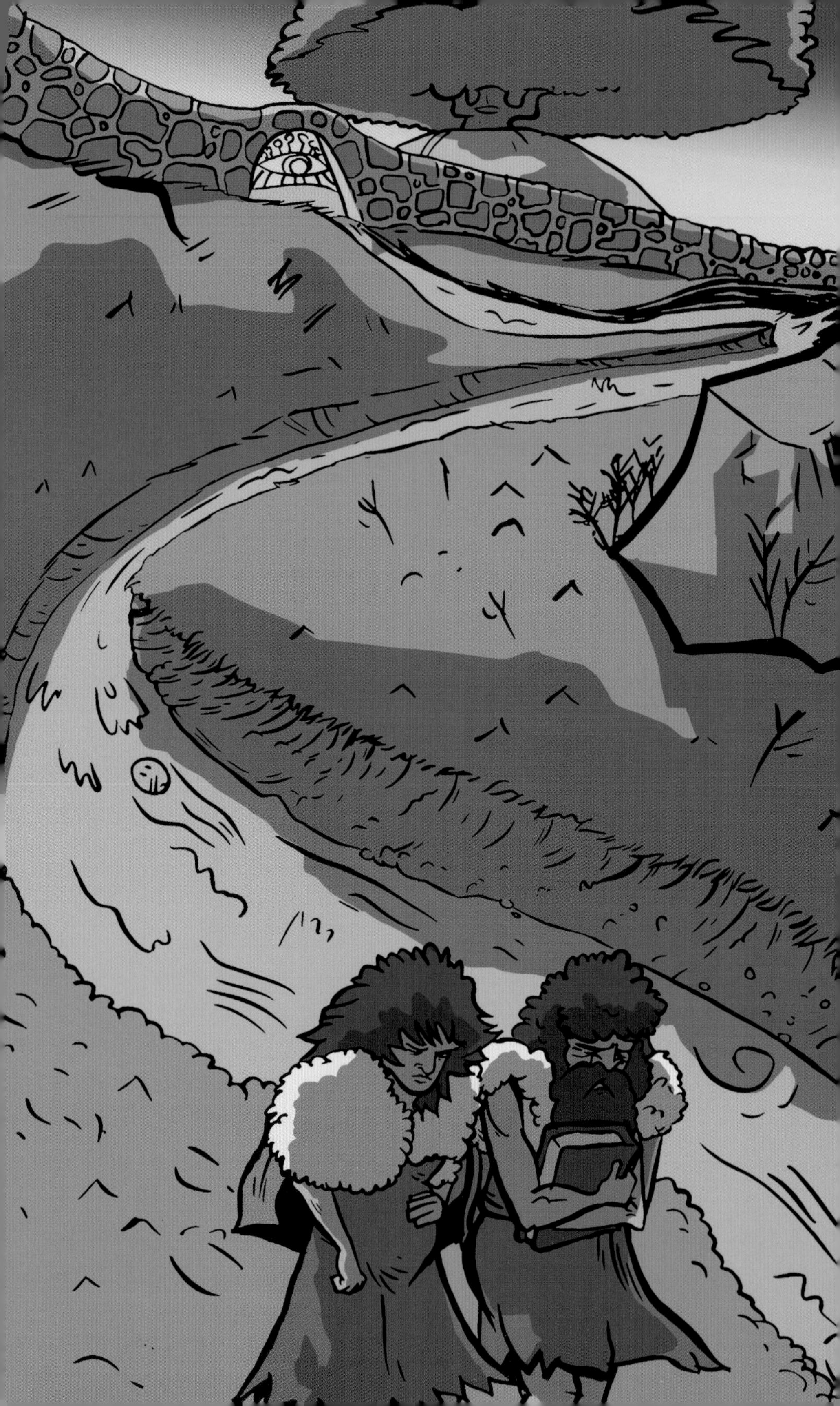

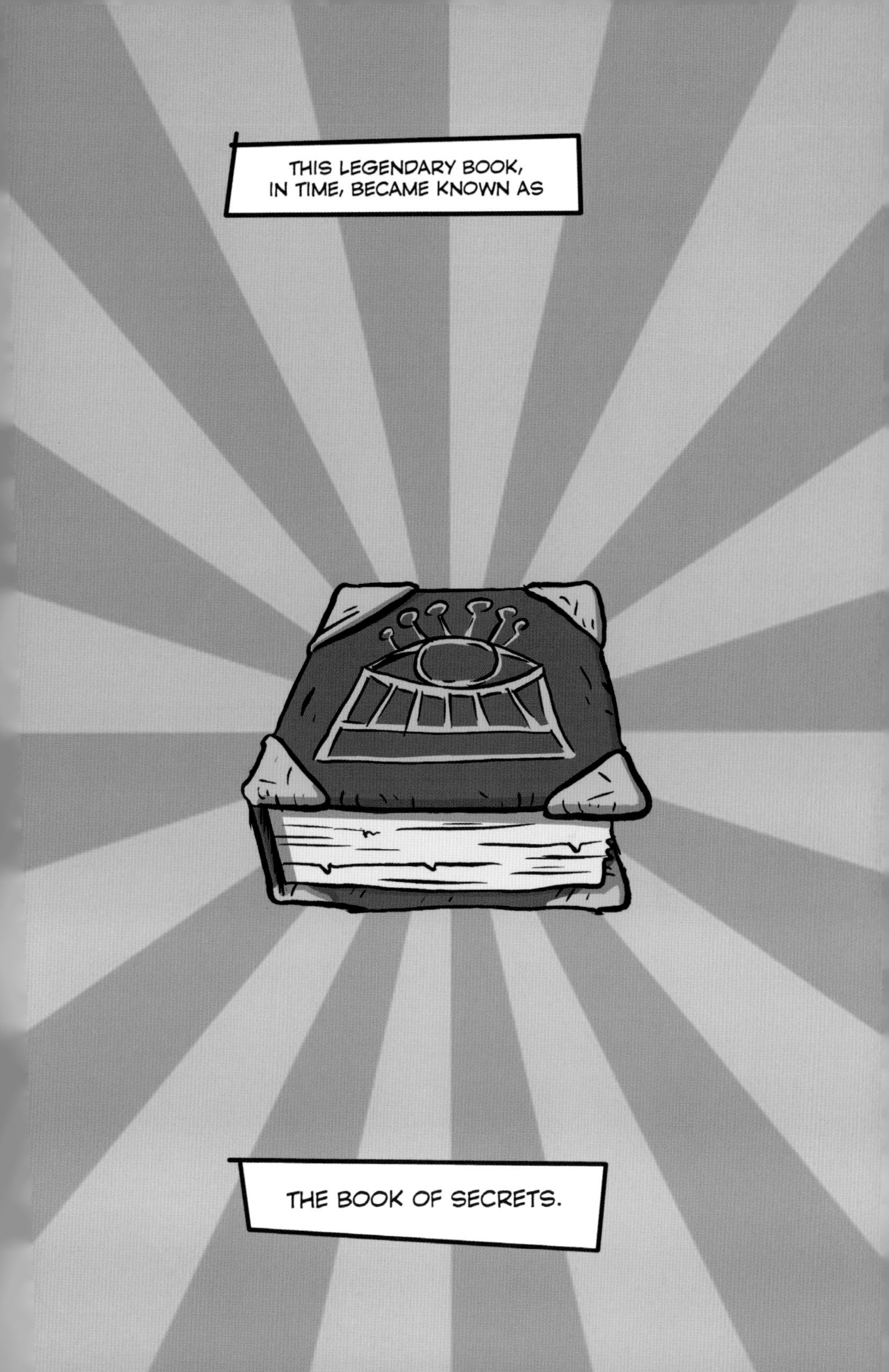
THIS LEGENDARY BOOK, IN TIME, BECAME KNOWN AS
THE BOOK OF SECRETS.

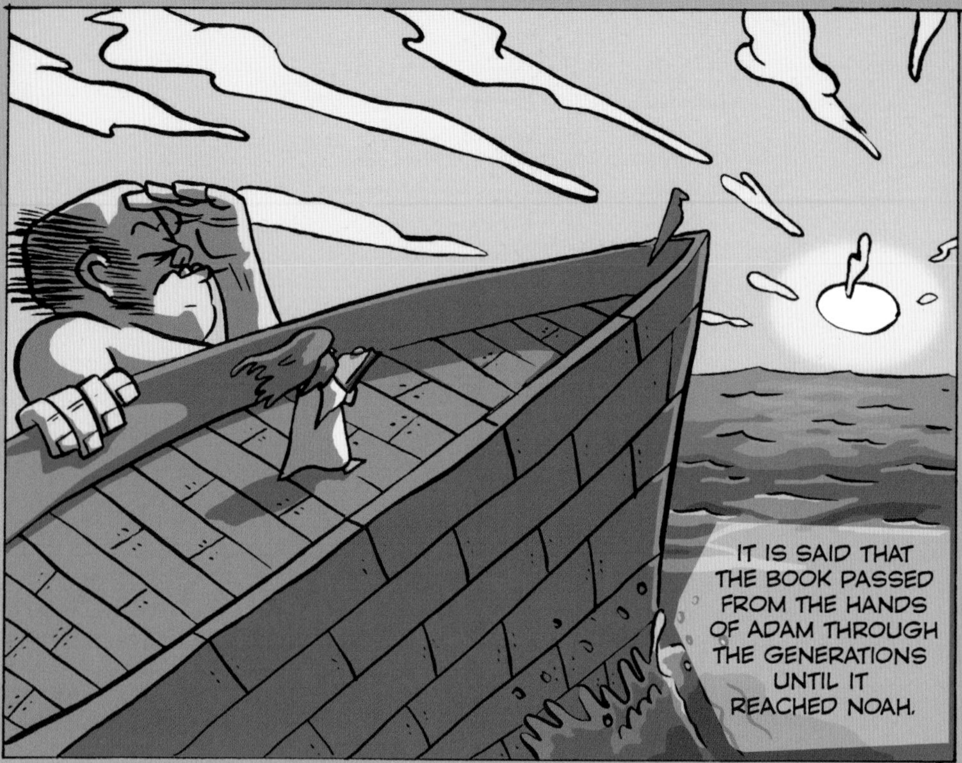
IT IS SAID THAT THE BOOK PASSED FROM THE HANDS OF ADAM THROUGH THE GENERATIONS UNTIL IT REACHED NOAH.

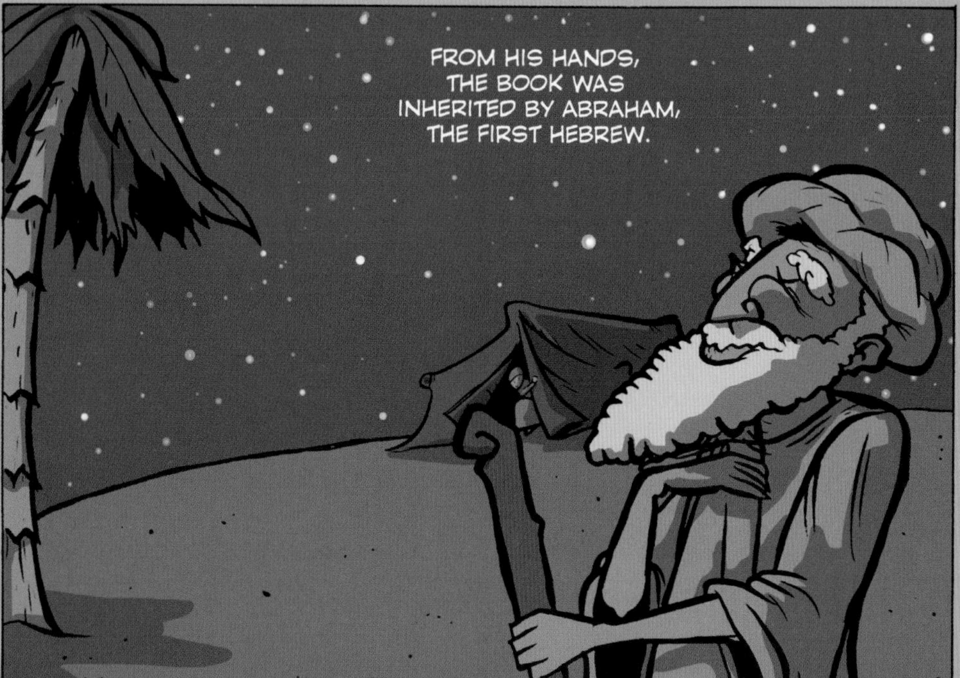
FROM HIS HANDS, THE BOOK WAS INHERITED BY ABRAHAM, THE FIRST HEBREW.

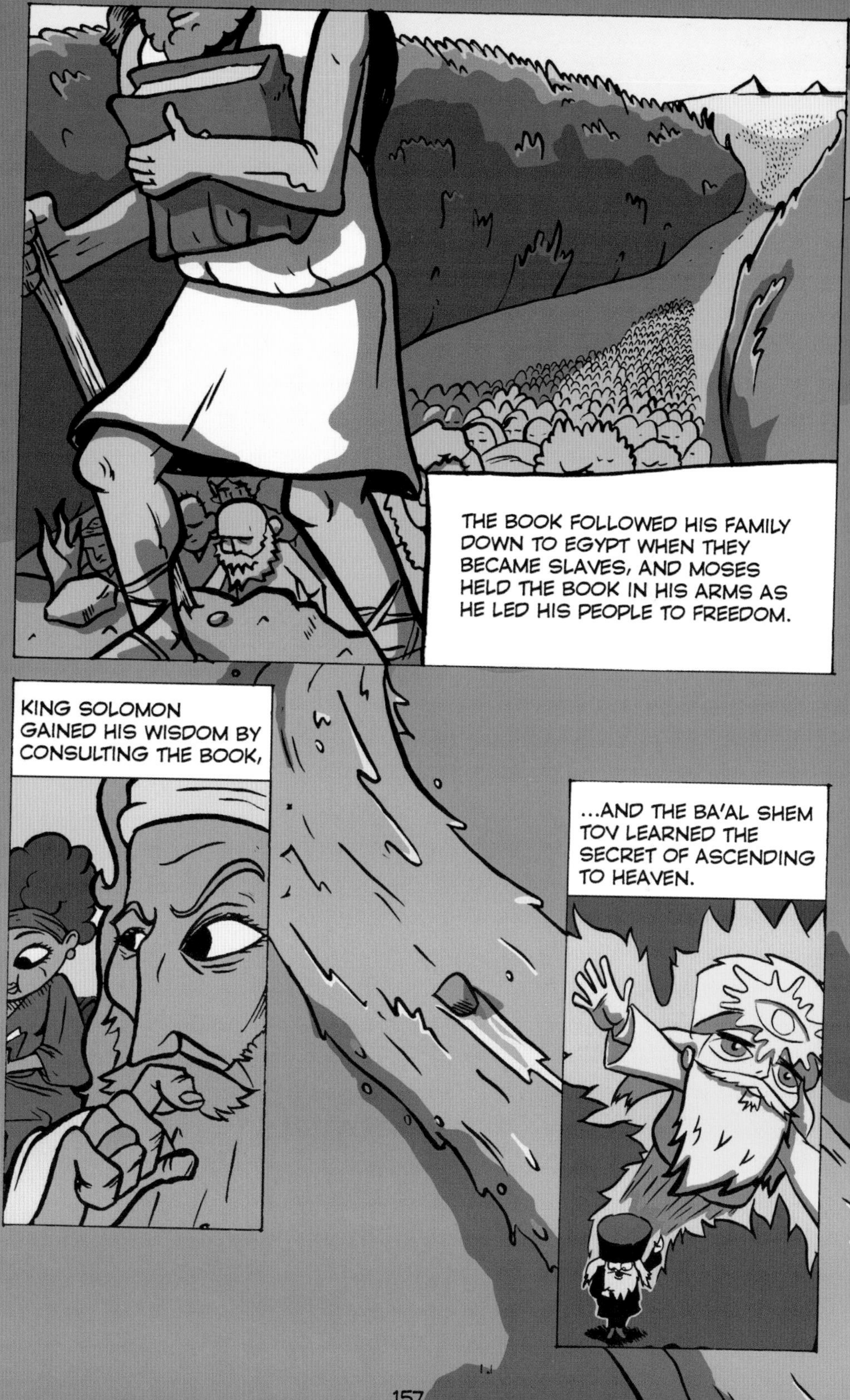
THE BOOK FOLLOWED HIS FAMILY DOWN TO EGYPT WHEN THEY BECAME SLAVES, AND MOSES HELD THE BOOK IN HIS ARMS AS HE LED HIS PEOPLE TO FREEDOM.
KING SOLOMON GAINED HIS WISDOM BY CONSULTING THE BOOK,
...AND THE BA'AL SHEM TOV LEARNED THE SECRET OF ASCENDING TO HEAVEN.

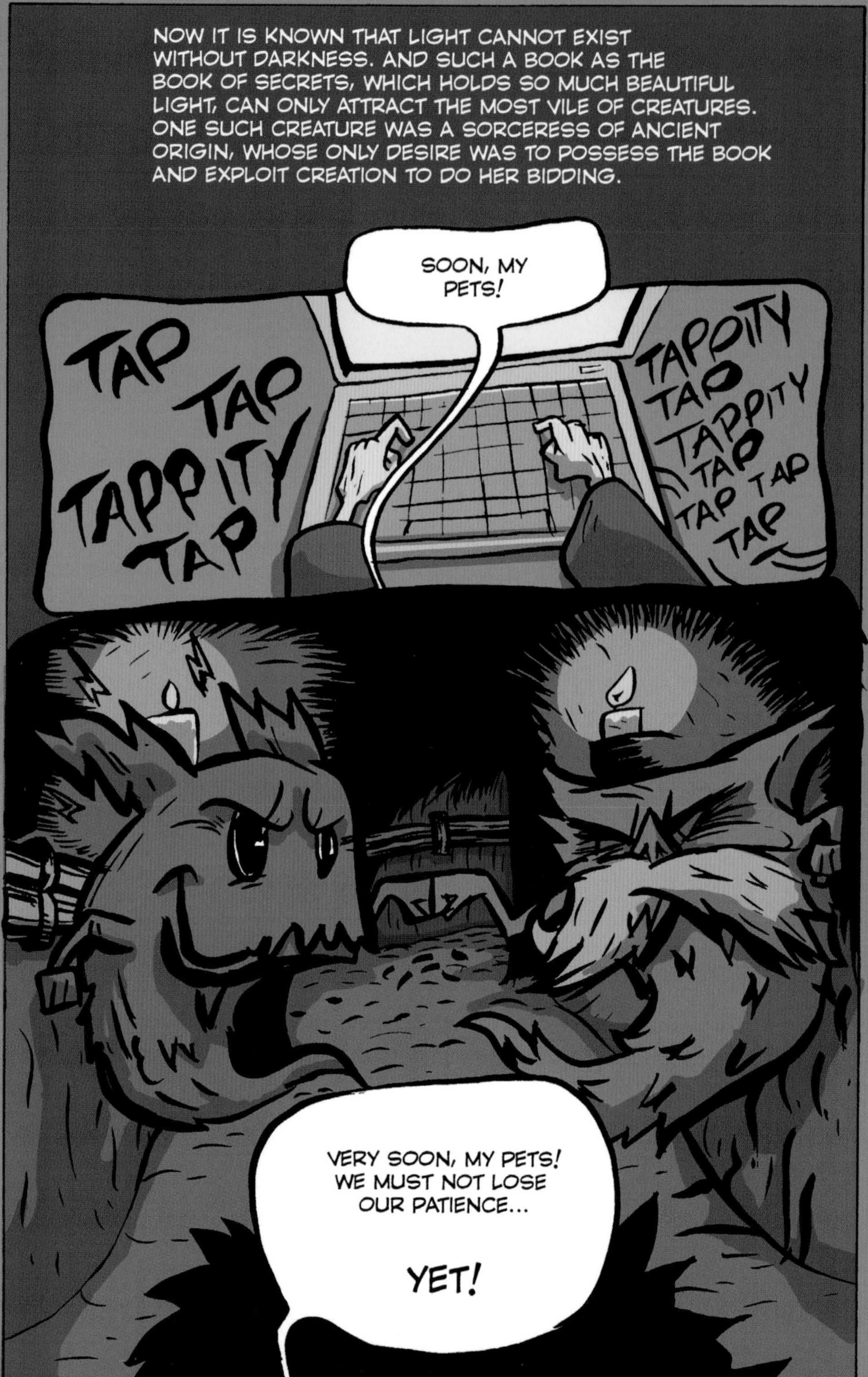
NOW IT IS KNOWN THAT LIGHT CANNOT EXIST WITHOUT DARKNESS. AND SUCH A BOOK AS THE BOOK OF SECRETS, WHICH HOLDS SO MUCH BEAUTIFUL LIGHT, CAN ONLY ATTRACT THE MOST VILE OF CREATURES. ONE SUCH CREATURE WAS A SORCERESS OF ANCIENT ORIGIN, WHOSE ONLY DESIRE WAS TO POSSESS THE BOOK AND EXPLOIT CREATION TO DO HER BIDDING.
SOON, MY PETS!
TAP TAP TAPPITY TAP
TAPPITY TAP TAPPITY TAP TAP TAP TAP TAP
VERY SOON, MY PETS! WE MUST NOT LOSE OUR PATIENCE...
YET!

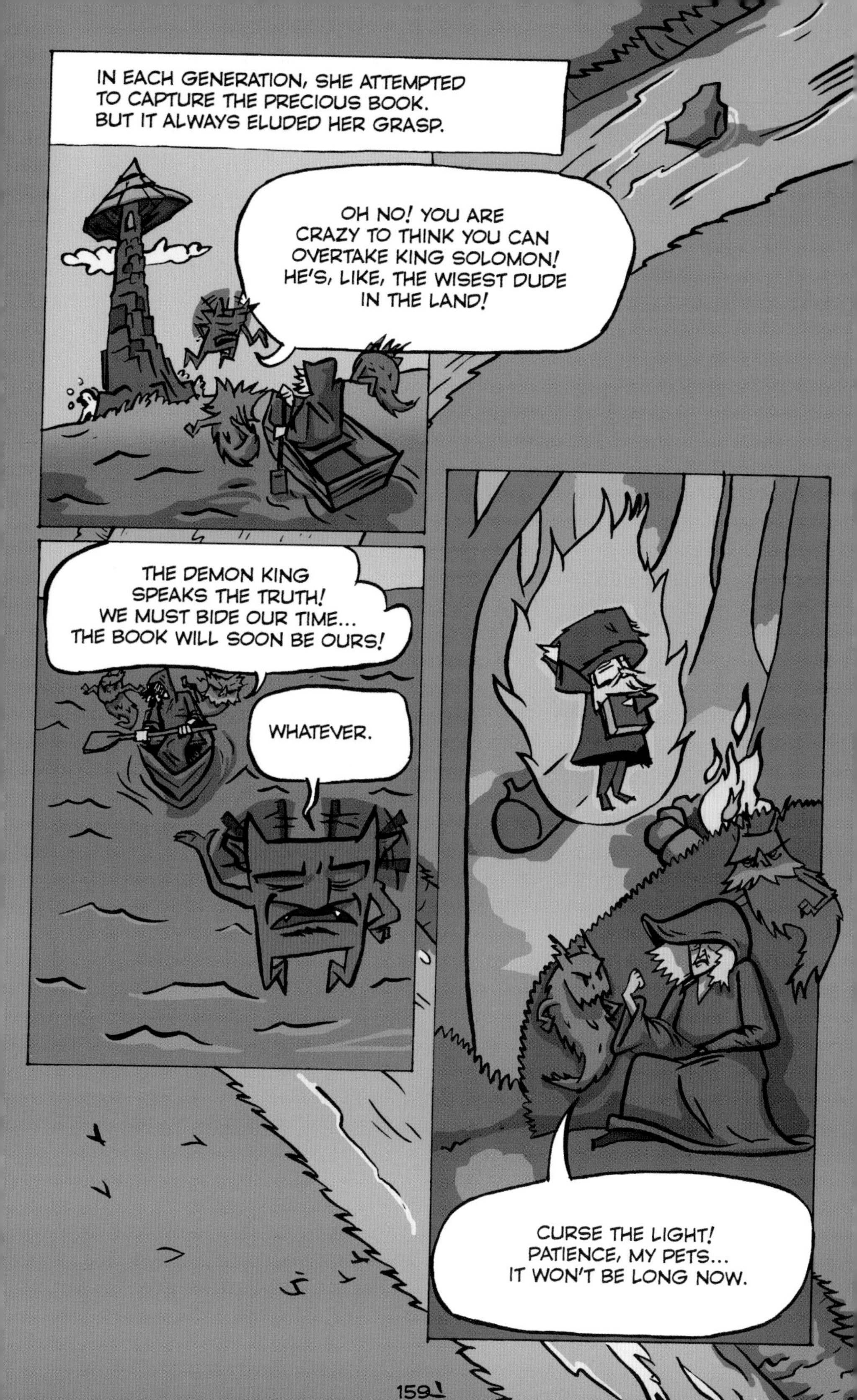

IN EACH GENERATION, SHE ATTEMPTED TO CAPTURE THE PRECIOUS BOOK. BUT IT ALWAYS ELUDED HER GRASP.
OH NO! YOU ARE CRAZY TO THINK YOU CAN OVERTAKE KING SOLOMON! HE'S, LIKE, THE WISEST DUDE IN THE LAND!
THE DEMON KING SPEAKS THE TRUTH! WE MUST BIDE OUR TIME... THE BOOK WILL SOON BE OURS!
WHATEVER.
CURSE THE LIGHT! PATIENCE, MY PETS... IT WON'T BE LONG NOW.

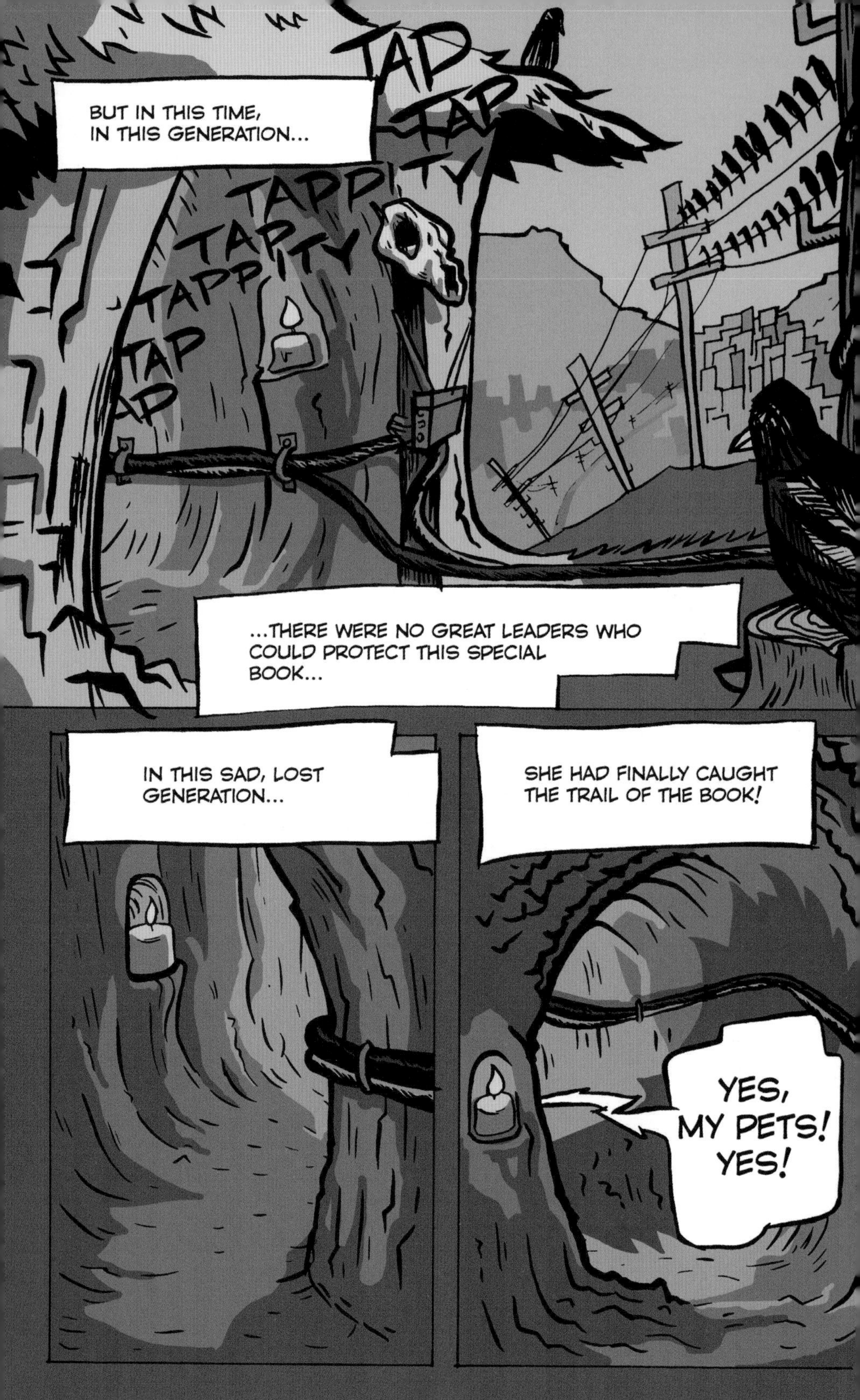
BUT IN THIS TIME, IN THIS GENERATION...
TAP TAP TAPPITY
TAPPITY TAP TAPPITY TAP TAP
...THERE WERE NO GREAT LEADERS WHO COULD PROTECT THIS SPECIAL BOOK...
IN THIS SAD, LOST GENERATION...
SHE HAD FINALLY CAUGHT THE TRAIL OF THE BOOK!
YES, MY PETS! YES!

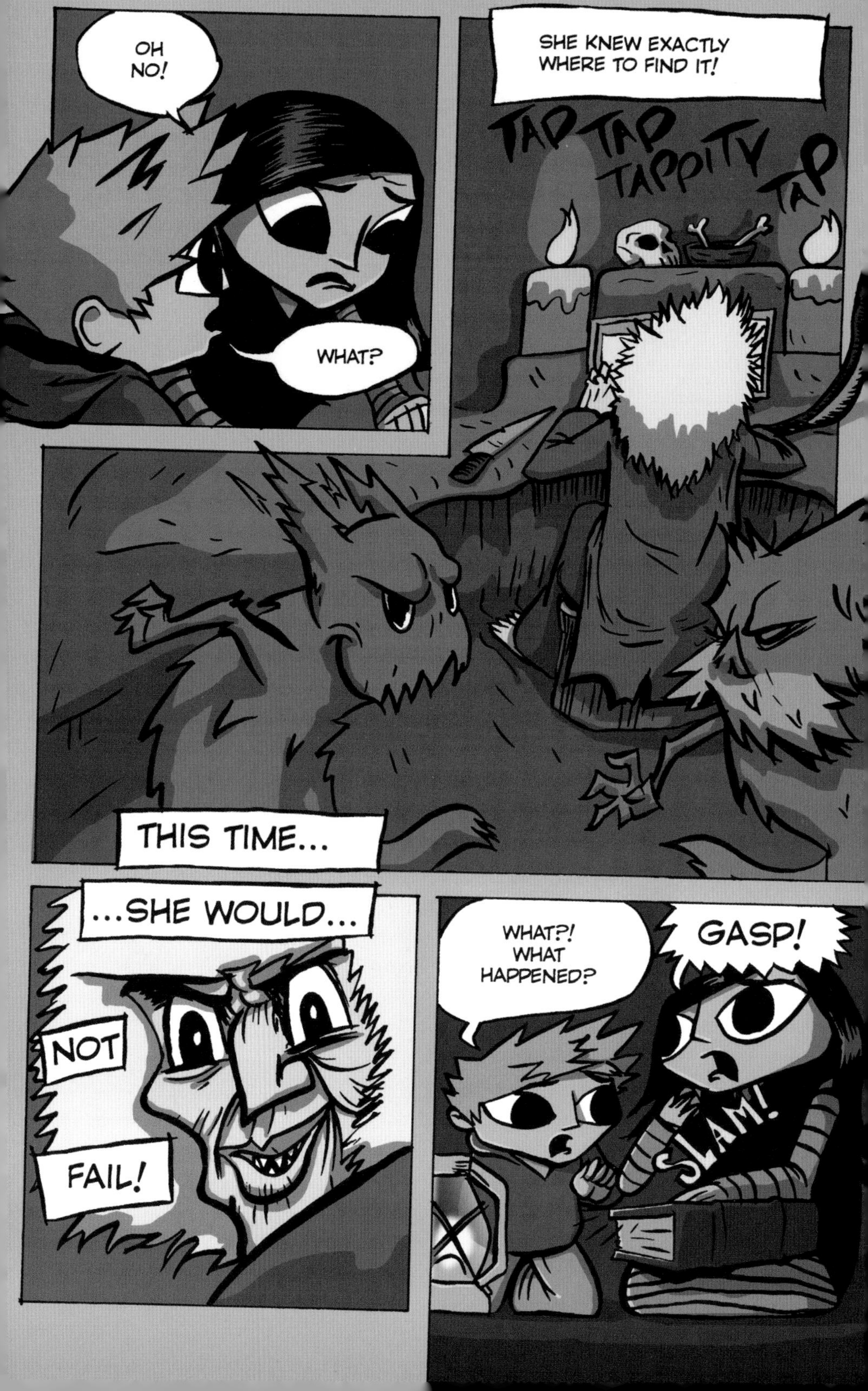
OH NO!
WHAT?
SHE KNEW EXACTLY WHERE TO FIND IT!
TAP TAP TAPPITY TAP
THIS TIME...
...SHE WOULD...
NOT
FAIL!
WHAT?! WHAT HAPPENED?
GASP!
SLAM!

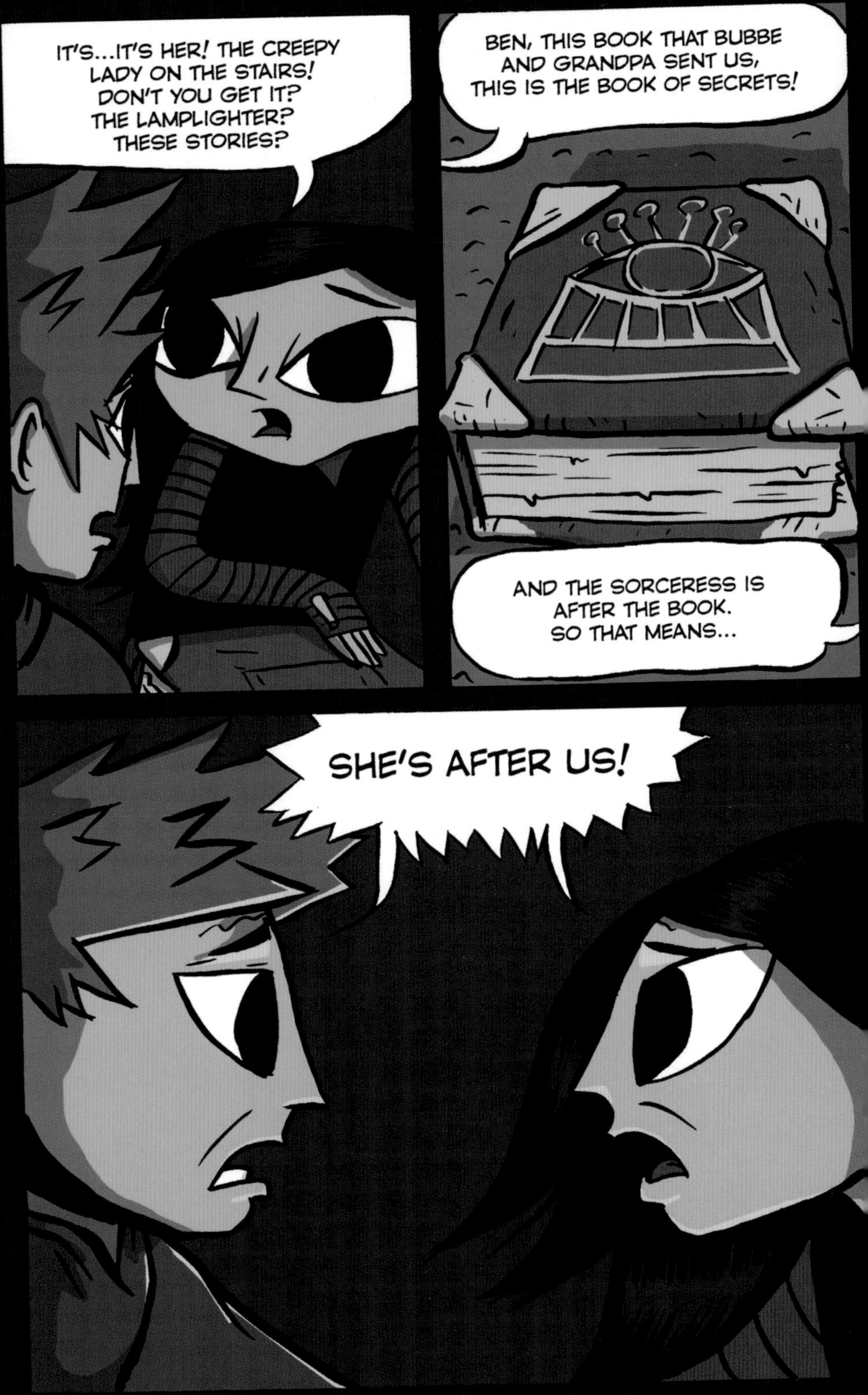
IT'S...IT'S HER! THE CREEPY LADY ON THE STAIRS! DON'T YOU GET IT? THE LAMPLIGHTER? THESE STORIES?
BEN, THIS BOOK THAT BUBBE AND GRANDPA SENT US, THIS IS THE BOOK OF SECRETS!
AND THE SORCERESS IS AFTER THE BOOK. SO THAT MEANS...
SHE'S AFTER US!

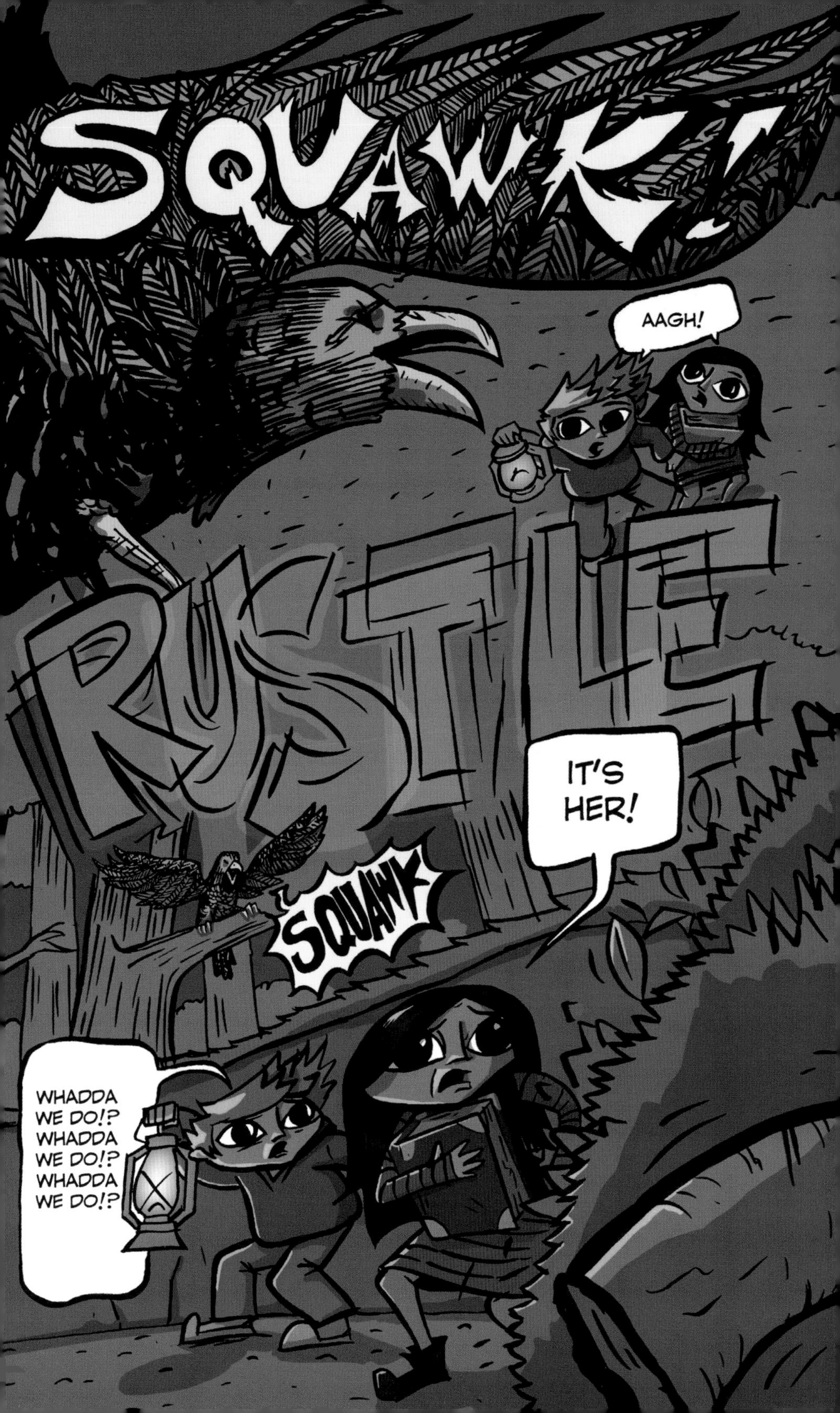
SQUAWK!
AAGH!
RUSTLE
IT'S HER!
SQUAWK
WHADDA WE DO!? WHADDA WE DO!? WHADDA WE DO!?

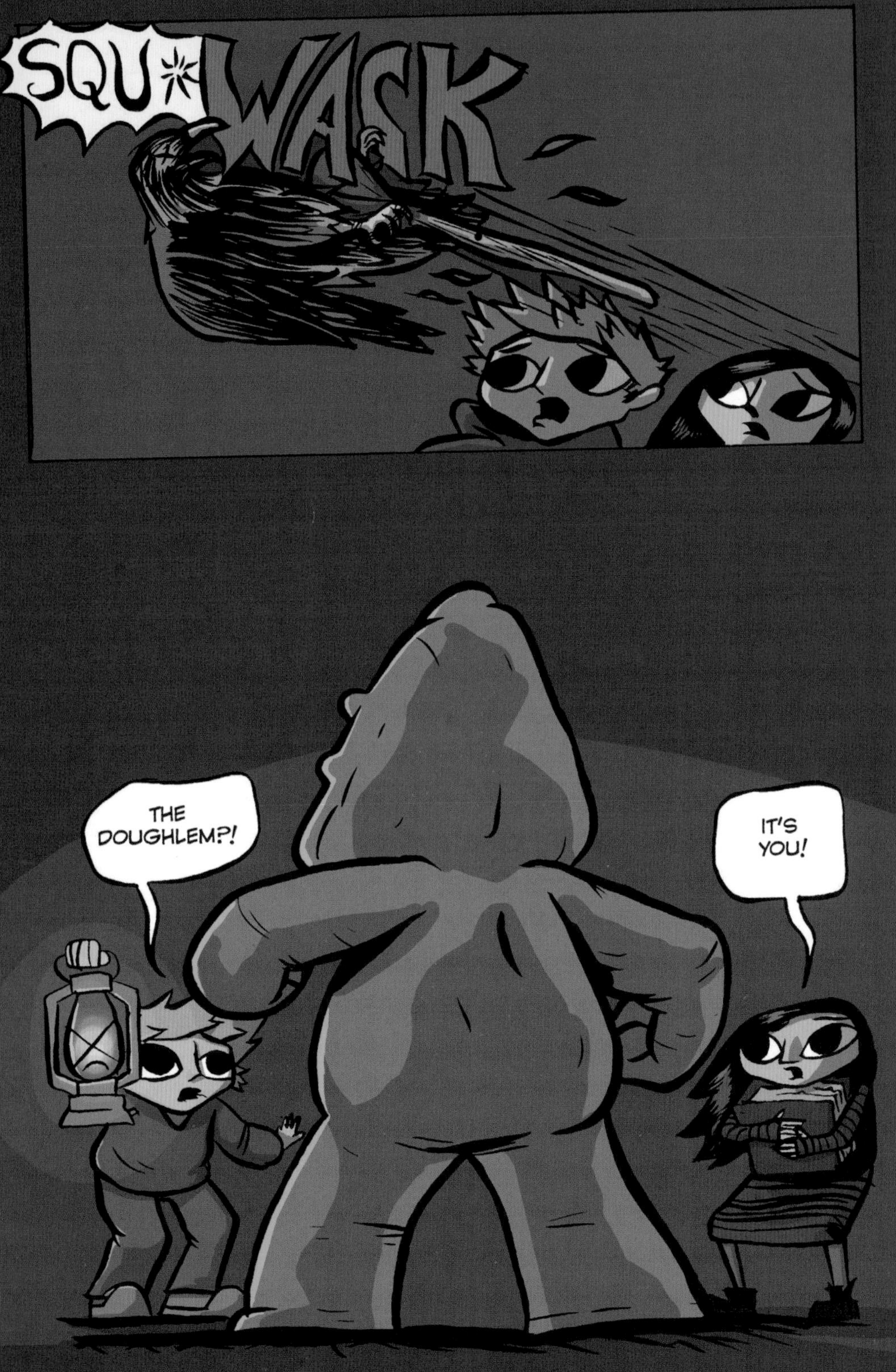
SQU*WACK
THE DOUGHLEM?!
IT'S YOU!

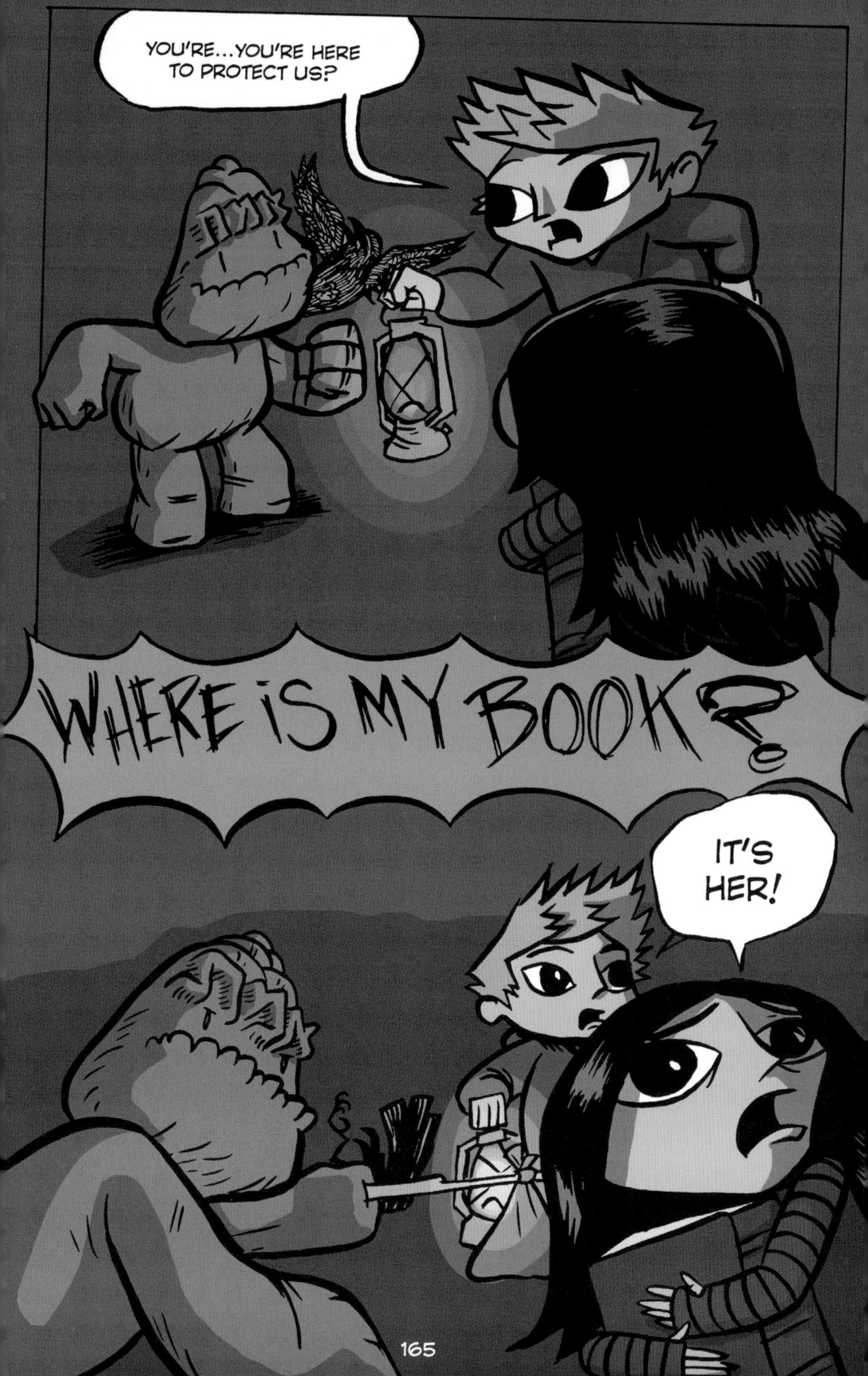
YOU'RE...YOU'RE HERE TO PROTECT US?
WHERE IS MY BOOK?
IT'S HER!

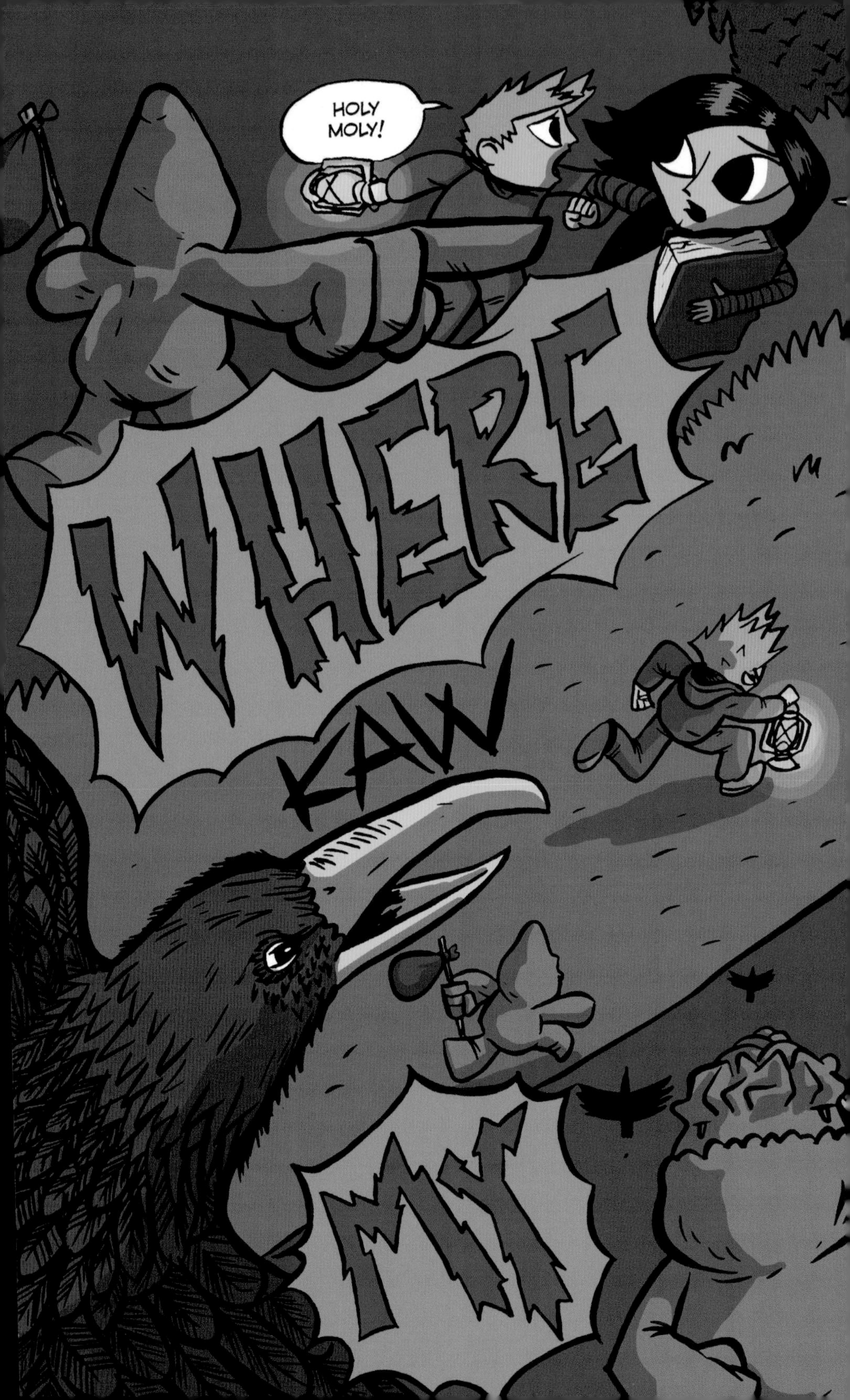
HOLY MOLY!
WHERE
KAW
MY

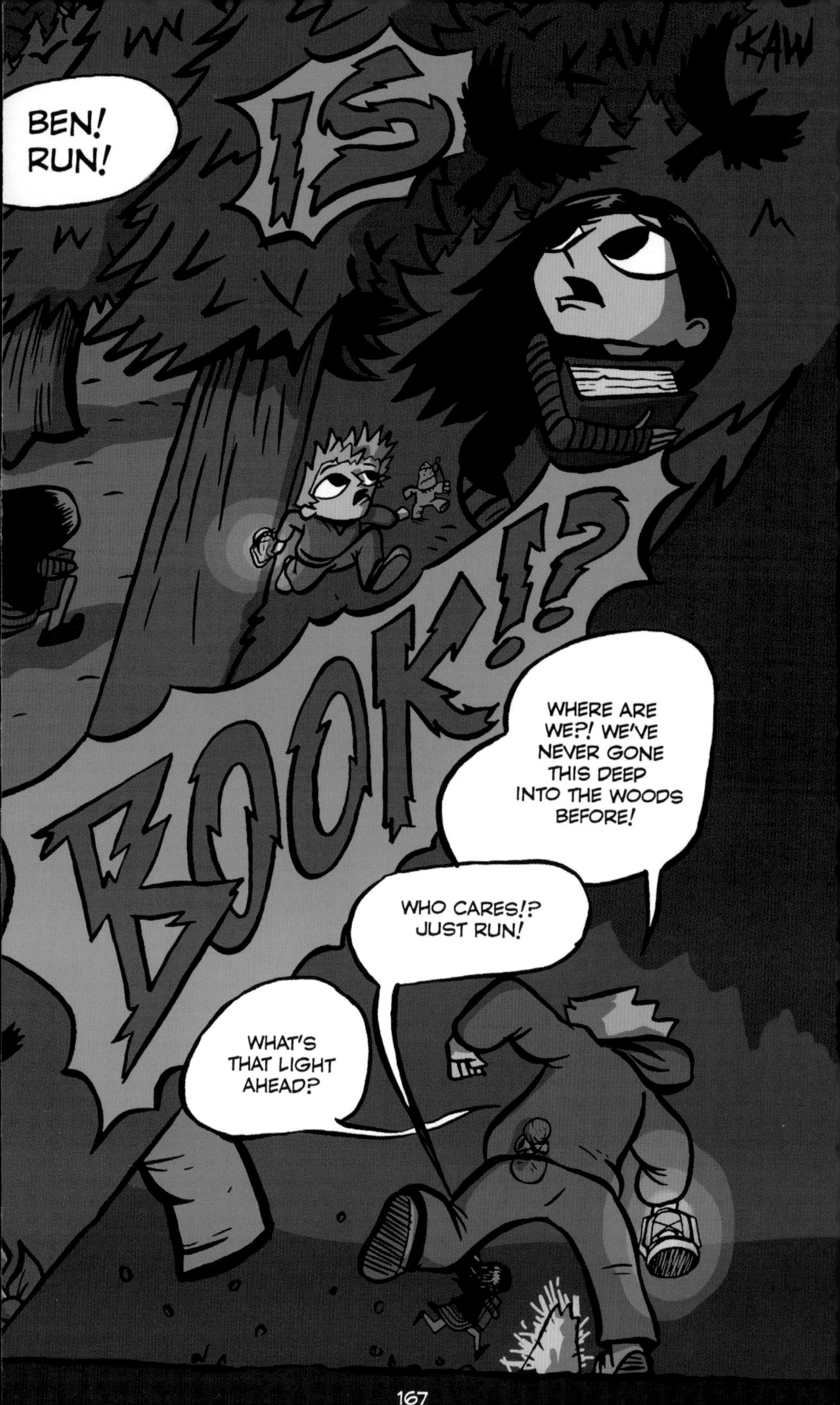

BEN! RUN!
KAW
KAW
IS
BOOK!?
WHERE ARE WE?! WE'VE NEVER GONE THIS DEEP INTO THE WOODS BEFORE!
WHO CARES!? JUST RUN!
WHAT'S THAT LIGHT AHEAD?

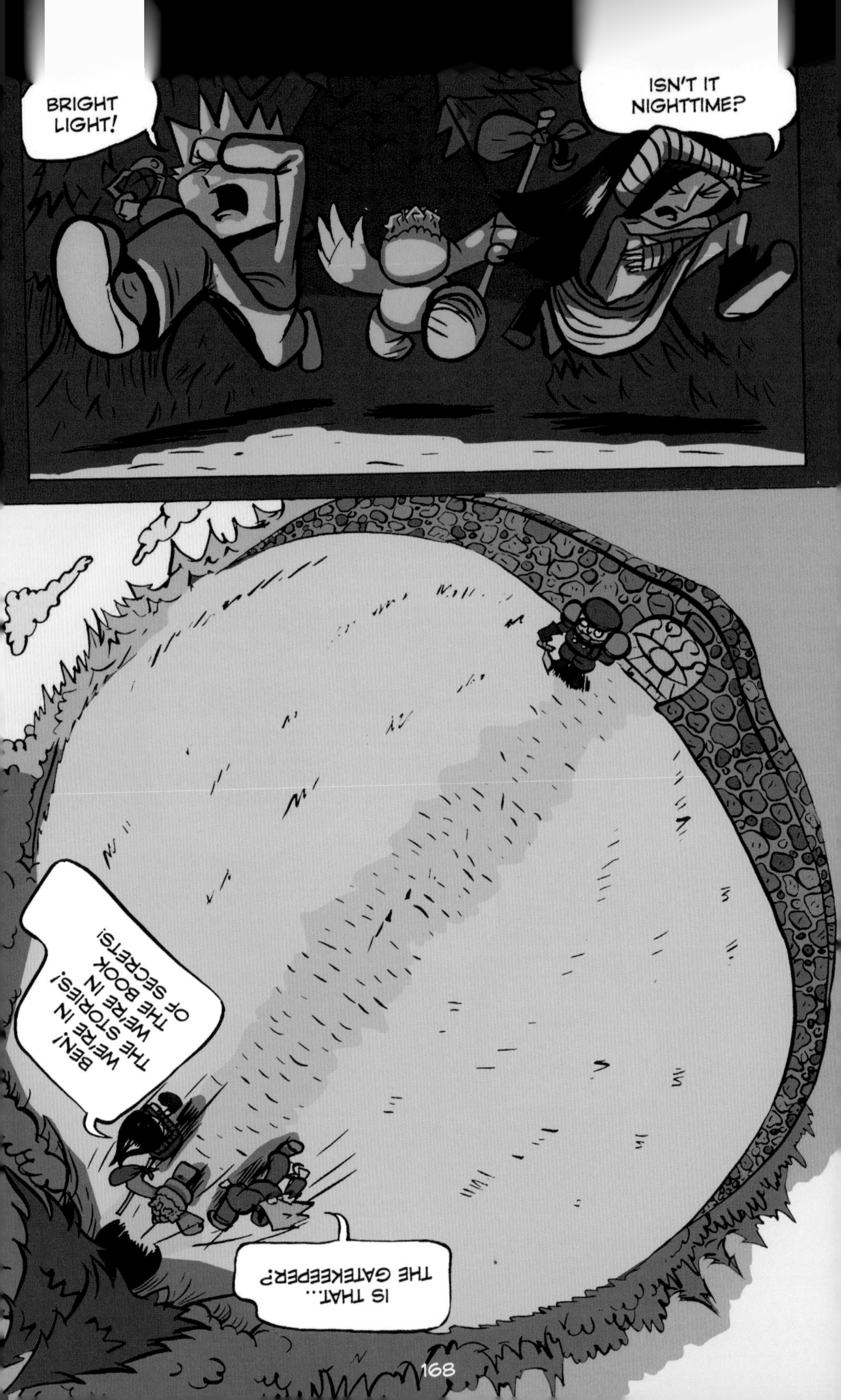
BRIGHT LIGHT!
ISN'T IT NIGHTTIME?
BEN! WE'RE IN THE STORIES! WE'RE IN THE BOOK OF SECRETS!
IS THAT... THE GATEKEEPER?

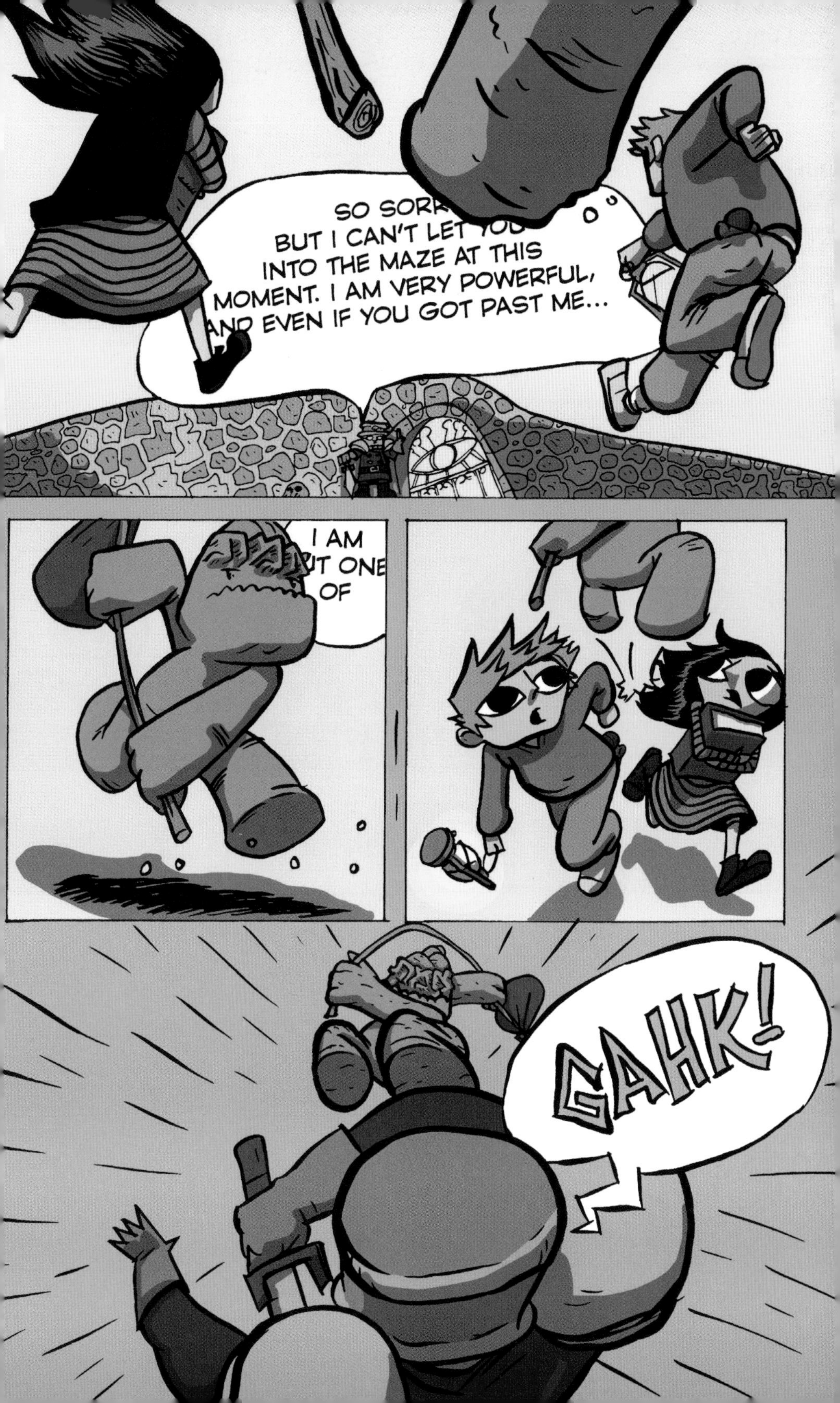
SO SORR
BUT I CAN'T LET YOU
INTO THE MAZE AT THIS
MOMENT. I AM VERY POWERFUL,
AND EVEN IF YOU GOT PAST ME...
I AM
UT ONE
OF
GAHK!

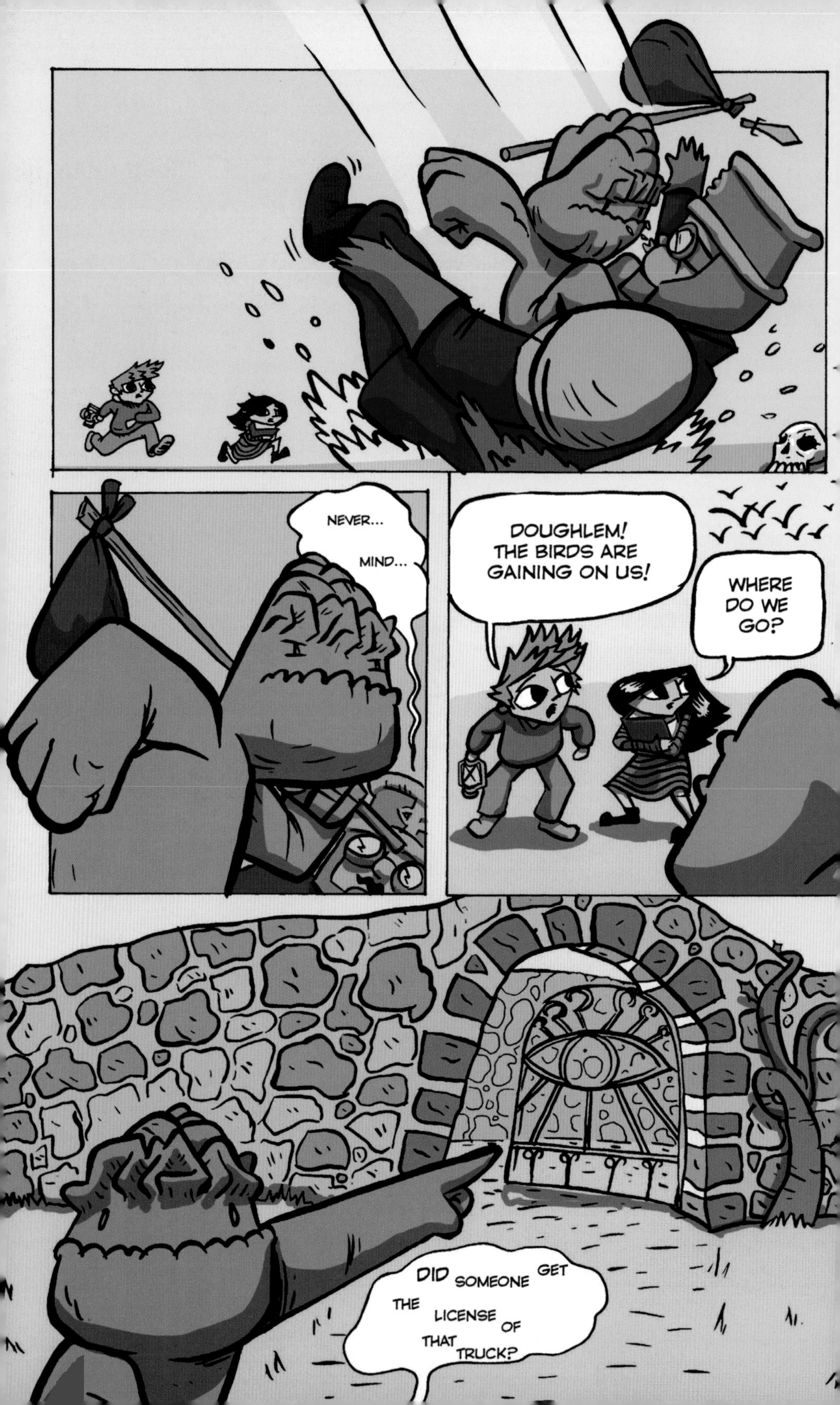
NEVER... MIND...
DOUGHLEM! THE BIRDS ARE GAINING ON US!
WHERE DO WE GO?
DID SOMEONE GET THE LICENSE OF THAT TRUCK?

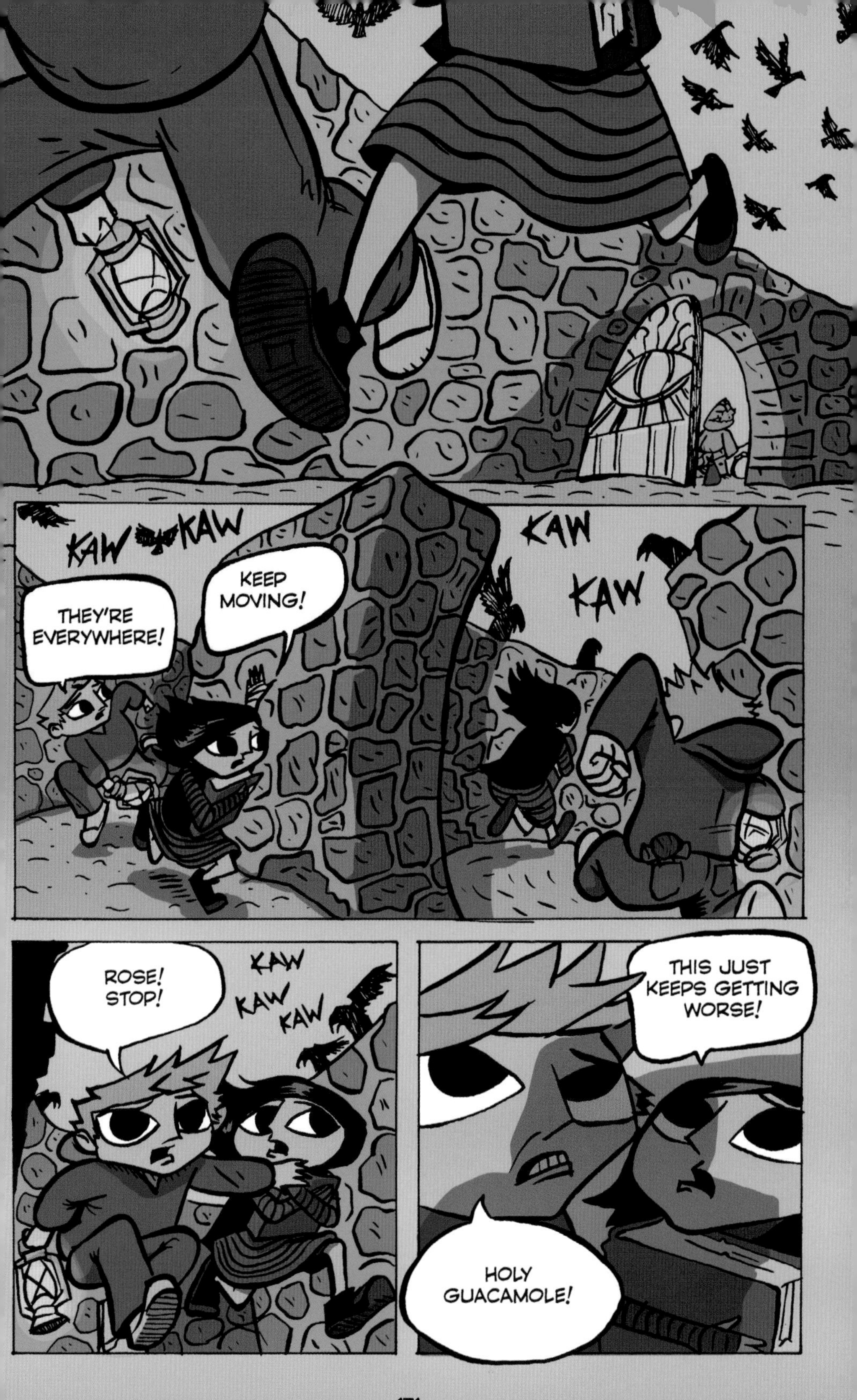
KAW KAW
THEY'RE EVERYWHERE!
KEEP MOVING!
KAW
KAW
ROSE! STOP!
KAW
KAW
KAW
THIS JUST KEEPS GETTING WORSE!
HOLY GUACAMOLE!

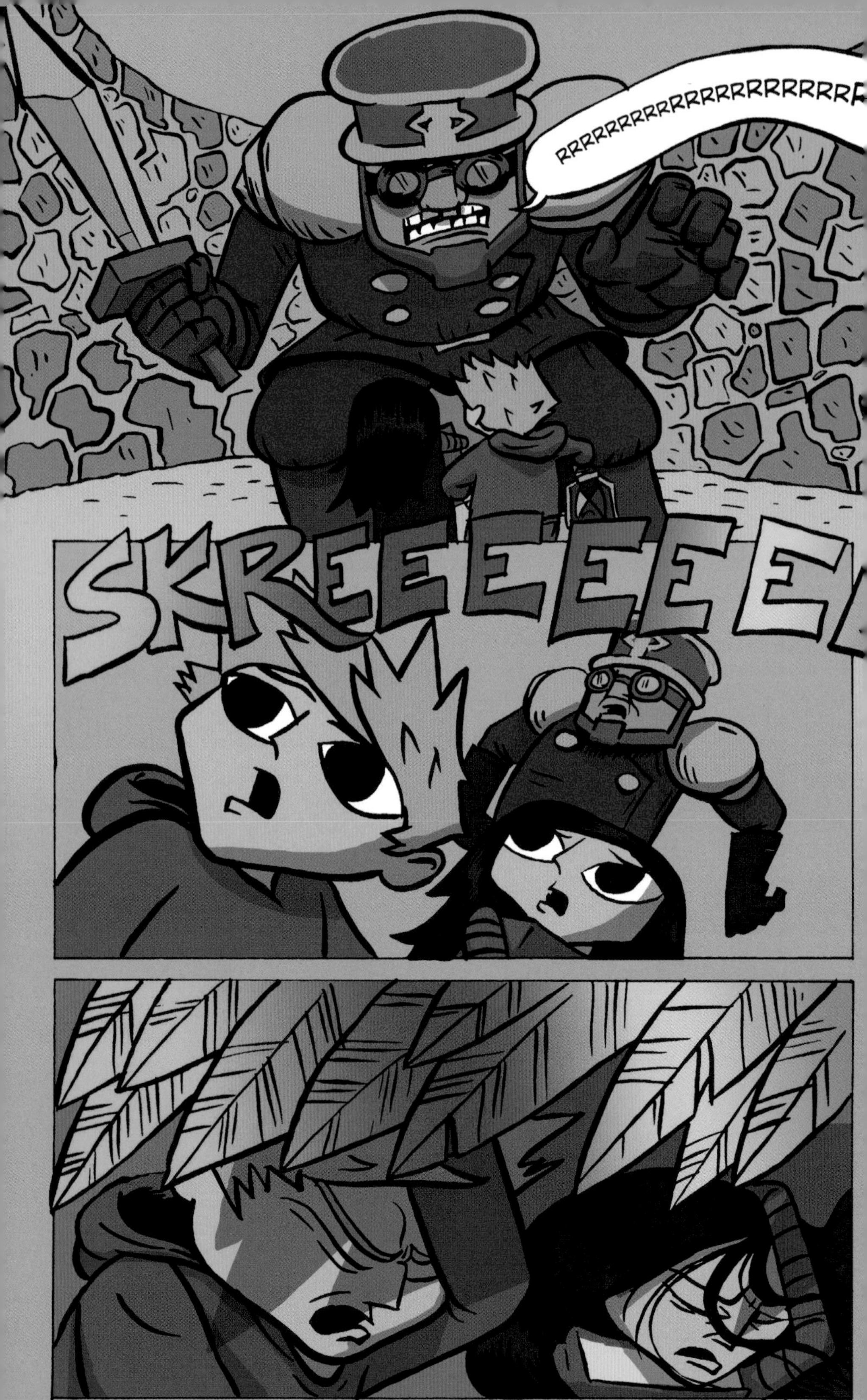
RRRRRRRRRRRRRRRRRRRRRRRRRR
SKREEEEEE

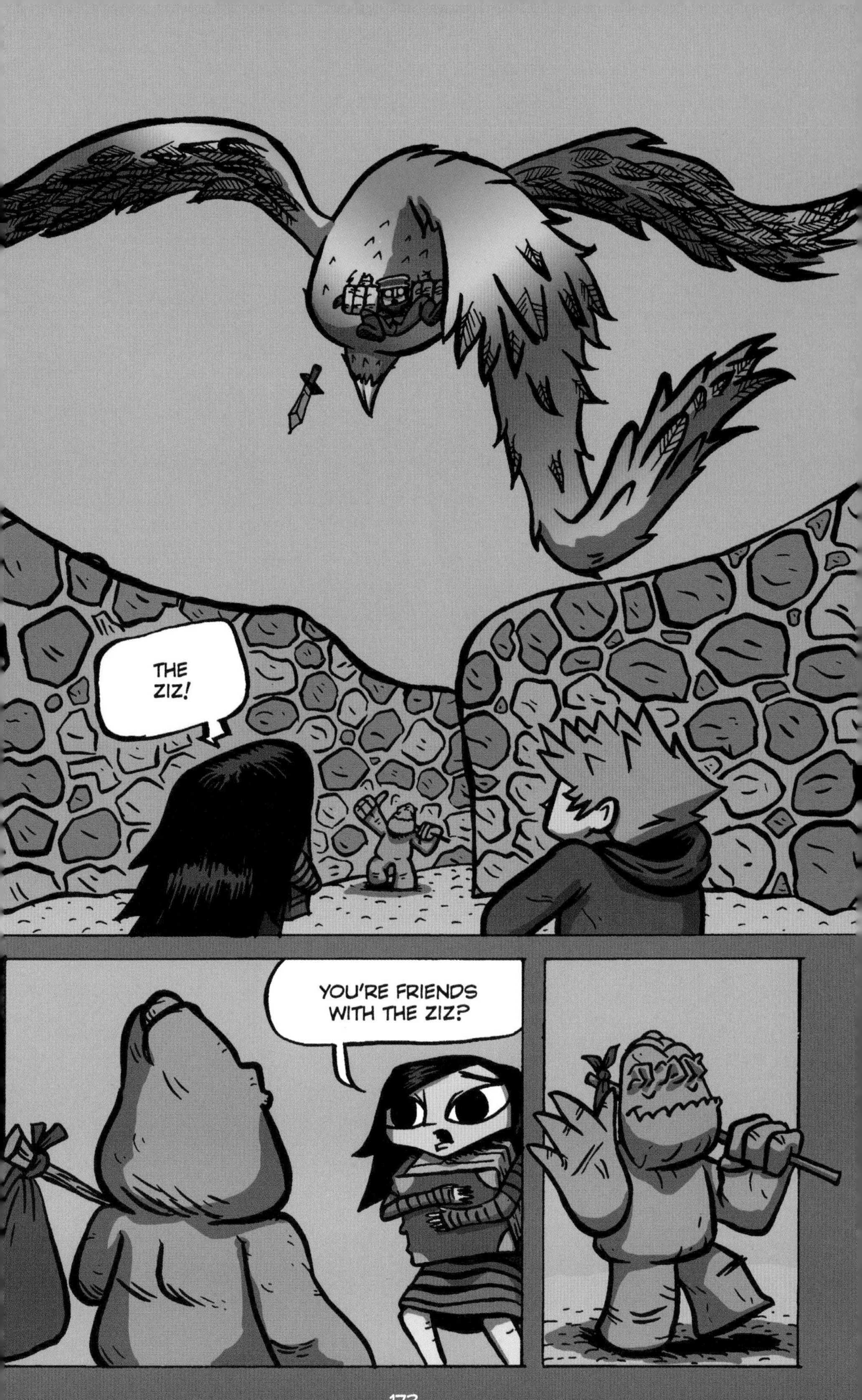
THE ZIZ!
YOU'RE FRIENDS WITH THE ZIZ?

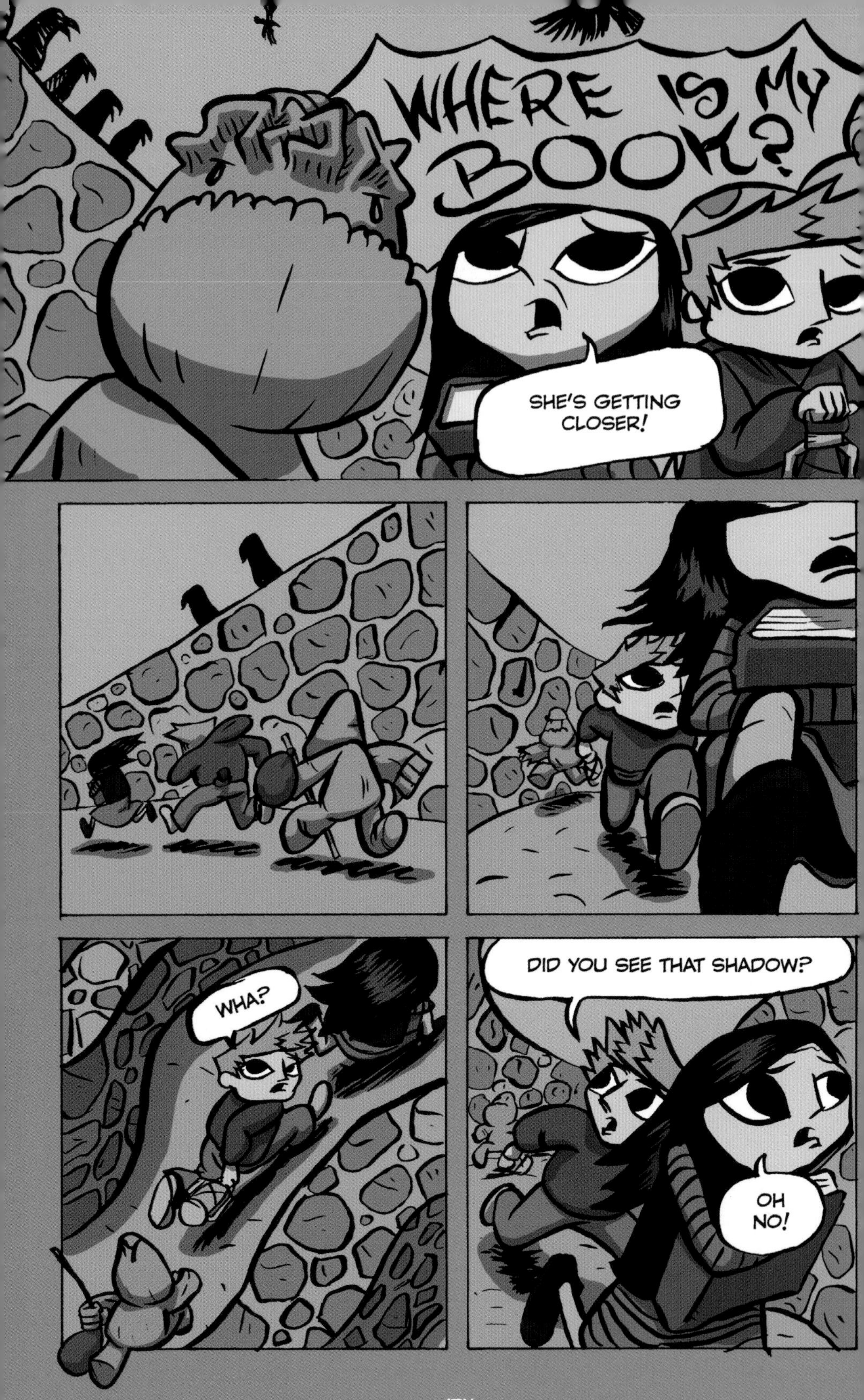
WHERE IS MY BOOK?
SHE'S GETTING CLOSER!
WHA?
DID YOU SEE THAT SHADOW?
OH NO!

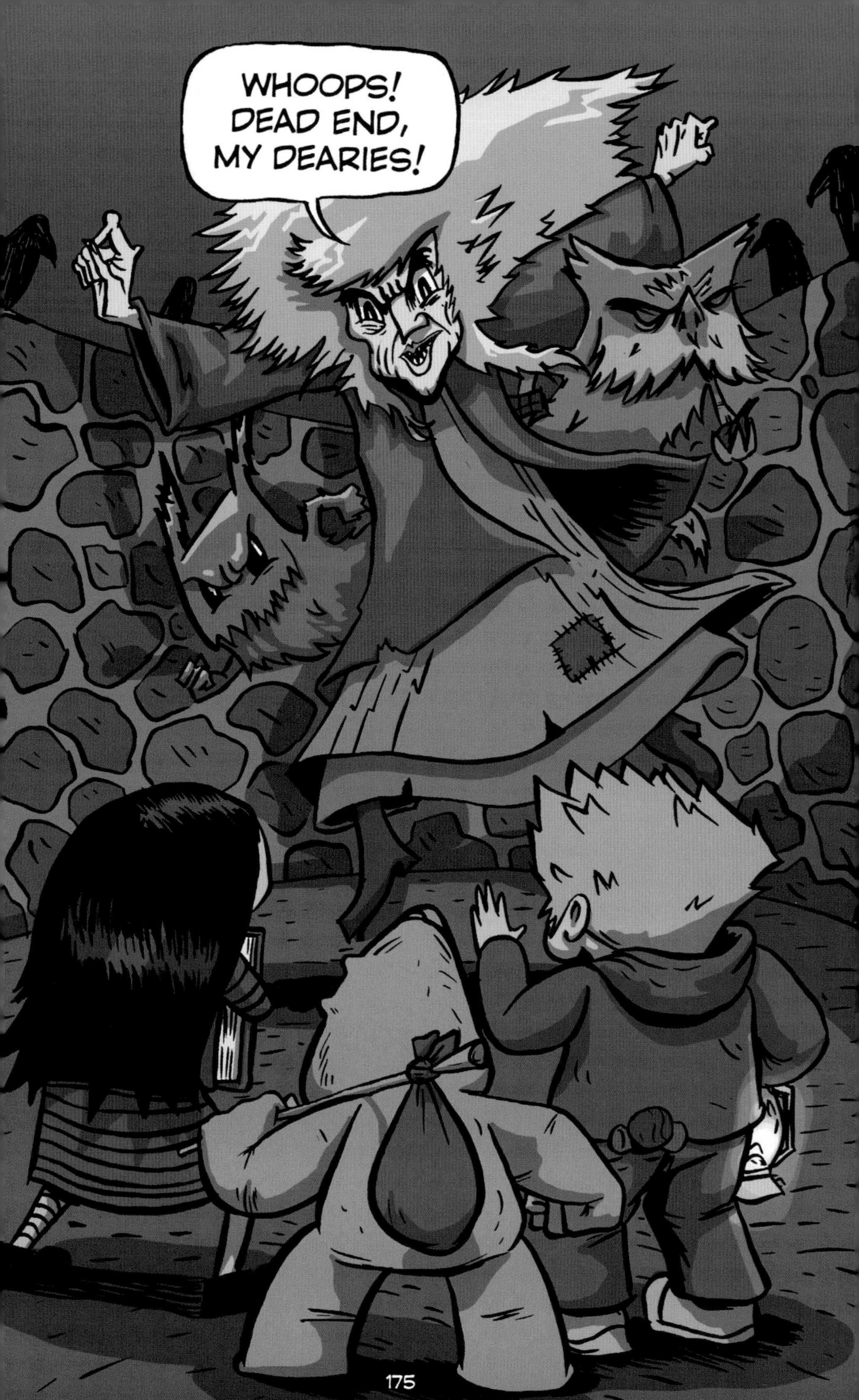
WHOOPS! DEAD END, MY DEARIES!

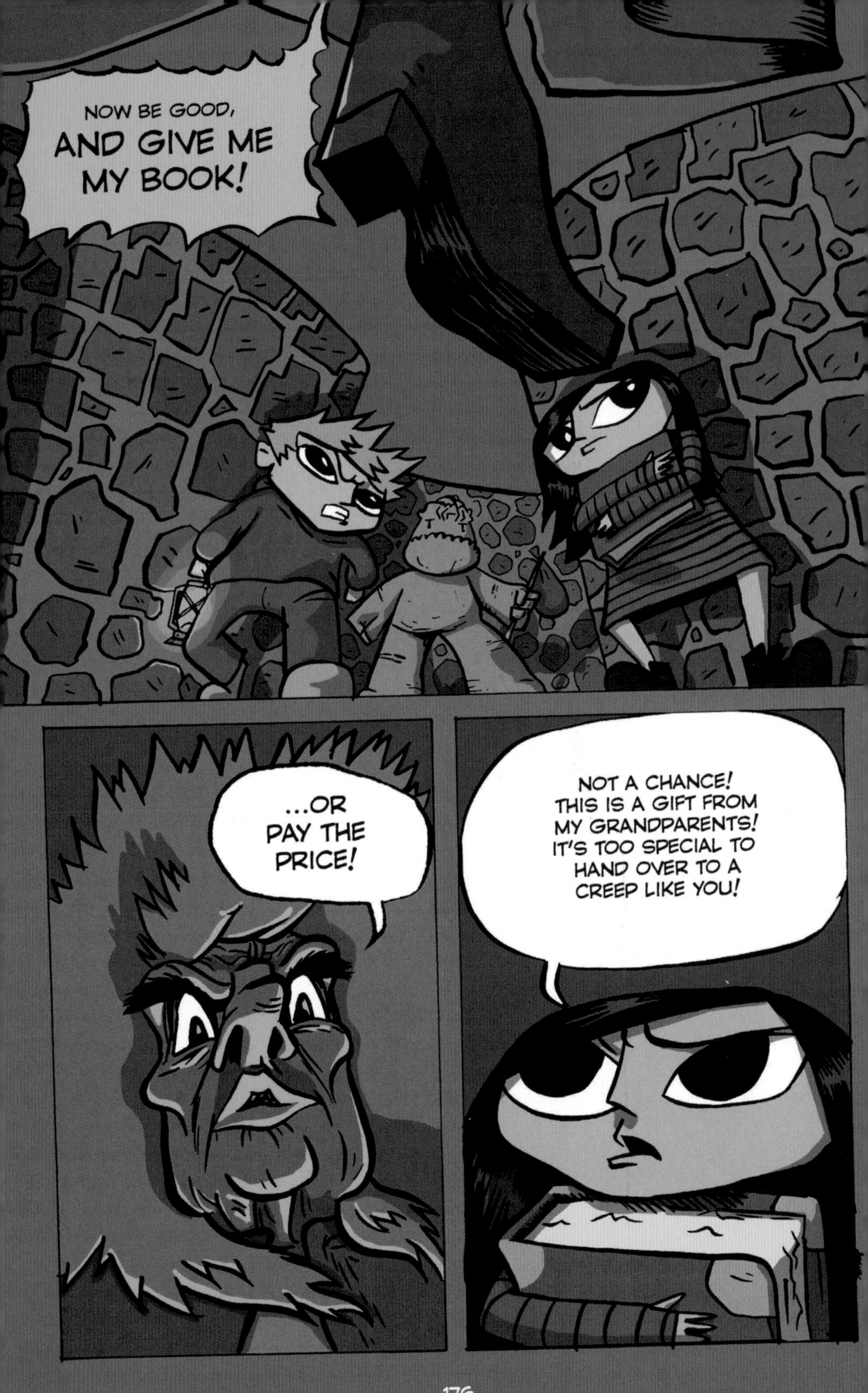
NOW BE GOOD, AND GIVE ME MY BOOK!
...OR PAY THE PRICE!
NOT A CHANCE! THIS IS A GIFT FROM MY GRANDPARENTS! IT'S TOO SPECIAL TO HAND OVER TO A CREEP LIKE YOU!

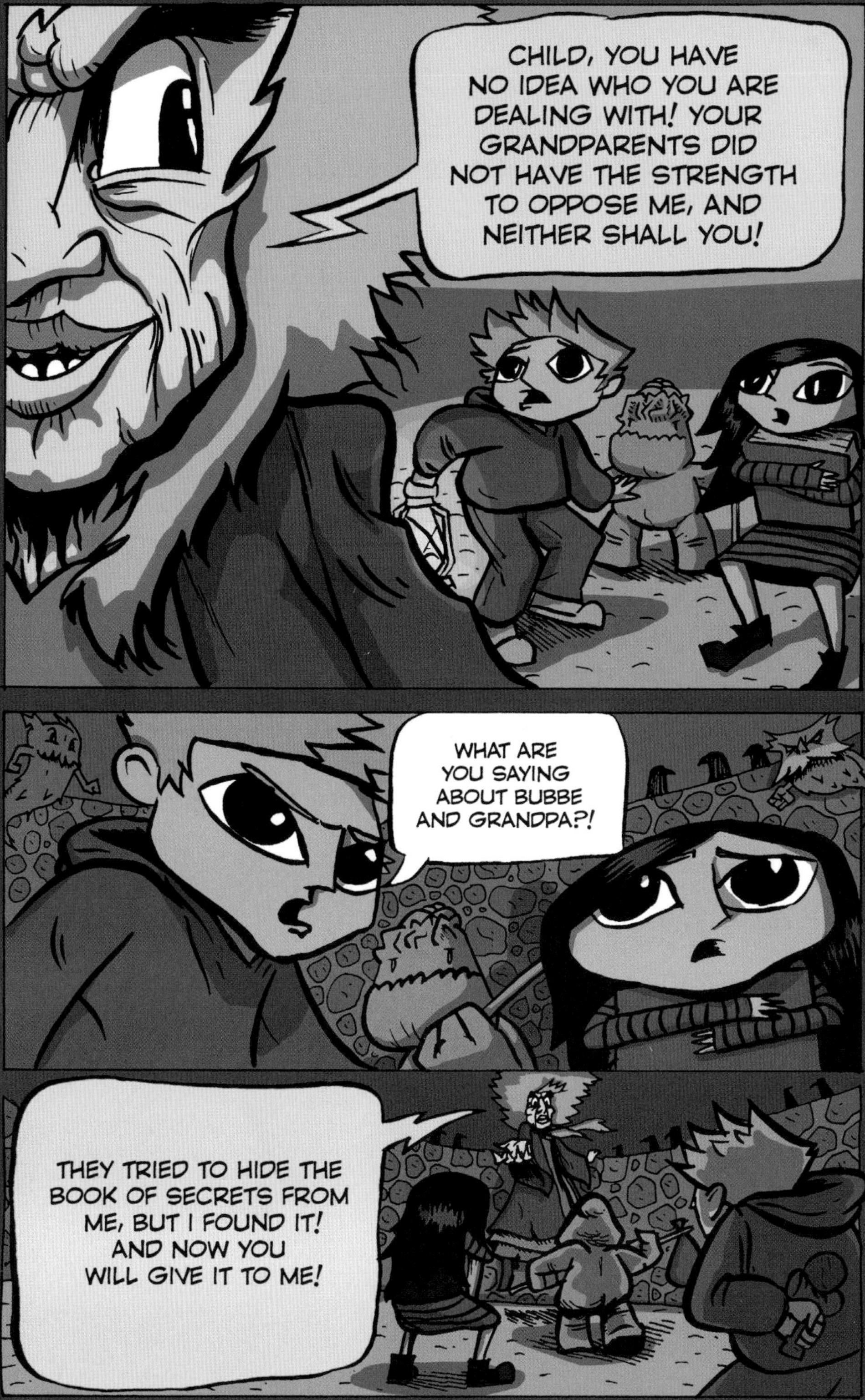
CHILD, YOU HAVE NO IDEA WHO YOU ARE DEALING WITH! YOUR GRANDPARENTS DID NOT HAVE THE STRENGTH TO OPPOSE ME, AND NEITHER SHALL YOU!
WHAT ARE YOU SAYING ABOUT BUBBE AND GRANDPA?!
THEY TRIED TO HIDE THE BOOK OF SECRETS FROM ME, BUT I FOUND IT! AND NOW YOU WILL GIVE IT TO ME!

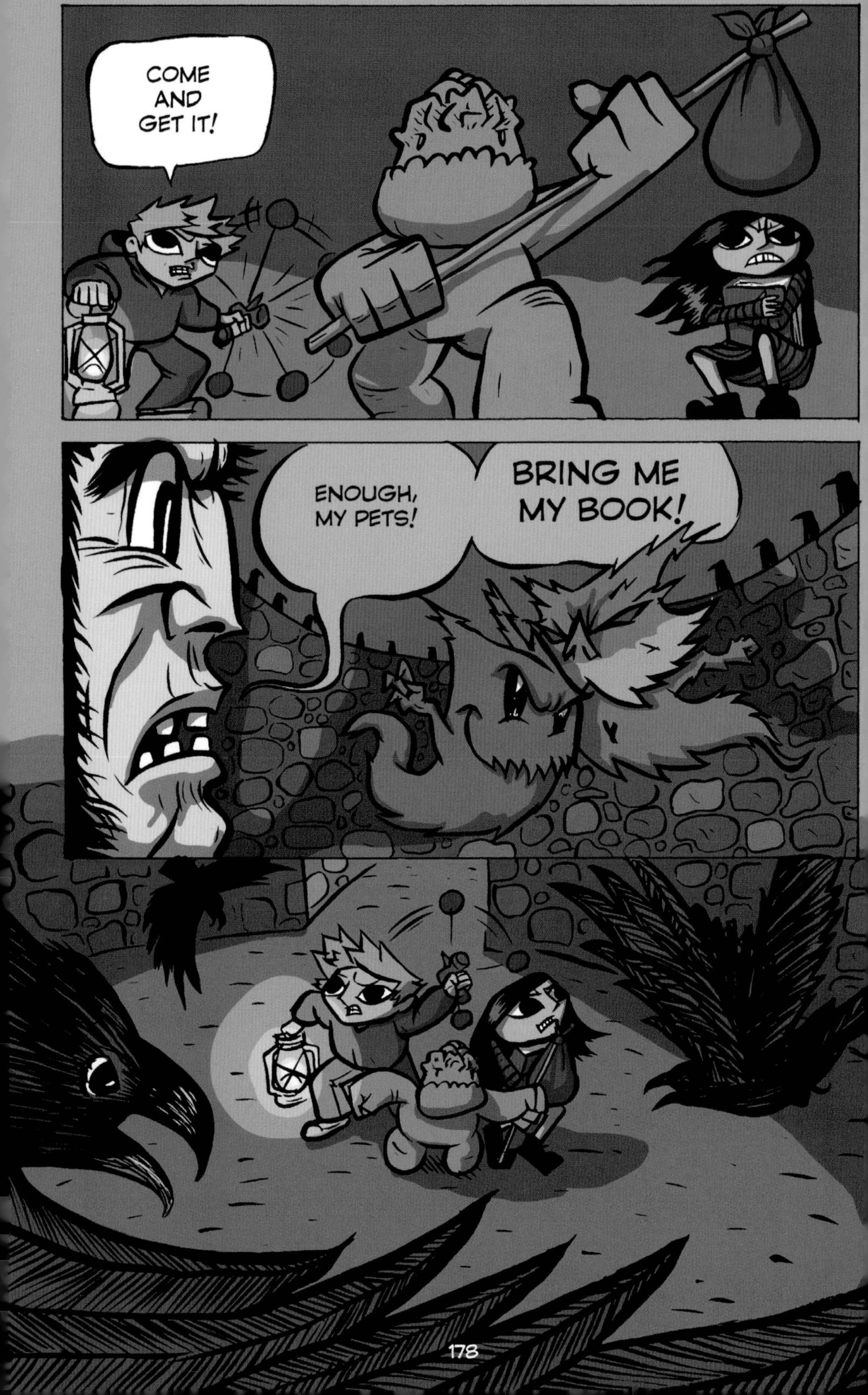
COME AND GET IT!
ENOUGH, MY PETS!
BRING ME MY BOOK!

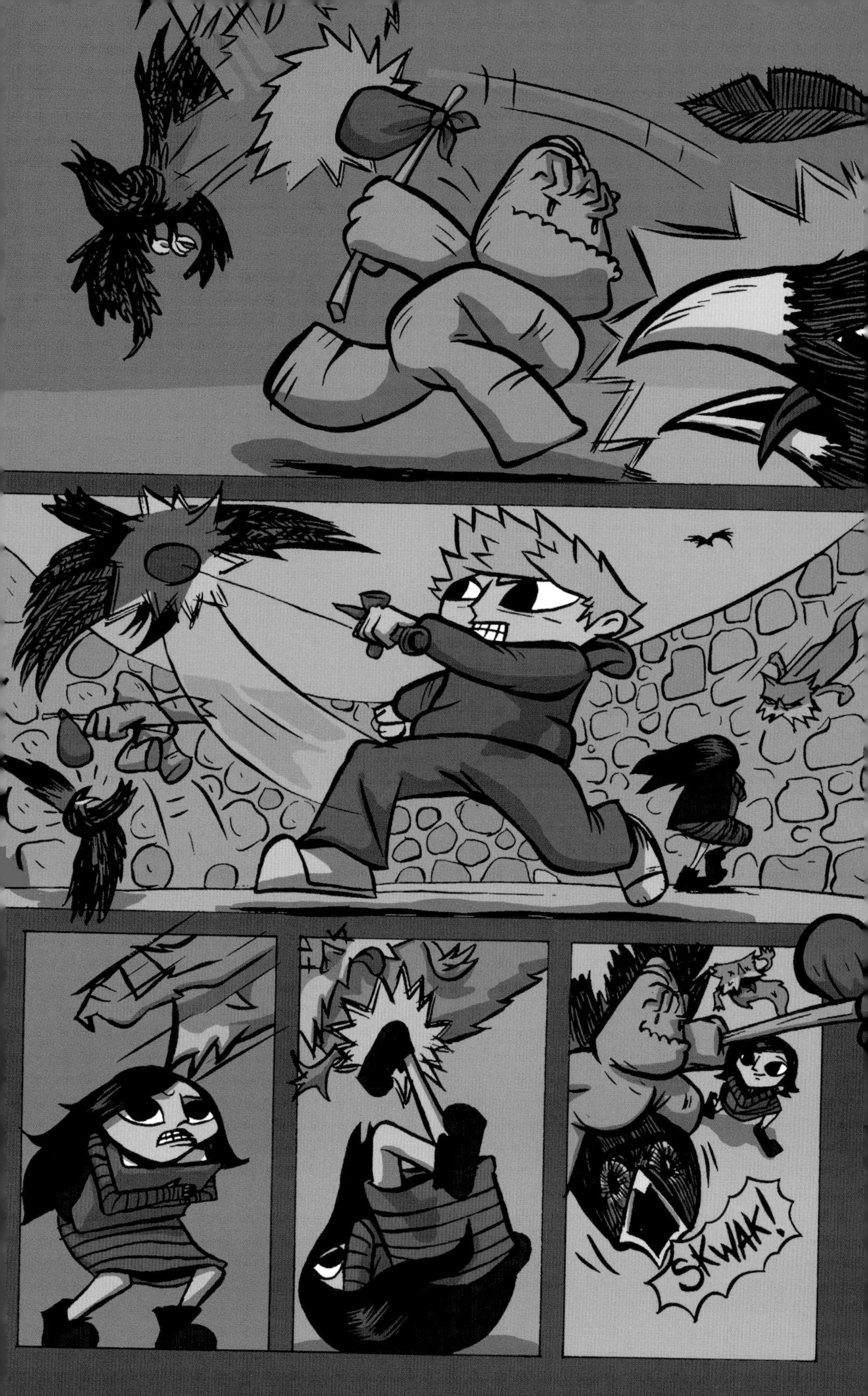
SKWAK!

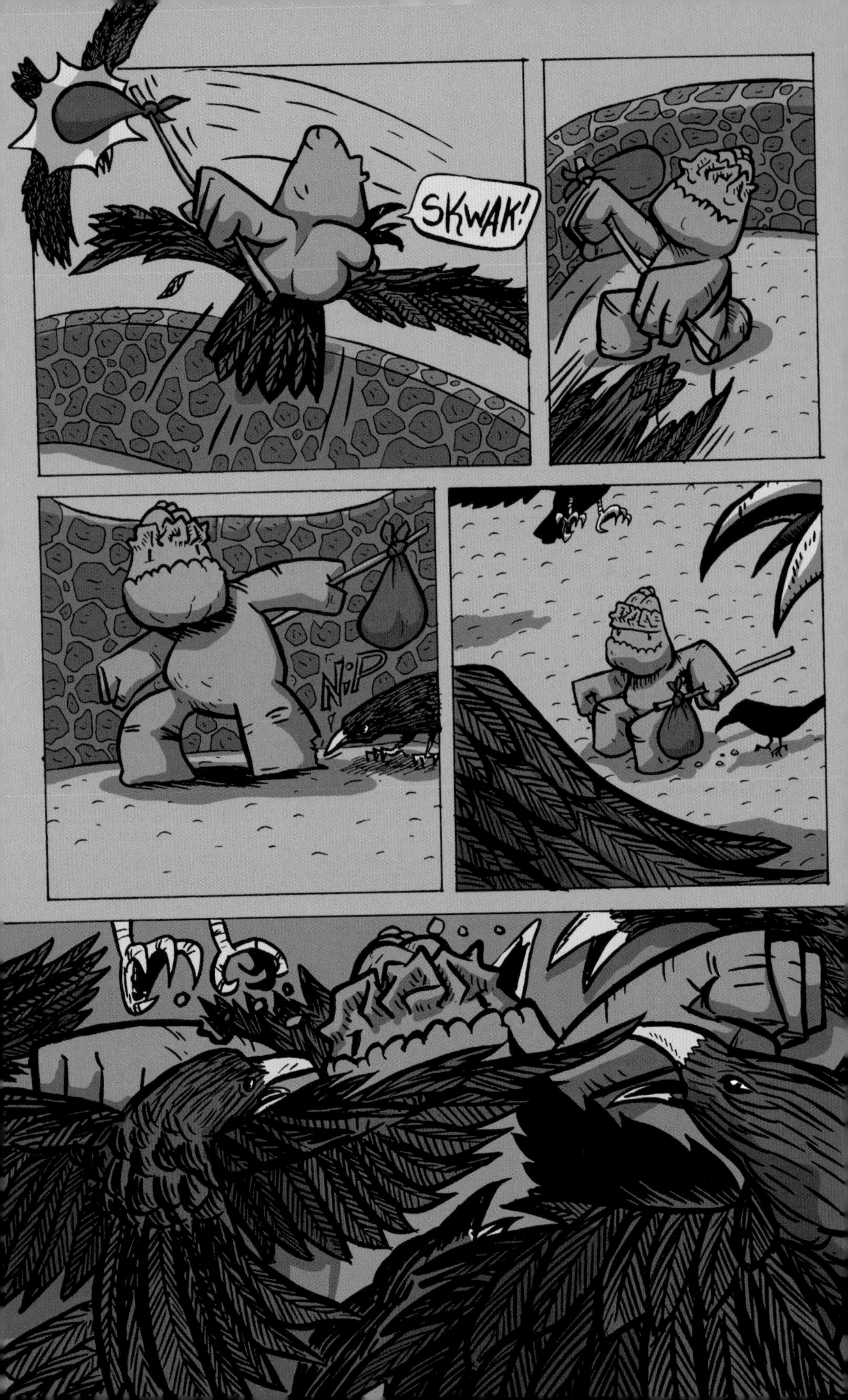
SKWAK!
NIP

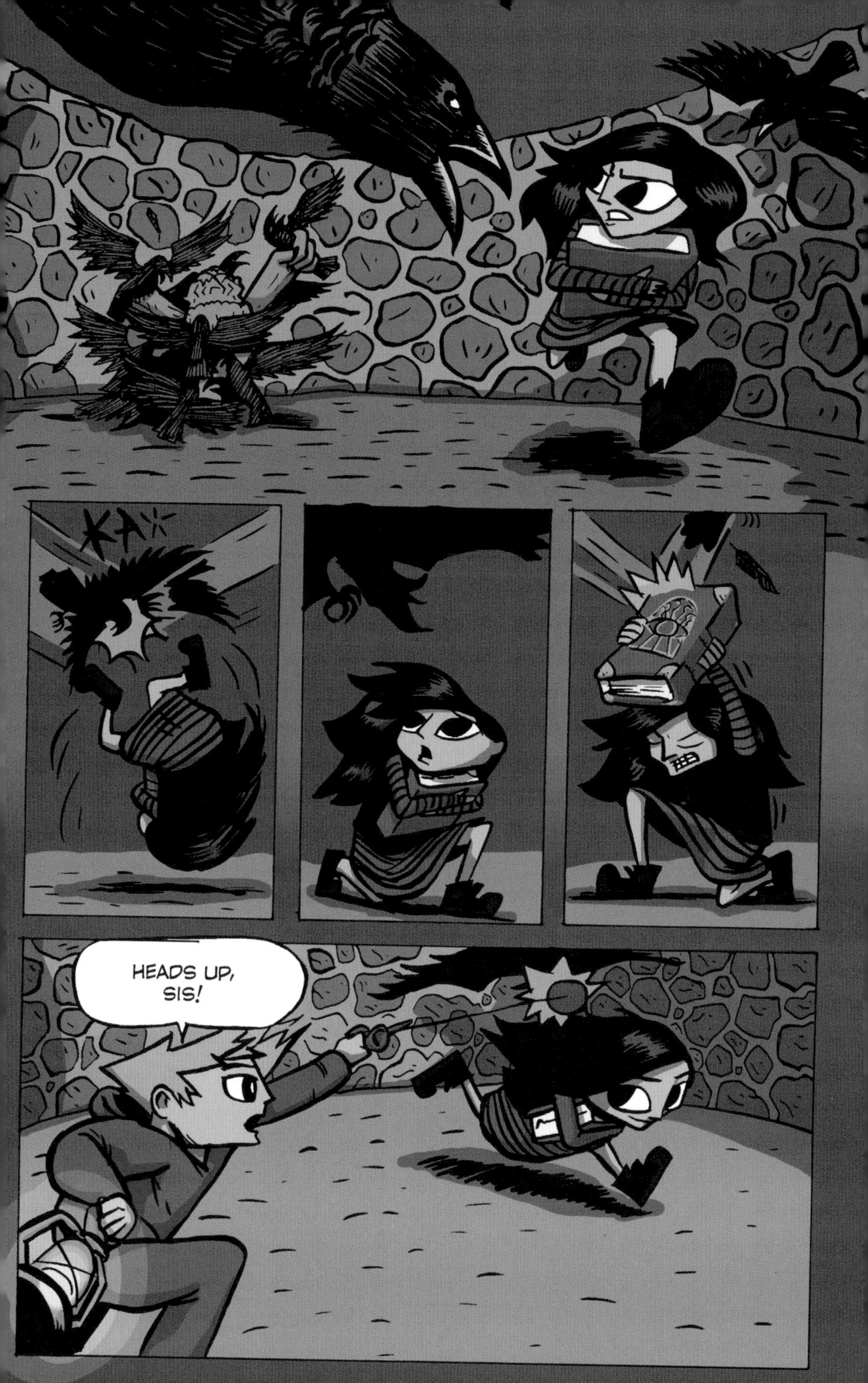
KA
HEADS UP, SIS!

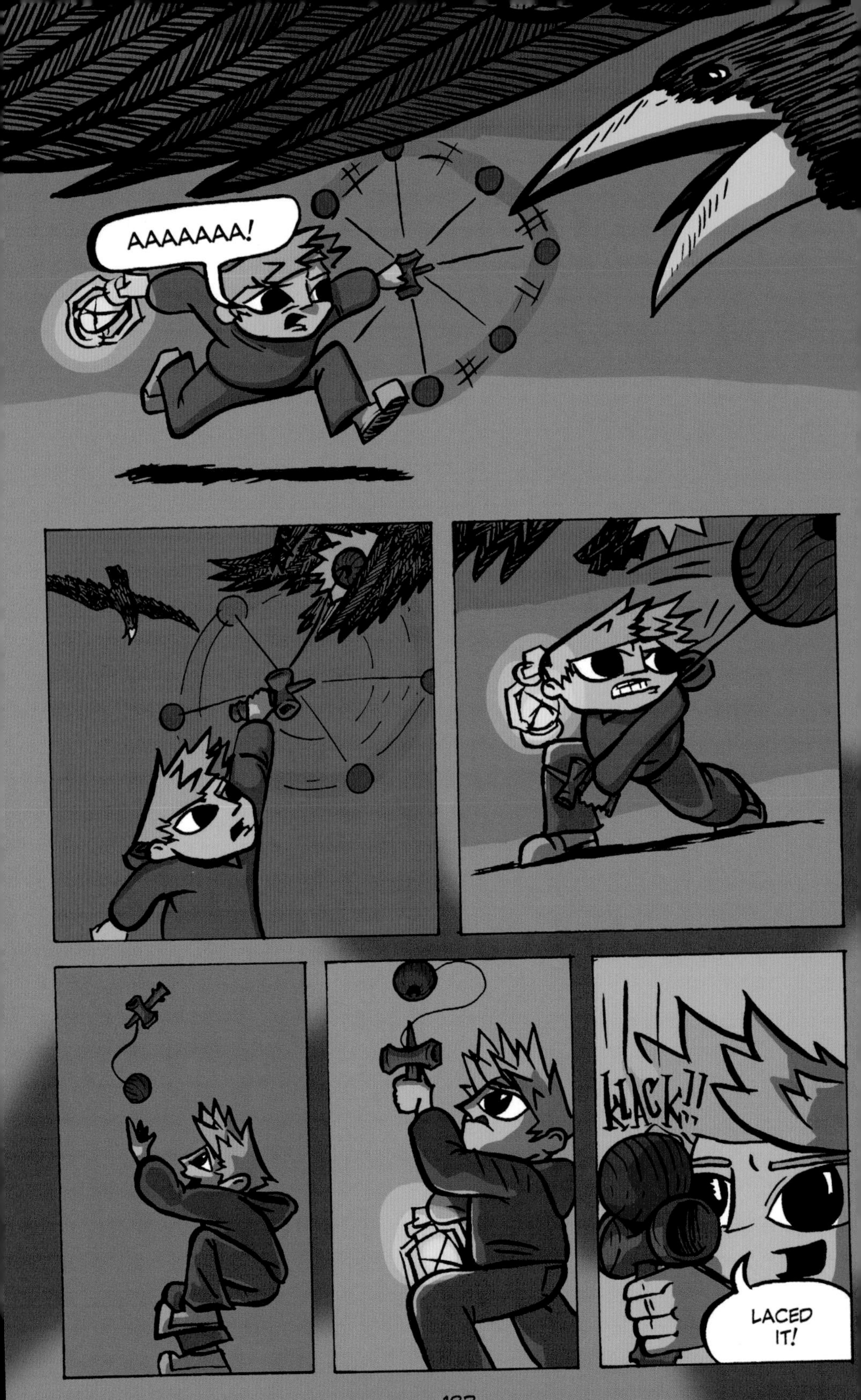
AAAAAAA!
KLACK!!
LACED IT!

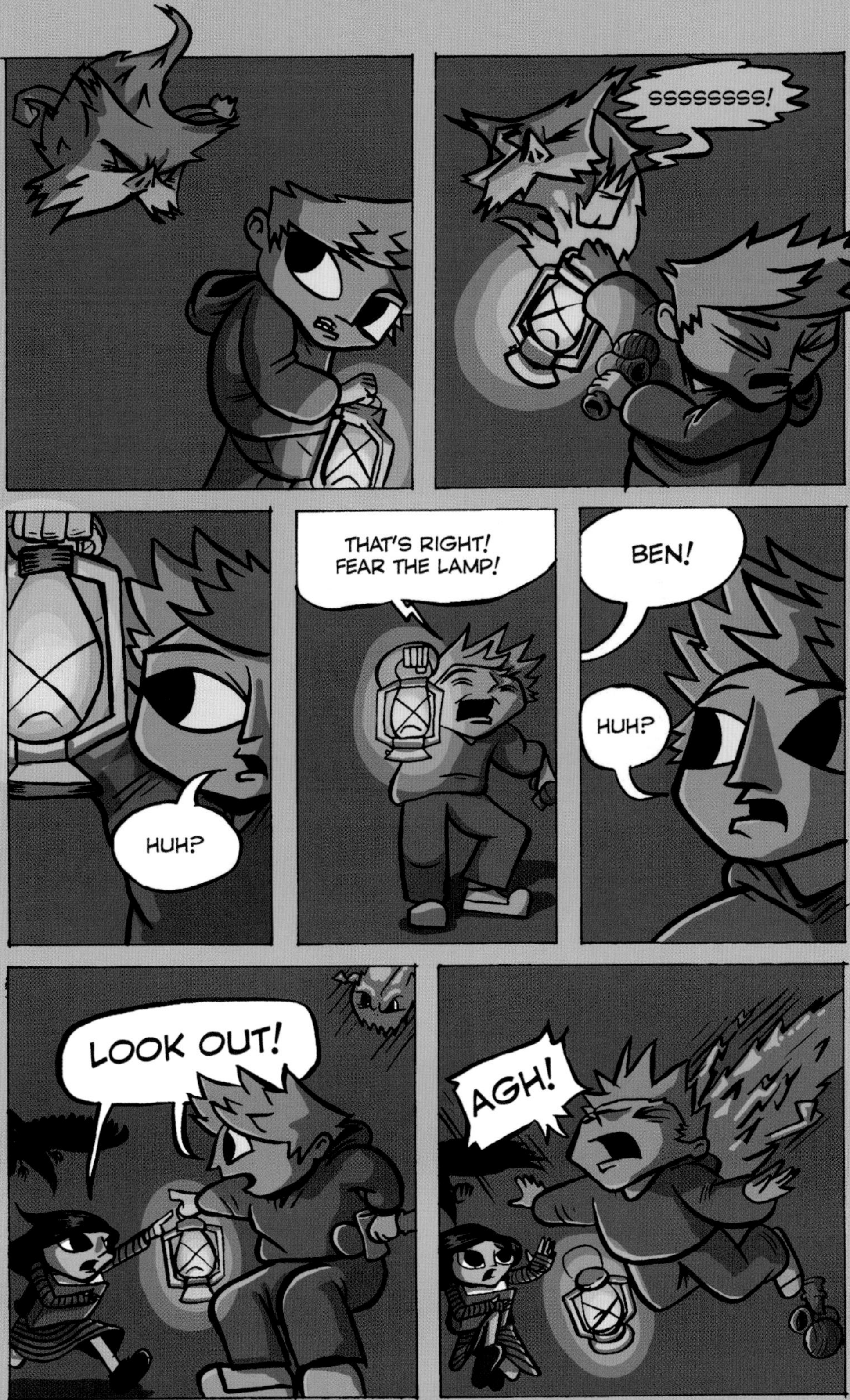
SSSSSSSS!
HUH?
THAT'S RIGHT! FEAR THE LAMP!
BEN!
HUH?
LOOK OUT!
AGH!

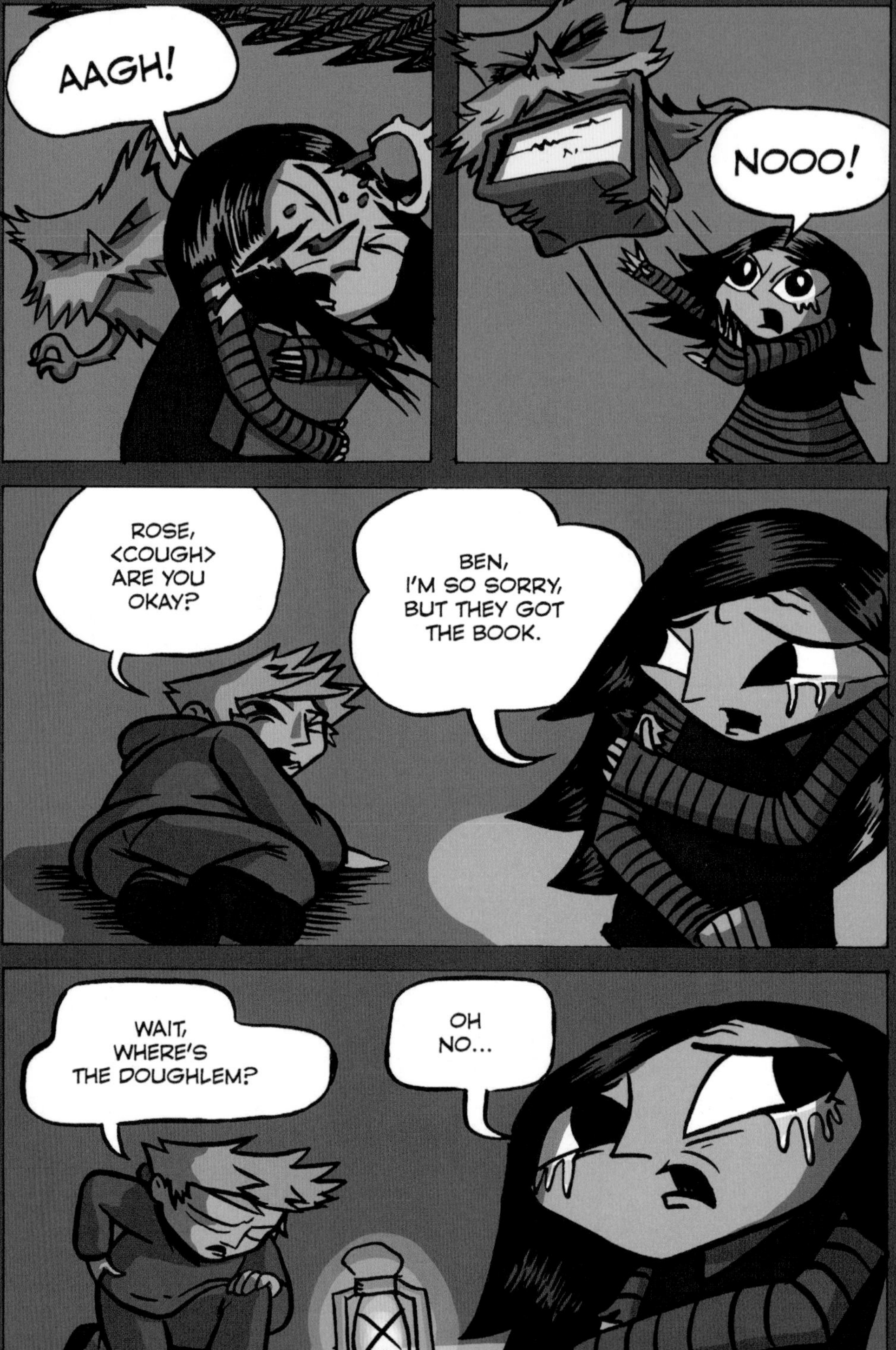
AAGH!
NOOO!
ROSE, <COUGH> ARE YOU OKAY?
BEN, I'M SO SORRY, BUT THEY GOT THE BOOK.
WAIT, WHERE'S THE DOUGHLEM?
OH NO...

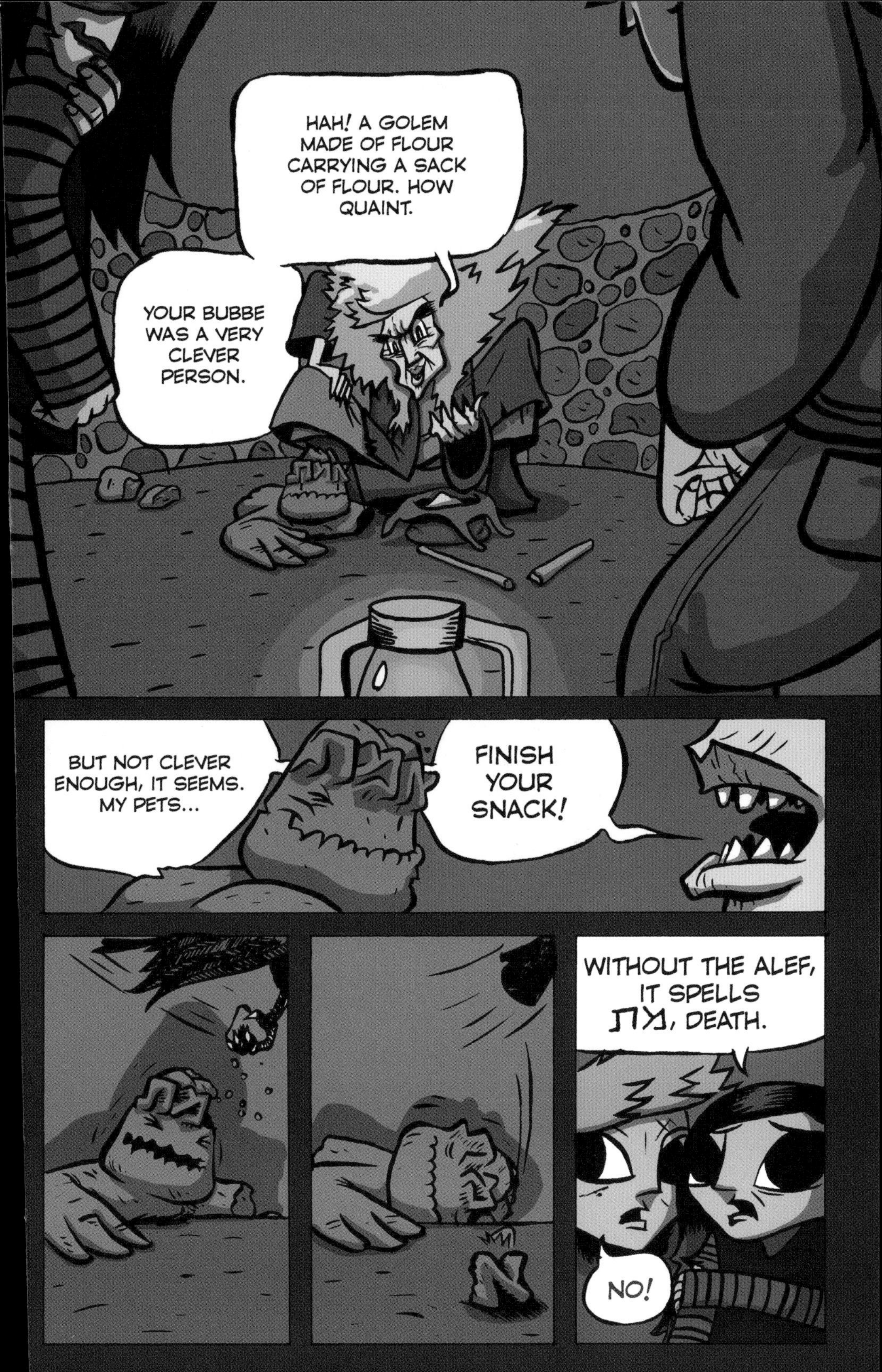
HAH! A GOLEM MADE OF FLOUR CARRYING A SACK OF FLOUR. HOW QUAINT.
YOUR BUBBE WAS A VERY CLEVER PERSON.
BUT NOT CLEVER ENOUGH, IT SEEMS. MY PETS...
FINISH YOUR SNACK!
WITHOUT THE ALEF, IT SPELLS מת, DEATH.
NO!

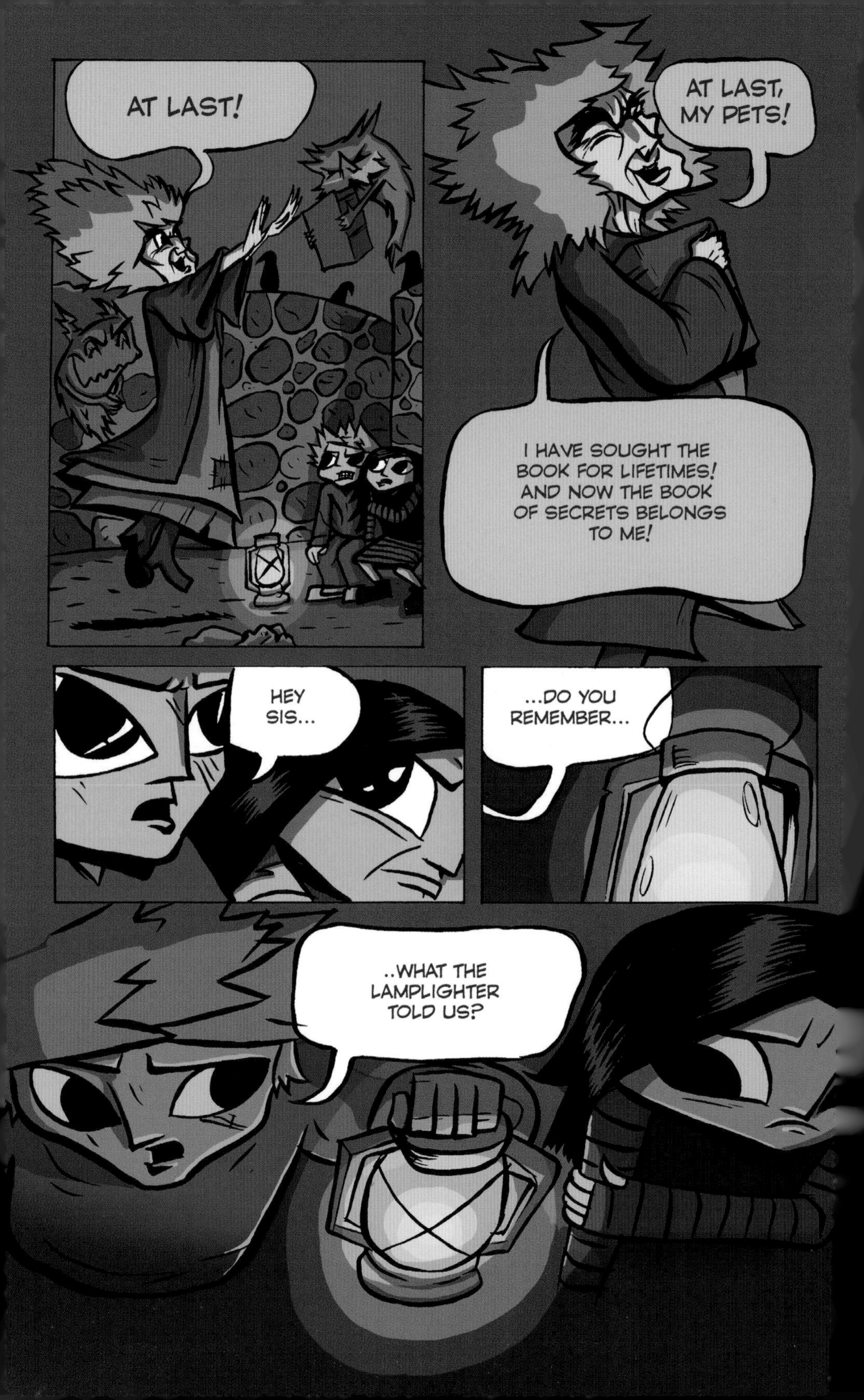
AT LAST!
AT LAST, MY PETS!
I HAVE SOUGHT THE BOOK FOR LIFETIMES! AND NOW THE BOOK OF SECRETS BELONGS TO ME!
HEY SIS...
...DO YOU REMEMBER...
..WHAT THE LAMPLIGHTER TOLD US?

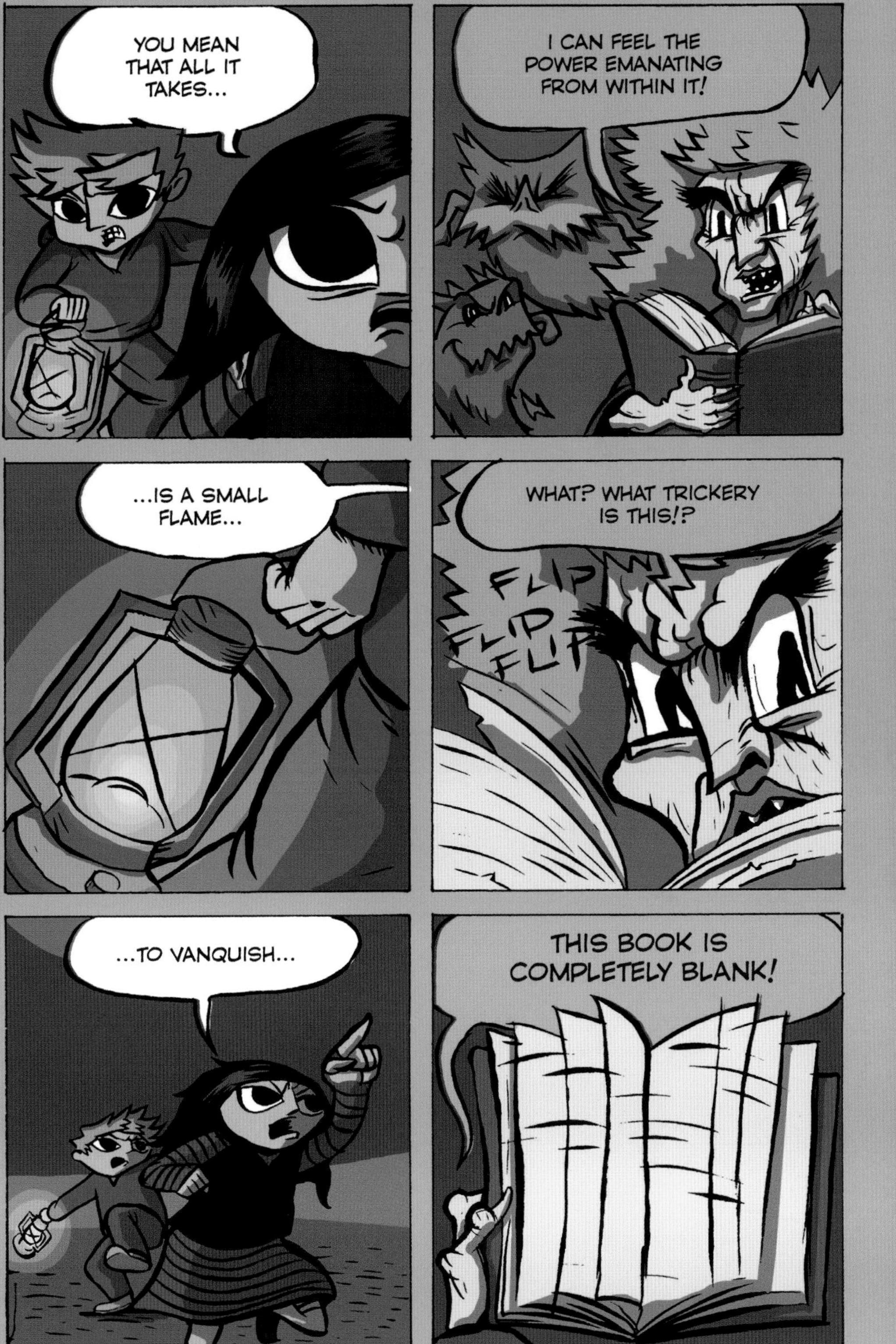
YOU MEAN THAT ALL IT TAKES...
I CAN FEEL THE POWER EMANATING FROM WITHIN IT!
...IS A SMALL FLAME...
WHAT? WHAT TRICKERY IS THIS!?
FLIP FLIP FLIP
...TO VANQUISH...
THIS BOOK IS COMPLETELY BLANK!

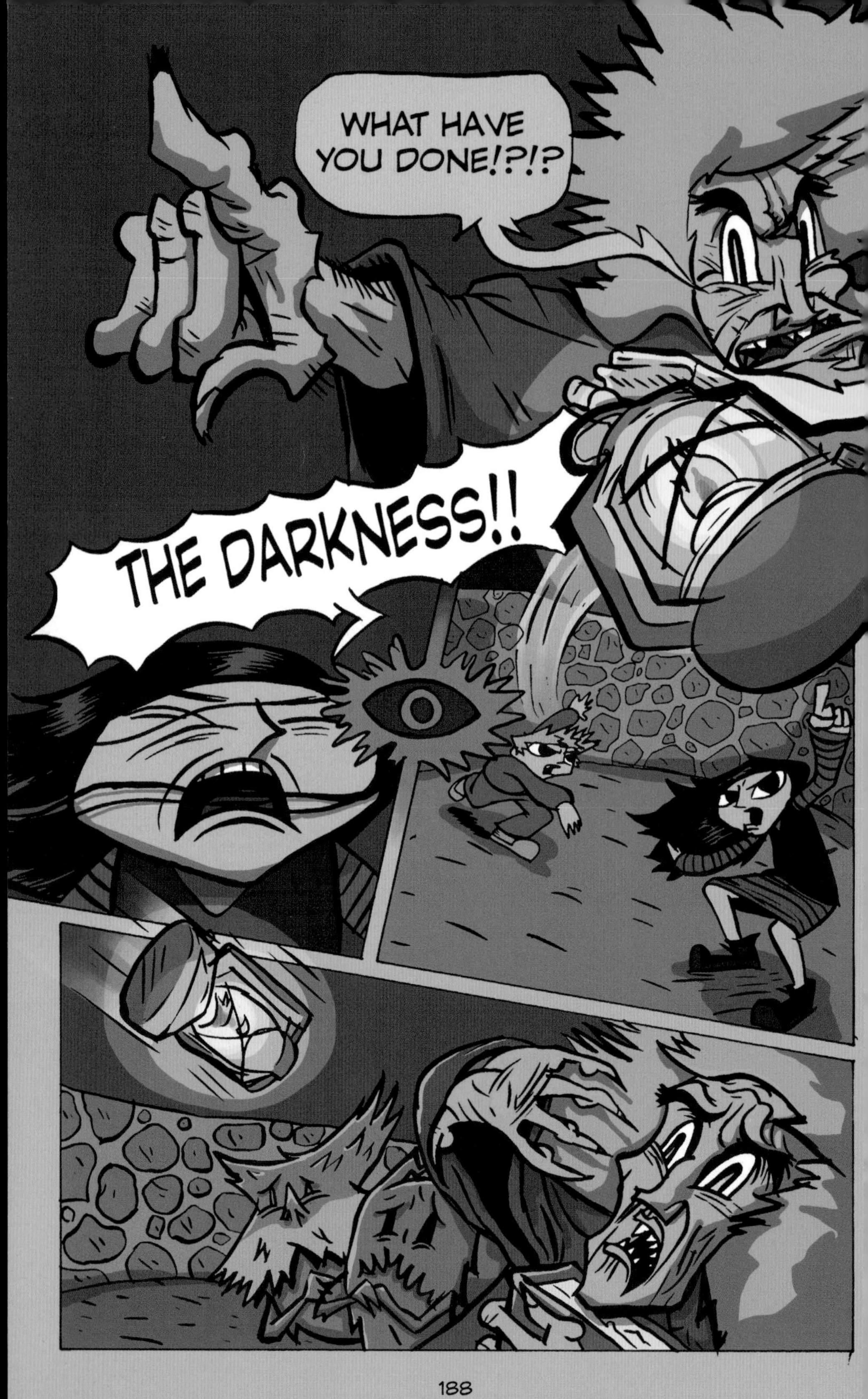
WHAT HAVE YOU DONE!?!?
THE DARKNESS!!

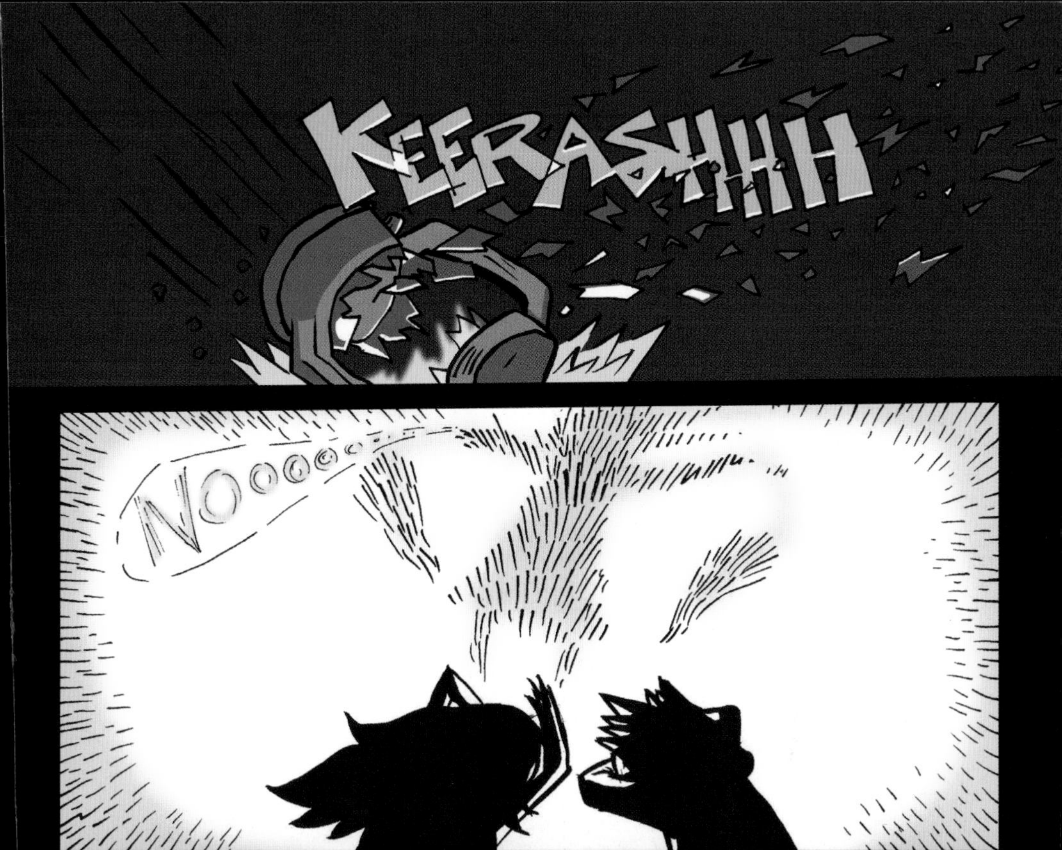
KEERASHHHH
NOOOOOO...

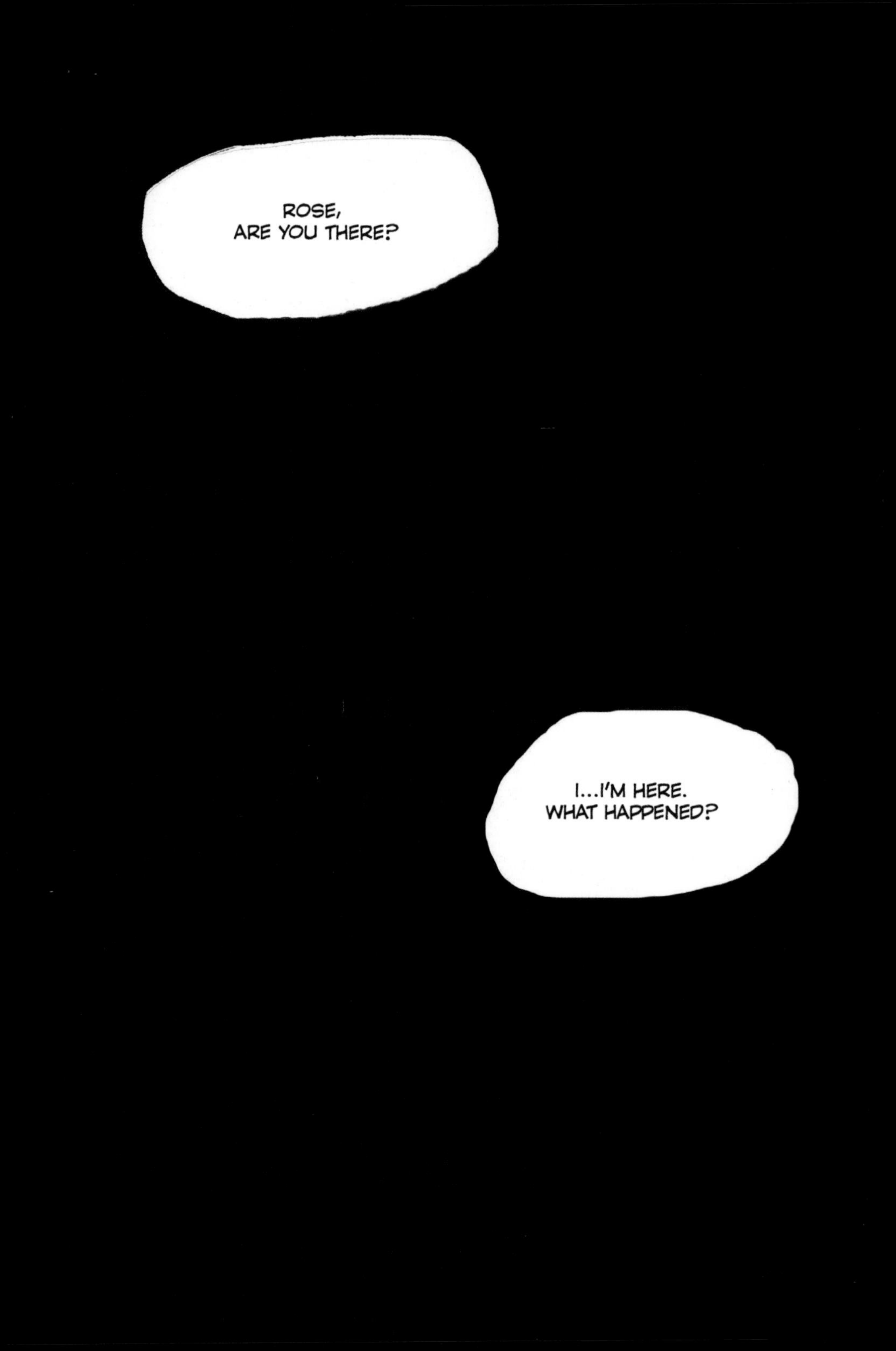
ROSE, ARE YOU THERE?
I...I'M HERE. WHAT HAPPENED?

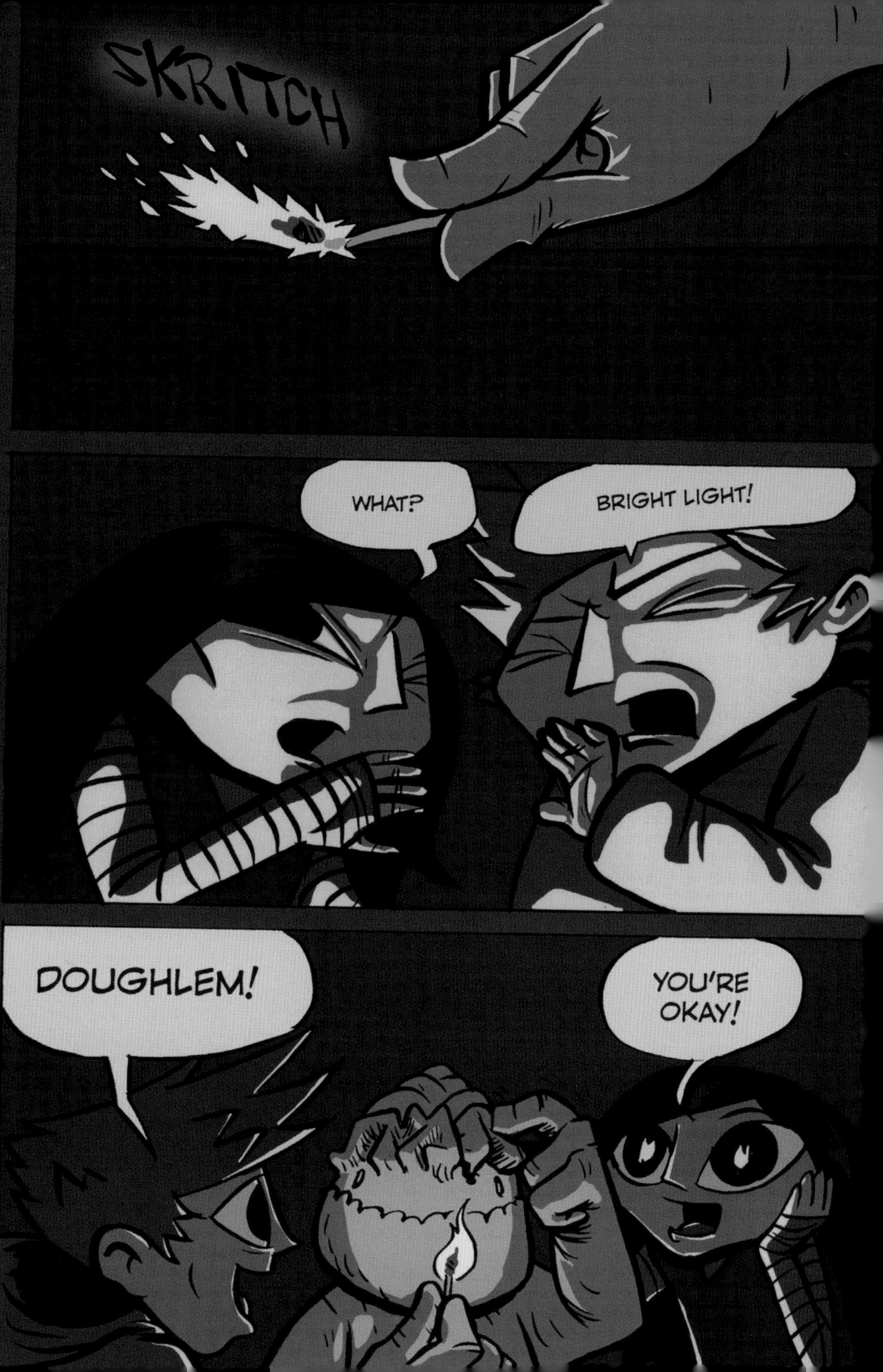
SKRITCH
WHAT?
BRIGHT LIGHT!
DOUGHLEM!
YOU'RE OKAY!

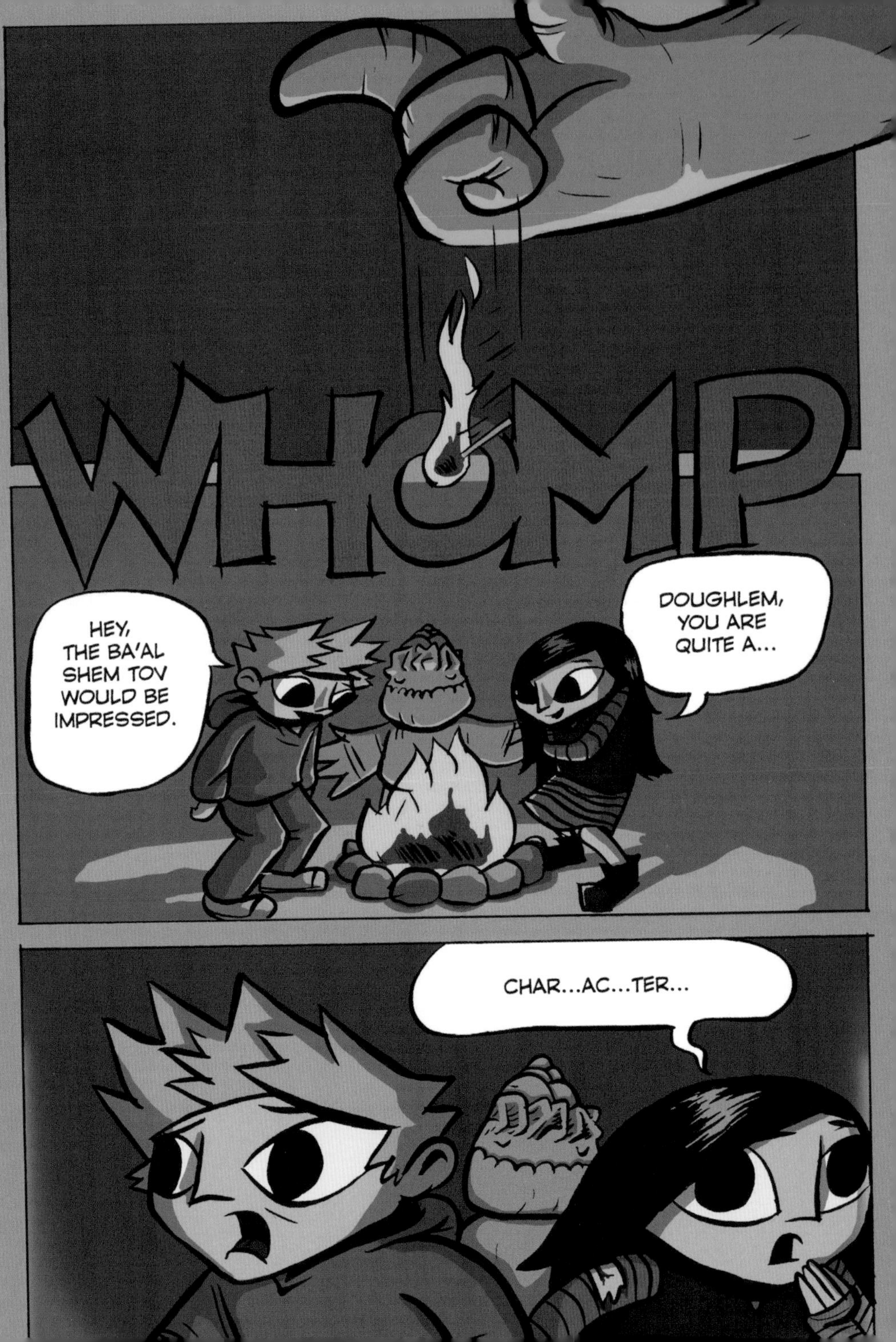
WHOMP
HEY, THE BA'AL SHEM TOV WOULD BE IMPRESSED.
DOUGHLEM, YOU ARE QUITE A...
CHAR...AC...TER...

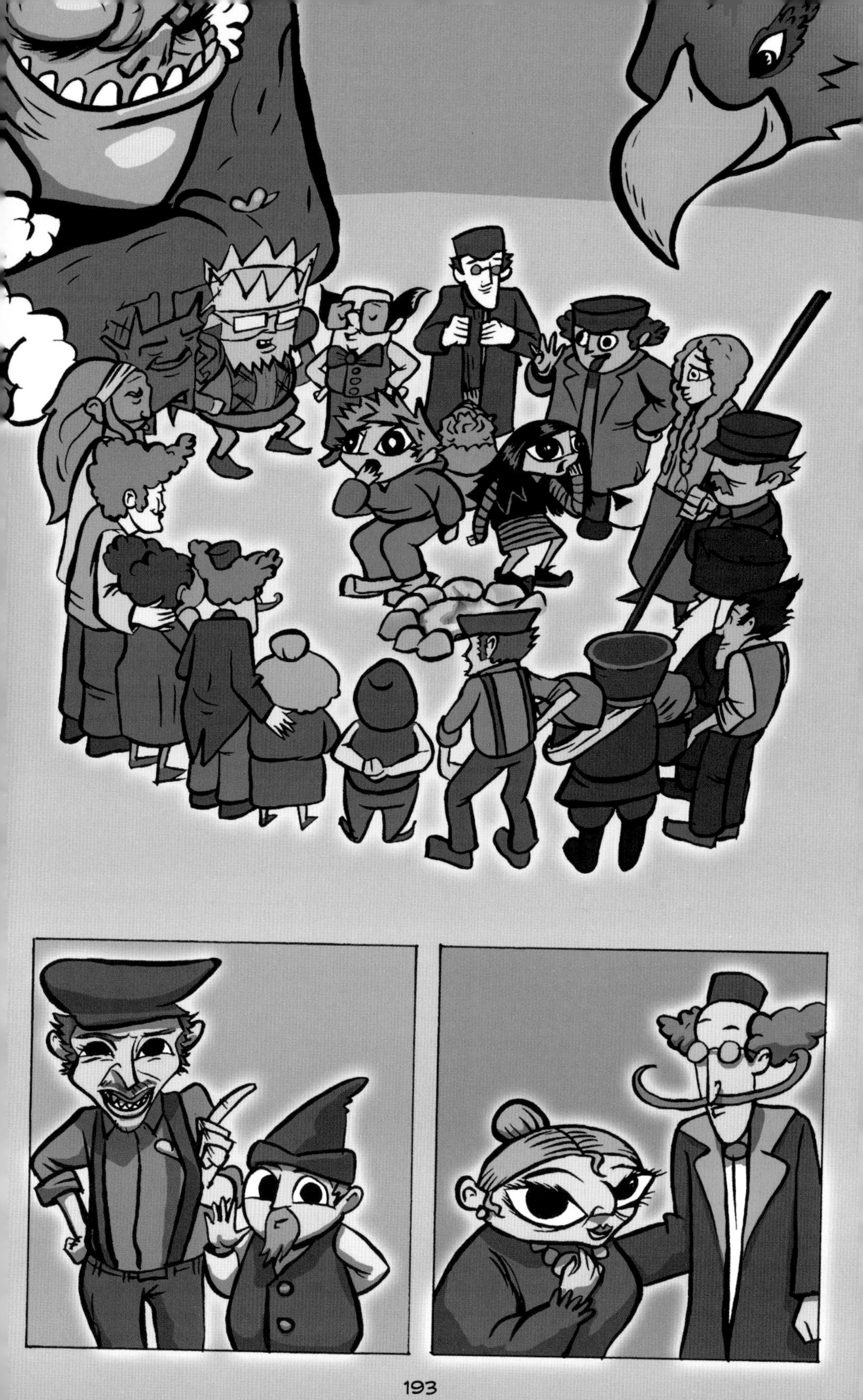

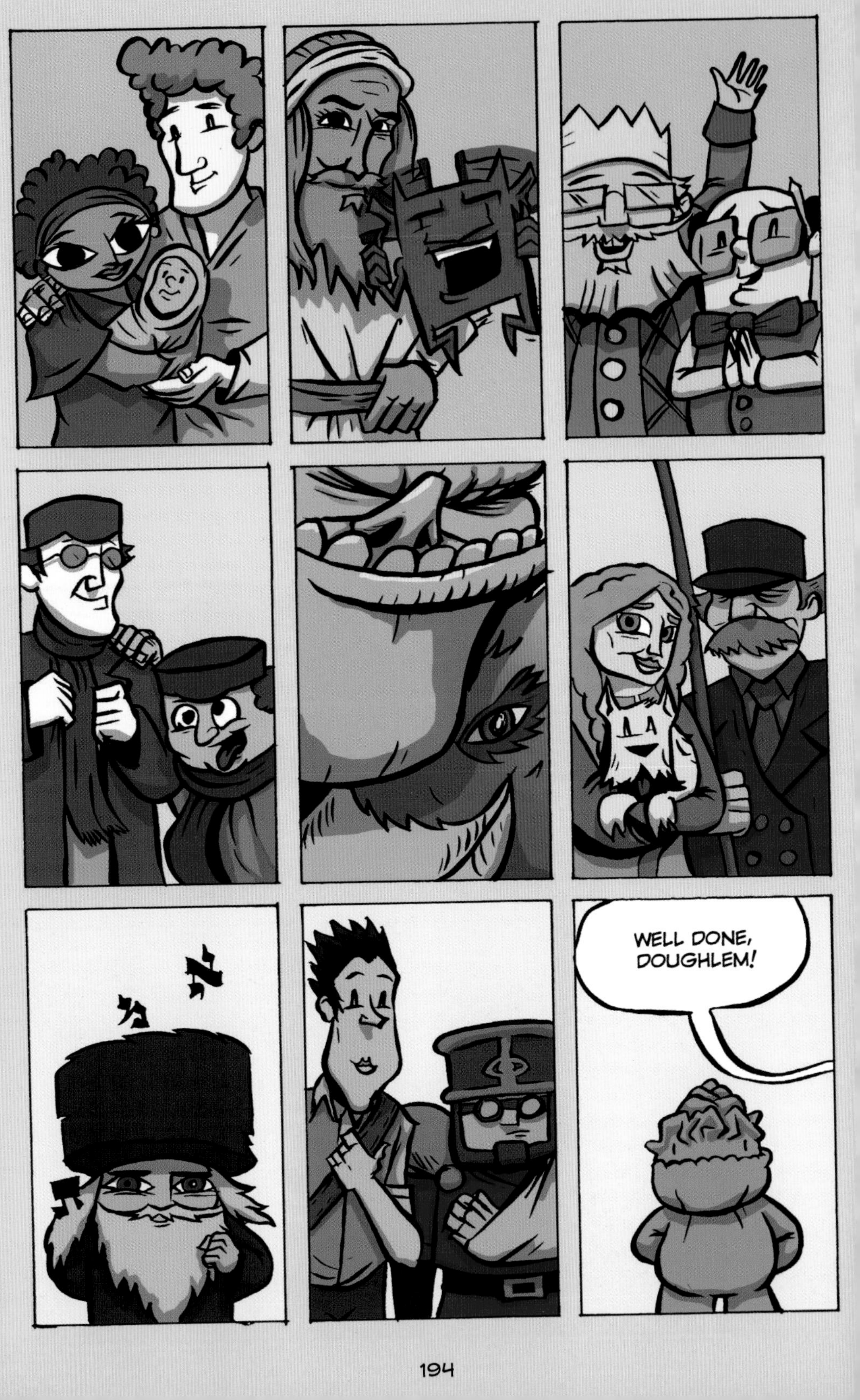
WELL DONE,
DOUGHLEM!

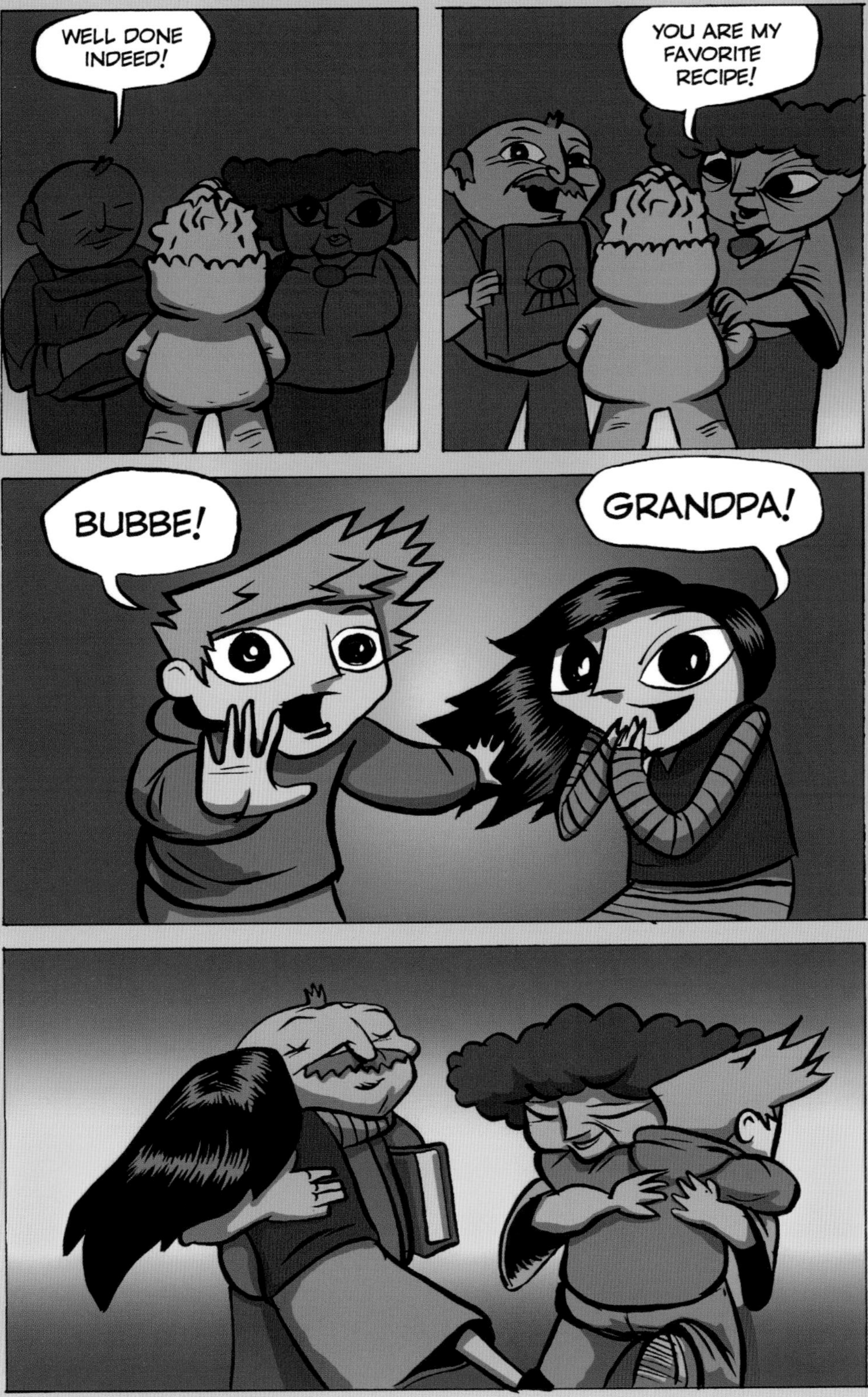
WELL DONE INDEED!
YOU ARE MY FAVORITE RECIPE!
BUBBE!
GRANDPA!

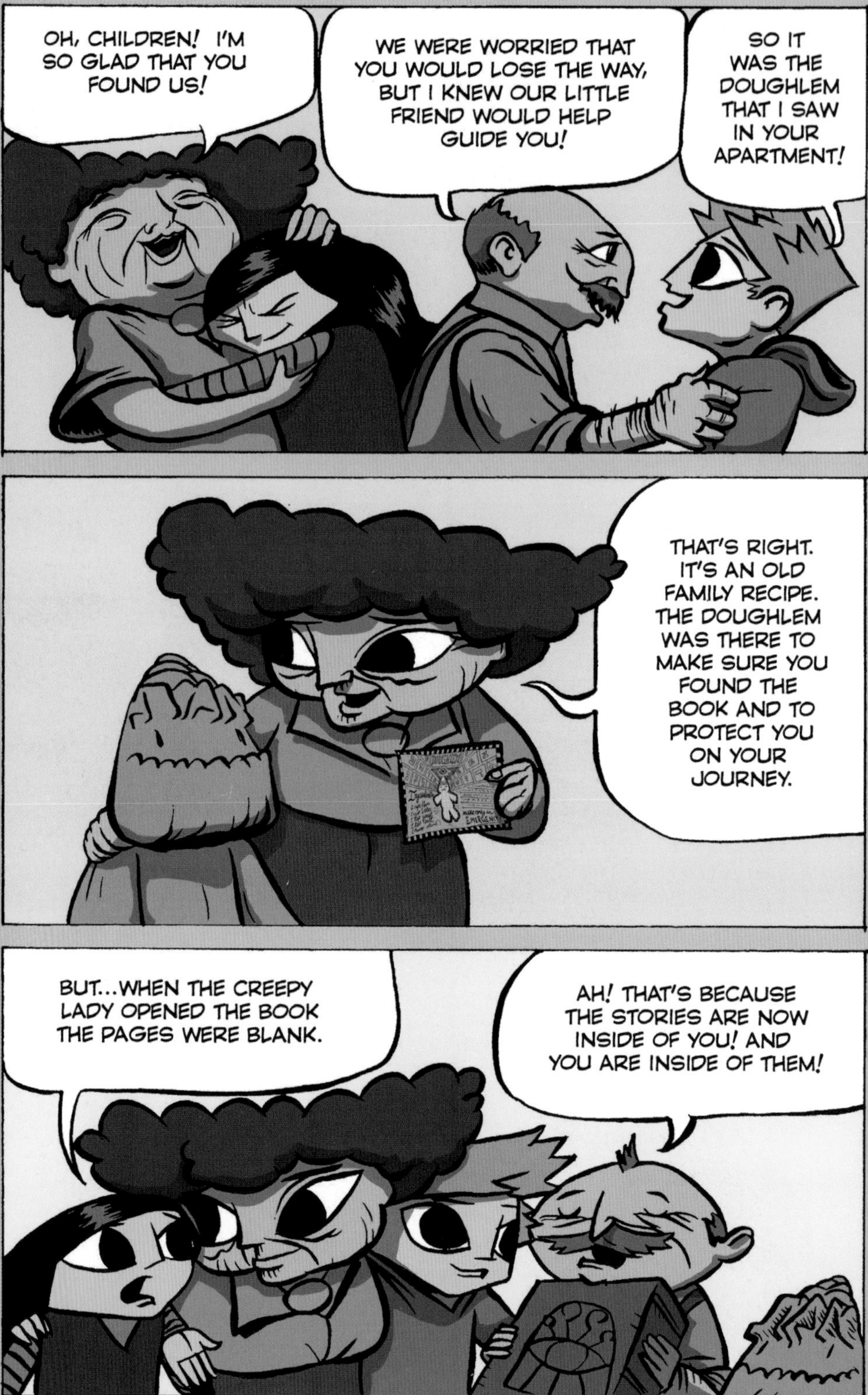
OH, CHILDREN! I'M SO GLAD THAT YOU FOUND US!
WE WERE WORRIED THAT YOU WOULD LOSE THE WAY, BUT I KNEW OUR LITTLE FRIEND WOULD HELP GUIDE YOU!
SO IT WAS THE DOUGHLEM THAT I SAW IN YOUR APARTMENT!
THAT'S RIGHT. IT'S AN OLD FAMILY RECIPE. THE DOUGHLEM WAS THERE TO MAKE SURE YOU FOUND THE BOOK AND TO PROTECT YOU ON YOUR JOURNEY.
BUT...WHEN THE CREEPY LADY OPENED THE BOOK THE PAGES WERE BLANK.
AH! THAT'S BECAUSE THE STORIES ARE NOW INSIDE OF YOU! AND YOU ARE INSIDE OF THEM!

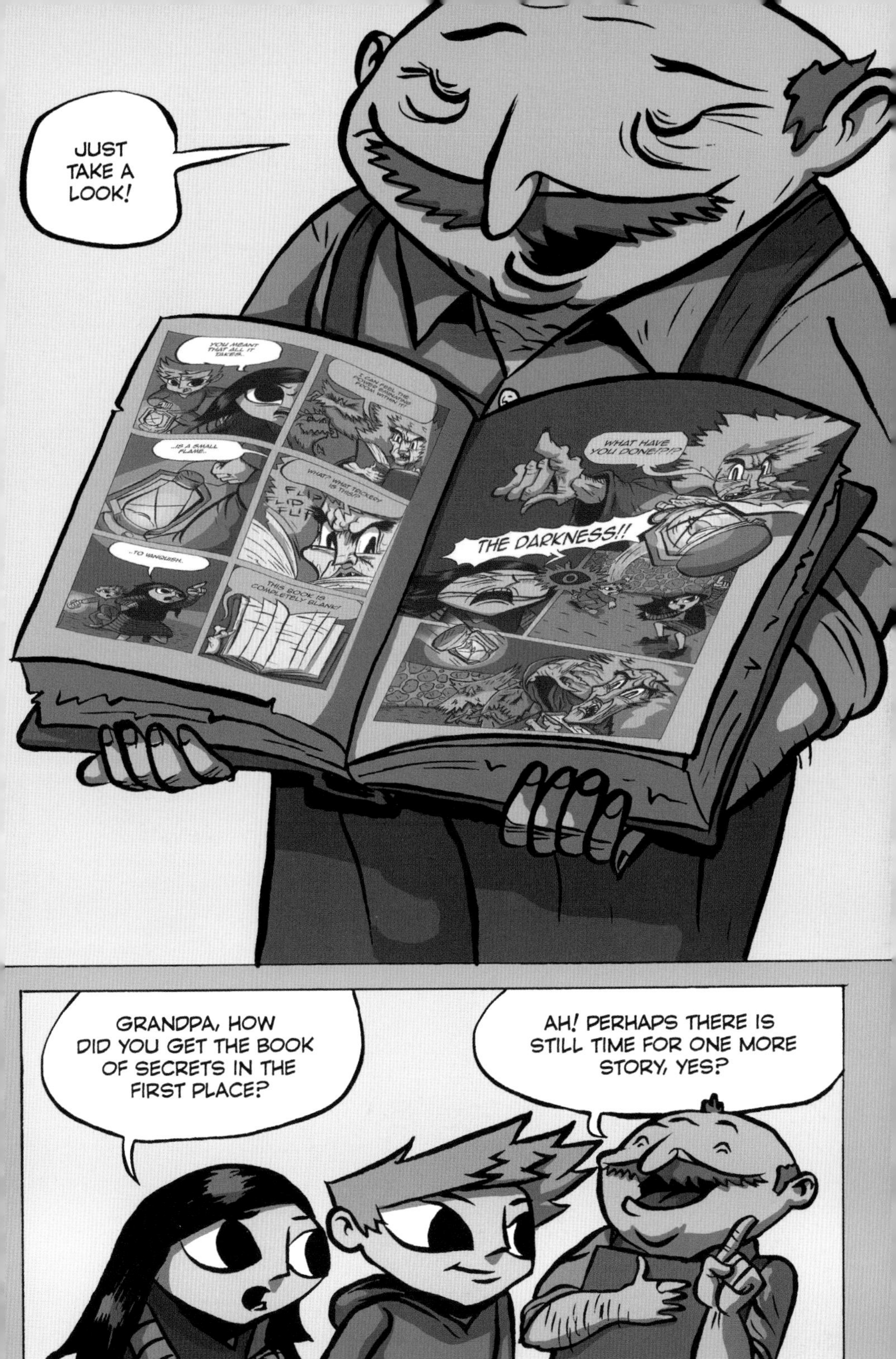
JUST TAKE A LOOK!
YOU MEANT THAT ALL IT TAKES...
...IS A SMALL FLAME...
...TO VANQUISH.
THIS BOOK IS COMPLETELY BLANK!
WHAT HAVE YOU DONE!?!?
THE DARKNESS!!
GRANDPA, HOW DID YOU GET THE BOOK OF SECRETS IN THE FIRST PLACE?
AH! PERHAPS THERE IS STILL TIME FOR ONE MORE STORY, YES?

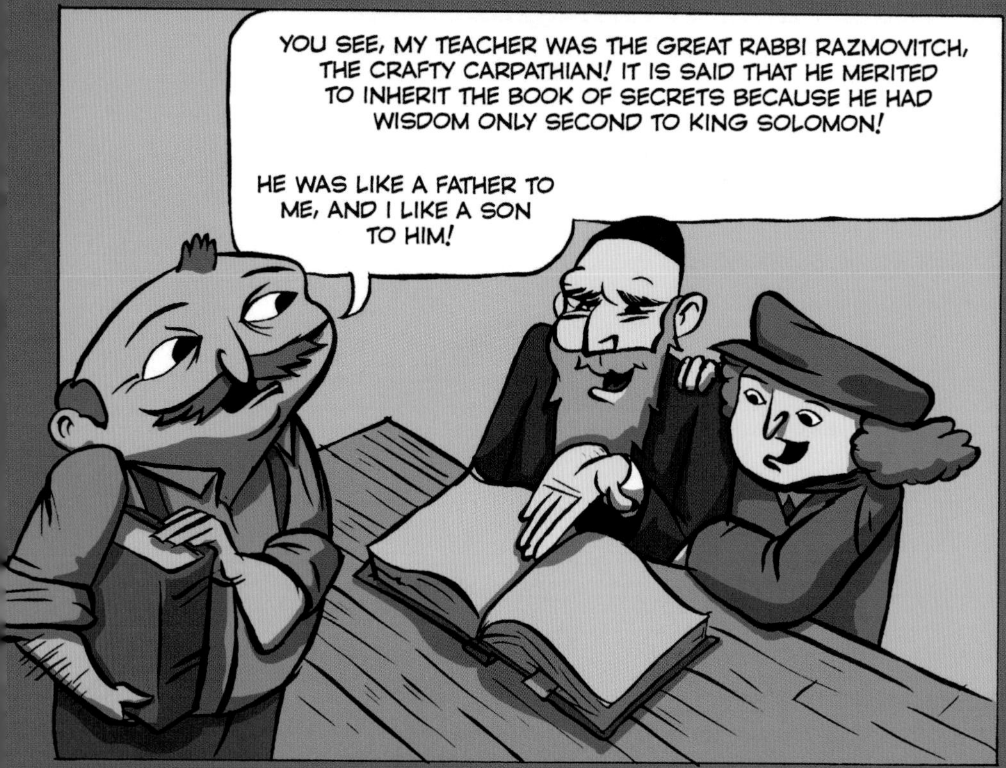
YOU SEE, MY TEACHER WAS THE GREAT RABBI RAZMOVITCH, THE CRAFTY CARPATHIAN! IT IS SAID THAT HE MERITED TO INHERIT THE BOOK OF SECRETS BECAUSE HE HAD WISDOM ONLY SECOND TO KING SOLOMON!
HE WAS LIKE A FATHER TO ME, AND I LIKE A SON TO HIM!

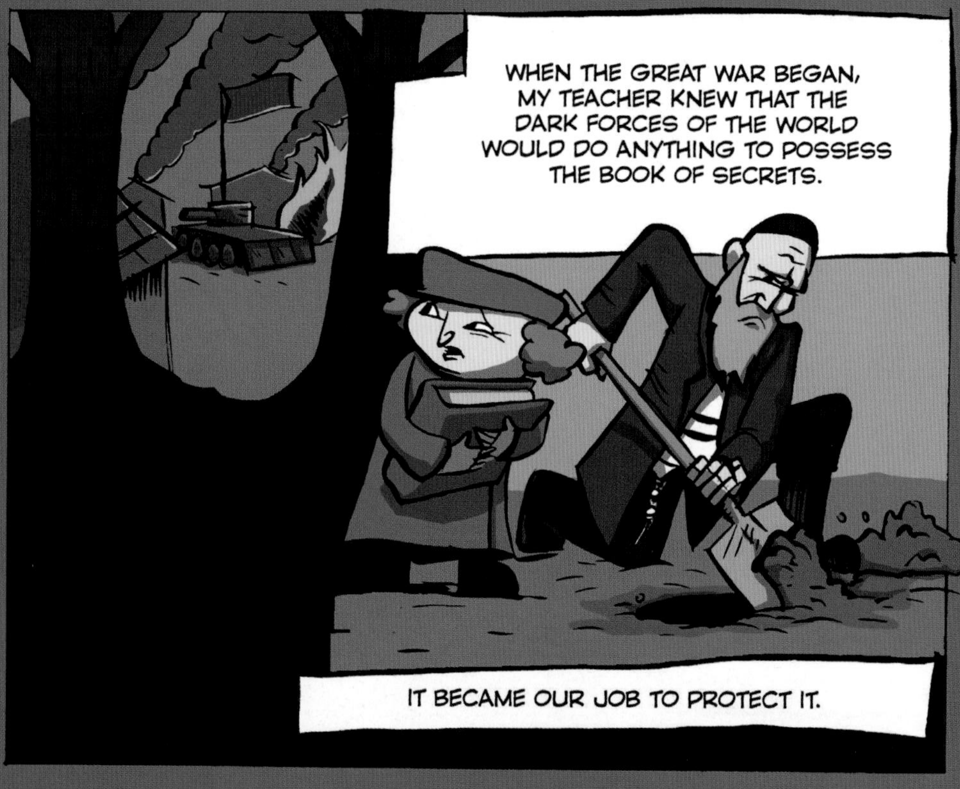
WHEN THE GREAT WAR BEGAN, MY TEACHER KNEW THAT THE DARK FORCES OF THE WORLD WOULD DO ANYTHING TO POSSESS THE BOOK OF SECRETS.
IT BECAME OUR JOB TO PROTECT IT.

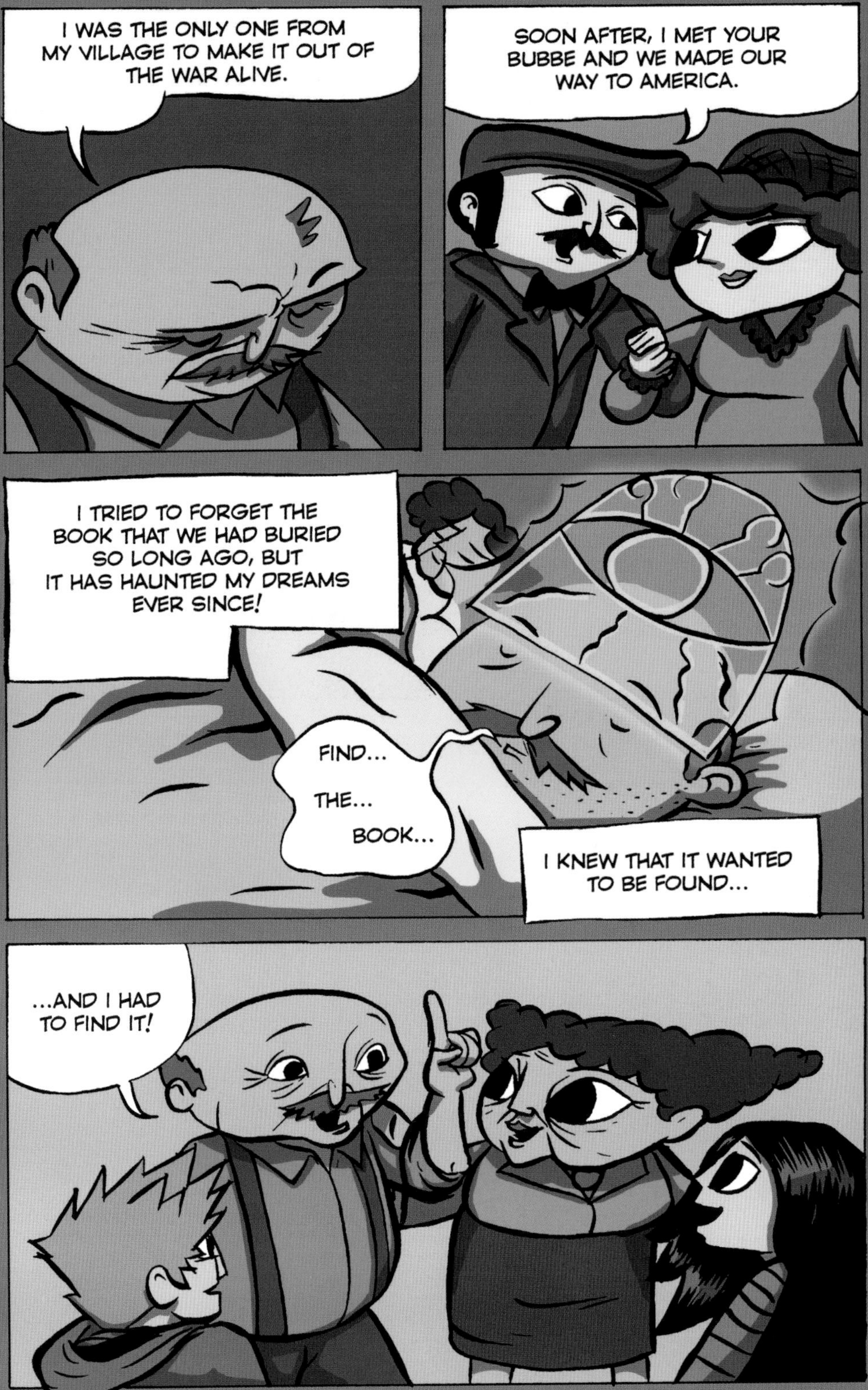
I WAS THE ONLY ONE FROM MY VILLAGE TO MAKE IT OUT OF THE WAR ALIVE.
SOON AFTER, I MET YOUR BUBBE AND WE MADE OUR WAY TO AMERICA.
I TRIED TO FORGET THE BOOK THAT WE HAD BURIED SO LONG AGO, BUT IT HAS HAUNTED MY DREAMS EVER SINCE!
FIND... THE... BOOK...
I KNEW THAT IT WANTED TO BE FOUND...
...AND I HAD TO FIND IT!

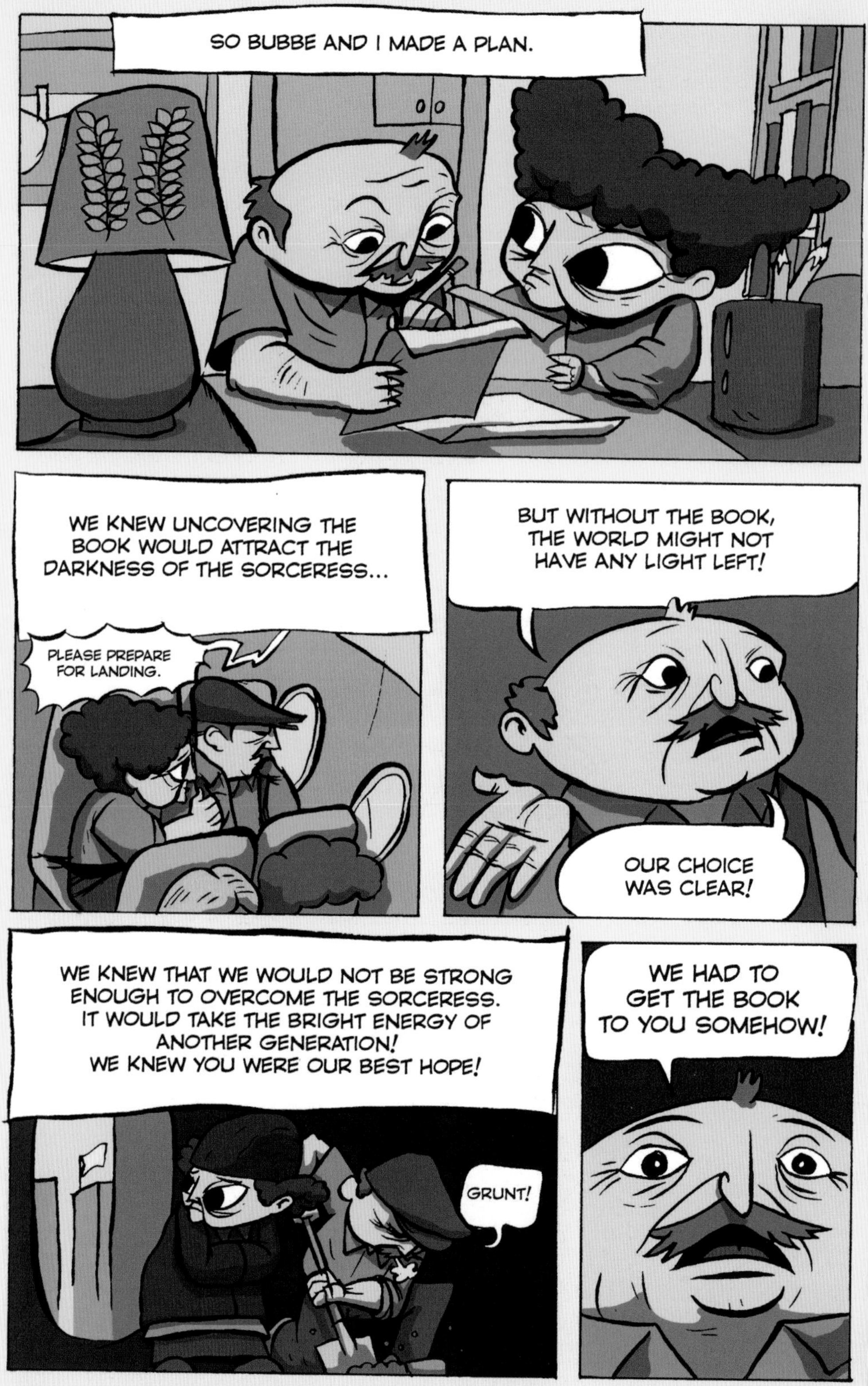
SO BUBBE AND I MADE A PLAN.
WE KNEW UNCOVERING THE BOOK WOULD ATTRACT THE DARKNESS OF THE SORCERESS...
PLEASE PREPARE FOR LANDING.
BUT WITHOUT THE BOOK, THE WORLD MIGHT NOT HAVE ANY LIGHT LEFT!
OUR CHOICE WAS CLEAR!
WE KNEW THAT WE WOULD NOT BE STRONG ENOUGH TO OVERCOME THE SORCERESS. IT WOULD TAKE THE BRIGHT ENERGY OF ANOTHER GENERATION! WE KNEW YOU WERE OUR BEST HOPE!
GRUNT!
WE HAD TO GET THE BOOK TO YOU SOMEHOW!

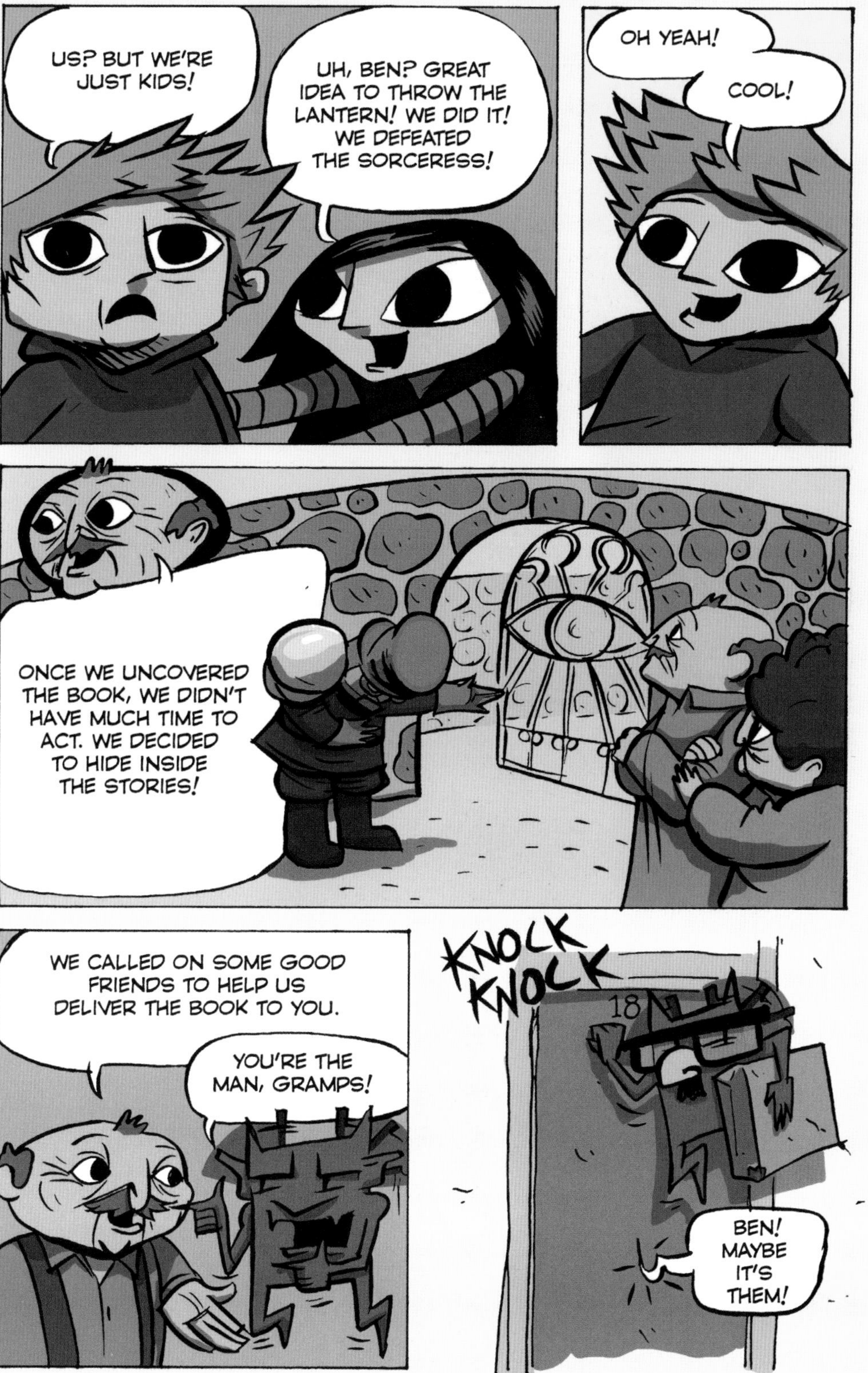

US? BUT WE'RE JUST KIDS!
UH, BEN? GREAT IDEA TO THROW THE LANTERN! WE DID IT! WE DEFEATED THE SORCERESS!
OH YEAH!
COOL!
ONCE WE UNCOVERED THE BOOK, WE DIDN'T HAVE MUCH TIME TO ACT. WE DECIDED TO HIDE INSIDE THE STORIES!
WE CALLED ON SOME GOOD FRIENDS TO HELP US DELIVER THE BOOK TO YOU.
YOU'RE THE MAN, GRAMPS!
KNOCK KNOCK
18
BEN! MAYBE IT'S THEM!

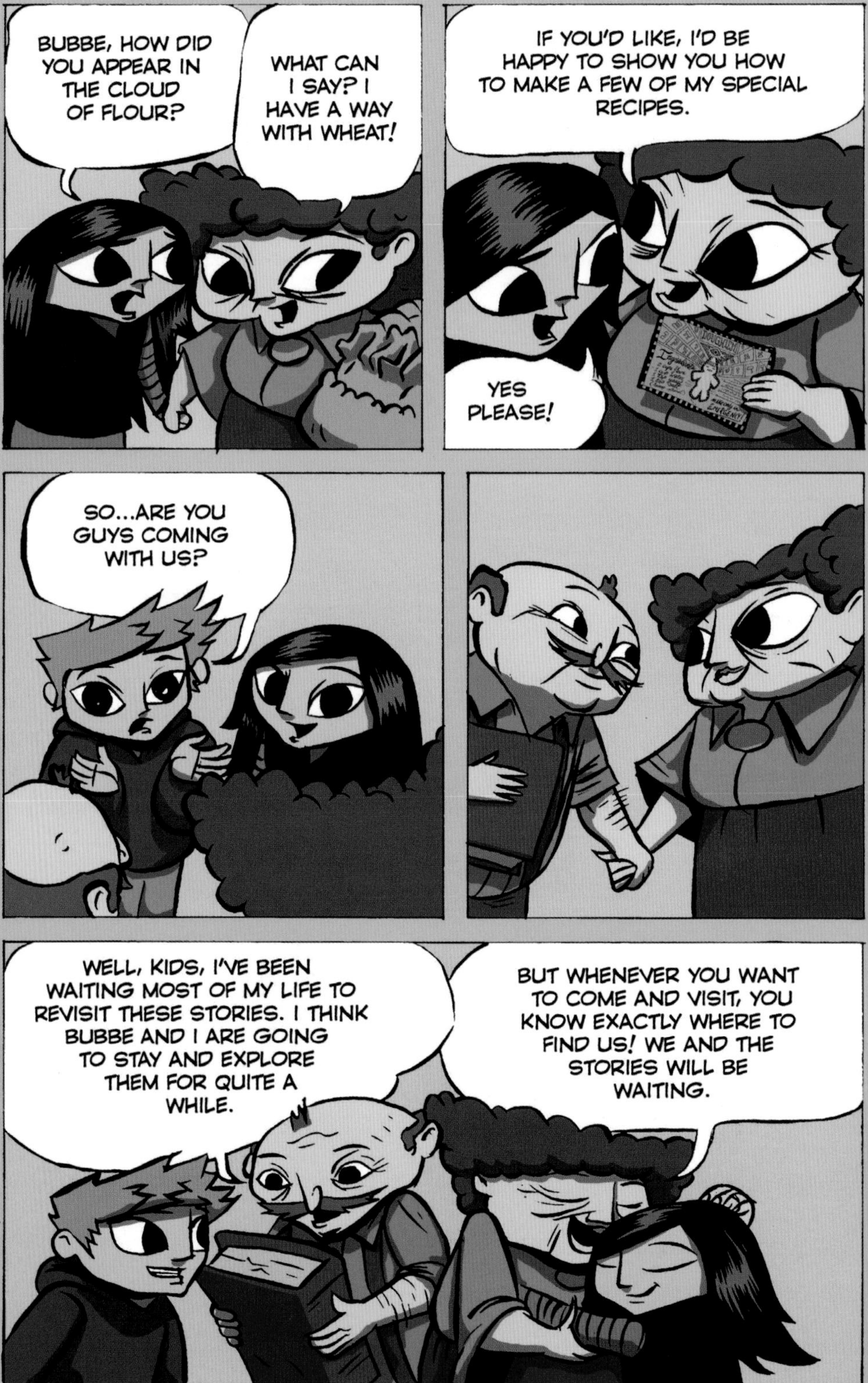
BUBBE, HOW DID YOU APPEAR IN THE CLOUD OF FLOUR?
WHAT CAN I SAY? I HAVE A WAY WITH WHEAT!
IF YOU'D LIKE, I'D BE HAPPY TO SHOW YOU HOW TO MAKE A FEW OF MY SPECIAL RECIPES.
YES PLEASE!
SO...ARE YOU GUYS COMING WITH US?
WELL, KIDS, I'VE BEEN WAITING MOST OF MY LIFE TO REVISIT THESE STORIES. I THINK BUBBE AND I ARE GOING TO STAY AND EXPLORE THEM FOR QUITE A WHILE.
BUT WHENEVER YOU WANT TO COME AND VISIT, YOU KNOW EXACTLY WHERE TO FIND US! WE AND THE STORIES WILL BE WAITING.

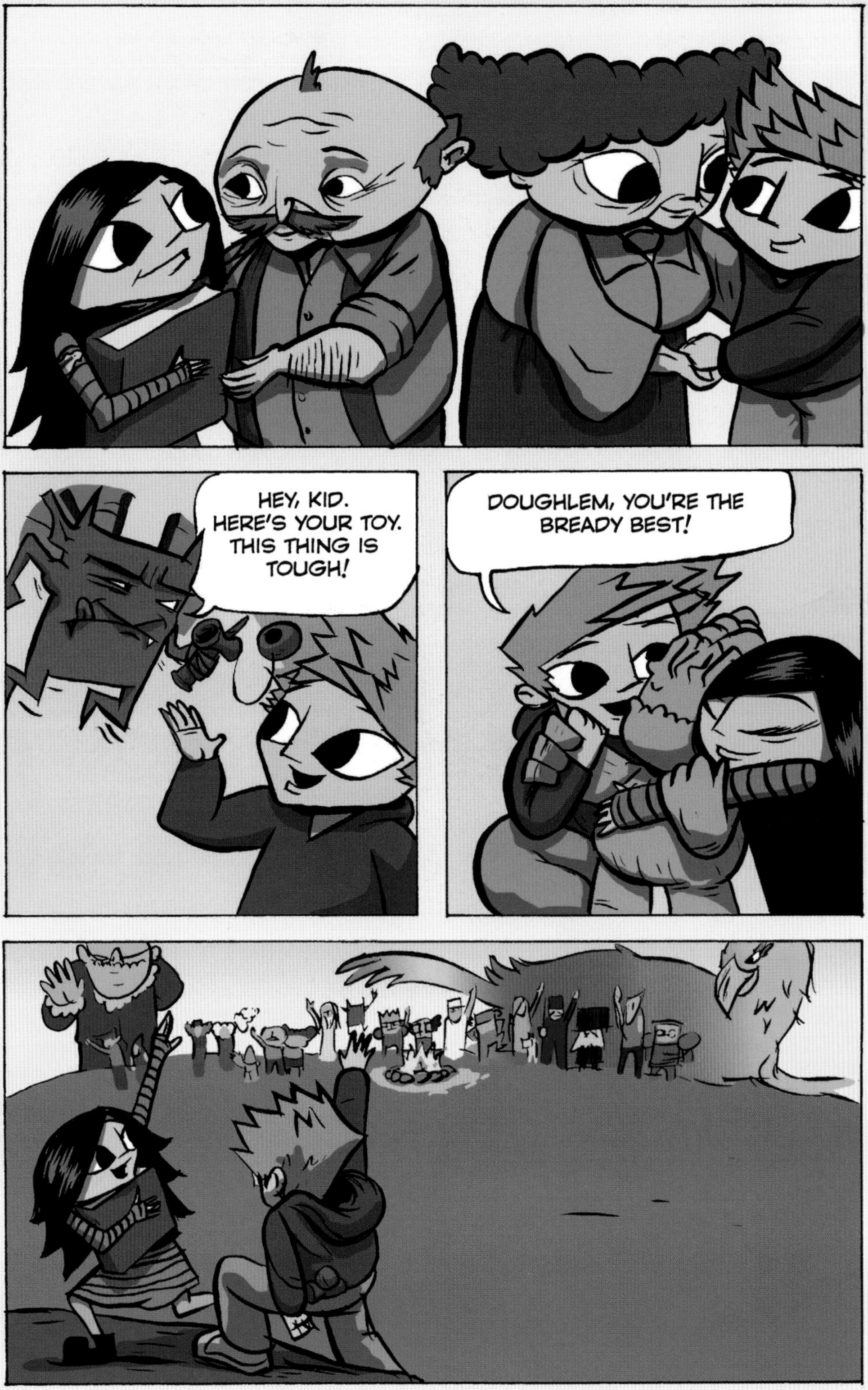
HEY, KID. HERE'S YOUR TOY. THIS THING IS TOUGH!
DOUGHLEM, YOU'RE THE BREADY BEST!

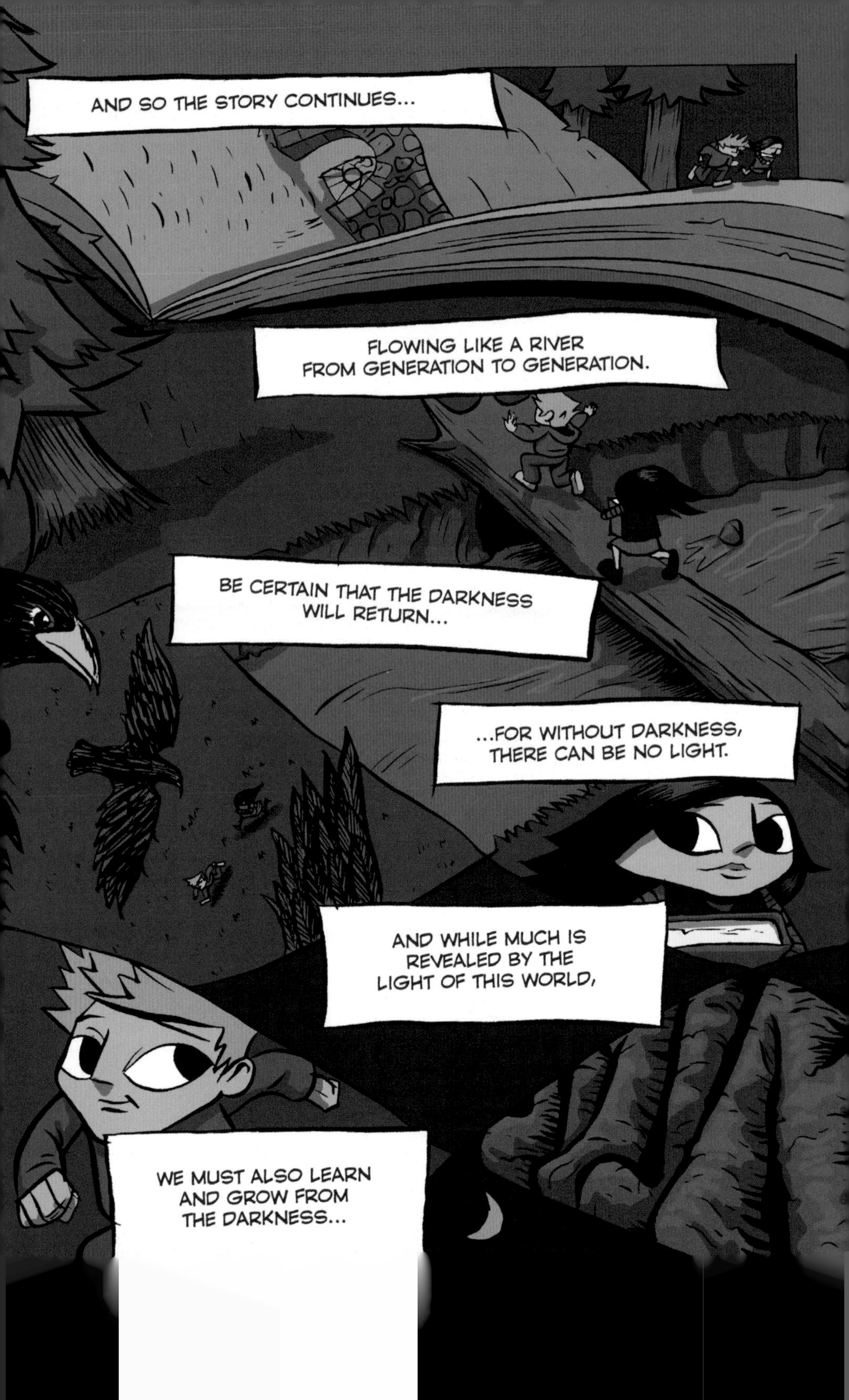
AND SO THE STORY CONTINUES...
FLOWING LIKE A RIVER FROM GENERATION TO GENERATION.
BE CERTAIN THAT THE DARKNESS WILL RETURN...
...FOR WITHOUT DARKNESS, THERE CAN BE NO LIGHT.
AND WHILE MUCH IS REVEALED BY THE LIGHT OF THIS WORLD,
WE MUST ALSO LEARN AND GROW FROM THE DARKNESS...

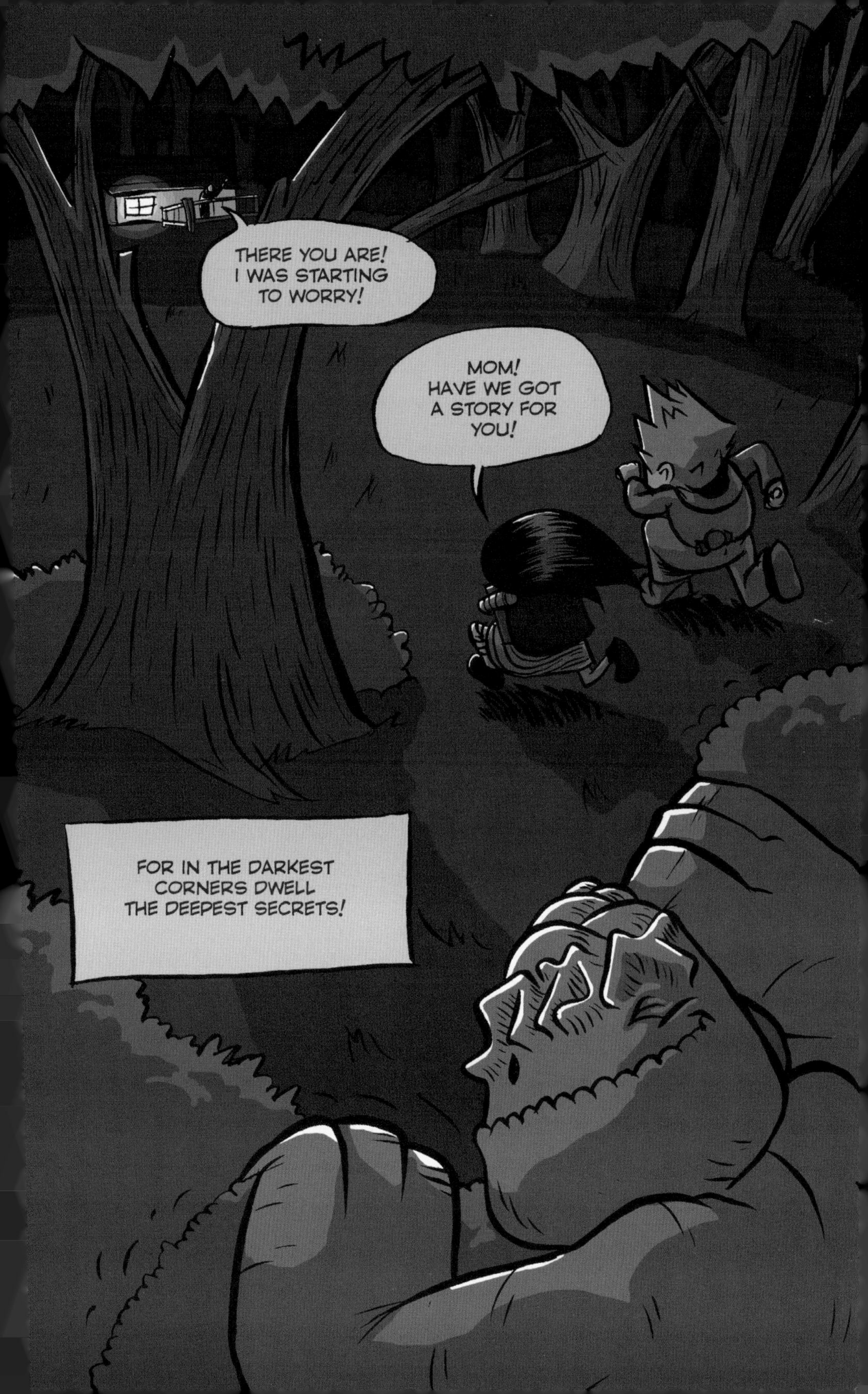
THERE YOU ARE! I WAS STARTING TO WORRY!
MOM! HAVE WE GOT A STORY FOR YOU!
FOR IN THE DARKEST CORNERS DWELL THE DEEPEST SECRETS!

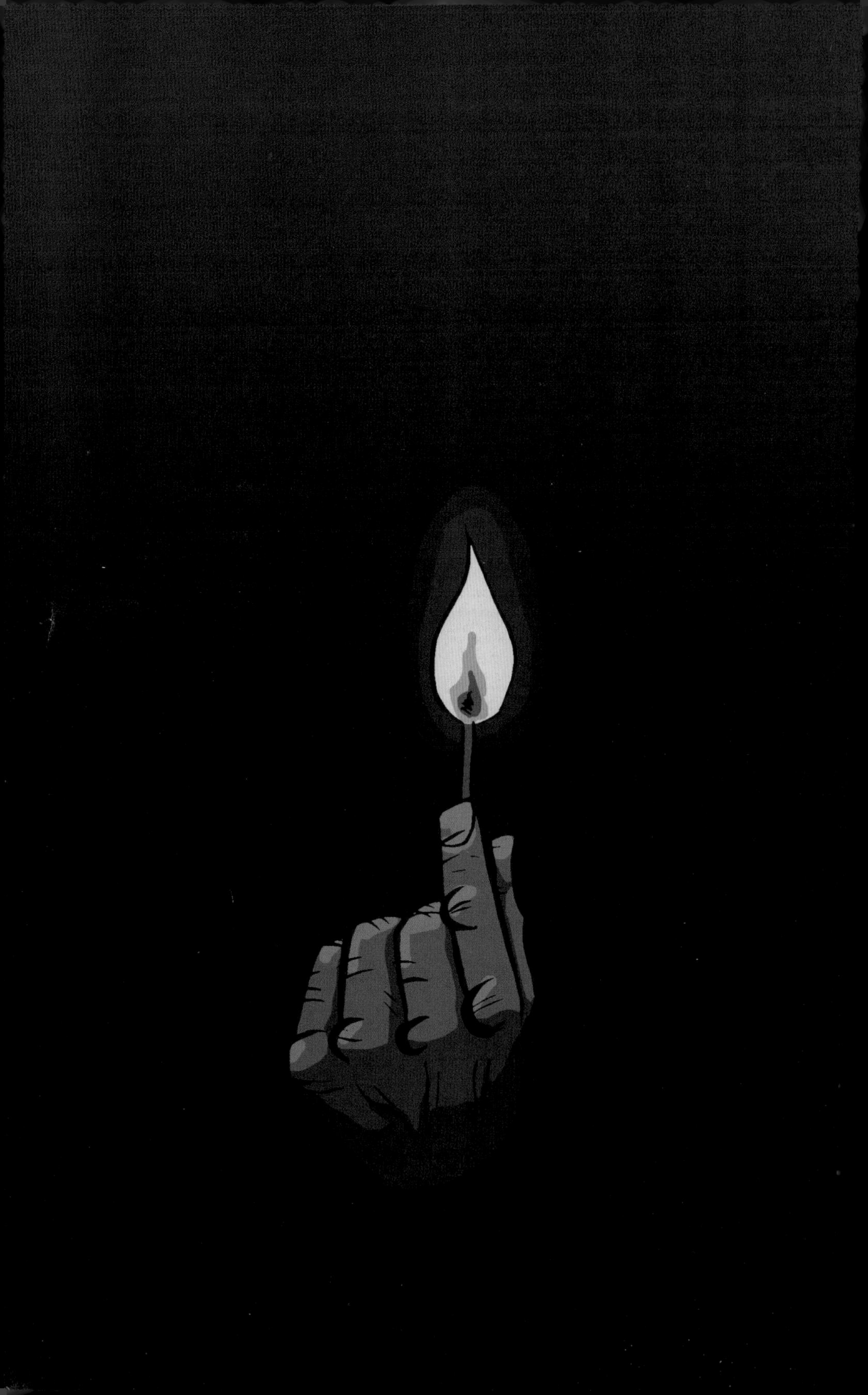

Author's Note

My thanks to the storytellers whose tales have inspired me.

THE BUTTERFLY IN THE HAND
Based on a Hasidic folktale

THE SCRIBE AND THE PRINCESS
Based on the Midrash Tanhuma B

THE TAINTED GRAIN
Based on Rebbe Nachman's Sippurei Maasiyot

OG AND THE TAILOR
Based on Brachot 54B, Pirkei De Rebbe Eliezer

UNDER THE BRIDGE
Based on Rebbe Nachman's Sippurei Maasiyot

BEFORE THE GATE
Based on the story "Before the Law" from The Trial by
Franz Kafka

AND THE STORY WAS ENOUGH
Based on a tale about the Ba'al Shem Tov

THE BOOK OF SECRETS
Based on the Midrash Tehillim 139

—Mat Tonti

About the Author

Rabbi Matisyahu (Mat) Tonti lives in Washington, DC, with his beloved wife and three kiddos. When he's not drawing comics, Tonti can be found bouncing on the trampoline, riding his bike, playing music, wandering through the woods, or learning Torah with his students and teachers. You can see and hear his ongoing artistic adventures on Instagram @rabbimatonti.